LONG GONE

Other Books By Denise Grover Swank

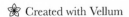

LONG GONE

Harper Adams

Mystery #2

DENISE
GROVER SWANK

Chapter 1

"Harper, what's taking so long with that file?"

I clamped my teeth together to keep myself from telling Becky, one of the paralegals at Morgan, Hightower, and Adams, that she could take the file in my hand and shove it up her ass.

I'd been working at my father's law firm for three weeks, and they'd been some of the worst weeks of my life. Which was saying something.

Five months ago, I'd been a Little Rock police detective with a high closure rate, well respected and with an exemplary record.

Oh, how the mighty had fallen.

"It's right here, Becky," I said in the best syrupy sweet voice I could manufacture as I handed it to her.

I couldn't embarrass my father and his partners or make them regret hiring me, which meant I had to do my best to remain polite and keep my temper in check. It wasn't lost on me that the some of the employees like Becky resented the hell out of me. If our positions had been reversed, I probably would have resented me too. Still, it wasn't like their jobs were

1

being threatened. I was doing everything they didn't want to do. At the same time, it was possible they knew what I did: the partners were paying me more than they should have for such a lowly position.

I needed the money, so I wasn't about to complain or offer to take less. Before leaving Little Rock, I'd lost my career, my savings, and the equity of my home. It had been sold to pay for my legal bills after I was investigated for shooting a teenager while on the job. With nothing left, I'd moved back to Jackson Creek and into the garage apartment in my parents' backyard six weeks ago. Then, a little over two weeks after I came back, my father had left my mother and moved into a small rental house.

My father was the one who'd encouraged me to come back to Jackson Creek and live in the garage apartment. My mother had been completely against it and hadn't tried to hide her feelings. I embarrassed her, and my presence was a constant reminder of my disgrace—and also that I had the nerve to be alive, while my younger sister was forever fourteen. My mother had only tolerated my residency because my father had insisted, something he rarely did.

My father and I had both expected her to evict me when he'd left, so he'd invited me to move in with him. But she'd surprised both of us by begging me to stay. There was still a part of me, buried deep down in my soul, that craved her approval and love, so I'd agreed.

I'd regretted the decision even as I made it. I was still regretting it.

My father kept trying to convince me to leave, but to my surprise, a Pollyanna dwelled deep inside me. I wanted to believe she could really change.

I already knew I was a fool. The hell she'd put me through the last three weeks was merely further proof. Becky kept piling on, and it was probably a matter of time before I went up like a powder keg. But I could keep it together for now. So I tried hard to give Becky a genuine smile, pretty sure I was failing. She snatched the file from my hand and gave me a cold look of dismissal.

Sighing, I turned back toward the file room. Debbie, the office manager, had been taken by surprise when I'd shown up for my first day. Turned out it had never crossed the minds of any of the three partners to tell her she had a new employee, and she'd scrambled to come up with jobs for me to do. After a rough first week or so, she'd finally settled on having me run the file room. A few days later, I'd presented a plan for reorganizing the room. She'd listened and agreed.

I was good at organizing, but it was tedious and so boring I'd actually nodded off more than once. The only thing that helped get me through the anxiety of my boredom was the water bottle I kept in my purse that was filled with half water and half vodka. As I entered the room and spotted my purse on the table, I felt a strong pull to it now.

I curled my fingers, my nails digging into my palms. I didn't need a drink. Sure, I was stressed and wanted something to help ease the tension, but I didn't *need* it.

But maybe a small one wouldn't hurt, because I was dangerously close to telling Becky exactly what I thought of her.

I took a step toward the table.

"Harper?" a man called out from behind me, and it took everything in me not to jump and make myself look suspicious.

I turned to face Mitch Morgan, one of my father's partners. He was in his mid-fifties and had a trim figure that was highlighted by his expensive suit. It was easy to see his salt-and-pepper hair was styled by someone who knew what they were doing, not Patricia at the salon on Main Street, or even any salon in Wolford, the nearest bigger town, ten miles to the north. His wife had died from cancer a little over a decade ago, and he'd never remarried. Instead, he chose to keep his options open and varied. But from what little I'd seen since coming back to town, the women he dated seemed to grow younger and younger.

He flashed me a warm smile. "Hey, I was wondering if you had time for a quick chat."

It was an unnecessary question. For one thing, he was my boss. For another, my job was mostly filing, which meant 99% of my day was available time for just about anything. There were very few filing emergencies. "Sure thing."

I followed him to his office, my stomach tightening with dread. Had they found out I'd been drinking on the job? I'd never gotten drunk at the office, and I was always careful to have mints or gum to mask any faint scent from the vodka I refilled my water bottle with every night.

Mitch's office was full of dark wood bookshelves and furniture. The seats were upholstered in tufted leather, and expensive artwork lined the walls.

I knew my father was worried Mitch, a defense attorney who'd recently won a couple of high-profile cases, might leave the partnership and open a practice up in Little Rock. Jackson Creek was a couple of hours away, and Mitch had needed to commute on his last case, staying in a short-term rental during the trial. It had gone well enough that he was getting more calls for cases up at the capital city.

"Have a seat, Harper," he said amicably as he gestured to the sofa underneath a landscape portrait.

I moved over to the sofa and took a seat as he shut the door, my stomach twisting into knots. I took his friendly tone as a good sign, but for the life of me, I couldn't think of a good reason he'd invite me for a private chat in his office. Maybe he wanted to ask about my father. My dad was acting like everything was normal, but he'd been married for thirty-nine years. Leaving his wife and filing for divorce was a huge life change.

Mitch took a seat in a leather chair across from me and rested his hands on the arms. "I thought I'd check in and see how things are going."

"With my father?"

He chuckled. "No. *You*."

"Oh." Did he mean in general or at the office? He'd never shown any interest in my personal life, so I went with professional. "Debbie seems pleased with my new filing system."

He tilted his head as he studied me. "I can't imagine you enjoy it much."

Oh. Lord. He was about to fire me? From a personal perspective, hallelujah, but I didn't have any other options, and at least this way I was making money. I kept a stoic face. "I'm grateful to have a job, Mr. Morgan, and I'm happy to help the firm in any way I can."

He released a chuckle and waved his right hand, which bore a large gold ring embedded with tiny diamonds. It flashed in the light of the table lamp next him. "It's Mitch. I've told you before, we're both adults. None of this Mr. Morgan stuff."

I forced a smile. "Then I'm grateful for the opportunity, Mitch."

"But this job is a hell of a lot different than what you're used to doing."

"True." I didn't know what else to say. That I hated it? That I was biding my time until I got my shit together and figured out what to do next?

"You know, your father is still holding out hope you'll go to law school."

I couldn't help laughing. "My mother too, but they'll both be disappointed. In the short time I've been here, I've realized that becoming an attorney isn't for me." Then, realizing I was talking to a lawyer, I hastily added, "No offense."

A bright smile spread across his face. "None taken. Honestly, I would have called you a liar if you'd said you were interested. I can see that being cooped up in the file room has you practically gnawing your leg off."

Oh shit. Had my boredom and frustration been that obvious? "I hope I haven't given the wrong impression, Mr. Morgan." I cringed. "I mean, Mitch."

"Relax," he said, patting the air. "You're not in trouble and you're not here because I plan on firing you. In fact, it's quite the opposite."

I breathed a sigh of relief...for the paycheck, not the job. But what did he mean? His words implied he was going to present me with an opportunity or a raise. Or both. I wasn't qualified to do anything other than filing and janitorial work, which would be a demotion.

"I've heard you're a very good investigator," he said. "There are rumors that TJ Peterman's daughter went missing a month ago, and you were the one who found her and brought her home."

I hesitated, trying hard to keep a poker face. While what he'd said was true, it wasn't public knowledge. "The police never officially declared her missing."

"No. I know they considered her a runaway and you disagreed with their presumption. It's also not lost on me that a Jackson Creek police officer was murdered by his brother in a murder/suicide the night she was returned home."

"What can I say?" I said, sarcasm slipping out before I could rein it in. "They say bad things happen in threes."

"So they do," he said, folding his fingers over his stomach as he continued to study me.

If he was hoping I'd spill the beans, he'd be disappointed. Peterman's twelve-year-old daughter *had* been kidnapped. But he'd insisted the police declare her a runaway, worried there would be a media circus otherwise that would impact his political bid.

Peterman's wife, Vanessa, happened to be the best friend of my deceased sister. She'd been more concerned than her husband, so she'd come to me for help finding her daughter. So I'd found her.

Drew Sylvester, the murdered Jackson Creek officer, had kidnapped Ava Peterman as a convoluted way of making me pay for his father's fall from grace. Turned out his father, Barry Sylvester, had been a Jackson Creek officer when my sister was kidnapped a little over twenty years ago. He'd discovered his other son, Drew's younger brother, Dan, had been sneaking around the kidnapper's house and taking voyeuristic photos of John Michael Stevens molesting my sister. So when Barry found out there was going to be a raid of the murderer's house, he'd warned the monster, wanting to make sure there were no signs of his son at the scene of the crime. If you asked me, they were all monsters.

Still. I may have recovered Ava Peterman, but I'd had nothing to do with Drew and Dan Sylvester's murders.

Those could be attributed to James Malcolm, the owner of Scooter's Tavern outside of Jackson Creek. The now-tavern-owner had once ruled a crime syndicate, and he'd made international headlines after he'd helped bring down an international drug cartel. He'd killed Drew while helping me save Ava, then killed Dan and staged their murder-suicide scene. If the Jackson Police Department found the situation questionable, they hadn't let on publicly. As far as I knew, the double homicide case was closed.

What Malcolm was doing in Lone County, Arkansas was anyone's guess, but if I were a betting woman, I'd place what little I owned on him being here for nefarious reasons, even if the sheriff couldn't currently find a single dirty thing about him. But while I suspected he was up to no good, I had no idea what he was actually doing. Other than taking care of the Sylvester brothers, he seemed to spend all his time running Scooter's Tavern. I still had no idea why I hadn't turned him in or why he trusted me not to. Sure, he'd caught me drinking while working the case, but it wasn't like I had a boss to answer to, which meant it wouldn't be mutual annihilation. Double murder charges trumped drunk on the job any day of the week. Of course, I could be labeled an accessory, but that wasn't what had held me back.

Mitch crossed his legs. "You have six years of experience as a detective in the Little Rock Police Department."

It wasn't a question, but I still nodded. "Yes, and eight years of experience as a beat cop before that. I also have a bachelor's degree in criminal justice."

"Impressive. I suspect you're more qualified to be a cop than all the officers in the Jackson Creek PD put together."

I wasn't sure how to respond. I believed he was right, but to admit so seemed pompous.

"Modest," he said with a chuckle. "You're a lot like your father."

I wasn't often compared to him, and it made my heart swell. My father had always been the softer of my two parents, and everyone used to say that Andi was like my father while I was more like my mother. Up until I'd left my job on the force, I'd tried hard to be seen as friendly and accessible, not hard and aloof, but looking back, I had to wonder if it had been a front. There was nothing soft about me now.

I gave Mitch a soft smile. "Thank you."

He studied me for a moment with a dramatic pause that gave me a small insight to how he dazzled a jury in a courtroom. He was drawing this out, putting on a performance. The question was why?

"Other than Peterman's daughter, have you ever looked for a missing person?" he asked.

"I never admitted to finding Peterman's daughter, but I have plenty of experience working missing person cases, both as a beat cop and a detective."

He uncrossed his legs and turned serious. "A client's

husband has been missing for five years. Hugo Burton. She wants to declare him dead so she can collect his life insurance, but officially, he's still a missing person."

"And you want me to find him?"

"Or prove he's dead. Clarice has lived in the shadow of his absence for far too long. She needs closure."

"And she also wants the life insurance money," I said dryly.

He leaned his head to the side. "True. I mean, if he's dead, she deserves to collect."

"How much money are we talking about?"

"Two million dollars."

My brow shot up, but I remained silent for a moment before stating the obvious. "That's a significant amount of money."

"Hugo was a prominent businessman and land developer in the county, so I would have been surprised if it had been less."

"I suppose you know the details of his disappearance."

He nodded. "He told his wife he had a late afternoon business meeting and never came home. She reported him missing that night and the police found his car at the Little Rock airport two days later."

"So he flew off somewhere?"

"There's no record of him flying anywhere."

"Surely there was security footage of the car being parked in the lot."

"The camera in the parking lot had been shot out."

I lifted a brow. "That's convenient."

"I know. There's also no record of him checking in for a flight, let alone booking one."

I recognized the familiar stirring in my gut. I'd always experienced this sensation when I started investigating a case. Slipping into detective mode was like sliding on a pair of worn slippers. "Did he get a new identity?"

"Possibly, but the police looked at the video footage from security, and there's nothing of him going through."

"So what's the going theory about the car?"

"The question is if he drove it there and dumped it, then found another mode of transportation or—"

"Or someone else dumped his car," I finished.

"Exactly," he said with a knowing look.

"If Hugo Burton was a land developer and had that much insurance, I take it he was a wealthy man."

"Wealthy is a relative term," Mitch said. "Turns out Hugo was broke when he disappeared."

"How broke?"

"His business account was practically empty, and he was on the brink of bankruptcy."

"So he fled?"

"One would think so, but Clarice is convinced he would never have willingly left her or their children. He was very involved in the kids' lives. In fact, they first grew alarmed when he missed his son's basketball game."

I heaved out a sigh. "She wouldn't be the first wife to be duped."

"And it's possible she was," he agreed with a good-natured nod. "The consensus among his family, friends, and business partners is equally split between him taking off and being murdered."

And they were probably torn on what to hope for. That he hadn't purposely abandoned them and left them with a mess or that he might come back someday.

"Any secret bank accounts?" I asked.

"If he had them, Clarice doesn't know about it. Maybe you can find out."

"Maybe. Any large money transfers leading up to his disappearance?"

"I have no idea. To be honest, I haven't looked into any of the finer details myself. Clarice came in this morning, and I only know what little I told you. That and what I know from the news reports."

I nodded. "Did you represent Clarice when Hugo first disappeared?" If Hugo had left to avoid prosecution, it wouldn't have been a bad idea for Clarice to hire an attorney to protect her interests.

"No, I only know her socially. I think she came to me because of my last case." We both knew he was referring to the one that made the news a few months ago. "I know you're not officially a P.I.," he continued, "but—"

"I am," I interrupted. "A P.I. I took the exam a couple of weeks ago when I took a day off to deal with some personal business in Little Rock."

His eyes widened. "Does your father know?"

"No one knows," I said. "Well, other than the licensing board of Arkansas. And now you."

A huge grin spread across his face. "What prompted you to take the exam?"

I wasn't about to tell him that Ava's mother had made the suggestion in a roundabout way. She'd been right—investigating was in my blood. There was no way any reputable law enforcement agency would hire me after what had happened in Little Rock, so becoming a P.I. was the only way I could legitimately investigate. But building a client base would take some time, and my plan was to work at the law office in the interim. "I miss investigating."

"That's only to our benefit," he said, smiling broadly, then his smile dimmed. "As for your hourly rate…" He made a face. "I presumed you weren't licensed."

Which meant he'd planned on paying me my current hourly rate, which was at least a fourth of what a P.I. would charge. But I was itching to investigate something, and I could likely use this case for my reference list. Ava Peterman's kidnapping was still pretty hush-hush, so I couldn't use her mother, Vanessa.

"I'm fine with taking my current hourly rate for this case. And if this investigation is successful, we can renegotiate for future cases."

He looked pleased with himself as he said, "I think we can work something out. Let's get started."

Chapter 2

Since Clarice had just shown up that morning, Mitch didn't have a file on Hugo Burton, but she knew he wanted to bring in a P.I. and had already said she'd be available to talk early afternoon should he find one quickly. He got up and wrote her name and number on a Post-it note, then handed it to me. "This is your sole responsibility for now. No more filing until this is done."

That was the cherry on top.

I took it from him, excitement rushing through my veins. "Thanks."

I headed out of his office and back to the filing room to grab my purse. Becky was standing just outside of the open door, her arms crossed over her chest. Her head was tilted forward so she could have the illusion of looking down at me even though I was probably three inches taller.

"Where have you been?" she demanded as I got closer.

"That's not really your concern."

"It is when I need a file and you're not here to get it."

"Then perhaps you should take your concerns to Mitch Morgan." I walked past her, heading into the room, and snatched up my purse.

"Where do you think you're going?" she snapped. "Your lunch break isn't for another half hour."

I walked to the doorway, but she blocked my path, her face screwed up with outrage. "I'm still talking to you."

I gave her a look that had made criminals stop in their tracks, and it seemed to have the same effect on her. "*You* are not my boss, Becky. Debbie is the office manager, and then the partners are above her. I take my orders from them, which means I don't have to explain a damn thing to you, so I suggest you move out of the way."

She started to say something before cutting herself off and moving to the side. I walked past her and headed down the hall to the exit, but she collected herself enough to sneer, "It must be nice working for your *daddy*."

I had half a dozen retorts on the tip of my tongue, but she'd already attracted the attention of several other office workers, who were standing in the hall gawking at us. I'd look like the bigger person if I walked away. Or I'd look guilty as charged. Lucky for Becky, I didn't really care what anyone else thought of me right now.

But that was a lie I had gotten good at telling myself. So good I almost believed it. The thought made my fingers itch to slip the water bottle in my purse out and take a swig.

I told myself I could wait until I'd gotten into my car.

I walked past the employees who were staring with gaping mouths and headed outside to my car. I needed to call Clarice Burton, but I wasn't going to do it with all those faces peering out at me. But I did take a big swig from my water bottle as I drove out of the parking lot.

A rush of heat filled my chest, and I basked in the comfort it gave me. I knew it would take a few minutes before I felt any real effects, and if I were honest with myself, it took a couple of gulps to get the same results a swig had given me months ago. But we all did things to get through the day, right?

In the beginning, I'd worried about drinking and driving,

but I wasn't drunk by any stretch of the imagination and a slight bit of alcohol took the edge off, making me calmer.

I headed to a gas station to fill up my Taurus. I suspected I'd be doing a lot of driving, so I might as well be prepared. While I filled up the tank, I called Clarice. She answered right away.

"Clarice Burton?" I asked. "I'm Harper Adams, a private investigator, calling on Mitch Morgan's request."

"Oh!" she gasped. "I hadn't been prepared for you to call so soon."

"Mr. Morgan wanted me to get started right away, so I've cleared my schedule to work on your case. I'd love to sit down and talk to you if you're free. Would you be available this afternoon?"

"I'm available now," she said breathlessly. "I really need to get this settled."

I cringed, grateful she couldn't see me. "I have lunch plans," I said, wishing it weren't true. My lunch plans were with my mother, and I already saw enough of her. At the same time, she'd be pissed as hell if I canceled. "Could we meet at, say, two?"

"That won't work," she said. "I have a prior commitment this afternoon and evening, and I'm volunteering at the food bank in Wolford all day tomorrow."

Which meant I couldn't talk to her until tomorrow night. If I accepted, I'd have to go back to the filing room for the next two days. I couldn't imagine walking in after the way I'd walked out. I would just have to deal with my mother's ire.

"That's not a problem," I said. "If you send me your address, I can head right over."

After she gave me her address and hung up, I steeled my back for what was sure to be a difficult call.

"Harper," my mother answered with a hint of irritation. "I hope you're not calling to cancel on me."

Was my mother a mind reader? Her guess was more likely

based on the fact I'd canceled on her two weeks ago when she'd asked me to go to the same bi-weekly historical society luncheon.

"I'm sorry, Mom. Something came up at work and I need to get on it right away."

"There can't be a *filing* emergency," she said in a snide tone.

"No," I said hesitantly, figuring she wasn't going to like where this was heading, but I wasn't about to hide it either. Especially not since I was hoping my filing days would soon be in the past. "I'm looking into the disappearance of a businessman."

She was silent for several long seconds. "I thought you put all that nonsense behind you."

"Which nonsense are you referring too?" I asked sweetly as I got back into my car and started to pull out of the gas station. "You'll have to be more specific since you find most of my life full of nonsense."

"For heaven's sake, Harper Leigh," she groaned, "no need to be so dramatic."

If that wasn't the pot calling the kettle black…

"I suppose a family as small as ours can only handle one dramatic one," I said, catching myself before I said drama queen. "But if you're referring to my career in law enforcement, then no, I don't see myself being employed by any agency any time soon."

"So you're doing this on your own," she said in a disapproving tone. "Like you did with Ava Peterman."

I still struggled with her hot and cold attitude over my search for Ava. She was the one who'd told me that she was missing. Sure, she'd pretended it was a more general warning to be careful, but she had to know me enough to realize I'd look into it. But during my investigation, she'd expressed her hostile disapproval, then barely acknowledged that I'd played a hand in Ava's safe return home.

"I'm not doing this on my own. It's part of my job."

"With Morgan, Hightower, and Adams?" she asked in disbelief.

"Yes, Mom. Mitch asked me to do it."

Her voice turned icy. "And your father approved of this?"

"Mitch is one of my bosses. I didn't run it by my *daddy*," I said in a snide tone.

"Harper Leigh! You will not take that tone with me."

I drew in a deep breath and held it for two seconds before blowing it out. I'd hoped to ease my irritation with a couple of sips from the bottle, but it hadn't helped. I unscrewed the cap and took another sip. "I didn't call to argue with you," I said as I screwed the lid back on. "I called to tell you I can't take you to the historical society luncheon."

"So what do you expect me to do?" she demanded. "I told them my daughter was coming last time, and now you're not showing up again. It's *embarrassing.*"

"Maybe you should tell them I have a *job*," I said flippantly.

She didn't respond for several seconds before she said, "I was hoping things could be different between us."

I let the words hang out there for a moment before I said, "You mean exactly the way you want them."

"I don't ask for much."

"I beg to differ." When my father had first left, she'd expected me to come over for dinner every night, then sit with her and watch TV, often some unrealistic police drama, until she went to bed at ten.

I'd agreed at first because, pathetic fool that I was, I'd craved her attention. Sure, the routine had bored me stiff, but a couple glasses of wine had helped move things along. But after a couple of weeks of thinly-veiled and not-so-thinly-veiled insults about everything from my weight to my clothes, my makeup and hair, my career choices, my overall attitude, and basically everything about me, I'd suggested my presence might not be necessary *every* night. Of course, then she'd started to cry and tell me how much she needed me.

I'd tried to be understanding because she began to cook my favorite foods and desserts and pulled back the edge in her voice, but the improvement had only lasted a few days. It was like she *wanted* to be more lovable, but she just couldn't keep from sliding back into her judgmental and snippy self.

How had my father lived with her all these years?

"Don't be tedious, Harper," she said, her voice stiff and formal. "Dinner will be at seven. Be on time." Dinner was always at seven, but I knew why she was "reminding" me.

"I have dinner plans with my friends tonight. I told you that."

"I'm making chicken parmesan."

One of my favorites, but she'd made it last week, so I suspected she had a roast thawed in her fridge. Knowing her, she'd pulled out the chicken parmesan suggestion to entice me to join her. "You can still make it. You can freeze it and save the leftovers." I knew better than to suggest she give them to me.

"So when will you be home?" she asked, her voice smaller.

"I don't know, Mom. I haven't had a curfew since I left for college."

"You don't have one now."

Maybe not technically, but she wanted to know where I was, what I was doing, and when I'd be home. I didn't live an exciting life. It consisted of work, home, and an occasional night out with my friends Louise and Nate. I didn't need to have that hammered home by constantly talking about it.

"I don't know when I'll be home. Don't wait up." Then I hung up before she could start arguing.

I really needed to find a new place to live. Sure, I was living in the garage apartment rent free, but it wasn't without cost.

I plugged Clarice's address into the map on my phone and

started heading to Wolford when my phone rang. Louise's name popped up on the screen.

"Hey," I said, feeling a rush of gratitude for our friendship.

"You're on your lunch break, right?" she asked.

Technically, I was, and I almost told her where I was headed, but for some reason, I was afraid I'd jinx it. Like Clarice would change her mind once she met me or realized who I was, and then I'd have to admit that I'd lost the job. Better to wait until after the interview, when I knew this was a real case. "You know it. Twelve on the dot."

"I'm on my lunch break too, eating in my car, so I figured I'd call to make sure we're still on for tonight," she said. "I know your mother gave you grief for meeting us at Scooter's Tavern last time. Didn't she call it Satan's den of iniquity?"

I laughed. My mother knew the tavern was owned by a hoodlum, as she called James Malcolm, and she worried I'd sully my reputation even more than I already had by frequenting it. Little did she know I'd worked a case with him. Fortunately for James Malcolm, his past created an appealing lure of danger to the general public, like Malcolm was a lion in a cage, even though the sheriff's department hadn't found even a whiff of impropriety, despite their many attempts to try. Then again, they didn't know about the double murder. It made me wonder what else Malcolm was getting away with.

"I think she called it the devil's playground," I said in a mock snooty tone. "And you're either psychic or your ears were burning, because I literally just hung up with my mother after she tried to guilt me into eating dinner with her. She even offered to make chicken parmesan."

"She's pulling out the big guns," she said with a laugh.

"I had dinner with her last night and the night before that and practically every other night I don't spend with you and Nate. I feel like I've earned my furlough. It's going to take more than chicken parm to get me to miss tonight."

"You really need to move out of that apartment, Harper," she said with a sigh.

"I know, maybe after another paycheck or two. Just a couple of days ago, Dad reiterated that I could move in with him, but…"

"Trust me. I get it," she said softly. "I could never move in with my mom, and we get along pretty great. You and your dad…"

She knew about our complicated history. He was finally trying to make up for his years of neglect and indifference, but moving in might throw things off. Besides, at least the garden apartment offered me some autonomy and privacy.

"The apartment over Nate's bookshop will be available for rent soon if you can hold out. The rent would be super cheap." He owned it and had decided to fix it up and rent it out, a plan he'd shared with us a few weeks ago. He'd given me a side-eyed look as he said it, subtly suggesting it could be the solution to my housing problem.

I had to admit I was tempted. But…

"I don't think it's a good idea," I said with a sigh.

"Because he likes you."

"Yeah, and while I have to admit I find him attractive, I just don't…"

"It's okay to not be interested in him," Louise said. "Even if he *is* cute."

"It's more complicated than that."

Nate Davis and I had reconnected when I was looking for Ava Peterman. We'd gone to high school together, and both of us had been in the brass section of our band. He'd asked me out to dinner, and I'd conditionally accepted, telling him I couldn't start anything until I wrapped up Ava's case. But that had happened four weeks ago and I'd continued to push him off, including Louise on all of our outings together. I knew I was sending him mixed signals, but the truth was I wasn't sure what I wanted.

My previous boyfriend had also been my partner in the Little Rock Police Department. He'd betrayed me after the shooting that had ended my career. The boy I'd shot had been carrying a gun—I'd seen it, clear as day—but no one had found it at the crime scene. Instead of taking my word for it, something he should have done as my partner in life and work, he'd doubted me. In fact, he'd encouraged me to lie and say I'd gotten it wrong. And when there were multiple break-ins at my house following the shooting, he'd treated me with derision as if I were either lying for attention or losing my mind.

I'd met Louise, who had been a Little Rock patrol officer, after the third and last break-in. She'd witnessed his degrading behavior at the scene…and she'd told me she suspected I'd been set up and that Keith was part of it.

I believed her.

She'd also told me she was quitting the department and taking a deputy position with the Lone County Sheriff's Department. Coincidentally, my hometown of Jackson Creek was in Lone County. We'd kept in touch, and when I'd moved back into my parents' garage, we'd started hanging out once a week.

"Just tell him you're not ready," Louise suggested.

"But then I'll be keeping his hopes up. The thing is, I'm not sure I'll ever be ready."

"I know," she said, not sounding happy about it. "But you know he's not going to take it well."

That was what I was afraid of. I really liked having Nate as a friend and didn't want to lose him, but he also wore his heart on his sleeve. I didn't want to hurt him.

When had I grown into such a coward?

"Are we still on for dinner and a movie in El Dorado on Saturday?" she asked. "It's been ages since I've seen a good romcom."

And it had been ages since I'd had a friend to hang out

with this way. I'd been close with my Little Rock roommate, Kara, but she'd distanced herself from me after the shooting. Looking back, we'd started to drift apart before that, when she'd started dating her current boyfriend.

Louise and I had gone to El Dorado a couple of weeks ago for lunch and some shopping, and I'd had more fun than I had in ages. Hanging out with her always made me feel lighter, like she helped burn off the dark clouds hanging over me.

"Of course," I said. "I'm looking forward to it." Even though I'd still be working this case, I wasn't expected to work on it 24/7.

"Great! Oops. Gotta go. I'll see you tonight," she said cheerfully as she abruptly ended the call.

It was such typical Louise behavior I couldn't help smiling. She was like a hurricane that swept in, spreading sunshine instead of rain, then ran back out to sea. She was exactly what I needed, and I was lucky to have her.

Now if only I could figure out what to do about Nate.

Chapter 3

Clarice Burton lived outside of Wolford off a county road.
The property was surrounded by farmland. Given the size of
her yard, her home had to be on at least a few acres. The
house was a large white colonial with huge pillars, with a side-
loading three-car garage that made it look even larger. An old
basketball hoop with a torn net was arranged at the back of
the driveway, which was empty of any vehicles.

I parked on the driveway, then took a moment to survey
the property. A large concrete, multilevel fountain sat in the
middle of a landscaped center in front of the house. I wasn't
surprised it wasn't running given that it was March and we
still had freezes in southern Arkansas at this time of year. But
the concrete was broken and chipped in multiple places,
suggesting it wouldn't have been running anyway.

I got out and walked up to the house, taking in the
chipped paint by the windows and the worn-looking roof. I
suspected the house was worth over one million, but if Hugo
Burton had disappeared with all the money, there probably
hadn't been much left behind to cover routine maintenance.

The front door opened before I got a chance to ring the
doorbell. The woman who answered was medium height,

probably an inch or two shorter than my 5'7", and looked trim in her expensive-looking athletic wear. Her hair was a salon-colored blond, and I guessed her to be in her early forties.

"You must be Harper!" she called out, walking out onto the front stoop. "Thank you again for coming so quickly."

"Of course," I said as I reached her. "I'm happy to help you find closure."

She reached for my arm and started to guide me inside. "Come in. I'm eager to get started and I want to make sure we have plenty of time. The police talked to me for *hours* after Hugo disappeared, so I wasn't sure how long you'd need."

I let her tug me into the foyer, then gently pulled myself free. The foyer had a white marble floor with a double staircase leading to a landing on the second floor. A multilevel crystal chandelier hung over a round, marble-topped table in the center of the space. A large, fake flower arrangement sat in the middle of the table.

"Would you prefer coffee, tea, water, or something else?" she asked, glancing over her shoulder as she headed into a living room to our left. "I guess it's too early to be hitting the hard stuff."

I supposed it was, but considered asking for a glass of whiskey anyway. Based on the money sunk into the furnishings of the house, I suspected they had top shelf. Then again, given her current money situation, maybe not. There was also the fact that drinking on the job was unprofessional. "Water is fine."

But I still salivated as I imagined the smooth whiskey sliding down my throat. James Malcolm and his attorney, Carter Hale, kept fine whiskey in their offices, and in the short time I'd spent working with them, I'd acquired a taste for it, making my usual go-to, Jack Daniel's, suffer in comparison.

Clarice continued walking through the living room, moving past the twin leather sofas facing each other, perpendicular to the marble fireplace and a dark wood grand piano in a corner. "I thought we could sit in the sunroom," she said as she neared the door, "even if it isn't sunny. Sometimes the sun peeks out and I soak it up when I can. I need all I can get and sometimes my stupid lamp isn't enough."

"Do you suffer from seasonal depression?" I asked as we entered a room with windows on two sides. Rattan furniture with bright, floral, overstuffed cushions filled the small space. Plants were everywhere, some flowering. I could see why Clarice preferred to be in here. It had a bright cheery atmosphere even I could appreciate.

"Yes, terribly. I'd love to move to Florida, which is part of the reason I went in to talk to Mitch this morning." Clarice moved to a tray arranged on a table between the sofa and a love seat. It already held two pitchers of water and crystal cut glasses filled with ice. She picked up one of the pitchers and poured water into both glasses as I sat on the sofa and looked out the windows into a small garden with dormant rose bushes. I could make out the edge of an in-ground pool behind the house.

I pulled out my phone and opened the recording app. "I hope you don't mind if I record our conversation. I'd like to be engaged in conversation with you, then take notes from the recording later."

"Of course. Whatever you need."

"Are you wanting to sell the house?" I asked as she handed me a glass.

"Yes, but Hugo's name is on the paperwork. If he's not here to sign, I can't sell."

"Which is why you're wanting him declared dead."

She sat down in the chair opposite me, her back to the windows overlooking the backyard. "I could file some kind of paperwork that would give me power of attorney due to his abandonment, but I'd rather have him declared dead."

"I take it you believe he's dead," I said, watching her closely to take in her reaction.

"Definitely," she said with a fire in her eyes. I suspected she'd been told that she was crazy to believe he hadn't abandoned her, and she was ready for a fight every time someone tried to convince her otherwise.

I instantly felt a kinship with her.

"How long were you married?"

A soft smile loosened the determination on her face. "A few months shy of twenty years when he disappeared. We were planning a party to celebrate."

"How did you meet?"

"In college, at a fraternity party. My sorority partnered with his fraternity at Ole Miss. We met our freshman year and fell in love. We married the June after we graduated."

"Were you both from Lone County?"

"Oh, no," she said with a short laugh. "Neither of us were, but Hugo had a friend in college who presented him with a business opportunity, so we moved here to check it out."

"Right after college?"

"Yes, we were in the process of moving and planning the wedding. It was pretty chaotic."

"I'm sure," I said with a smile. "So where are your families?"

"Hugo's parents died in a car accident when our son Anton was five, and my father died of a heart attack shortly after Hugo disappeared. My mother still lives in Mississippi."

"Do you have any other children?"

"We also have a daughter, Mary Ann."

"How old are your kids and where do they live?"

Her face beamed with pride. "Anton just graduated from the University of Arkansas in Little Rock last May with a nursing degree. He works at the surgery center in Wolford."

"And Mary Ann?"

"She's currently a sophomore at Ole Miss."

"How old were the kids when your husband disappeared?"

"Anton was seventeen and Mary Ann was fourteen."

I held her gaze with a sympathetic look. "I'm sure that was difficult for all of you. How did they handle his disappearance?"

She frowned. "Honestly, not well. They were very, *very* close to Hugo and refused to believe he'd left them."

"Would either of them be willing to talk to me?"

Her eyes widened. "Is that necessary?"

"They might have a fresh take that you don't." When she hesitated, I added, "You can have a roomful of people watch the same event, and every one of them will have a slightly different version. We all see things through the lens of what we've experienced, and sometimes it makes us see things differently. That doesn't mean their versions are wrong. They're just different."

She studied me for a moment, then nodded. "I'm not sure speaking to them is necessary."

"You don't want me to speak to your children?"

"I don't want to worry them about this."

At some point, they'd figure out that she was working on declaring him legally dead, but it wasn't my job to question her decisions. I'd let it go for now but circle back around to it later. For the present, I decided to switch gears. "From what little I know, most people think your husband ran off. Why do you think he's no longer living?"

Her fingers toyed with the fringe on a throw pillow next to her as she trained her gaze out the window. "Hugo turned out to have been somewhat of a fraud." She swallowed hard, then turned to face me. "But one thing I'm sure of is that he loved me deeply and he loved our kids. He would do *anything* for them. *Anything*. He never would have left us—and especially them—with this mess."

"And when you say mess, what exactly do you mean?"

Sighing, she sat back, took a sip of her water, and then set the glass on the table next to her. "Hugo had multiple business deals in the works when he disappeared. He was into land development and often worked with corporations to set up new locations for their franchises."

"He was like a real estate agent?" I asked, genuinely curious.

"No, although he talked about getting his license."

"So he was like a liaison between the realtors and the corporations?"

"No." She shook her head and frowned. "It was much more hands-on. He kept his ear to the ground and seemed to know when a potentially lucrative property would come on the market. He'd snatch it up, do a bit of development to the land, then find a buyer who would pay him more."

"The people he was purchasing the properties from didn't know what he was doing?"

She shrugged. "Maybe? Maybe not. He didn't usually talk to the landowners unless the property wasn't for sale. Otherwise, he dealt strictly with the listing agent. But for the properties that might fall in an area he thought would be good for development, he was known to approach the owner and make them an offer."

"Did he approach landowners very often?" If one of them sold their land and then found out Hugo had resold it for more profit, it could have incited one of them to murder him.

"Only a few times that I know of. But that was ages ago, back when he first started. Later he let his real estate agent handle contacting landowners."

"Seems like a risky gamble," I said. "Buying land he didn't know he could resell."

"He had a map of Lone County and the surrounding counties in his office," she said quietly. "And he was familiar with a lot of liaisons in corporations. He knew what they were looking for." Her chin lifted. "And he didn't just turn around and resell the property. He had studies done on the land.

Drainage. The cost of bringing electricity, water, sewers if they were applicable, otherwise septic systems. The logistics of roads for trucks. All of that took time and money."

"Sounds like a lot of work," I said.

"It is. No corporation was going to make an offer on land without that information," she said. "They either work with land developers or hire their own people to handle the logistics. The people who worked with Hugo appreciated that he'd already done the heavy lifting for him."

"I wouldn't think there would be that much business moving into the county," I said.

"You'd be surprised. Hugo and a group of other men were interested in growing the area."

"A group of other men?"

"The Colter Group. They were trying to bring in more business. Hugo played a huge role."

"Did the group continue after Hugo disappeared?"

"It disbanded about a year later, but Brett Colter, the head of the group, continued doing the work."

I made a mental note to talk to Brett Colter.

"Did Hugo own any land when he disappeared?"

"Several properties, but Brett had a legal agreement with Hugo for the development of one of them. A high-end strip mall. Brett took over after Hugo disappeared."

"What's going on with the properties now?"

"Not counting the one Brett took over, there were two in Hugo's company's name. Burton Management."

"Did Brett Colter pay you Hugo's portion for the property they were jointly working on?"

"No," she said softly and seemed to shrink a little. "When I approached Brett, he told me I had some nerve coming to him after Hugo had financially screwed him by leaving like he did."

"Did you have an attorney look over the contracts?"

She shook her head. "I don't have copies."

"I would think you're entitled to copies. Did you ask Mitch Morgan to get them for you?"

"He agreed to take my call for a consult as a courtesy because he's a friend of a friend, but he's a defense attorney. He says I need a probate lawyer, but he's going to find one for me."

"My father is a property attorney," I said. "I can see if he'll look into it."

She clasped her hands together. "Would you?"

"I can't guarantee he'll be able to find anything, but if he can't, I'm sure he'll point us in the direction of someone who can."

"Thank you."

"Do you have any paperwork at all about these deals? Addresses or surveys or anything to help with the locations would be great."

"I don't. They were all at Hugo's office, and when I went to collect Hugo's stuff about a month after he disappeared, the office manager had already packed it up into a box."

I glanced up in surprise. "He was still a missing person, legally speaking. I would think they would have given him more time." I considered what she'd said. "I take it the paperwork wasn't in the box?"

"No. Just personal items, such as family photos. A civic award and a trophy from a charity softball tournament."

I tilted my head. "Nothing else?"

"Nope. They said everything else was office supplies and they'd tossed them."

That seemed hard to believe. He must have had business files. What had happened to those? I paused. "You said Hugo worked with the Colter Group. Was he an employee or a consultant?"

"Definitely a consultant, but Hugo said the contracts stated that he was to get a percentage of the net proceeds, plus bonuses."

"And Colter didn't give you anything?" I asked.

A shadow crossed her face. "No. Brett said they used the amount Hugo would have received and used it to help cover the money the group lost because of him."

"How did Hugo cost them money?"

"I don't know." A bitter look filled her eyes. "He said it was too complicated for me to understand." She shrugged, looking sheepish. "Honestly, he was probably right. I rarely understood what Hugo was talking about."

"Did Brett or anyone else with the group give you any financial statements or documents?"

"No. Nothing."

That sounded like bullshit, and I planned to look into it. "Where was Hugo's office? Did the office manager say why they boxed up his property so quickly?"

"He said Hugo was two months behind on the rent. So when he heard Hugo was missing, he boxed everything up and threw out what he considered trash. I...I only found out because I went there looking for his business checkbook."

My brow shot up. "Did you ever get it?"

"No. It wasn't in the box of items they gave me. Nothing pertaining to his business was in the box."

"What made you think the checkbook was at his office?"

"Because he always kept it there." Her jaw set and her tone darkened. "When I mentioned all of this to the sheriff's department detective, he told me that Hugo had probably taken the checkbook with him when he ran off. And he figured he'd probably destroyed the files intentionally."

"You told the police about his office being cleaned out without your consent?"

"Yes, and they told me I could file a police report, but I chose not to. The sheriff's department had already made up their minds, and I was tired of trying to change them." She paused. "Maybe that's why I want to have him declared dead. It would be like a big FU to them for not looking harder."

I could understand why she felt that way, but the sheriff's department had more information about the case than she did. Hopefully, they'd reached that decision after a thorough investigation. "Did the detectives have anything to say about his office? Surely, they searched it."

"They did, although I didn't remember them telling me they'd gotten a search warrant. It doesn't mean they didn't, though. I don't remember much from that first week he was missing. There was a flurry of activity, making posters and posting in Facebook groups and such." She sniffed. "It's all a blur."

The week my sister had gone missing was the same. It was a blur, yet there were still some excruciating details I'd never forget. Like the crumbs hanging from Chief Larson's mustache when he came to tell us Andi was dead. And the shoestring that hung from a tree next to John Michael Stevens's head when he'd approached us in the park with a gun and told my sister to come with him.

"So I know they searched his office," she continued, "but they wouldn't confirm whether they'd found the checkbook."

"Instead they suggested he may have taken it with him," I said. Which meant they must not have found it. I couldn't see a reason why they would hide it from her.

"Mitch said that the bank accounts were empty when he disappeared," I continued. "Do you know where the money went?"

"If you think Hugo transferred the money to a secret bank account, you're wrong," she said bitterly. "There were no large transfers other than the down payments for various pieces of land and loan payments. Hugo didn't shuffle the money some-where so he could go live on a beach. He was trying to keep everything all afloat."

"At the time of his disappearance, did you know he was in financial trouble?"

Tears filled her eyes. "I had no idea."

"You didn't notice the low balances in the accounts?"

Her cheeks flushed. "I'm embarrassed to say I didn't pay attention. I never had anything to do with the business accounts, and he took care of our personal accounts too. Hugo said all the money stuff would stress me out, so he gave me a monthly allowance for the household and for things for myself. If I needed more, I'd ask him, and he always gave it to me."

The furnishings and her clothes suggested she had expensive taste. If Hugo had never denied her, had he felt pressured to make sure money was always available for her? Had he taken risks to keep her living in the style she'd become accustomed to? And if it had gotten to be too much, would he have run off rather than risk telling her the truth?

"How did Hugo handle conflicts?" I asked. "Did he try to avoid them? Confront them head on? Or somewhere in between?"

"He wasn't a fan of conflict, but he had difficult conversations with his clients all the time. Especially at the end. He didn't tell me what the conversations were about, but he told me that he'd had to deal with investors who were upset when investments weren't progressing as quickly as they would have liked."

"Did he seem like himself before he disappeared?" I asked. "Any changes to his personality or behavior?"

"He was preoccupied and a little distant, but the morning he disappeared, he told me he was working a big deal that would turn things around. He had a potential new investor who could change everything. I was surprised, because I had no idea he needed things to turn around. When I asked if we were in trouble, he confirmed that we were and said he hadn't told me because he didn't want me to worry. He left for a lunch meeting, then worked at the office and called me around four to tell me he'd meet us at Anton's basketball game, but he might be a little late because of his meeting."

"Do you know the location of the meeting?"

"No. He didn't say."

"Do you have any idea who he was meeting?"

She frowned. "No."

"What about his lunch meeting? Do you know where it was or who it was with?"

She shook her head. "He didn't tell me things like that. Like I said, he kept his business life mostly separate from his family life. Money and meetings too."

"I realize you don't know much about your husband's business dealings, but is there any chance you know if the meeting was in Jackson Creek or Wolford?"

"It could have been in either place. Or maybe even El Dorado. He'd occasionally go as far as Little Rock, but he'd usually tell me first. I know the afternoon meeting wouldn't have been in Little Rock or even El Dorado. He wouldn't have had enough time to get there and be back for Anton's game."

"Did Hugo keep a paper appointment calendar or a digital one?"

She nodded. "A paper day planner, but it would have been with him or in his office, and I didn't get it in my box of his belongings."

Which meant the sheriff's department had it if it had been in his office. I said as much, and she scowled.

"Who knows if they have it. If they do, they didn't tell me. Unless it had the details of his supposed escape, I doubt they'd care much about the planner. Especially since they refuse to consider that anything bad happened to him."

And she refused to believe something bad hadn't. I suspected she wasn't on friendly terms with them.

"If they think he ran away and they have some kind of proof, I suspect they'd close the case, or at least stop actively investigating it. Unless…" I held her gaze. "Did your husband lose other people's money?"

Her back stiffened. "Hugo wasn't a thief."

"I'm not accusing him of that, but you said he was dealing with investors who were unhappy that they hadn't gotten a return on their investment. I'm guessing they didn't get their money after he disappeared."

Her cheeks flushed. "No. Some of his investors weren't happy and let me know."

"I'm sure that was difficult, especially when you had no knowledge of his business practices."

Her eyes lit up and she leaned forward. "Yes. You get it."

I gave her a sympathetic look. "If the sheriff's department thought Hugo defrauded people out of money, they might be waiting to potentially file charges against him."

"You mean they may want to *arrest* him?" she asked in dismay.

"Honestly, I have no idea what they're thinking, but if people lost money, they may have filed reports. And since the police haven't found Hugo's body, they haven't declared him dead, which means the cases would still be open." Tears filled her eyes. "Did no one warn you that might be a possibility?"

She shook her head, and a tear slipped out. "No."

While I found that hard to believe, I didn't call her on it. "I'm going to set up an interview with the lead detective. Which police department is handling the case?"

"The Lone County Sheriff's Department. Wolford PD started the investigation when he went missing, but since his office is in Jackson Creek city limits, they tried to take over. There was some squabbling, but the Lone County Sheriff's Department was ultimately given precedence."

"Do you happen to remember the name of the detective handling the case?"

Her lips pressed into a tight line. "Matthew Jones. He wasn't very helpful."

I made note of his name, debating on asking why he'd been unhelpful, but decided to make my own decisions about the detective. I suspected she found fault with him because he didn't agree with her conclusion about what had happened to Hugo. "Also, I'm going to need copies of bank statements for at least a couple of years before his disappearance, and statements for six months afterward too. I'll need them for any bank account with his name on it—personal and business. And I'll also need anything related to his properties or business deals."

She wrung her hands in her lap. "I've already gathered the bank account information. Mitch told me you'd probably need it."

That gave me pause. "You just happened to have two years of bank statements available that quickly?"

A wry look crossed her face. "You're not the first person to have asked for it."

"And what was the consensus of the person or persons who looked previously?"

She grimaced. "I'd rather you made your own conclusions."

Just as I'd suspected.

Chapter 4

Clarice went to her home office to get the bank statements. I waited in the sunroom until she returned with a manila folder stuffed with a thick stack of papers. I asked her if Hugo had kept anything in a home office before his disappearance, but she insisted he kept business firmly outside of the house. Something I found difficult to believe. Then again, if he'd been shuffling money to secret bank accounts, he probably wouldn't have wanted his wife to stumble upon evidence of it. Not that she was looking.

I took the folder and made sure Clarice had my phone number in case she thought of anything else or simply wanted to check on my progress.

Once I was in my car, I looked up the sheriff's department administrative number and called, asking for Matthew Jones. To my surprise, he was available.

"Detective Jones," he grunted into the phone when he answered.

"Detective Jones, this is Harper Adams calling on behalf of Clarice Burton. I'm looking into the disappearance of her husband, Hugo Burton. I was wondering if you could find some time to speak with me about the case."

He was quiet for several seconds, long enough that I started wondering if we'd become disconnected. "Detective Jones?"

He cleared his throat. "Sorry. It took a moment for all of that to sink in. Harper Adams?"

I cringed, grateful this was a phone call so he couldn't see me. "Yes, do you have a problem talking to me, Detective?" I asked in a brisk tone. *Here we go.* Someone else who thought I had murdered that boy in Little Rock.

"No," he said with a little chuckle. "It's just I don't think I've ever taken a call from someone so infamous."

I ignored his statement and moved on to the reason for my call. "Do you have time in your schedule to talk about Hugo Burton? His wife hired me to look into his disappearance."

"Hired? You doin' P.I. work?"

"Since I'm calling you about a case, I have to say you have very good deductive skills, Detective. I even have a shiny license number to go with it. Now about a meeting…" It occurred to me that perhaps I shouldn't be so adversarial, but it was my go-to defense mechanism lately. Still, he wasn't required to take a meeting with me. He didn't have to tell me *anything.* I needed to play nice.

But my attitude didn't seem to bother him.

"Sure," he said amicably. "What the hell? I'm free this afternoon. Does that work for you?"

"As a matter of fact, I have a few free hours. What time is convenient for you?"

"Meet me at the sheriff station at three. I'll tell you what I can."

"Thank you. I'll see you then."

I hung up and looked at my clock. I had about an hour and a half before I needed to be at the station, which was located at the edge of Wolford city limits. I didn't have time to go to the courthouse and look up Hugo's property records. Then again, I doubted they'd be in his name. He would have purchased them his LLC, Burton Management. I decided to head to the library and see what came up when I ran a search on Hugo's name.

The library wasn't crowded on a Tuesday afternoon, so I didn't have any trouble getting access to a computer. When I typed in Hugo's name, hundreds of hits popped up. The top searches were about his disappearance and updates to the case, including his car being located at the Little Rock airport.

I spent an hour at the library, then decided logged out of the computer. I had just enough time to run by the liquor store before I headed to the sheriff's station. I definitely didn't want to be late since this would be my first time meeting with a detective about a case when I wasn't in an official position. I hated to admit that I was nervous. Detective Jones had no reason to be forthcoming with information, and we both knew it. His cooperation would depend on whether he was willing to deal with me.

Some detectives welcomed fresh eyes on an old unsolved case, while others didn't like their work being scrutinized. The problem was that police and sheriff budgets only allowed so many detectives in the department, and if they were over-whelmed with cases, some cases were pushed aside, like it or not, especially if they'd hit dead ends.

I almost skipped the liquor store so I could show up early, but I always bought my whiskey and vodka in Wolford, and since I was already here, I might as well drop in and stock up.

Once inside, I headed to the back to get my bottles. I'd picked up my bottle of whiskey and was trying to decide between a large bottle of vodka, since I'd recently gotten paid, or a smaller one. I figured I wouldn't be drinking as much since I wouldn't be trapped in the file room.

I was grabbing the smaller bottle when I heard the front door ding, and an all-too-familiar voice said, "Hey, George. I'm here to pick up my special delivery."

I cringed. Shit. Just who I didn't want to see.

"I've got it in the back," said George, the store manager. "Give me a second to grab it."

"No problem," James Malcolm replied good-naturedly.

George hurried past me toward the back room, and I weighed my options: hide back here until Malcolm left, or head up front and act like I wasn't doing anything wrong.

Which I wasn't. I was thirty-six years old. It was perfectly legal for me to buy alcohol.

Even so, I didn't want to face Malcolm outside of his tavern. Sure, I'd seen him at least once a week since we'd found Ava Peterman, but I'd always been with Louise and Nate, and neither of us had ever mentioned our collaboration or the fact that I knew he'd killed Drew Sylvester and made it look like he'd been murdered by his brother. I'd order drinks and he'd give me jabs about my drinking, but only when other people weren't around to hear. Even then, I tried to avoid him.

At first, I told myself it was because he was a murderer, but I knew the real reason.

It was the fact I hadn't turned him in.

Perhaps I hadn't told the police because, deep down, I thought those men had seen more justice than they'd ever find in a courtroom. And perhaps I'd avoided James Malcolm because if I didn't face him, I didn't have to come to terms with what that meant about me. I could pretend I hadn't condoned the murder of two men.

Just like I could keep pretending I was fine. Everything was okay.

So I stayed in the back, clutching both bottles to my chest while I waited for George to return to the front with two bottles of whiskey. George rang him up, an astronomical total of over a thousand dollars—no wonder his whiskey was so smooth—and a couple of minutes later the bell on the door dinged, announcing Malcolm's exit.

When I walked up to the counter, George gave me a curious glance.

"Took you longer than usual to make your selection, Harper," he said as he scanned the first bottle.

I told myself it wasn't a big deal that the liquor store owner knew me by name. Hell, he'd recognized Malcolm, too, although I had to wonder why Malcolm was buying expensive bottles of whiskey here when he could surely acquire them through the tavern.

I already had my debit card out before George gave me my total, which seemed paltry in comparison. I scooped up the bag and headed out the door, then stopped in my tracks when I saw Malcolm resting his ass against my driver's door.

He gave me a lazy grin, and I told myself the flutters in my stomach were because I'd forgotten to eat lunch.

The sun reflected off his hair, creating more shades of brown than when he was in the tavern or out at night. He was wearing jeans and an unzipped leather jacket, exposing a solid black T-shirt underneath. He didn't have his bag, so he must have put it in his car while he waited for me to come out.

I'd looked Malcolm up after we'd found Ava, wanting to know more about the man I'd worked with. There was surprisingly little personal information about him, but I did know he'd been born in a rural Fenton County, Arkansas town and was forty-four years old. He'd never been married and, as far as I knew, didn't have any kids.

"You know, this is the behavior of a stalker," I said dryly as I approached him.

"Or a friend waiting to say hello."

"I wasn't aware that we were friends," I said, stopping a few feet in front of him.

He smirked, his eyes lighting up. "Acquaintances doesn't feel right, and we definitely aren't co-workers or partners."

I shifted the bag to my hip. "Why do we need a label?"

He looked pleased. "True."

"We both know you didn't stick around to say hello. Are you here to bust my ass for buying alcohol?"

"You're a grown-ass woman. You're allowed to buy whatever you want."

I gave him a look of disbelief. "Yet you make snide comments about my drinking at the tavern and…before."

His face became expressionless. "We were working a case before, and your drinking was interfering with that."

"Is that why you're here? Because of *the case*?"

"Maybe I waited to see how you're doing."

"Doubtful."

He drew in a deep breath and stood straighter, then started toward his car.

Could that actually be why he'd waited? "Why didn't you ask me at the tavern?"

He stopped. "I was under the impression you didn't want anyone to realize we actually know each other."

He had a point. I hadn't.

"You're not here because of…"

He lifted his brow. "Because of how things were ultimately resolved? No. I figured if you had a problem, you would have let me know by now or a sheriff's deputy would have shown up at my door. Since neither has happened, I figured we were square."

I took a step closer, my voice taut with anger. "You know I was a police detective. How do you think I could be okay with what you did?"

He held my gaze with steely eyes. "Actions speak louder than words, Detective." Then he turned on his heels and strode to his car again. I stood there like an idiot watching him drive away, wondering once again what the hell I was doing. I should grab my phone and call the sheriff right now and tell him what Malcolm had done. I could say I hadn't come forward sooner because I'd felt threatened by him. But that would be a flat-out lie, and I refused to tell it. So I told myself I wasn't reporting him because I didn't want to sink back into legal trouble.

But that was a flat-out lie too. I just didn't call myself on that one.

Chapter 5

The Lone County Sheriff's brick and glass main building looked relatively new. After my encounter with Malcolm, I'd had a long drink from my water bottle, but I was still on edge when I pulled into the parking lot, so I took several more sips before exiting the car. I popped a couple of breath mints as I walked to the entrance. When I entered the foyer, I reached for my badge to show the receptionist, but I no longer had a badge. The realization hit me with a sharp pang.

I'd based my entire identity on being a cop, and being a P.I. felt like playing dress-up. Like I was pretending to be the real deal but never would be again. It was a hard pill to swallow.

Clearing the lump out of my throat, I walked up to the counter and told the receptionist I was there for a three o'clock appointment with Detective Matthew Jones. She told me he was expecting me and would find me in the waiting room.

There were plenty of empty seats, but I remained standing. I was glancing around at the décor when I heard Louise exclaim in surprise, "Harper?"

She was coming through a back door, wearing her brown

deputy uniform. Her long dark hair was pulled into a bun at the nape of her neck.

"What are you doing here?" she asked, worry in her eyes.

"Don't worry. I'm fine. I'm here on business, but I didn't let you know I'd be here because I thought you'd be out on patrol."

"I just finished up some reports." She scanned the waiting room, her gaze skipping over a middle-aged man on the other side of the room. "What business are you here about?"

"Kind of a long story, which I'll tell you about tonight, but I'm meeting with Detective Jones."

"Matthew?" she asked in concern, then panic filled her eyes. "Oh my God. Did something happen?"

She knew I'd faced more than my fair share of hostility since coming back to Jackson Creek. While the majority of people had accepted my past, there were still a few citizens who weren't happy I'd returned home after the shooting last October, and they weren't shy about letting me know. While most of harassment had been relegated to verbal confrontations, a few threatening notes had been left on my car at the grocery store and in the parking lot of the law office. I'd refused to file any police reports, worried the local agencies would think I was making it up for attention.

"No, I'm fine," I said again, placing a reassuring hand on her arm. "I'm here to ask him about an old case."

She squinted in confusion, but I could also see she was dying to know what was going on.

"Like I said, long story, but I'll tell you over drinks tonight. I'll even buy with my paycheck, which was deposited into my previously empty account last Friday."

"Rolling in the big bucks now," she teased half-heartedly while glancing back at the door she'd used to enter the space.

The door opened, admitting a man in a white dress shirt, red tie with white stars, and navy dress pants. If it were Halloween, he'd have a good shot at winning a costume contest for dressing like an American flag. "Ms. Adams?" he asked, he gaze firmly on me.

"I'll talk to you later," Louise said under her breath, then headed out the front door even thought it was clear she wanted to stay.

I turned toward the back doorway. "Thank you for agreeing to meet with me, and so expediently."

"Call me curious," he said with a twinkle in his eyes I hadn't expected. I was used to the animosity I'd been facing from the Little Rock and Jackson Creek PDs.

He led me down the hall to an interrogation room. A file sat in the middle of the table. "I thought we'd have more privacy in here," he said, following me in and shutting the door behind us. He hesitated. "I should have asked if you want something to drink."

"I'm fine." Especially after my sips in the car.

I sat at the table and pulled the notebook out from the deep pocket of my coat. "Looks like you're ready for me." I took all the folders on the table to be a good sign.

He sat down across the table and watched me for several long seconds. I studied him as well. I guessed him to be in his early forties, but he didn't have a paunch like a lot of detectives in their forties got. He was fit and was attractive. I was sure he used that to his advantage. I couldn't help wondering if he was planning to use it now. Too bad for him, my ex-partner/boyfriend had also been a fit and good-looking detective in his forties. I was immune to his type.

"You said you were looking into Hugo Burton's disappearance?" He scooted his chair back and assumed a relaxed pose, but I could see through the ruse. Why was he on guard? Because he didn't trust me? Or was this about the case?

"Yes, Clarice Burton has hired the Morgan, Hightower, and Adams law firm to help declare her husband dead so she can move on with her life."

He snorted. "And collect the massive life insurance policy."

I wasn't surprised he knew about the policy. I would have been more surprised if he didn't. "If he's dead, then it's owed to her."

He leaned back in his chair. "He's not dead."

"You have evidence proving that?"

"I don't have anything that suggests he is." He leaned forward, resting his arm on the table. "He was in financial trouble and had a shitload of people who were probably about to sue him, not to mention he was possibly facing fraud charges. His car was found at the airport, sure, but his passport was missing. So was all of the documentation about his business. Including his checkbook." He stuck out a finger with each point.

"Did he pack a suitcase?"

"No, but—"

"Seems to me he would've taken the trouble to pack if he planned on leaving the country."

"He may have left in a hurry."

"Perhaps he intended to leave at a later date," I conceded, "but then the perfect opportunity presented itself and he took it. It sounds like you think he planned his exit. Did he move any money after he disappeared?"

"Two hundred grand to an offshore account."

I stared at him in surprise. Especially since Clarice claimed he hadn't moved any money.

"It was online, late on the day he disappeared. Late enough it didn't post until the next morning, not that anyone was looking that evening."

"What did the financial auditor say after looking at Hugo's bank account records?"

His face flushed slightly. "We didn't have an auditor review them."

I stared at him in surprise. "Weren't you planning on filing fraud charges? Seems to me you'd need hard proof."

"The state would have filed the fraud charges, but they weren't interested in pursuing it until we found him."

"Do you know who owns the offshore account?"

"Not a clue."

"An auditor could have helped with that."

"Look," he said, irritation flashing in his eyes before he quickly covered it. "We're not a big city. We're a small county sheriff's office doing the best we can with limited resources. Why pay an auditor when the state was gonna do it anyway? Besides, that bank transfer was as plain as day."

I held up a hand in surrender. "You're right. It's pretty damn easy for me to come in and play armchair quarterback five years after the fact. I'm sorry."

He nodded, but it was stiff. Then he added, "And the state investigator who took over the case when it hit a dead end couldn't find out who owned it, but the consensus was it was Burton's."

"Did you entertain the idea of murder?" I asked.

"Of course, but the money transfer was pretty damning, especially since it occurred at nine p.m. and he was supposed to show up at his son's basketball game at five. Even if we ignored that, there wasn't any evidence to suggest foul play."

"Clarice said she got a call from Hugo around four, saying he'd be late to the game. I'm presuming you checked both their phone records to confirm that."

"We did, and she was telling the truth. There was a call placed from his number at 4:03 that lasted four minutes. It was placed outside of Jackson Creek, around the area of Highway 20."

Four minutes seemed like a long time to tell someone they were going to be late, but they were married. They probably talked about other things.

"You said he committed fraud," I said. "What about the

investors who lost money? Were any of them pissed enough to have killed him?"

"We interviewed all of them. They had alibis for the window of time when Burton went missing."

"How many defrauded investors were there?"

"Six. I can't tell you who they are, but one is known for his own land development deals."

"Brett Colter?"

He lifted his brow with a smirk, looking impressed. "I can neither confirm nor deny."

He'd confirmed enough. Besides, Clarice herself had told me about it. "Hugo's wife said he owned multiple properties at the time of his death. One of them was jointly owned with Brett Colter," I said. "A strip mall."

"Yes. The property was owned by the Colter Group, but he had two other properties in the name of his own corporation, Burton Management. One was a smaller property, kind of the centerpiece of a property he'd hoped to use to lure a Japanese automaker into building a parts plant. He was in the process of purchasing the land around it, and he'd been working on it for less than a year. But it was the second property that got him into trouble and sucked up more time and money than he'd likely planned. The Sunny Point property."

"Sunny Point?"

I was surprised when he pulled a bulky folded document out of a file and unfolded it multiple times to reveal a map of the county. "The Sunny Point property was right here, to the southwest of Wolford." He pointed to an area outside the city limits. "He was in the process of creating a luxury neighborhood with multiple-acre lots, homes starting right around one million dollars."

My jaw dropped. "There's enough money in the county for homes in that price range?"

"The Colter Group was bringing in businesses and corporations with upper management folks who were used to owning homes in California and the East Coast. One million would be nothing to them. But when he started running into trouble, he pivoted and decided to add a separate neighborhood with slightly less expensive homes. He called it Phase Two."

"So what happened?"

"Burton's first problem began when he was conducting studies on the original land. Turns out there's an endangered bird species that lives in a marshy part he'd planned on draining. It sucked up multiple acres and he left him scrambling. The marshy area was where he'd planned on putting the clubhouse and pool, and the drawings of that part of the development and walking trails cutting through the countryside were front and center on the website and brochures. Plus he'd sunk a good couple of hundred thousand or more coming up with the plans and environmental studies. He was pretty much back to the drawing board."

"So he sought out investors?" I asked.

"He already had a few investors at that point, but he definitely needed more. The two original investors balked at his request for more money. They'd each invested 100K, and the second one had already contributed an additional 50K. The first one still refused to put up more money when Burton came back a third time, but the second investor added another investment of 50K."

"So the first investor was in for hundred thousand, and the second was in for two?"

"Yep."

"Where on the timeline did Burton go back and ask for more money?" I asked.

He smiled. "I'll get to that soon."

I nodded. It made sense to keep things chronological. "What did the investors buy into and what did they expect to get out of it?"

"Their initial investments were for financing the

infrastructure of the neighborhood, and the extra money was supposed to help him come up with plans for moving the clubhouse and pool. When Burton added Phase Two, they had to purchase more land. Which took more money."

"Why buy more land and add to his financial burden? Why not just deal with what he had?"

"The plan was that the investors would get a percentage of the lot sales, based on how much they'd put in. When Burton bought the first parcels of land, he purchased them at two thousand dollars an acre. He was planning to sell one- to five-acre lots, starting at fifty thousand an acre."

"Buyers were willing to pay that much for a lot?" I asked in disbelief. "Two hundred and fifty thousand?"

Detective Jones grinned. "I never said he sold any lots."

"Wait. He never sold any lots?"

"Nope, he was still in the development stage when he disappeared. Five years after he'd started. Which was why he was also working on the land for the Japanese car part facility to the east. He was hoping to make a significant profit he could then roll into Sunny Point, which included both Phase One and Two; however, he simply called it Sunny Point. He was smart enough to get all new investors for the land for the Japanese auto manufacturer. None of the Japanese auto land investors were part of Sunny Point."

"What was the hold-up on Sunny Point? You said he had multiple investors, so obviously he managed to pull in more money."

"He seemed to run into trouble at every turn. Just one bad luck situation after the other. It was like the poor guy was cursed. And it wasn't like he was new at this. He'd successfully developed another neighborhood to the north of Wolford, as well as several other business sites. But Sunny Point seemed to do him in. He had to clear the land and bring in electricity, internet cable, and water. Roads and drainage. But he seemed to hit a roadblock with everything and was paying out money hand over fist until he ran out. By then existing investors were getting pissed, especially the two original investors. They'd been told it would only take two years max before they'd see a return on their investment."

"Couldn't Burton have gotten loans?"

"His credit was maxed out. When he disappeared, he was behind on the payments for the loans on the land and was facing foreclosure."

"So where did the money come from that he transferred into the offshore account?"

"Remember when I said Burton had asked the original investors for more money a third time? He hit up all of his investors with a request for more money a few weeks before he disappeared. Unbelievably, five of the six gave him money. The total nearly came to two hundred thousand. We think he realized he was never going to get out of his mess and decided to cut his losses. So he took the money and ran."

"And left his wife and kids behind? For only two hundred thousand?"

"Hey," he said with a lackadaisical shrug. "Two hundred grand isn't exactly chump change."

"I've been to his house. Two hundred grand wouldn't support the lifestyle he's accustomed to."

"Maybe not, but I'm sure it's better than prison."

"True," I agreed. "But I doubt he would have been put away for long. It sounds like he wasn't intentionally defrauding his investors."

"He wasn't until he fled, although the state was looking into pressing charges. A few of his investors had approached the state together after his third request for more money, but they both assured me they hadn't told Burton. So I doubt that he knew. The investigator had barely gotten started."

"If they had contracts with him, then I doubt they had grounds for fraud charges before his disappearance. Any lawyer worth their salt would have built in a risk clause."

"True, but they definitely had grounds *after* he transferred the funds to another account without their consent and fled."

"So the evidence points to Hugo taking the money and running." But I wasn't buying it. Not when I knew Jones had cut corners with his investigations.

"That's the way we saw it," he said, then shifted in his seat. "Besides, in regard to your question about his family, he and his wife were having marital issues."

"Oh really?" I asked, though I wasn't necessarily surprised. Clarice Burton wouldn't have been the first spouse to hide issues in a missing person case. "When I met Clarice a few hours ago, she never hinted at that, of course."

"She wasn't exactly forthright with me either. Mrs. Burton didn't have a job outside the home and her husband gave her a monthly allowance. When I spoke to her, she painted their marriage as pretty damn perfect, but her friends and family didn't see it that way. They said Burton had started giving her less money, and Clarice wasn't happy about it. At all."

"When was the life insurance policy taken out?" I asked. "And who was the beneficiary?"

He chuckled. "We considered her as a suspect for his potential murder too, but she has an alibi for the entire day."

"That must mean she's the beneficiary—no surprise since she's his wife—but when was it taken out?"

"Two months before his disappearance. For a policy that large he had to have a full physical and he was the picture of health."

"And for that kind of potential payout, Clarice Burton could afford to pay someone to do the job for her."

He sat back in his chair and chuckled. "I thought she was your client."

"She is, but I was hired to find out what happened to Hugo Burton. Clarice wants the information to declare him dead. It would be pretty stupid of her to hire me if she were the one behind it. Also, while she wants proof that he's dead, *my* goal is to find out what happened to Hugo Burton. Period. I just need hard evidence. And preferably a body, either dead or alive."

He laughed. "Dead or alive. That's cold, Adams."

I didn't respond to his comment, getting back to the topic at hand. "What about the three investors in the small property southeast of Wolford? You said there was no crossover between the investors on the two properties?"

"No. I doubt the Sunny Point investors would have given him more money for a second project when they were so frustrated over his lack of progress on the first."

"Hugo didn't ask them for more money?"

"No, but I suspect he was planning to before he left. The manufacturer he was in talks with needed more land, so his realtor was in the process of coming up with a list of properties Hugo could purchase to expand. The realtor was still working on the list."

I took a moment to consider what to ask next. "I know Hugo's business documents were missing, but did you find anything useful when you searched his office? A planner? Post-it notes?"

"Nope. Like I said, we're pretty sure Burton took it all with him."

"So he took his passport and all his legal documents, but no luggage?" My disbelief came through loud and clear.

He gave me a lazy shrug and grin. "As you said, an opportunity presented itself and he took advantage. That was our working theory too."

"If his car was at the airport and you found no evidence of him in the surveillance footage inside the airport, then how did he get away?"

"We weren't entirely sure on that part, but our best guess is he had the car dropped at the airport as a decoy. We think maybe he purchased a junker car and used it to drive somewhere else."

"If he left the country, wouldn't there be a record? Did he have forged documents?"

"We're thinking he drove down to Mexico, crossed the border with a fake ID, and then flew to wherever he was going from there."

It wasn't a preposterous idea. It was plausible, but it just didn't feel right. Then again, the only person I'd met with any connection to Hugo was his wife, and she'd deceived me about the state of their marriage.

"I keep hearing how important his kids are to him. I suspect y'all confirmed that."

"We did. And they were. He coached all their sporting teams, put them to bed when they were little, and did nearly weekly activities with them, both together and one on one."

"Do you really think he'd walk away from that?" I asked without any hint of accusation. Jones had interviewed countless people on this case. He'd have a better idea than I would.

His face softened, and he sat back in his seat, suddenly looking uncomfortable. "If I'm honest, that's that part that makes me wrestle with him fleeing. By all accounts, that man lived for his kids. It's hard to marry the idea of him running off forever with the man who was obsessed with his children. A few family members say they think he would have divorced his wife if he could have handled not spending every day with them. I confess, there are times when I wonder if we got it wrong."

His statement caught me by surprise. "When we started this interview you told me that you were sure he ran off. Now you're saying you don't believe that?"

"Oh, the evidence tells me he ran off. But…" Some of the confidence left his eyes as he held my gaze. "I've had a daughter since Hugo Burton disappeared."

I nodded, understanding sinking in. "You're a father and you've experienced that connection." Now I understood why he was so eager to meet me.

A pang shot through me as I thought of my own father. I suspect the thought of losing me wouldn't have stopped him from running off if it meant saving himself. I hoped Detective Jones loved his daughter more than my father had loved me.

I swallowed the lump in my throat. "I also suspect," I continued, grateful that my voice didn't waver, "you had time to let the case simmer. Given those two factors, you now look at it through different eyes, a different lens." I held his gaze. "Do you still believe Hugo Burton ran off and abandoned his kids?"

He hesitated, then glanced down at the table before he looked up with a hard look in his eyes. "I'm no longer one hundred percent convinced he did."

Chapter 6

While I was surprised Detective Jones was willing to admit he might have gotten it wrong, it made me respect the hell out of him.

I nodded. "I plan to find out what happened to him, one way or the other. Anything you can give me to help with the investigation would be greatly appreciated."

He drew in a breath, then sat up straighter. "It's still an ongoing case, and you're not with a law enforcement agency, so obviously I can't give you everything, but if you'll give me some time, I'll put as much information as I can together and send it to you."

"Honestly, that's more than I expected."

He laughed. "I figure fresh eyes are good. All I ask is that you keep me in the loop. And if it turns out he was murdered, and your client had something to do with it…"

"I'll bring you everything I dig up," I assured him. "I think we both want the same thing—to find out what really happened to Hugo Burton. And if Clarice Burton had something to do with it, I have no intention of hiding that from you."

He gave a sharp nod, and I thought we were done, but he

sat back in his chair, looking relaxed. "So you decided to become a P.I., huh?"

While I wanted to stay on good terms, I didn't feel like discussing my life choices with him. "Obviously," I said with a half smile.

"I guess that makes sense. I hear you have a good track record." He shrugged. "Other than the shooting, *obviously*."

"Is there a purpose to this conversation or are we making idle chit-chat?"

He laughed. "Just trying to figure you out."

"That's really not necessary, but I can assure you that I'm a damn good detective, whether I'm wearing a badge or not."

"It'll be a lot harder without the badge," he said, still amiable. "You can't call in a forensics team."

"The way I see it, I'll be taking cases that have already occurred and the crime scene will have been cleaned up."

"Which means you'll be dependent on guys like me sharing what we know."

I wasn't sure where this was heading, so I sat back in my seat and kept my gaze steady. "I'm not in competition with you, Detective Jones. I was a detective in Little Rock for six years. I know how tough it is to give all your assigned cases the time and attention they deserve. There's no judgment on my part unless there's full-on negligence. Consider me your backup team."

He laughed. "You're like a relief pitcher."

"Given how little I know about baseball, I'll have to take your word for it. Again, I'll ask you to remember that we want the same thing."

"You plannin' on stickin' around Lone County?"

"Is that information pertinent to this case?"

He gave me a lazy grin. "I guess not."

"Then I guess we'll both find out."

Picking up the file, he stood as he pulled out a business card and handed it to me over the table. "Fair enough. If you leave an email address, I'll send the files to you, probably later tonight."

I took the card and got to my feet, extending a hand. "Thank you, Detective. I appreciate anything and everything you can share with me."

He took my hand and shook, his grip firm but not hard enough to send a message. "Let's hope you find something."

After he led me to the front, I headed out to my car. The interview had gone better than expected. Almost too good. Like he'd choreographed the entire thing.

Anxiety simmered in my gut, shooting out waves of paranoia.

Paranoia. That's what it was. I had nothing to base my wariness on other than the fact that I'd been burned by other law enforcement agencies. Detective Matthew Jones had no reason to sabotage me. He wasn't out to get me. He wanted to close a five-year-old case and recognized that I could be the one to help him do it.

I wasn't totally convinced as I got back in my car. I still felt jumpy, and the intrusive thought about my father hadn't helped. Was that one of the reasons I hadn't wanted to move in with him? He'd abandoned me once, even if he'd physically been present. Sure, he'd made an effort over the last couple of months—he'd asked me to come home and then helped get me a job at the law firm—but I had to admit I didn't completely trust that he wanted to make things right between us.

I didn't even consciously think about what I was doing when I grabbed the water bottle and took several sips. But thankfully the panic began to ease.

I shoved my thoughts about my father to the side. They wouldn't help with this case and were nearly twenty years in the making. They weren't going to be resolved in a matter of weeks.

As far as I saw it, I had one choice: I could let my fear

send me running from this case, or I could suck it up like I had done since the day Andi was stolen right in front of me and keep going.

It wasn't really a choice at all, so I grabbed my phone and looked up a name.

Brett Colter.

I needed to talk to him but the more I knew going into the interview the better…presuming he'd even take my call.

The top hit was a website listing for the Colter Group. I spent several minutes perusing the slick site filled with images of shiny construction projects and smiling faces and only found a vague description as to what the Colter Group actually did. There was some bogus mission statement about bridging communities and civic-minded businesses to build a better tomorrow.

So Brett Colter was a bullshitter.

Not that I was surprised. I suspected Hugo Burton had been a bullshitter too. He must've been a good one if he'd gotten people to keep investing in a project that had yet to turn a profit.

There was one way to find out, and that was talking to the guy. I called the number on the site, and a woman answered, "The Colter Group. How may I help you?"

"Hi," I said in a friendly tone. "My name is Harper Adams. I'd like to set up an appointment to speak to Brett Colter about Hugo Burton."

"Oh." It was one word, but I heard the trepidation in her voice.

"Do you know if he'd have any availability tomorrow?" Then, hoping he'd be more open to taking a meeting if it didn't sound ominous, I added, "From what I understand, Mr. Burton ran off and left Mr. Colter with a huge financial burden. I'd like to speak to him about that."

"And how are you involved in this?" she asked hesitantly.

"I'm a private investigator working for Mrs. Burton. We're

working to have him declared dead." I paused. "Which I'm sure would be to Mr. Colter's advantage."

I was operating on the assumption that Brett Colter was a savvy businessman, and would realize that he might be entitled to some financial compensation if Burton were declared dead.

"If you'll please hold, I'll check on Mr. Colter's availability."

"Of course."

I knew she was putting me on hold to check with her boss, not that I blamed her. I'd do the same thing in her situation.

A minute later, she came back on the line. "Mr. Colter says he has some availability tomorrow at nine a.m. here at the office. Will that work for you?"

It worked better than she knew. I'd start my day with his interview and use it to point me where I should go next. "That works perfectly with my schedule."

After she gave me the address, she said, "See you tomorrow." I took her cheerfulness as a good sign. Colter hadn't just agreed to meet with me. He was looking forward to it.

I hoped that meant he'd be chatty.

I decided to head home and do some research there. I had the copies of bank statements from Clarice and now that I was an official P.I., I had limited access to records that the average citizen didn't. I planned on taking full advantage.

I got to work as soon as I returned to my apartment, surprised that my mother wasn't waiting at the back door to complain about how all her friends had looked down on her because I had missed the historical society luncheon.

I couldn't begin to fathom why she'd wanted me there so badly when she was so obviously embarrassed by me. The few times I'd brought it up, she'd dismissed me as being dramatic. Pot, meet kettle.

I wanted to look at the land Hugo had owned to find out who had taken the properties over after the foreclosures, but I didn't have any identifying information to look them up, so I started on the bank statements. There had been multiple deposits of varying amounts in the days leading up to his disappearance. Then the night of the day he was last seen, there had been an online wire transfer to another account— presumably the offshore account Detective Jones had told me about. I had to admit it was pretty damning. The basketball game was at five, and the transfer was made at nine p.m.

If I went with the assumption that he'd been murdered and he'd made the wire transfer himself, then I had to wonder why he hadn't gone to Anton's game. Had he purposely missed it or had he been kidnapped, then forced to make the transfer before his murder? Or maybe someone had murdered Hugo and had access to his accounts to make the transfer into their own.

Why had Clarice lied about the transfer? She'd had the bank statements. Surely, she'd seen it. I wanted to ask her but decided to get more information first.

Detective Jones had been secretive about the list of investors, but at the back of the thick packet of bank statements, I found copies of the five checks deposited into his account. All written from the investors' personal bank accounts.

Brett Colter

Tim Heaton

Pete Mooney

Skip Martin

Bill O'Murphy

The only name I recognized was Colter's, but a quick internet search showed me that three of the five investors were dead. Bill O'Murphy had died of colon cancer the year before at the ripe old age of eighty-seven. Tim Heaton had been in a car accident several months after Hugo disappeared, and Pete Mooney had been found beaten in a Little Rock alley less than a year later. The news reports said Mooney been mugged, but it still seemed suspicious. I couldn't find much more about him via an internet search other than he'd been forty-three years old and was from Pine Bluff. What had he been doing in Little Rock? I planned to dig into it more.

Skip Martin, the second investor who was still alive, owned a Ford dealership on the south side of Wolford. Based on the photos I found in my search, he appeared to be in his fifties and had a couple of grandkids. He also supported several ball teams and gave money to the Wolford High School.

I became so absorbed in my work that I hadn't realized it was getting darker. I glanced at the time on the bottom screen of my laptop with a start. It was nearly seven, and I was supposed to meet Louise and Nate in a few minutes. I shot them a quick text that I was running late, then quickly changed into a pair of jeans and a sweater. Snagging a jacket and my purse, I rushed out the door and down the steps leading to the backyard.

As I got to the car, I realized my mother's house was dark. She always had the lights on by dusk, especially the exterior ones.

I paused next to my car, wondering if I should go inside and check on her, but I suspected that was exactly what she wanted. This was another act of manipulation. She'd give me a face-to-face lecture about how I was failing in my duties as her daughter, and I didn't have the time or patience. Instead, I sent her a text apologizing for canceling lunch, then tucked my phone in my pocket and started the twenty-minute drive.

For any other bar, a full parking lot on a Tuesday night would be an oddity, but not for Scooter's Tavern. It was always busy. Then again, it was the most laid-back place to hang out in Lone County, not that there was much competition unless you included Our Lady of the Lake's Bingo night.

When I walked in, I saw Louise and Nate in a booth in the back. Louise lifted a hand to get my attention. I waved back, then made a stop at the bar to order a beer, my mouth watering at the thought of a Jack and Coke. I'd had the urge to make one all afternoon, but I'd held off, telling myself that I would be able to have a beer tonight. But now that I was here at the counter, all of the bottles of hard liquor in front of me, a beer didn't seem like enough.

Too bad it had to be.

Malcolm was at the other end of the bar and after our encounter that afternoon, I had no desire to run up to him and order a drink. If he noticed me walk in, he didn't let on. I walked up to the counter where Misti, a bartender I'd met the first time I'd come in, was standing. She greeted me with a warm smile. "Hey, Harper. How's it hangin'?"

I laughed. "It's not too bad, actually. How are things with you?"

Misti and I hadn't been introduced under great circumstances—Malcolm had made me hand over my keys and sit at the bar with a glass of water and a basket of nachos on the house until she deemed me fit to drive. I hadn't been drunk, but I didn't hold the messy situation against her. It wasn't her fault her boss was an asshole, and she'd been pretty cool about the whole thing. But now I was more careful about what I ordered and how quickly I ordered my next drink. I knew she and Malcolm were watching.

"Not too shabby," she said, shaking her head as she reached for a beer mug. Her long dark hair shook behind her. It was layered and curled, different than her usual ponytail look. "You want your usual?"

"Yep. You're definitely not *lookin'* shabby," I said with a grin. "You got your hair done."

"My cousin is in beauty school and cut and colored it for free. You like?"

"Love!" I said. "I could use a trim myself."

Her brow rose and she looked down at me. "You could use more than a trim."

"Ouch," I said with a laugh.

"You know what I mean."

I did, but I'd never been one to color my hair. I'd always pulled it back when I was working, and since I was almost always working, I'd seen no need to do anything with it. Kara, my old roommate back in Little Rock, had always said a haircut and color made her feel like a new woman. Maybe they both had a point; I could use a new hairstyle to go with my new life.

"I can give you my cousin's name," Misti said. "They do it at the beauty school, and it's pretty cheap."

"My mother always says cheap's not better." As soon as the words left my mouth, I was horrified. Mostly because I couldn't believe I was quoting my mother.

Misti laughed. "It worked out pretty well for me."

"I can't argue with that. And my mother is a snob, so I'm not sure why that tumbled out. Sorry."

She set my glass of beer on the counter. "Hey, no offense taken. My cousin's name is Emily, and she's at the beauty school in Wolford on Tuesdays and Thursdays."

"Thanks," I said as I grabbed the glass, resisting the urge to gulp down half the mug.

"You startin' a tab?" she asked.

"Yeah, and add Louise and Nate's drinks to it. I got my first paycheck and I owe Louise a drink or twenty."

Misti grinned. "Got it."

Heading over to the booth, I glanced around the room. It was an old habit of assessing for threats, and it didn't die easily. I'd noticed Louise do the same thing on more than one occasion.

Louise scooted over when I reached the table, and I slid in next to her. "You owe me a story," she said, bright-eyed. "What were you doin' at the sheriff's office?"

"First things first—I'm buying the drinks tonight. This is a celebration."

"Getting your first paycheck?" Louise asked.

"That too." I paused and glanced at each of them. "I did something a couple of weeks ago that I didn't tell either of you about."

Louise's eyes danced with excitement. "You joined Tinder!" She didn't seem to notice Nate flinch.

"No," I said adamantly. "I definitely did *not* join Tinder." I drew a breath. "When I was in Little Rock a couple of weeks ago, I sat for the Arkansas P.I. exam. And I passed."

"You did?" Louise squealed.

"I should *hope* you'd pass," Nate said dryly, but a grin tugged at the corners of his lips.

"So you're quitting your father's firm?" Louise asked.

"No. Not exactly. One of the partners asked me to look into the disappearance of a businessman from five years ago. Hugo Burton. Ever heard of him?"

Louise considered it, then shook her head. "I was busy enough dealing with the crime in Little Rock. I sure as hell wasn't paying attention to what was going on in Lone County. Hell, five years ago, I didn't even know Lone County existed."

"You didn't know the geography of your own state?" Nate asked with a laugh.

"Do *you* know every county in the state?" she countered.

Nate lifted his beer bottle and lifted it to his lips. "Point taken."

"So why are you lookin' into this guy?" Louise asked.

"The sheriff's department investigated his disappearance, but they never came up with anything conclusive. They think he ran off, which seems plausible. But his wife insists he'd never have left her and the kids."

Louise grunted, then picked up her beer, saying dryly, "That's what they always say."

"Yeah, I know, but Clarice Burton thinks her husband was murdered, and Detective Jones says he's no longer so sure that's not a possibility."

Louise's eyes grew wide. "He actually admitted that?"

"I was just as surprised as you are. He said the man seemed to live for his kids and he spoke to a lot of people who backed that up."

"So what's his deal? Why would he run off?" Nate asked. "And no, I never heard of him. I might have known that Lone County existed five years ago, but I was too busy grieving my wife to care."

His statement could have been a downer, but the more time we spent with Nate, the more we realized he used humor to deal with the painful parts of his life. Maybe one of us should have called him on it, but it seemed easier to go with it. We weren't close enough friends to cross that boundary yet. Besides, I had no desire for either of them to bring up my own pain.

"He was a land developer," I said. Then, after swearing Nate to secrecy, I told them everything I'd learned about his business dealings. "I have an appointment with Brett Colter tomorrow at nine, and I've spent the last hour or so looking into the investors."

"Which was why you were late," Nate said. "You got absorbed in your work."

"Yeah," I said with a grimace. "Sorry."

"Don't be sorry," he said. "I haven't seen you so excited since we won the marching band contest in El Dorado back in junior year."

"Umm..." I said dryly, "I think you're confusing me with *yourself*. I was in my moody teenage girl stage and didn't get excited about anything."

"You were excited about winning the contest," he said with a grin. "You just remember it differently because you thought you were too cool to care."

"Y'all," Louise said, holding up a hand in protest. "Who gives a shit about a band contest from the dark ages?"

"Says you," Nate said haughtily. "We had a huge rivalry with Magnolia, and we kicked their asses. It was a coup."

"I'm sure it was the sweep of the century," she mocked. "And I agree that Harper's got a sparkle in her eyes." She leaned forward. "Which is why I guessed she'd joined Tinder. A guy can definitely give a girl sparkly eyes."

"Enough about my eyes," I said, shaking my head. "I didn't have lunch and I'm starving. I'll go to the counter to order our food. The new waitress looks like she's got her hands full. Dinner's on me too."

Malcolm must have hired new waitstaff, because I didn't recognize the young woman standing at a table of about eight guys who were all showing off for her. Malcolm had taken notice behind the counter, and from the way he was eyeing the table, he was ready to step in if things got out of hand. I could see why they were interested. She was blond and blue-eyed, and filled out her Scooter's T-shirt nicely, but the guys must be newbies because everyone knew Malcolm didn't let customers treat his staff disrespectfully and their behavior was about an inch shy of crossing the line. Stepping over it was a sure-fire way to not only get kicked out on your ass but get a lifetime ban.

"Look at you, big spender," Louise said, giving my arm a slight push.

I laughed. "I'm making fifteen dollars an hour. So don't be thinking you can order a steak dinner."

"Scooter's doesn't have steak," Nate countered.

I gave him a dry look.

"Oh. I'm being too literal again."

Louise touched her fingertip to her nose while pointing to him with the other hand.

"Just tell me what you want," I said, "and I'll go order for us."

After they gave me their requests, I headed up to the bar, straight to Malcolm, who still seemed to be fixed on watching the new waitress and the table full of men.

"Detective," he said dryly as I rested a hand on the counter, his gaze not moving off the men.

"Malcolm," I said just as dryly. "You too busy giving death stares to take an order? Or should I head over to Misti?"

He still kept his gaze on the table. "I can watch the table and make a Jack and Coke at the same time."

"Too bad my order's more detailed than that, and a Jack and Coke's not on the list."

He turned to face me, and just like this afternoon, my stomach flip-flopped. There was no denying James Malcolm was a handsome man. His dark brown eyes seemed to see past my flesh and deep into my soul. I suspected he'd used that gaze to control his underlings and his enemies when he'd been an active crime boss. He was still wearing the solid black T-shirt I'd seen under his jacket, and the ends of the short sleeves were stretched by the bulging muscles underneath. Crow's feet surrounded the corners of his eyes, and his cheeks and chin were covered in dark stubble mixed with a few white hairs.

"You ready, or do you need to write it down?" I asked mischievously. "You know what they say about short-term memory when we get older." I was only eight years younger than him, but I couldn't resist.

One of his eyebrows arched menacingly, but then he cracked the barest hint of a smile. "I think I'll be okay."

I gave him the order, which was incredibly easy—a cheeseburger, a chicken sandwich, and buffalo wings, all with fries.

"Got it," he said, but when I didn't head back to the table, he said, "Wanting the Jack and Coke pretty bad, huh?"

I hated that he was right. I'd been eyeing the bottle of Jack Daniel's on the counter behind him, but I'd rather die than admit it. "You don't know shit, Malcolm. I was about to ask you if you know anything about Hugo Burton or Brett Colter."

His left eye twitched and he turned serious. "Let me get this order in first."

So he *did* know about them, or at least one of them. Asking him had been a long shot. I'd done it partly on impulse and partly to distract him from the drink he knew I wanted. But he seemed to know a lot about the activities in the county, so it seemed like a worthwhile shot.

He headed to the window to the kitchen to place the order, then came back and stood in front of me, casting a quick glance at the table full of men before giving me his attention.

"Why are you asking about Burton and Colter?"

"So you know of them?"

"I know Burton's missing."

"And Colter?"

He was silent for a moment, then said, "I know of him."

I found it interesting he knew about either of them. Five years ago, Malcolm had lived in Fenton County, and from what I understood, he'd been dealing with a turf war. I found it odd that he would know about a small-time developer about a hundred miles away in a two-bit, rural county. Then again, men like him didn't get into power unless they had a wealth of information, and there was a chance he'd only learned about the pair after moving here.

"Hugo Burton's wife thinks he's dead, while the sheriff's department thinks he ran off. I'm looking into what really happened to him."

His brow cocked slightly. "Why?"

"Because I'm being paid to do so."

"Someone hired you?" he asked, sounding surprised.

I decided to ignore his reaction. "Do you have an opinion one way or the other about what happened to Hugo Burton?"

"You're assuming I give a shit either way."

"Come on, Malcolm," I cajoled. "If you know about him, you have an opinion."

"Who said I know anything about him? Maybe I just heard his name in passing."

He was playing games, and I didn't want to play. I was too busy trying not to salivate at the thought of drinking a Jack and Coke. So I turned around and walked back to the table. I'd get more out of him later.

Chapter 7

"What were you talking to Malcolm about?" Louise asked with a wary look.

"I gave him my order, then suggested he try being less overprotective of his waitstaff." A flagrant lie that made me feel guilty, not only because it was a lie, but because I found it oddly endearing that he cared so much for their welfare. I never would have expected it of a man with his past and position.

I asked Nate about his week at the bookstore. He told us several cute stories about the children who frequented his store.

"You know why your customer base is so toddler heavy, right?" Louise asked as the new waitress brought our food to the table. Her name tag read Angie.

Nate groaned as he took his basket of wings from her. "Not this again."

"*I* want to know why he has so many toddlers in his book-store," Angie said eagerly. "You own Morty's Bookstore, right? I've been in there before and you helped me find a poetry book." Blushing slightly, she gave him a quick, appraising look, and the smile on her face suggested she liked what she saw. Truth be told, it wasn't the first time a woman had looked at him like that since we'd started meeting here once or twice a week over the last month. But the looks usually came from other patrons and Nate never seemed to notice.

Louise leaned across the table toward her. "Because their mothers are bored, and they imagine Hot Nate boning them against the bookstacks."

Nate's face turned bright red as Angie's grin spread. "I can see that." She handed the chicken sandwich to Louise, and I took the hamburger.

"That is *not* true," Nate choked out in protest.

"You're cute when you blush," Angie said and started to turn around.

"Hey, Angie," Louise called out. "Can you bring us another round of beers?"

"Sure thing," she said, then flounced back to the bar.

"I'm never going out with you two again," Nate protested as he reached for several napkins from the holder at the end of the table.

"Lies," Louise said. "You need us. Your social life is just as pathetic as mine."

His brow rose and he gave her a death stare.

"But the good news is that it's better than Harper's, so there you go."

"Ouch," I said with a laugh, picking up my burger.

Louise squirted ketchup into her basket. "Yet it's the truth."

She was right, but she and Nate had lived in the area longer than I had. And I wasn't much interested in a social life.

"So tell us about your week, Louise," Nate said. "Anything weird or wacky in the world of Lone County's law and order?"

She laughed. "As a matter of fact…" She took a bite of

her chicken sandwich and pointed to her mouth to mime that she couldn't tell us yet.

I shook my head with a grin. When I'd met Louise, she'd been uber serious, but then again, police cover-ups tended to make a person act that way. She was a different woman here —lighter, freer, happier. It gave me hope that the same thing could happen for me someday.

Once she swallowed, she told us about a traffic stop she'd had the day before when she pulled over an older woman in a 1970's Volkswagen bug for speeding.

Nate snorted. "That's the best you've got?"

"Hold up, Judgy McJudgy Pants," she said, waving a fry at him. "I'm not done." She paused for dramatic effect, then said, "The backseat was stuffed with bags of marshmallows."

"When you say stuffed…" Nate prodded. "Are you saying she had several bags on the backseat?"

"Obviously you don't know the meaning of the word stuffed," Louise said, giving him a piercing look. "Which I could make a very dirty comment about, but for some inexplicable reason, I'll refrain."

I burst into laughter, which made all of us start laughing.

It felt good to laugh. I hadn't had much laughter even before the shooting incident last October. Hanging out with Louise and Nate made that all too clear.

When we settled down, Louise continued, "I'm talking she had bags of marshmallows crammed into the back from the seat to the ceiling. She couldn't see out the back window. There must have been *hundreds* of bags of marshmallows in her car."

"Why?" I asked. "What was she going to do with them?"

"I tried to find out, of course," she said. "Only I didn't come right out and ask. I asked if she was on her way to a bonfire to make s'mores, although if she was making s'mores, she had enough marshmallows to give s'mores to the entire county."

"But she didn't have the graham crackers and chocolate," Nate said, "so she must have been doing something else."

"They could have been in her trunk," I suggested to play devil's advocate.

"There's no way enough graham crackers would fit in the trunk, let alone the chocolate bars."

Louise shot him a grin. "She didn't confirm one way or the other. She just chuckled nervously and asked if she was free to go."

"Weren't you suspicious?" I asked.

"Of course. I had no idea what she planned to do with all those marshmallows, but try as I might, I couldn't come up with a devious reason for her having them. So I gave her the speeding ticket and sent her on her way."

"And now we'll never know," Nate said with a sigh, then turned to me. "What about you, Harper? Anything interesting?"

"Well, other than getting a case to investigate, not really. Unless you call Becky losing her shit in front of the entire office interesting."

They wanted details, of course, and I was sure that Nate would use this story as gossip currency. He was a huge gossip, not that I usually minded. He'd provided me with helpful information during my investigation of Ava's disappearance, both about her father and how the tide of public attitude had changed about me since I'd moved back to Jackson Creek. Plenty of people in the office had witnessed her meltdown, so the stories wouldn't necessarily be tracked back to me. Not that I cared if they were.

After we finished eating, we headed over to the pool tables to play a round of pool. While we played, I asked Louise if she knew anything about Detective Jones, and she said she hadn't had much interaction with him, but everyone seemed to like him.

We finished our game close to ten, and Louise said she needed to head out so she could get up for work the next day.

"I should head out too," I said. "I'm hoping to get more research done before my meeting with Colter in the morning."

"Keep me updated on how that goes," she said as we headed over to the table so she could get her coat and purse. She cast a glance to the bar. "You sure you don't want me to help with the bill?"

"Absolutely not. How many meals did you buy me when I got back to town? I *want* to do this, so don't fight me on it."

"Okay," she said, then gave me a hug. "Love you, girl. Be careful."

"You too. We'll talk later in the week about Saturday." I watched her go and realized that Nate was in no hurry to follow her out. He was shifting his feet, looking nervous.

"What's up?" I asked, deciding to take the direct approach.

He sat down in our booth, and I reluctantly sat across from him. I had a feeling I knew what this was about.

"I know you said you needed more time because of your job and your father divorcing your mother..."

My stomach sank. So, this was it—the place where all my avoidance had led.

"I know," I said, still unsure whether to be brutally honest or gentle. I went with the latter. If I told him a flat-out no, he might avoid me for a while. Or possibly permanently, and I really didn't want to lose him as a friend. "I'm just not ready to open myself up to someone right now. You're a great guy—"

He leaned his head back and groaned. "Here we go with the great guy speech..."

"Look, Nate," I said, feeling uncomfortable. "I don't want to date *anyone*. At. All. So don't take it personally. I've been to hell and back. I feel like I can barely keep myself together right now, let alone manage a relationship." I gave him a warm smile. "You deserve better than that."

"As long as you're not just blowing me off," he conceded. "If you're not interested in me, then I want you to tell me."

"Honestly, I'm not sure what I want, but I'm flattered that you want to go out with me, despite all my issues. But," I added, "I have no idea how long I'll be messed up, so if one of those hot toddler mothers turns out to be single and makes a move, feel free to go for it. You deserve to be happy."

Thankfully, he didn't look upset. "You deserve to be happy too, Harper."

I wasn't sure I agreed with that assessment, but I knew better than to tell him so. Better to go home, make myself a Jack and Coke, and drown my feelings in my work. It had worked for years until last fall—the losing myself in my work part, not the drinking. But I was also self-aware enough to know it hadn't ever really worked before, even without the drinking. I'd just kept all the trauma of my sister's kidnapping and murder buried. The shooting of that teenager last fall had dragged it all to the surface.

"Thanks, Nate. And thanks for understanding."

Angie walked over and placed the bill on the table in front of me. "I heard you were covering the bill tonight."

"Word gets around," I said with a chuckle, then reached for my wallet and pulled out my debit card. I took a look at the bill and saw a note on top.

If you want to hear what I know about Colter and Burton, meet me at the back door in ten minutes.

I glanced at Angie, who didn't seem interested in my response, and handed her my debit card and the bill.

"You can head out, Nate," I said. "You don't have to wait for me."

"Are you sure?" he asked, looking uncomfortable. "It doesn't feel right leaving you here to walk out into the parking lot alone."

"I have to go to the restroom before I leave, and also, I was a police detective," I said with a laugh. "I'm pretty sure I'm qualified to take care of myself."

He made a face. "Yeah. I guess so." He grabbed his jacket and gave me another look. "I'm glad things seem to be working out for you."

"Thanks," I said. "That means a lot."

He headed toward the door as Angie returned with my card and the receipt. I gave her a twenty-five percent tip, then went to the restroom before walking out the door into the parking lot.

I made sure no one was watching, then headed around the back of the building, stopping outside a solid metal door. I only had to wait about twenty seconds before the back door opened and Malcolm's face appeared. He didn't say a word as he pushed the door open wide enough for me to enter. I followed him, letting the door shut behind me as we moved down the hall and to the left. He guided me to a partially open door, and before we entered it, I could see it led into an office, only it was nicer than it should be. I'd worked a few restaurant jobs in college, and those offices had dirty white walls, ugly metal desks, and fluorescent lights. This room had wood paneling, a leather sofa and chairs, and a wooden desk.

"Looks like you're trying to compete with your attorney for the nicest office," I said as he shut the door behind us.

I'd visited his attorney's office after the Jackson Creek police chief had suggested I'd kidnapped Ava for attention. Malcolm had insisted I use his attorney during my questioning with the chief. Of course, it hadn't been a favor. He'd loaned me Carter Hale to make sure I didn't spill any of his secrets.

"Hardly," Malcolm said, walking over to a dry bar and pouring two glasses of whiskey. "His office is pretentious." He handed me a glass, then motioned to the sofa as he made his way to a chair. "I often spend eighteen hours or more a day here, and I'm not living in some cheap-ass room. I won't apologize for that."

"Fair enough." I looked down at the drink in my hand, wondering if this was a test. I sat down on the sofa, intending to set the glass on the coffee table, but I couldn't seem to make myself put it down. "I take it you have information about Hugo Burton or Brett Colter that you don't want people to know about."

He sat in his chair and leaned back, lifting the glass to his lips. "Something like that."

"So why are you sharing it with me in private?" I asked, genuinely curious.

A wicked light filled his eyes. "Maybe I'm just being nice."

I gave him a pointed look. "Doubtful."

He laughed, then took a slow sip of his drink. When he lowered the glass, he said, "Let's say I'm going to share what I know because I'm curious to see if you can solve this."

That also seemed unlikely, but I decided not to call him on it. "So tell me what you know."

"Hugo Burton was in some deep-ass debt. He'd maxed out with his creditors, and he was looking for suckers to give him money for his dumbass projects."

"When you say dumbass projects…?"

"Don't play stupid with me," he scoffed. "You had to know he was balls deep in his Sunny Point project and the Japanese car parts plant. If you didn't know, then you don't have any business investigating shit."

"I know about them," I said, trying not to sound defensive. "I guess I'm surprised you do. He disappeared back when you were living in Fenton County."

"I like to know what's going on where I live." He gave me a cheesy grin. "I'm civic-minded like that."

I gave him a dubious look. "You've never struck me as a man who lives for his community, Malcolm, so tell me why you really know about Burton."

"You don't need to know that part, and I don't need to tell you shit. So if you can't just take what I know and accept it without asking a ton of questions, you might as well head out to your car and back to your mommy's garage."

I hadn't told him I lived in my parents' garage apartment, but I wasn't surprised he knew. It should have freaked me out, but instead it made me trust his intel.

"I can live with that," I said, but I didn't add the *for now*. I didn't believe for one minute that he was doing this to help me. He wanted something out of it. I was just patient enough to bide my time to figure out what it was. "You don't think the residential neighborhood was going to work."

"It probably could have...if the right person had run the project."

"And Hugo Burton wasn't the right person?"

"Hugo Burton had his head up his fucking ass. He couldn't develop a doll house, let alone a multi-million-dollar neighborhood."

"Then how did he get people to invest in it?"

"Because he was a fantastic salesman." He took a sip of his whiskey. "Or so I'm told. Plus he'd developed some successful baby projects in the past, but they didn't come close to the scope of Sunny Point. He floundered."

He'd known Hugo Burton. Or at least knew in-depth information about him. *That* was interesting.

"So he conned people out of money?"

"No, he was stupid enough to believe his own bullshit."

"Where does Brett Colter come into play?"

"Why ask about him?" he asked with a coy look.

"His wife brought him up. She said her husband was part of the Colter Group, and that they had some big project go through after Burton left that made millions. I guess she didn't get any of it. Colter said Hugo had owed him what he would have gotten from the deal and more."

He stroked his chin. "Interesting."

Did he really know not know this or was he bullshitting me? I was guessing the latter. "Clarice Burton also said the Colter Group disbanded after Hugo went missing. What do you know about that?"

"Nothing worse than trying to get a bunch of rich assholes to play nice together. I'm sure the egos sucked the air out of the rooms they were in."

"Are you suggesting it didn't have anything to do with Hugo Burton?"

"I don't see how it could. They were two entirely different things."

"A source told me that the reason Hugo was developing the land for a Japanese automaker was because he wanted to move the money into Sunny Point."

His brow lifted. "A source?"

I shrugged and started to lift the glass to my mouth, then stopped. I lowered my hand but still couldn't bring myself to set the glass on the table.

Malcolm didn't let on that he'd noticed, but I knew he had. I was pretty damn sure nothing escaped him.

"I don't know about any plan to move money around," he said, "but I *do* know Burton was accused of cheating the investors on the neighborhood project."

"What about the auto parts project?"

"I didn't hear much about it other than he hadn't gotten enough land to suit the car maker. After Hugo defaulted, Brett Colter bought the land from the bank. Rumor has it he tried to revive the Japanese auto parts plant deal, but they'd already moved on."

"So what did he do with it?"

"He built a warehouse and leased it to an online pet supply distributor. Dudley."

Interesting. I had more questions to ask Brett Colter in the morning.

"What about Sunny Point?"

He paused. "It was sold to a corporation. Larkspur Limited."

"Who owns Larkspur Limited?"

"That's the question of the hour."

"*You* can't track down who is behind Larkspur Limited?" I asked in disbelief.

"Didn't waste the time and resources to do so."

More bullshit. But Malcolm and his henchman Carter Hale seemed privy to a lot of information. It was surprising they couldn't track down this particular fact. I suspected that was why he was interested in my investigation. But why? "What did they do with it?"

"Not a damn thing that I know about."

While I planned to verify the transfer of ownership, for now I decided to switch gears. "What do you know about Brett Colter?"

"He's a well-respected citizen of Wolford and Lone County. He's on the board of commissioners for the county and sponsors several youth sports teams."

I gave him a wry look. "Is he dirty?"

He laughed. "How can you accuse such a civic-minded man of being dirty?"

"You just claimed to be civic-minded and you're rolling in shit."

He didn't look offended. "Not anymore."

"Does what happened to the Sylvester brothers change that claim about being clean?"

I hadn't meant to bring that situation up, but I'd had multiple beers and the opportunity had just presented itself.

His eyes grew cold. "No. I was making the world a better place."

We stared at each other for several seconds before I mentally said fuck it and took a long sip of the whiskey. Especially since I couldn't bring myself to mourn the brothers' passing. The whiskey went down smooth, and I resisted the urge to groan with satisfaction. "This is good whiskey."

"I don't drink that Jack Daniel's shit," he said, his voice tight. "And I wondered when *that* topic would come up."

We both knew he wasn't talking about the whiskey.

"I should have turned you in," I stated, sweat breaking out on the back of my neck. No one knew I was back here. He could kill me and get rid of my body. I had something huge to hold over his head, and he was trusting me with his secret. Then again, we both knew I was part of the whole showdown, and if I tried to turn him in, I could end up implicating myself.

If I were an honorable person, I would have done just that, outcome be damned.

We both also knew that I wasn't going to do it.

"Do you really want to talk about that?" he asked dryly. "I thought we covered that this afternoon."

I took another sip of my drink, a smaller one this time, letting it linger on my tongue. God this was good.

"No," I finally said. "I don't."

He nodded in acknowledgment. After a moment, he said, "You like filing at Morgan, Hightower, and Adams?"

"Would I be looking into Hugo Burton's disappearance if I did?" I asked with a wry laugh.

"Thought about working somewhere else?"

I sat up, wondering if he was about to offer me a job. I needed to shut that down ASAP. "I got my P.I. license. This is my first official case."

His eyes brightened. "Is that so? You freelancing for now?"

"This case is for my father's firm, one of the partners, but yeah, I think I'd like to start my own business."

He took a sip from his glass. "Hale could probably throw a few things your way."

"Why would you help me?" I asked, suddenly on guard. "I understand why you're giving me information about Hugo

Burton and Brett Colter, but why tell me that Hale might have work for me? What's in it for you?"

He laughed, his eyes sparkling with it. "Are you always so suspicious?"

"Yes."

"You said you know why I'm giving you info on Burton and Colter. What did you deduce?"

I took another sip, my gut beginning to warm as the muscles in my neck began to loosen. "Obviously, you're interested in finding out what happened to Hugo Burton. I don't know exactly why, but you hope to gain something from it."

"Why can't I just want to help out a down-on-her-luck fired police detective?"

"First of all, I wasn't fired, and second, you're not the altruistic type."

He took another drink, finishing off his whiskey. He set the empty glass on the arm of the chair. "We worked well together on your last case. Maybe we could work on this one too."

I narrowed my eyes. "Which man are you interested in?" I held up my free hand. "Wait, don't tell me. Brett Colter."

He was silent for a moment before he said, "Let's just say one of the men involved in this did something truly heinous, and I intend to make him pay for it." The look in his eyes was murderous.

Colter or Burton? Did he want to find Burton and exact his revenge? But what could Hugo Burton have done that was truly heinous? And what was the connection to Larkspur Limited?

"And you plan deliver your own justice," I said flatly. "Just like with the Sylvester brothers."

He gave me a dark look. "You think the law is on our side?"

"Hey, I'm not on your side. I'm on the side of truth."

"Maybe I'm on the side of truth too," he said.

"I could lie and tell you I'm tempted to use your help, but

I'm too tired." I finished off the whiskey and set the glass on the table. "I think I'd like to try to solve this one on my own."

"So what are you doin' here, talking to me?"

"In case you haven't noticed, I'm not clairvoyant. I can't read minds and I can't read the future or the past. I was curious what you had to say, and now that my curiosity is satiated, I'll think I'll head home."

His jaw tightened, and I knew I'd pressed some kind of nerve, but damned if I knew what. I hadn't been lying. I was too tired to play this game tonight.

I stood. "Thank you for the information."

Malcolm didn't say a word as I headed for the door and walked out.

I hoped to God I hadn't just made him an enemy.

Chapter 8

When I got home, the lights inside my mother's house were off, but the front porch light was on, so I decided I had nothing to worry about.

I made a Jack and Coke before I started looking through Hugo's financial documents. It wasn't long before I noticed a deposit from an LLC that I'd missed before, Larkspur Limited. The check was for ten thousand dollars, and it had been deposited a month before Hugo disappeared.

Malcolm said Larkspur Limited had purchased the Sunny Point land but hadn't done anything with it. Why?

I was tempted to keep looking into the company, but I was meeting Brett Colter in the morning and needed to prepare for our meeting. The information I'd found said he was from Mississippi and had gone to Ole Miss around the same time as Hugo and Clarice. Had he and Hugo known each other in college? Was Brett Colter the reason Hugo Burton had moved to Lone County?

I remembered that Detective Jones had said Brett Colter had bought the Japanese car part land and then developed it for Dudley, the national online pet store, and did a quick search. There were several articles about the company moving in and then the grand opening, but it looked like they'd only been in operation for a year.

My eyes felt dry, and I realized it was after midnight. I had to get some rest before tomorrow, so I closed my laptop and got ready for bed. I was still keyed up, which made going to sleep nearly impossible. My thoughts kept returning to the whiskey bottle underneath my kitchen sink, but I'd had two Jack and Cokes since coming home. I didn't need another drink.

I couldn't stop thinking about it, though, my brain telling me one sip wouldn't hurt. Just one. What was one more after all the drinks I'd had today? Besides, a wheedling voice in my head insisted, I hadn't had that much to drink today. I'd only had two beers with Louise and Nat. My brain knew it was a lie, but it kept pushing…

I got into bed and turned off the lights, waiting for sleep to take over. Instead, my brain became fixated on getting a drink. I tossed and turned in bed, for at least fifteen minutes, then told myself that I'd have one drink for medicinal purposes. It would help me go to sleep so I'd be on top of my game when I met with Colter in the morning.

I got up and turned on small lamp on the kitchen counter, then grabbed the half-empty bottle from under the sink. After snagging a juice glass, I poured the glass half-full, then turned off the light and sat upright in bed, fluffing the pillows behind me.

I tried to sip it slowly, but as soon as the alcohol passed over my lips I already missed the good stuff I'd tried in Malcolm's office. I gulped it down, feeling the burn all the way down my esophagus, hating myself.

Tomorrow I'd do better. Tomorrow I'd give this up for good.

When I woke up the next morning, it felt like a drum line was performing in my head. I'd downed another glass of whiskey before I'd finally fallen asleep. But I'd had much worse hangover headaches before. This was nothing.

I washed down a couple of ibuprofens with a freshly made latte, then took a long, hot shower, staying in until the water started to cool. I got out, dried off, then dressed in dark gray pants and a silky white button-up, laying my dark gray suit jacket over the back of one of my dining chairs. I put on minimal makeup and left my shoulder-length hair loose. My goal was to look professional but approachable.

I still had an hour before I had to leave, so I ate a piece of toast as I resisted the urge to add some whiskey to my coffee. Today was the day I was weaning myself off alcohol.

Of course, I'd told myself the same thing multiple times over the past several weeks. Most days I made it to lunchtime before I caved, but I'd actually made it to three one afternoon. That had to be progress.

Deep down, I knew my problem had become serious. Normal people didn't fill their water bottles with water and vodka. Normal people didn't wake up wondering when they were going to have their first drink of the day. They didn't have to negotiate with themselves over how many drinks they had. Still, there was a difference between sort of acknowledging I had a problem and doing something about it.

I didn't want to need help. I'd been independent most of my life. So my life had been shit, and I'd used alcohol as a crutch. So what. Now that I was investigating again, I wouldn't be in such a self-destructive spiral. I wouldn't need to drink because I'd be occupied with my cases.

Okay, so I drank yesterday while I was working the case, but I'm easing myself back in. Once I get going, I won't even think about it.

But my brain obsessed over adding whiskey to my coffee until I got up and added a bit just so I could concentrate on preparing for my interview with Colter.

Once I took a couple of sips and I tasted the whiskey on my tongue, the tight hold on my mind loosened and I could focus on performing another internet search for Larkspur Limited. I came up with nothing.

Since corporations in the United States filed in states, I searched the Arkansas database for hits. When I came up with nothing there, I went to a national database that searched Secretary of State offices in all fifty states. I had to set up an account and purchase a week's pass, but I finally got results. A search found a Larkspur Limited to be an LLC registered in New Mexico, incorporated by Lark Spur Trust. New Mexico was a state that allowed anonymous corporations.

Malcolm had known it was an anonymous LLC and couldn't find who owned it..

He was hoping I could identify the owners for him. He was after a man who had done something truly heinous, and Hugo Burton wouldn't have had money to invest in a separate company. Did that mean Brett Colter was behind Larkspur Limited and Malcolm intended prove it because the company was responsible for something heinous? And what would Malcolm consider heinous?

Unfortunately, I had a lot more questions than answers, but as far as I could tell, the only business Larkspur Limited had ever done was purchase that one large piece of property.

My alarm went off on my phone, which meant it was time to leave for Brett Colter's office, but I didn't regret the way I'd spent my time. I felt better prepared than I had an hour ago.

The sky was overcast, and the wind had picked up. A storm was blowing in, but it looked far enough west that I thought I could get to Colter's office before it hit.

The Colter Investments office was a three-story building with a parking lot that had to have had at least thirty cars parked in it. After I parked, I grabbed an umbrella and headed inside. The lobby had a white marble floor and a dark wood wall behind a desk staffed by a middle-aged security guard with a name tag that read Mike.

My shoes clicked on the stone, echoing through the two-story lobby as I approached. "I'm Harper Adams. I have a nine o'clock meeting with Mr. Colter."

Mike gave me a tight smile. "Good morning, Ms. Adams. Mr. Colter is expecting you. Just take the elevator to the third floor."

I walked over to the single stainless-steel elevator and pushed the button next to it. A sign listing several other businesses and their office numbers was pinned to the wall next to the elevator. The stainless steel doors slid open almost immediately, and I entered the car and pressed the third-floor button. When it opened on three, another reception desk was directly in front of me, only this one was staffed by a young woman with full, long blond hair and a friendly smile.

"You must be Harper Adams," she said sweetly. "Mr. Colter is expecting you." She rose from her chair and walked around the desk. "If you'll come with me."

I followed her through an open office space with eight desks, all filled with people who seemed intent on their jobs.

We walked past them and down a short hallway, stopping in front of a partially closed door at the end.

The receptionist knocked, then pushed the door open. "Mr. Colter? Ms. Adams is here to see you."

"Come in. Come in," a man called out good-naturedly, and she pushed the door all the way open, moving aside so I could enter.

I stepped into the sleek, contemporary office space, my gaze landing on the fifty-something man sitting behind a glass, metal-framed desk.

"Ms. Adams. Please, take a seat." He gestured to a couple of chairs inside his office.

I'd started in that direction when the receptionist asked,

"Can I get you something to drink, Ms. Adams? Coffee? Water?"

I would gladly offer up my hypothetical firstborn for a really good cup of coffee—and there was a chance I'd get one here—but I didn't want the distraction. "Thank you, but no."

"Brett?" she asked.

His gaze lingered on her with a hint of lust, which he quickly tried to cover. "No thank you, Miranda. That's all for now."

If he wasn't sleeping with her, he was hoping to.

I was still halfway to the chair, but I turned to look out the wall of windows overlooking a wide stretch of undeveloped land. About half was covered in fields, but the rest looked like dense woods.

"It's beautiful, isn't it?" he asked in a soft tone that surprised me.

I turned to look at him, but he was staring out at the view.

"I have to say," I said as I came to a stop in front of one of the chairs, "I'm surprised you haven't developed it."

Chuckling, he turned to face me. "I guess you would think so. And maybe most developers would. All that space just waiting to be…"

"Developed?" I asked my brow rising.

He chuckled again. "I do more than develop, Ms. Adams. I create something out of nothing. I help provide stability and job security. I help a town grow and thrive."

"So you consider land developing to be an honorable profession?" I asked as I sat down.

Surprise filled his eyes. "You don't?"

"Honestly?" I asked as I sat back and crossed my legs. "I hadn't ever really thought about it one way or another. People and corporations buy land. They put something on it. They make money. Then they move on to the next project."

He leaned forward, an earnestness washing over his face. "Well, I see it differently. Sure, any fool can buy a lot and put a

McDonald's on it, and don't get me wrong"—he held up his hands in a defensive maneuver—"towns need McDonald's, but I do so much more than that."

"You're very civic-minded," I said, using the term Malcolm had used the night before. "You support multiple youth sports teams. You're a booster for the high school athletic program. You're on the county commissioners board—"

"A thankless job," he interjected.

"You support multiple fundraising charities in the town of Wolford and the county."

He held out his hands. "What can I say? I love this town."

"But you're not from around here, correct? You're from Mississippi?"

"That is correct," he said, a flash of surprise flickering in his eyes. He shifted in his seat. "I'm sorry. I was under the impression you were here to ask me questions about Hugo Burton."

"Oh, I am," I assured him with an eager look. "It's just that I looked you up to see what kind of business you had with him, and all that other stuff came up. I was impressed."

Some of his hesitation faded, and his self-importance reappeared. "Well, like I said. I love Wolford."

"I'm surprised you haven't run for city council or mayor," I said. "My father was mayor of Jackson Creek back when I was young. He loved the town and saw it as his way of giving back, so I appreciate someone who's so dedicated to their community."

His smile spread. I had him back.

"But my father was born and raised in Jackson Creek. I guess I'm just curious how you came to live in Wolford. I'm sure there's a good story there."

"Oh," he said, some of his brightness fading. "It's not all that interesting. I was offered a job here right after college. It was supposed to be temporary, but I just loved the place so much, and then I met and fell in love with my wife"—he turned a picture frame around on his desk so I could see an old photo of him with an attractive middle-aged woman and three children—"and the rest is history." He turned serious. "Miranda said you were here to ask me some questions about Hugo because you're helping poor Clarice have him declared dead."

He didn't want to talk about his past before he came to Wolford. Interesting.

"I am," I said. "I know you were working on a project with him with the Colter Group at the time of his disappearance, so I was hoping you could help me understand what he was up to, both with your business dealings and his own."

He frowned, drumming his fingers on his desk, expelling nervous energy. "Of course, I'll help any way I can, but I'm just not sure how much help it will actually be."

He was already acting dodgy, which I didn't take as a good sign. He could kick me out at any minute, so I sucked down my irritation and pretended to be grateful. "Anything you can tell me will be helpful." I paused, then said, "Maybe start by telling me about the Colter Group."

"Sure. Sure." He sat back in his seat and locked his fingers over his stomach, which looked pretty trim for a man in his fifties. I suspected he visited the gym fairly often to impress poor Miranda. "I started the Colter Group with five investors with the purpose of bringing outside employers into the area. We were hoping to bring more jobs to the county, and we pooled our resources to do so."

"How long before Hugo's disappearance did you create the group?"

"Honestly, not all that long," he said with a frown. "We all knew each other because we were all civic-minded." He made a face. "The other three men were business owners—Skip, who owns a Ford dealership."

That had to be Skip Martin, who had also invested in Sunny Point.

"Doug owns multiple fast-food restaurants, and Dickie owns a grocery store."

"Skip Martin, right?" When he nodded, I added, "Do you have last names for Doug and Dickie?"

"Sure, but why?"

"So I can ask them about Hugo, of course."

"They really didn't have much interaction with him, and besides, Doug sold his restaurants and he and his wife moved to North Carolina to be closer to his ailing mother-in-law."

"Still…"

He sighed. "Doug Skelton and Dickie Troost."

Why didn't he want me to talk to them?

"And Hugo was part of it too," I said.

He lifted a shoulder in a lazy shrug. "True. I only brought Hugo on because, well, we went way back, and he was in the middle of developing some of his own properties that happened to be bigger than the ones he'd completed before. I figured I'd bring in his expertise." The frown on his face looked a little over the top, but I decided to take the bait anyway.

"I take it he wasn't as good of a resource as you'd hoped?"

"No. Not in the slightest." He drew in a breath. "Everyone had to contribute to the group. I invested fifty percent and the others invested smaller amounts, but Hugo's was the lowest. Only five percent. He argued that his knowledge would help pay for his lack of funding."

"Why didn't he contribute more?" I asked.

"He didn't have the money. He was stretched thin with Sunny Point when we first started the group. He'd already purchased more land for what he called Phase Two, then he started his cockamamie auto plant project." He shook his head. "I told him he needed to focus on one thing, that stretching himself on three projects was too much. Of course, when I brought him on, I had no idea what a mess Sunny Point was or I never would have offered him a spot." His lips pressed tight. "Damn near ruined my reputation when the fool took off."

"So you think he ran off?" I asked. "You don't think he was murdered?"

Releasing a heavy sigh, he gave me a sympathetic look. "I know Clarice thinks he was murdered, but I think he realized he was never digging himself out of his hole and ran off with the money." He tapped the desk with the tip of his finger. "A few weeks before he left, he went around and gave his poor investors a sob story about his kid getting sick and how he needed more money and that he was so fucking close to getting a contract with the Japanese automaker. Once that went through, he'd have more than enough money to complete Sunny Point." He grimaced. "Excuse my language. I try not to curse in the presence of a lady."

I nearly told him I wasn't a lady, but instead I held up a hand. "I'm not offended. In fact, I appreciate your frankness."

He nodded.

"I didn't hear anything about his kid being ill."

"That's because he wasn't. Hugo made it up. Some of the poor fools gave him more money to help with Anton. Hugo took off a week or so later."

"So you're sure he ran off? Do you think one of his investors could have found out his son wasn't sick and gotten pissed enough to kill him?"

Colter laughed. "Have you met Hugo's investors? I doubt any of them are capable of murder."

"I haven't, but I've found that people you would never suspect are capable of murder under stressful situations."

He chuckled nervously. "I'd hate to meet the people you know."

Obviously he didn't know about my history, and I planned to keep it that way. "You mentioned meeting Hugo's investors, but three of the five men who gave him more money have died since his disappearance."

He looked genuinely shocked. "Really? I knew about O'Murphy, but who's surprised? The man was as old as Methuselah. Who were the other two?"

"Tim Heaton and Pete Mooney."

He pursed his lips for a moment. "I guess I'd forgotten about Tim Heaton, but I've never heard of Pete Mooney." He leaned forward, resting his forearms on the desk. "Where was he from? What did he do?"

"Mooney was from Pine Bluff. I'm not sure what he did for a living."

"Hmm." He seemed lost in thought as though trying to reason that out.

"There's one more investor," I said. "Do you happen to know who it is?"

He shook his head. "I was one of the two original investors. I have no idea who the other one was."

"Could it have been Pete Mooney?"

"No. It was someone local and Hugo said they wanted their anonymity."

Could they have been part of Larkspur Limited?

"Clarice says the Colter Group had a deal go through after Hugo left, but you refused to pay her for Hugo's share of his investment."

He shook his head, looking like he was trying to hide his disgust. "I told Clarice that Hugo didn't have anything to do with the deal. Not to mention all the legal and PR expenses we accrued trying to defend our reputation after he left. Those far exceeded his investment."

"Do you have a copy of your agreement with Hugo?" I asked without any hint of accusation. "Clarice says she doesn't have a copy. She told me that when she asked you for one, you failed to produce it."

He shook his head. "That's because there wasn't a legal

agreement. I was a fool back then, and I relied on our friendship to be our bond. It was all verbal."

"You had four investors and formed an LLC, but you
didn't have a legal agreement with them?" I asked in disbelief.

"The verbal agreement was only with Hugo, and besides,
around these parts, a man's word used to mean something."

I gave him an incredulous look, but quickly tried to hide it.
I was ready to move on to my next question and I was interested in his response. "Do you know what happened to the
two properties that Hugo was trying to develop?"

He didn't appear all that surprised by my line of questioning. "I make no secret of the fact I bought the smaller property Hugo intended for the car maker from the bank, but
before you start thinking I did something sketchy to acquire it,
I'll have you know the bank had it up for sale for two years
before I made an offer. If I was gonna kill Hugo to get it,
seems to me I would have purchased it sooner."

I lifted a brow. "I never accused you of murder, Mr.
Colter."

"It doesn't take a fool to see that you're turning over rocks
hoping to find something crawl out, so I figured I'd face this
head on. I didn't kill Hugo, and I wasn't interested in that
piece of property until about three years after his disappearance."

"Fair enough. What about Sunny Point?"

"I heard some corporation bought it, but nothing ever
came of it. As far as I know, it's still sitting down there, just the
way Hugo left it."

It was hard to believe he'd purchase the property intended
for the Japanese car company under his own corporation,
then use a secret one to purchase Sunny Point. Which wasn't
to say he didn't know more than he was pretending.

"Do you know anything about the corporation who
bought it?"

He shook his head. "Nope."

"It's called Larkspur Limited. Ring any bells? They were incorporated in New Mexico." I paused a beat. "It seems strange they didn't do anything with it."

He shook his head, showing no reaction at the corporation's name. "Never heard of it, but it's not so strange that they bought the land and did nothing to it. Sometimes property takes time to develop. That was Hugo's first mistake—telling his investors they'd see a return in a couple of years. He should have pushed that date out and happily surprised them by delivering sooner."

That made sense and made me question Hugo's business sense. Then again, maybe that was exactly what Brett Colter was trying to do. I had to admit that Malcolm's prejudice against Colter might be clouding my opinion. "Hugo was supposed to have a business meeting the day his disappeared," I said. "He had a business lunch, then he was supposed to go to the meeting, followed by his son's basketball game. Only he never showed up at the game, obviously."

"Obviously," he said in a tight voice.

I decided to try a bluff. The worst he could do was accuse me of having erroneous information. "I know you met with him for lunch. Did he happen to mention his afternoon business meeting?"

Colter's face paled. "How do you know we met for lunch?"

"It was in his calendar."

"I thought his planner was lost."

"The police had his planner," I lied. "I saw a copy."

He swallowed. "I met with Hugo to tell him that the other investors and I wanted him out of Colter Group. That we were worried his name was going to hurt us."

"How did he take it?"

"How do you think he took it? He was pissed, then he started to cry. I told him to man up." He shook his head in disgust. "He told me that he had a meeting that afternoon with a potential new investor. He asked if I'd bring him back on board if the deal went through. I told him I'd consider it, but I had no intention of bringing him back, and I was considering demanding my investment back. I was one of the original investors in Sunny Point, and according to the contract, I could have demanded my initial hundred thousand investment back at the six-year mark."

That had to freak Hugo out. Especially since it looked like he didn't have a hundred grand to pay Colter back. Still, part of this didn't make sense. "If you were going to call in your marker, then why did you give him a check for fifty thousand dollars a week or so before?"

His mouth pressed tight, and his eyes flashed with irritation. "That was a moment of weakness. At lunch, I confronted Hugo about Anton's health and asked how he could be a starting basketball player if he was so ill."

"I suppose he didn't take that well."

"He tried backtracking, but there was no denying he'd lied. I wouldn't be surprised if that's why he left town. If the truth was that obvious to me, then everyone else was going to find out."

I had to admit, it was a pretty compelling reason for Hugo to run. "Do you know who Hugo's afternoon meeting was with?"

"No idea. He refused to tell me, but he said it was an outside investor."

"What does an outside investor mean exactly?"

"I took it to mean someone outside the county."

"Do you know where he planned to meet this person?"

He shook his head. "Nope. He was pissed at me, and he left the restaurant before we'd even finished the meal."

"Do you remember where you ate?"

"His office was in Jackson Creek, so I went to him to soften the blow. We ate at Roots."

I nodded, my mind racing. Deputy Jones hadn't told me

about Hugo's lunch meeting with Brett Colter. Had he intentionally kept it from me, or did he not know about it? I decided to bluff again. "Why didn't you tell the sheriff's investigators that you were dumping him from the group?"

His face paled. "Who says I didn't?"

"I had a meeting with Detective Jones yesterday afternoon. He never mentioned it, and as important as that is, I believe he would have."

Colter swallowed hard and shifted his gaze to the side. "It didn't seem important. The man ran off. No need to make him look any worse."

Or maybe Colter didn't want to give the detective anything to make himself a suspect. What if Hugo threatened to make waves, and Colter decided to shut him up permanently?

Or what if Hugo had damaging information against Colter and threatened to release it if Colter dropped him from the Colter Group? It was a stretch, but not impossible.

I changed topics. "When did you hear that Hugo was missing?"

"The day after our lunch meeting. Clarice called me that morning and asked if I knew where he was. I told her the truth—I had no idea."

"And when you heard, what did you think had happened to him?"

"Honestly? That he ran off. I still think that, although I hope for Clarice's sake she can claim the policy." He glanced at his phone on the desk. "I'm sorry, but I have another meeting that I need to get to. I wish I'd been more helpful."

"You were very helpful, Mr. Colter," I said, getting to my feet. "Thank you for your time."

I headed out the door, my mind spinning. Colter had information he was holding back. I just needed to find out what.

Chapter 9

I got in my car and headed to the Wolford County courthouse. I needed to find out more about Hugo's properties, but I also wanted to talk to his kids. If he was really as close to them as everyone was leading me to believe, I wondered if they'd noticed anything before he left.

I pulled into the parking lot of the courthouse and called Clarice.

"Do you have something already?" she asked, hopeful.

"No, sorry. I know you don't feel comfortable with me talking to your kids, but I would like to get their perspective on this."

She hesitated. "I really don't want you to do that."

My suspicions were immediately on alert. "Why? They're both adults now."

"Mary Ann's in college," she said in a snippy tone. "I wouldn't call that an adult."

"Your son is a nurse in Wolford. I think he would qualify."

"Anton and Mary Ann have been through so much. I don't want them to relive this any more than they already have."

"I understand," I assured her, "but I really think their perspective could be helpful. Especially Anton's."

She paused for several seconds.

"Tell you what," I said. "Why don't you tell Anton I'd like to talk to him, give him my name and number, and we'll leave it up to him whether he wants to contact me. If I don't hear from him, I'll let it go." It went against every instinct not to talk to him, but I couldn't force her to put us in touch, and considering she was the client, it wouldn't be right to circumvent her and contact her son on my own.

"Okay," she said, but she definitely didn't sound happy about it.

"Thank you."

"So have you made *any* progress?"

"I'm still doing my initial digging. Trying to get up to speed."

"So that's a no?" Her tone was short.

"As I said, I'm still getting caught up on what everyone else knows."

"I'm not paying you to find out what everyone else knows. I'm paying you to find new information."

Here was the snippy Clarice Burton that Detective Jones had alluded to. "Clarice, if you're unhappy with my progress, then feel free to contact Mitch and let him know you'd like someone else to handle the case, but I assure you that no one would have new information at this point. It's too early in the investigation."

I wasn't thrilled with the idea of her pulling the case. It would be a blow to my ego. Nevertheless, I wasn't going to put up with unrealistic expectations.

"No," she said, her voice tight. "I'll leave it for now. And I'll call Anton and tell him you want to talk to him. But if he says no, you need to leave it alone." Her tone turned menacing. "But you have to stay away from my daughter. I won't drag her into this mess."

"Agreed," I said, not adding the silent *for now*. If Anton agreed to speak to me, I planned to ask him his thoughts on why his mother wanted to keep him and his sister out of my investigation.

I hung up, reevaluating my opinion of Clarice Burton. The case hadn't been solved in the five years since her husband's disappearance. Did she really think I'd solve it in less than twenty-four hours? Then again, she'd gone years without answers. No doubt she was impatient to wrap things up and move on with her life.

I headed to the courthouse and was about to walk inside a few minutes later when my phone rang.

"Harper Adams," I answered, standing on the courthouse steps.

"Ms. Adams? This is Anton Burton. Hugo Burton's son."

While I'd hoped he'd call, I hadn't expected him to call so quickly. I took that as a good sign.

"Anton, thank you so much for calling," I said. "I'm sure you know that your mother hired me through Morgan, Hightower, and Adams to help her declare your father legally deceased. I was hoping to talk to you about him."

"Do you think he ran off and left us?" he asked bitterly.

"I don't have an opinion one way or another," I assured him. "That's part of the reason I'd like to talk to you. To get your perspective."

"But not Mary Ann?"

"Your mother prefers I leave her out of this."

He paused for several seconds. "That sounds like my mother. She's always been overprotective of Mary Ann. Like she can pretend our father never disappeared and everything will be okay."

"I take it you don't approve of her tactic."

"Mary Ann's messed up, likely because we never talked about it." He cleared his throat. "So when would you like to talk? Today? Tonight?"

"Whenever is convenient for you," I said. "We could meet

for lunch or coffee if you want to do it during the day. Or I could come to your home tonight."

"I'm free for lunch. Want to meet at Sarah Jane's Café in downtown Wolford? Say a little after noon? That's when I get my lunch break."

"I happen to be in downtown Wolford right now. I can see the café across the square."

"Okay," he said, and I noted the eagerness in his voice.

I hoped I wasn't getting his hopes up only for him to be left with no answers when I was done. "I'm wearing a gray jacket and pants with a white shirt," I said. "I have shoulder-length dark hair."

"I'm wearing blue scrubs." He took a breath. "Do you think you'll really find out what happened to Dad?"

And there was my confirmation. "I don't know, Anton, but I intend to try."

After he hung up, I headed into the courthouse. I had less than an hour to get the information I needed before it was time to meet him.

The property department was on the first floor, and when I walked into the waiting area, I could see two women sitting behind the counter. An older woman with white hair who looked like she would have been eligible for retirement two decades ago sat at a desk stacked with papers, and a younger woman, probably in her early twenties, was walking out of a back room.

"Hi," I said as I approached the counter. I knew the properties wouldn't be in Hugo's name, so I made sure to use his corporation's name. "I'd like to see what you have on land owned by Burton Management and also Larkspur Limited. And any plot maps you might have as well as the history of the properties."

The younger woman wrote the names on a piece of paper, but the older woman's eyes narrowed. "Why're you askin' about Burton Management?"

"I'm researching one of the partners." Sure, Hugo had been the sole owner, but they didn't need to know that.

"Hugo Burton?" she asked.

So much for that.

The fact she could put all that together so quickly caught me off guard. "Yes. I know he had two properties at the time of his disappearance, so I'd like to see what you have on those as well as anything else he might have owned."

"We don't just give that out to anyone," she snapped.

"Actually, I think you're required to," I said. "Freedom of Information Act."

The older woman pursed her lips tightly, then approached the counter. "You'll have to fill out a request. We have ten to fourteen days to perform a search."

"Ten to fourteen days?" I asked, trying to hide my dismay.

"That's the best I can do." She shoved a form in front of me. "Fill that out, and I'll need to see some ID."

I pulled my driver's license out of my wallet and handed it to her. She looked it up and down with suspicion, then glanced up at me with a frown. "I need to make a copy."

"Of course," I said with a smile that took a ton of effort to form.

When the older woman disappeared into the back, the younger one gave me a sympathetic look. "Sorry about Lucinda. She's retiring next week and she's pretty cranky about it. They're kind of forcing her out and...well..."

I guess I had the retirement part right.

I started filling out the form, and the young woman kept chatting.

"Lucinda hates when people request records like yours. She says she'd rather have a root canal."

Looking up records was her job, but I refrained from saying so, because the younger woman was talking, and I wanted to keep her talking.

"Plus," she continued, lowering her voice. Lucinda was in

the back of the room, standing in front of a copy machine. "She's probably not happy that two people have requested the same thing within such a short period of time."

My brows shot up. "Someone else has been asking about Burton Management and Larkspur Limited?"

At the same time, it made sense. They hadn't asked me for clarification because they'd heard the request before.

"Oh yeah, a man came in late yesterday afternoon asking about High Tower."

"Not Larkspur Limited?"

She made a face. "No, I don't think so."

"Do you remember what the man looked like?"

"I don't know," she said, making a face. "I was in the back, and I only heard him asking about it. Lucinda wasn't very happy about him asking either."

"Did you happen to hear his name?"

"No. Sorry."

"But surely Lucinda took his license too," I said. "Is there any way you can find out who was inquiring?"

Her gaze narrowed. "Why?"

What was I going to tell her? I decided to go with the truth.

"I'm a private investigator, and I find it weird that someone was asking about his land the day I started looking into Hugo Burton's disappearance."

"You're a private investigator?"

I nodded.

She glanced over her shoulder at the back room before turning to face me again. Her lips turned down. "I wish I could help you, but I can't. I don't want to get in trouble." Her face brightened. "You can come back in a couple of weeks after Lucinda retires."

I really didn't want to wait a couple of weeks, but I didn't want to make an enemy of her either. If I started a P.I. firm, there was a good chance I'd be back, requesting information for another case. But if the clerk had a description, even a bare bones one, it might help.

"Sorry…" I said, "what was your name?"

"Marissa."

"Marissa, I'm not sure what you remember about Hugo Burton's disappearance five years ago. You may not have even heard about it."

"I heard about it," she said. "Everyone knew about it."

"Well, you probably heard he ran off, because that's what everyone other than his family thought, but I'm trying to find out what really happened to him. His family's been stuck in limbo for five years, so anything you can remember about the guy from yesterday will help *them*."

Guilt filled her eyes. "I really don't remember much. I was in the back doing my job, and Lucinda was doing hers. I didn't pay much attention."

"Surely you heard him talking," I suggested. "Do you remember anything they said? Or what his voice sounded like?"

"He wasn't loud, but he wasn't quiet either." She shrugged. "It was just a guy's voice."

"Was he polite? Demanding? Arrogant? Young? Old?"

"He wasn't yelling at her, so I guess he was polite. He didn't sound like an old man, but he didn't sound like a kid either," she said, sounding frustrated. "I wish I could help more."

That didn't narrow it down much, but it was better than nothing. "No, that's great. Do you know if Lucinda gave him anything?"

"No. I think she told him he had to wait too."

Movement behind Marissa caught my attention. Lucinda was heading toward us from the back room, so I nodded to the side slightly to warn Marissa that her boss was coming.

The older woman plopped my driver's license on the

counter with a smacking sound. "The fee to pull the information on two properties is forty dollars."

I hadn't finished filling out the form but pulled out my wallet and placed two twenty-dollar bills on the counter.

She snatched them up. "I don't know what you're doin' here, but you should go back to where you belong, *Harper Adams.*"

So she knew about my notoriety.

The younger woman's eyes bugged out and her jaw dropped, but I gave Lucinda a tight smile. "I see you're a member of my fan club, but sorry, Lone County is my hometown too. I'm not going anywhere."

I had to wonder why I kept insisting I was staying in the very place I hated.

Chapter 10

When I walked out of the courthouse, I still had fifteen minutes before I was supposed to meet Anton. I needed to get my hands on a map of the county. Lucinda was obviously in no hurry to help me, but Anton might have a general idea of where his father's former property was located. I headed into a shop a few businesses down from the café that looked like it sold tourist tchotchkes. I had no idea why Wolford would need a store that sold tourist crap, but I wasn't going to question it.

The only person inside was the cashier, an older man wearing a white button-down shirt with black pinstripes paired with a black bow tie. He gave me a cheerful hello when I walked in.

The store sold all things Arkansas with a major focus on Razorback décor but close to the register I found a stand with foldable maps. Some were for state parks in the surrounding area, but I found a beat-up looking copy of a map of Wolford stuffed in between some state maps. When I opened it, I could see that it showed a good chunk of unincorporated land outside of town. I carried it up to the register and the older man looked over his reading glasses in surprise when he saw what I was purchasing.

"I didn't realize we still had one of these," he said. "It's gotta be at least ten years old."

"Even better," I said, taking my wallet out of my purse.

He waved with his free hand and passed the map back to me. "It's yours for nothin'. If I'd known it was there, I woulda thrown it away."

"Thanks," I said as I took it. I started to walk out the door, then stopped and turned back. "Say, do you know anything about the disappearance of Hugo Burton?" It was a long shot and anything he knew would probably be gossip, but gossip could sometimes yield a clue or two.

His nose scrunched up as he pondered it, then his eyes lit up. "That businessman who stole all those guys' money?"

"Yep, that's him."

"Not much. Only that he stole the money and ran. Left his family in the lurch. Ruined a man's life."

I inclined my head. "Ruined a man's life?"

"Poor Bill O'Murphy. His son practically disowned him for spending his inheritance on that land project."

"Mr. O'Murphy was an older gentleman, right?"

He nodded. "That's him. He was a frugal man all his life, and then he decided to hand over nearly three hundred thousand dollars to that shyster. Shawn O'Murphy never forgave his father."

Shawn O'Murphy sounded like an entitled asshole.

"Did Shawn ever try to confront Hugo Burton?"

He laughed again. "Nah. He sure would have liked to, but nobody could find the man."

"So he found out after Hugo disappeared?"

"His daddy confessed a few weeks afterward that his money was gone. Shawn was livid and even tried to find the man himself. Of course, that was wasted effort. Burton was long gone."

Interesting. If he had his timeline right, Shawn O'Murphy

wasn't a potential suspect, but it might not hurt to check him out.

"What about Tim Heaton?" I asked. "Do you know anything about him?"

He shook his head and tsked. "He sunk a lot of money into that land too, but he wasn't in as bad as shape as poor ol' Bill."

"I heard he died in a car accident."

"He did, and left his wife a lot of insurance money. Lots of rumors goin' round that he ran into those trees on purpose, if you know what I mean."

"Suicide?" I asked.

"Yeah, but the sheriff told his wife it wasn't. Said there were skid marks on the road and there was a dent on the side of his car."

"Like someone ran him off the road?"

"They didn't come right out and say it, but they sure insinuated from what his wife said. But she was grateful, 'cause the insurance wouldn't have paid out for suicide."

Interesting.

"What about a man named Pete Mooney?" I asked. "Know anything about him?"

He pursed his lips before he said, "Nope. Never heard of 'im."

"I'm guessing you know Brett Colter."

He made a face. "Suurrre do."

I rested my hand on the edge of the counter and leaned closer. "I take it you don't think much of him."

"Thinks he's God's gift to this town and he ain't even from here. He's from Mississippi."

"I heard he's brought in a bunch of businesses to the area."

He released a bitter laugh. "If he says so."

"He hasn't?"

"If you ask me, he's almost as much of a shyster as that Burton fella."

"He's taken people's money?"

"In a roundabout way." He leaned closer and lowered his voice. "He's on the county board, and he makes sure that contracts and such go to his own businesses."

"I'm pretty sure that's not legal," I said.

He shrugged. "He covers his tracks by having corporations that don't have his name on them get the winning bids, especially his construction company, but if you dig deep enough, you'll find that he owns them."

Corporations without his name on them? Was Brett Colter behind Larkspur Limited after all? His side corporations were definitely worth looking into.

"What about Skip Martin? Do you know anything about him?"

He paused. "He lost money in his dealings with Burton, but it didn't do him in. He owns the Ford dealership here in town."

I'd definitely be talking to him.

I glanced at my phone and saw it was almost time to meet Anton. "Thank you for your time, Mr...?"

"Name's Carl Edmonds," he said with a grin, sticking out his chest. "And I'm happy to help a fellow officer of the law."

I stared at him in surprise.

He chuckled. "It wasn't that hard to tell you're a cop."

"I'm currently a P.I."

"But you *were* a cop, and I'm glad someone's finally trying to find the bastard."

"You said fellow officer of the law?" I prompted.

"I was in the Lone County Sheriff's Department for nearly thirty years before I retired and opened this store, although I'm not sure how much longer I'll keep it open. Business ain't what it used to be."

"I'm sorry to hear that."

He shrugged, not looking concerned. "It's the way of the world, and besides, my wife has been begging me to retire for years. I just don't know what I'll do with myself. I kind of like being downtown, seeing what's going on."

I thought of my own semi-retirement. "I understand completely."

He narrowed his eyes. "I suspect you do."

His scrutiny made me uncomfortable, like he could see right through me.

I lifted the map. "Thanks again for the map, Officer Edmonds."

"Anything I can do to help. If you're looking into any older cold cases, feel free to come back and ask me questions. I might remember something from back in the day."

"Will do," I said, meaning it. Carl Edmonds could prove to be a valuable source. He'd already helped more than I could have hoped.

After my lunch with Anton, I planned to pay a visit to Skip Martin.

When I walked into the café, I didn't see a younger man in blue scrubs, but it was busy, with only one table left. Thankfully, a waitress greeted me in passing and told me to take a seat.

A couple of minutes later another waitress, a woman who couldn't have been older than twenty, walked over and handed me a menu, then took my drink order: a water with lemon.

I had just started to open the map when I saw a man in navy blue scrubs standing in the doorway. He looked remarkably like the photos I'd seen of Hugo—same dark hair, same nose and mouth.

I waved to catch his attention, and he nodded in acknowledgment, then headed over as I stood and offered my hand. "Anton?"

He took my hand with a firm grip. "That's me."

"I'm Harper Adams. Thank you for agreeing to meet with me."

He released my hand and took the seat opposite me. "Yeah, of course. Anything I can do to help find my dad."

His gaze lowered to the partially opened map.

I sat back down and folded it. "I was hoping you could tell me about your father's properties."

"Sunny Point and Martindale?"

"Martindale?" I asked.

"That's what Dad called the property that he was trying to develop for the Japanese auto manufacturer."

I nodded. "No one I've talked to has called it that."

He shrugged with a sheepish look. "I'm not surprised. I think that was kind of an inside name between my dad and me."

"Where did the name come from?"

"We saw a purple martin out there." When I gave him a blank look, he grinned. "It's a bird. So I started calling it Martindale. Dad did too, but I guess he didn't with everyone else." His eyes misted and a soft smile played on his lips.

"I'm sure you miss your dad," I said softly. "I've heard you were really close."

"We were," he said, his eyes filling with tears. "That's why I'll never, *ever* believe he left of his own free will. He would never have left me and Mary Ann."

"But he *would* have left your mother?"

His face paled. "You caught that?" When I didn't respond, he said, "Mom and Dad weren't getting along all that great when he disappeared. They fought a lot over money."

Definitely not the impression Clarice had given me, although it fit with what Detective Jones had told me. "Do you think they were heading for a divorce?"

"I don't know,' he admitted. "I think they loved each other, but Mom didn't understand the way his business worked. She was upset that Sunny Point kept running into problems, but she got downright pissed when he started working on Martindale."

"She didn't approve of him purchasing that property?"

He snorted. "Not only no, but hell no. She said he needed to focus on selling lots in Sunny Point and getting some homes built before moving on, but Dad tried to convince her the property needed more development before he could even think about letting contractors build houses. He told her that Martindale would help fund Sunny Point. He planned to make money with Phase One, but Phase Two was when he and the investors would rake in the money."

"Do *you* think it would have funded Sunny Point?"

He made a face as he considered it. "I was a senior in high school. I didn't know shit about investing and land development. I took my dad at his word." He shrugged. "Sure, Dad took me to see the place, but the part I liked was driving the utility vehicle around. The business end of it didn't interest me."

I gestured to his scrubs. "I see you didn't follow in his footsteps."

He laughed. "No, I had no interest in it. At all. Not even before he disappeared. I was always more interested in biology and life sciences. Then after he left, I *really* didn't want anything to do with it."

"I understand," I said.

He paused as though considering his words. "You really are going to try to find out what happened to him, aren't you?"

I held his gaze. "Yeah, Anton. I am."

He nodded and started to say something, but the waitress walked over and set a glass with a dark liquid in front of him.

"Hey, Anton," she said with a warm smile. "I figured you'd want your usual Coke. Want your usual lunch too?"

"You know it," he said with a smile.

"One club sandwich with chips coming right up." She turned to me, confusion clouding her eyes. I'm sure she was trying to figure out why I was eating lunch with a man a good decade younger than me. "Have you figured out what you want?"

"Do you have a chef's salad? If so, I'll take one of those with ranch dressing."

"Sure." She gave Anton a flirty look before heading to the kitchen, but if he noticed he didn't let on.

I got back to business. "Your mother said your father was supposed to go to your basketball game the day he disappeared."

He nodded and took a sip of his water. "He never missed a game. Like *never* missed a game. Even if he was sick. When he didn't show that night, I knew something was wrong. He'd told me that he was meeting someone out at Sunny Point before the game, so when it was over, instead of celebrating with the team, I headed out there to see if he'd had car trouble or something."

Hugo had planned to meet the investor at Sunny Point? No one else I'd spoken to had seemed to know that.

"Did you try to call your dad?"

"I did, but it went straight to voicemail, which wasn't that uncommon. Cell service was spotty out there, which was one of his many, many issues with the place."

"Did you find anything when you went out to the property?" I asked.

He shook his head. "His car wasn't there, but I was pretty sure he'd been there. The property had a few asphalt roads, but most of it was either trees or cleared land. He kept a utility vehicle in a shed at the end of the paved road. I checked the shed, and it was inside, but the wheels were muddy, like he'd driven around the property."

"Could it have been old mud? Maybe from driving it another day?"

He shook his head. "We'd had it out the weekend before and the wheels were clean. Plus, it wasn't dried mud. It was fresh."

"Did you tell the sheriff about the wheels?"

He rubbed the back of his neck and made a reluctant face. After dropping his hand and resting it on top of the table, he said, "My mother insisted that I speak to the police as little as possible. So the answer is no, I didn't tell them about any of this."

I stared at him in shock. "Why wouldn't she want you to tell them?"

"She said it didn't matter. That they already knew he had a business meeting. It wouldn't help them to know about muddy tires. Or that he'd even been out there at all."

"The sheriff's investigator I spoke to said they knew he had a meeting, but they didn't seem to know who it was with or where. They didn't even know if the meeting had actually taken place."

His eyes widened and he looked sick. "You're saying if I'd told them what I knew, they might have been able to find my dad?"

"I don't know," I said, hoping to ease his guilt. "It might have, but there's every chance it might not have."

If possible, he looked even more stricken. "Oh. God. It could have made all the difference."

"It *could* have helped," I conceded. "We don't know for certain, but it definitely gives me a new angle to look into." I held his gaze. "And I promise, I *will* look into it."

"Okay." He looked slightly appeased.

"Do you happen to know who he was meeting?"

"No. He didn't give me a name, but I know he'd been talking to someone with a company called something lark."

"Could it have been Larkspur Limited?"

His face brightened. "Yeah. That was it."

I'd already wondered if Larkspur Limited might have been the possible new investor, and this confirmed it. "Did your dad happen to mention anything about Larkspur Limited before telling you about the meeting?"

"Not really. I know he thought they could help turn Sunny Point around. He said they had a ton of money, and they were willing to put it into the project. Mom was worried that Dad's profit was going to plummet and that he wouldn't make much money if he brought in a huge investor, but he said he didn't have a choice. That he was going to go bankrupt if the investor didn't buy in."

According to Anton, Clarice obviously knew more about her husband's business than she'd let on to me or Detective Jones. I wasn't sure what to make of that. It sure didn't paint her in a good light. Neither did the way she'd coached her son.

"So you think your father was meeting someone from Larkspur Limited at Sunny Point before your game?"

"I don't think. I know."

"I'm guessing he would want to show them the property, but what would that entail?"

"He would take them on a tour. When he had someone out there, he'd take them around on the roads he'd put in, usually on the utility vehicle so he could go across the land too. That was probably how the tires got muddy." He sighed. "He'd shown the land to enough people for me to know. I went with them on a few tours. Especially in those last few months. Dad really wanted me to get into the business, so he was showing me the ropes."

The waitress arrived at our table with two plates. She set

the food in front of us and gave Anton a huge smile. "Can I get you anything else?"

"Nope, I'm good," he said.

"You sure?" she asked, batting her eyelashes.

"Yeah."

She started to walk away, and I called after her, "Thanks, I'm good too."

Anton cringed. "Sorry. She kind of has a crush on me."

I could see why. He was a handsome guy and about her age. His gaze didn't follow her, though, so I suspected it was one-sided. Or that he was much more interested in the topic at hand.

I took a sip of my water, then said, "So, if the investor took the tour and said no thanks, what would have happened to your father and the property, financially speaking?"

He swallowed hard. "My father would have declared bankruptcy. This investor was his last hope."

"Did that scare him? Was he prepared to deal with that if it didn't work out the way he was hoping?"

Fire filled his eyes. "Are you trying to suggest that he ran off if the investor said no?"

"No, not at all. Everyone says you and your sister were his entire life. He might have considered leaving Wolford and Lone County, but he could have just moved away. Why abandon his family, and why do it immediately after the investor meeting? Why not sell your house and move?"

He shook his head. "Mom would never leave. She loved it here."

"But she wants to leave now."

Confusion covered his face. "What?"

"She says she wants to move to Florida."

His forehead creased as he set down his fork. "What are you talking about?"

"She told me she wants to move to Florida and that

declaring your father dead will free things up legally for her."
No need to mention the life insurance money. At least not yet.

He was silent for several long seconds. "I'm not sure she'd
do that. She's queen bee here, and she'd have to start over
somewhere else. You have to understand…" He paused and
looked away for a few seconds before turning back. "My
mother loves attention, and she got plenty of it when my
father went missing. Sure, there was a scandal because so
many people lost money, but no one blamed her or Mary Ann
and me. Everyone said he took the money and abandoned us.
She claimed she had no idea what my father was up to, which
was a flat-out lie, but she knows my sister and I would never
publicly call her out on it." He shook his head again and
picked up a fry. "My mother would never leave Wolford."

"Your mother led me to believe she wasn't privy to your
father's business dealings." Not to mention she'd told Detective Jones the same thing.

His mouth shifted to one side. "I suspect she didn't know
everything, but she knew enough. We all did. Dad talked about
it at dinner." He took my silence as confusion. "We ate dinner
together every night. My dad insisted we have family time."

I nodded. "I'm sure it helped make your family closer."

His gaze dropped to his plate, and he said quietly, "Yeah."

"Brett Colter said your father got more money from the
investors by telling them you were ill and needed the money.
Do you know anything about that?"

He shook his head, his eyes wide. "No. He wouldn't have
done that. It would have been a lie."

So either Colter had lied to me to make Hugo look bad or
Anton didn't know his father as well as he thought he did.

I gave him a second to let his emotions settle before I
asked, "Did your mother know about Larkspur Limited?"

"She knew Dad was meeting with a potential new investor,
but I don't know if he told her the name of the group. Just
that the meeting was happening."

"How did *you* know?"

He reached for his glass but didn't pick it up. "He told me more than he told her. I was probably his best friend, and in hindsight, he might have told me too much. It was a pretty hard burden for a kid to know how bad things were for his dad." He lifted his glass and took a drink.

"I'm sorry."

He shrugged, trying to look nonchalant as he lowered the glass, but I saw the pain in his eyes. "It is what it is."

Realizing I hadn't touched my food yet, I picked up my fork and started to mix up my salad. "So if the meeting with the investor went badly," I said, "and your father *hadn't* disappeared, how would he have reacted? Would he have gone to your game?"

His jaw set. "Absolutely. Like I said, he *never* missed any of my games."

"But this would have been particularly bad news. Do you think he would have needed to regroup before he went to the game? Is there some place he would have gone? Maybe a bar? The gym to work off his frustration? A nature spot?"

He took a bite of his sandwich with a pensive look. When he swallowed, he said, "I'm racking my brain, but can't think of any place like that. I really think he would have come to the game and pretended like everything was okay." He paused. "I've given this a lot of thought, and he would have known that he was about to let all of us down. He wouldn't have made it worse by not going to the game." His mouth twisted into a half smile that didn't reach his eyes. "Does that make sense?"

"Yeah, Anton. It does."

"It's just...Mary Ann and I were everything to him. He pretty much lived for us. He would have come to the game."

I stabbed some lettuce with my fork. "Let's say your father showed up. What would he have done after the game?"

"We would have all gone home and had a late dinner."

"Would he have told the family that the meeting went poorly?"

"Yeah. I think so. We all knew the meeting was that afternoon, and we knew it was important. We would have asked."

"Do you think the pressure of telling your family could have been too much for him?"

His face reddened. "I told you he wouldn't have run, Harper."

I leaned closer, lowering my voice. "Anton, he obviously went *somewhere*. If he was murdered, I'm trying to figure out the timeline. Where would he have gone? And if he *was* murdered, by whom and why? Murder by a stranger is extremely rare, but it *does* happen." I knew that all too well from my sister's kidnapping and murder. "Was it a case of a robbery gone wrong? Or was it one of his investors?"

His cheeks turned pink. "Sorry. I know you're trying to help, but for the past five years, I've had dozens of people tell me I'm deluded to believe he didn't run off. I guess it's hard to accept you think there might be another explanation."

"It's okay," I said. "I understand your frustration, but I *will* tell you that I'm not making up my mind one way or the other yet. While I think it's less likely he ran away, I'm not ruling it out. I need to look at all the angles, so don't be offended by my questions."

"Yeah, I get it." His gaze dropped to the table, and he repeated, "I'm sorry."

"And I'm sorry you've had to live through this, but every piece of information you can give me, even if it makes him look guilty of deserting you, will help." I held his gaze. "I know you don't know me and have no reason to trust me, but I'm asking you to anyway. I'm likely the first person who has actively investigated your father's disappearance in years. If you want me to find out what happened, I need you to be honest with me."

He studied me for a moment, then said softly, "Yeah. Okay. I will."

I nodded and took a bite of my food, giving him a moment to absorb everything. I needed to establish a timeline of the last places he'd been. "Your father had a lunch meeting with Brett Colter, but I'm not sure what else he did that day. Do you know what time he was meeting his investor?"

He shook his head. "No. I just know it was in the afternoon."

"I know they must have toured the property, but were they meeting there or somewhere else?"

A sheepish look washed over his face. "I'm not sure. I only know they were going out there. We'd had a lot of rain the night before, and he was worried the utility vehicle would get stuck in the mud."

"And the wet ground would have made the tires of the utility vehicle muddy. Which is how you're sure the tour happened that day."

"Yeah, definitely. Certain parts of the land were really prone to getting soggy and muddy, like the marsh. That's where the birds lived. The ones that halted his project."

"Do you know what happened to Sunny Point after your father disappeared?"

"I know the bank foreclosed on it."

"Did you know it was bought soon after the bank put it on the market?"

His eyes widened. "I knew Brett Colter bought Martindale, but I didn't know what happened with Sunny Point."

"Brett Colter bought Martindale years later. How did you know about that purchase and not the other?"

He made a face. "They announced that Dudley, that online pet store, was putting in a distribution site and that Brett was behind it. It didn't take much effort to put together that it was on Dad's land."

"Do you know if the sheriff's department searched Sunny Point or Martindale?"

Guilt covered his face. "I don't know."

"They should have searched them," I said. "It was common knowledge he was supposed to meet an investor. It stands to reason they'd do it on the property." I needed to see the Sunny Point property, even if it was owned by someone else. "You saw the map I was looking at when you came in. It's of Wolford and the surrounding area. Do you think you could show me where Sunny Point was?"

"Yeah," he said. "I knew that place pretty well."

I shoved my salad to the side and opened the map again, turning it to face him as I pulled a pen out of my purse.

He pushed his own plate to the side and pointed to a highway which ran through Wolford down to El Dorado. "It was off Highway 20. If you're coming from Wolford, the entrance was right after you cross Meadow Creek. The road is paved and there's still a sign there, but it's faded now. The road goes a good quarter mile or so before it dead ends at the shed." He ran his finger from the highway onto the land. "The northern border is the creek, probably to about here." His finger stopped a good bit away from the highway. "Then it goes down to here." He trailed it south on the map, then back over to the highway. "It angles back so the entrance is narrow —probably about five hundred feet—but it's wider in the back."

"Can you draw it?" I asked, handing him the pen.

"It won't be perfect."

"A guesstimate is good."

He drew it in and I stared at it in amazement. "This looks huge."

"It is. It's five hundred acres. It started out at three hundred, then he bought two hundred more, realizing the project wasn't going to move quickly enough if he was just moving large-lot luxury homes. He planned to put more affordable homes on that back section with access from this county road." He pointed to where the property touched County Road 71.

"You know a lot for being in high school when all of this was going on and not being interested in joining your father's business."

He made a face. "Like I said, he wanted me to make it a family business. I hadn't told him I wasn't interested. I liked that he included me." He was silent for a moment, looking close to tears. "Sometimes I think it was good something happened to him. That way he never had to find out the truth."

"Obviously I never knew your father," I said gently, "but everything I've heard so far suggests differently. He might have been a bit disappointed at first, but I'm sure he ultimately just wanted you to be happy."

Chapter 11

Anton told me he needed to get back to the clinic, then tossed money on the table and said he'd cover the bill.

I had barely touched my salad, so I took a few more bites then grabbed my bag and headed out the door. As soon as I reached my car, I pulled out my phone and called Detective Jones. I had never asked him if they'd searched the land, and I wanted a clear answer. Thankfully he answered before it went to voicemail.

"Ah, Harper Adams," he said, sounding amused when he answered.

"Got my number saved in your phone?" I asked, not sure how I felt about that.

"I expected to hear from you again," he said with a laugh. "Figured I should be prepared for your questions."

"Then I suppose it's not a surprise that I'm calling to ask if you searched either of the properties Hugo Burton owned at the time of his death."

"You mean like search for a body?"

"Or anything helpful."

"Well, first of all, the Sunny Point property is over five

hundred acres. Do you know how much manpower that would take?"

"So that's a no?"

"I never said that," he grumbled. "I asked if you knew—never mind." He didn't sound happy. "The answer is yes. We searched both properties, but I admit that we didn't canvas them like we would if we were looking for a missing kid or person."

"But Hugo Burton *was* a missing person."

"We believed he'd ran off. We'd found his car in Little Rock. Do you know how much money a search like that would have cost?"

I didn't answer. I had no idea how much it would cost here, but back in Little Rock it would have taken a small fortune.

"I take it you found something," he said quietly.

I'd agreed to keep him updated on my search, but something felt off. I wasn't sure if it was my general paranoia and distrust at work, or whether my instincts were kicking in. But hiding what I knew for at least a few days wouldn't cause any harm. Not after five years.

"Just asking questions," I said, trying to keep my tone light.

"I see," he said, obviously not believing me.

"I promise to let you know if I find anything important."

"That's all I can ask," he said grudgingly.

"I do have one favor to ask," I said, my brain fixating on the abandoned car. "Can you get me any information on Burton's car at the Little Rock airport? A report about how it was found and photos?"

"I already gave you information I shouldn't have yesterday," he said, his voice tight.

"Then let me come into the office and look at them. I need to have a better understanding of what I'm working with." When he didn't respond, I pushed a little harder. "If you were working this case, wouldn't you want to see them?"

"I *did* work this case," he snapped back, but it wasn't full of venom. More like exhaustion mixed with defensiveness. "Remember? Five years ago."

"And you needed that information," I said. "Just like I need it now."

He cursed under his breath, then said, "I'll see what I can do. If I let you have it, I'll send it in an email."

"Thank you, Detective Jones," I said, meaning it. He could have chosen to be a complete asshole and not share anything with me, yet he was cooperating. I felt guilty that his openness hadn't eased my suspicious nature.

"Don't thank me yet," he grumbled. "I said I'd see what I could do."

"Yeah. Sure. I understand," I said and hung up. I knew he was going to send it, though, which made me fall back into the trust him camp.

I really needed to quit flip-flopping. What the fuck was wrong with me?

Back in Little Rock, I'd been known for my calm, meticulous investigations. I didn't get riled up. I followed the trail and let my instinct drive me. But my instincts seemed to have shriveled up.

I just had to trust they would come back.

I wanted to search the property, but I also wanted to talk to Skip Martin, so I searched for the number for the Ford dealership and called, asking for Skip.

"May I ask who's calling?" asked the man who'd answered.

"My name is Harper Adams and I need to speak to him about an investment he made several years ago. Is he available today?"

The man hesitated, then said, "Hold please."

Some cheesy elevator music played over the line for about

ten seconds before the man said, "He's available this after-noon at three."

"That fits with my schedule. Thank you."

After he hung up, I sat in my car, contemplating what to do for the next two hours. I decided to drive down Highway 20 to check out the Sunny Point property. Anton had said there was a paved road onto the property. I could drive down the road, maybe look around a bit, then head back for my three o'clock meeting.

It seemed like a great plan until I crossed Meadow Creek and saw the sun-faded navy-blue letters on a white sign: *Coming Soon! Sunny Point Executive Homes! From Burton Management.*

I pulled off the side of the road to the entrance, then parked perpendicular to the long metal bar blocking the entrance to the property.

Anton had neglected to mention the gate.

I shut off the engine and got out of the car. The gate was actually two rusted metal bars held together by a short stretch of silver metal chain and a keyed padlock. The vegetation on either side of the faded asphalt had grown up to the edge, making it impossible to drive around the obstacle.

A *No Trespassing* sign was nailed to the bottom of the sign.

After a short risk analysis, I tucked my keys in my pocket and walked around the gate. If I was arrested for trespassing, I'd invoke Detective Jones and hope he'd clear me. Worst case scenario, I'd get arrested and have to pay a fine.

The wind was picking up, making the edges of my coat flap open. I held it together as I walked the stretch of road to the end. I guessed it to be longer than the quarter mile Anton had mentioned, but otherwise I found it unremarkable. If Hugo had done any work, the vegetation had either grown back or the infrastructure was underground, as suggested by the utility flags sticking out of the tall, dead weeds on either side of the road. Water. Electricity. Gas. If Hugo had been forced to pay for running the utilities from the highway, it must have been expensive.

The utility shed was still at the end of the road. When I opened the door, it was empty. I suspected Clarice had sold the utility vehicle. It was what I would have done.

I stood in place and made a full sweep of the property. It looked like whoever had bought it had done absolutely nothing with it.

Why?

I really needed those property records to find out how much Larkspur Limited had purchased it for and compare it to what Hugo had paid for the two properties. Foreclosure properties were notorious for going for less than their worth. Had someone from Larkspur killed Hugo so they could buy the property for themselves for a massive discount? If so, *why*?

A couple of paved roads broke off from the one I was on, one on either side. A cul-de-sac was on the south side, with about five white PVC pipes sticking out of the ground, several hundred feet apart. If the pipes were the utilities for houses, then Hugo had planned for them to be distant from their neighbors. Then again, I suspected that's what most executives would want. The lots were mostly tree-filled, ensuring the homeowners' privacy.

Spots of land had been cleared around the other road, but I didn't see any pipes. I followed that road as it curved and meandered through trees to the southeast until it dead ended about three football lengths from the main road.

I headed back to the shed and scanned the land again, looking for anything that might stick out. The only remarkable thing I noticed were a hint of ruts running in multiple directions, presumably from Hugo's tours. I wanted to see the land, but I couldn't do it with my car and it would take forever on foot. Besides, I didn't have time today.

I headed back to the highway, and about halfway down the road, I saw a dirt road I'd missed walking in. It led down a hill, and I could catch a glimpse of what appeared to be Meadow Creek. Had that been where the pool and clubhouse were supposed to go? Why would he build a clubhouse in a marsh?

After a stop through a coffee shop drive-thru, I added a little whiskey I kept in the glove compartment. I'd done so well and hadn't had anything to drink since breakfast, but I told myself I was cold, and it was just to warm up, but deep down, I knew it was a lie. I told myself I'd start again tomorrow. By the time I pulled up to the Ford dealership at 2:55, I'd not only warmed up but eased my guilt as well.

I finished off my coffee, then popped a few breath mints as I walked through the front doors and told the receptionist I was there for a three o'clock meeting with Skip Martin. She picked up a phone to tell him his appointment was there, and a few seconds later, a man in jeans and a long-sleeve button-down shirt emerged from the back and walked straight toward me, extending his hand. His salt-and-pepper hair was styled, and he was wearing loafers.

"Skip Martin," he said, shaking my hand then releasing it and taking a step back. He held his hands up in front of him. "I hear you're here to talk about an investment of mine. If it's about that waterpark, I didn't know anything about the safety issue when I bought in. I swear."

"No," I said, slightly confused, reminding myself to possibly investigate that later. But it also assured me that no one had called warning him that I was asking questions. "I'd like to speak to you about another project." I glanced around the showroom, then back to him. "Can we talk in your office?" I reasoned that if he was hesitant to talk about Sunny Point, he'd have a harder time getting me out of his office than he would walking away from me at the receptionist desk.

His forehead furrowed. "Sure, come on back."

I followed him to a small office, the desk covered in paperwork and stacked folders. I would have expected something more glamorous for the owner, but then again, he wasn't dressed in flashy clothes. Maybe he'd preferred the bare-bones space.

He stood at the entrance and let me in, then shut the door behind him as he took a seat at the desk. "I think I know what you're here for, and to be honest, I'm surprised someone didn't come by sooner."

I lifted a brow. "What do you think I'm here for?"

"Sunny Point and Hugo Burton."

"What do you think I'm going to ask?"

"Ask?" he countered. "I thought you were here to give me an update about the fraud case against Hugo."

"You still haven't heard anything about the case?" I asked in surprise.

He leaned back in his chair, the seat hitting the wall. "The last I heard, they couldn't bring charges against Hugo unless he turned up somewhere, and I couldn't get my investment from the bank after the property was foreclosed on."

"I hate to be the bearer of bad news," I said, "but I don't know anything about the fraud case."

He sat up straighter in his seat. "Then why are you here?"

"To ask you questions about Hugo and Sunny Point."

He groaned. "I already told you all everything I know."

"Mr. Martin, I'm not sure who you think I'm with, but I'm a private investigator who was hired to find Hugo Burton."

Disbelief covered his face, followed by irritation. "Who hired you?"

"It doesn't matter," I said in a casual tone. "If I find Hugo Burton, then the state will arrest him for fraud, and while I doubt he'd have any money to repay you, you'd at least have the satisfaction of knowing he'd rot in prison for a while." I shrugged. "Then again, maybe he made more money, and he does have enough to repay you. Either way, it's in your best interest to tell me what you know."

His lips pressed together. "Okay. I'll tell you what I can, but I doubt it'll help you find the bastard."

"Why don't we start with how you knew Hugo?"

"I met him about fifteen years ago at some charity function. He was a land developer, doing small stuff. We were friendly when we saw each other, but we weren't buddies or anything."

I nodded.

"But then about ten years ago, he asked me out to lunch. I was surprised since we weren't close, but then he told me about a neighborhood he was working on—Sunny Point. I was intrigued, not to mention I wanted to build a house out there myself. So I gave him money...and waited. Then I gave him more money. And waited. He hit me up the third time right before he left town. I was pissed he was asking for more, even though there was so little progress out there."

"But you gave him a check anyway."

"It's the damn cost sunk fallacy, only I was too stupid to see it. Hugo convinced me by offering me a better payout than before. He told me he had a big-time investor interested. Hugo was going to take a smaller cut so we could get a bigger one. I know it sounds stupid, but I'd already put in so much already. I really wanted to get it back." He released a bitter laugh. "I not only lost what I'd put in but twenty thousand more."

"Hugo didn't tell you that he needed the money because his son was sick?"

"Anton?" He shook his head. "No. Was Anton sick?"

"No, but Brett Colter told me that he and some other investors gave Hugo more money because he needed it for Anton, who was sick."

Skip shook his head. "Hugo was a bastard for running off with our money, but I can't see him lying like that about his kid. Wolford's not all that big. It would have come out sooner rather than later."

"But likely not until after Hugo left," I said.

He pushed out a sigh. "Yeah, I guess you're right." He was silent for a moment. "Honestly, I still find it hard to believe he ran off and left his kids. They were his life."

"Several people have told me that. Do you think that there's a possibility he didn't run?"

"You mean someone killed him?"

"Maybe."

He was quiet for several seconds. "Yeah, I considered it, but the detective who was looking into it was so sure he ran off that I took his word for it."

"Surely the other investors were just as pissed at him as you were. Could one of them have been angry enough to confront him?"

"Bill O'Murphy was fit to be tied, but he wasn't the murdering type. He was more the praying them straight type."

"What about the other three investors?"

"Other *three*?" He narrowed his eyes. "I only knew about four of us—me, Brett, Bill, and Tim Heaton. Who are the other two?"

"One is a man named Pete Mooney."

He shook his head again. "Never heard of him."

"He was from Pine Bluff. He died in Little Rock soon after Hugo disappeared."

He grimaced, then his eyes widened. "Tim died a few months later, and so did Bill. Is someone going to come after me?"

"Tim died in a car accident and Bill died of colon cancer."

"How did this Mooney guy die?"

I hesitated. "He was mugged and murdered."

He nearly jumped out of his chair.

"Mr. Martin, I'm positive you're safe. All three men died

less than a year after Hugo disappeared, one by natural causes and the other in a car accident. I'm sure it's coincidence." But I wasn't about to admit it was too big of a coincidence to suit me, particularly given what I'd learned about the car accident.

"But people say Tim was run off the road…"

"Again, if something was going to happen to you, I believe it already would have happened."

He settled back in his chair, but he didn't look convinced.

"You said Hugo mentioned a big-time investor," I said. "Did he happen to tell you anything else about the person?"

"Not really, although I know it was a man because Hugo kept calling him a 'he.' I also know he wasn't from around here. He said he'd been talking to the guy for a while and that he was finally ready to invest. He was pretty hopeful."

"So why did he need more money from you if this mysterious guy was about to invest?"

"Something about showing the guy he could raise more capital." He shook his head. "Stupid. I know."

"You seem like a successful guy, so I suspect Hugo Burton was pretty convincing."

"That's for damn sure."

"If the big-time investor wasn't from around here, did Hugo mention where he was from?"

"Somewhere in the state, but not Little Rock." He forehead creased as he seemed to ponder my question. "I think he said the guy was from El Dorado."

"El Dorado. How sure are you of that?"

"Not one hundred percent, but pretty damn sure."

Clarice had mentioned Hugo going to El Dorado for work lunches. Maybe he'd met the big-time investor there. "That's helpful, Mr. Martin. Thank you."

"Sure," he said with a wave of his hand. "Anything else you want to know?"

"Yeah, one more thing. Do you happen to have a copy of the contract you signed with Hugo for Sunny Point?"

He shook his head. "No. I gave my copy to the state attorney general. I never got a contract for the payback restructure." He made a face. "See, stupid."

But Skip Martin didn't seem like a stupid man. Hugo must have had enough of a silver tongue to sell beachfront property in Arizona. "I know this may seem like an illogical question, but do you know anything that could possibly help me locate Hugo Burton?" I asked. "Anything at all."

He snorted. "If I did, I would have gone and gotten him myself."

That was fair. Skip seemed like the kind of guy who liked to settle things personally, without involving other people. "Well, thank you for your time."

I stood and headed for the door.

"What did you say your name was again?" he asked.

"Harper Adams."

"Ms. Adams, if you find Hugo Burton and my money, I'll pay you a thousand dollars if you tell me first."

"A very interesting offer, Mr. Martin, but I'll be telling my client first."

I headed out to my car, trying to decide on my next move, but I saw I had a text from Carter Hale.

Drop by my office. I may have something to help.

Chapter 12

I wasn't surprised that Malcolm had told his attorney about my interest in Hugo Burton. The real question was what he might have to help me. I was intrigued enough to head back to Jackson Creek.

I walked through the front door of his office, a change from the last time I'd visited, so I was surprised when his receptionist recognized me.

"Ms. Adams. Mr. Hale is expecting you. You can go on back."

I walked down the hall and stopped outside his cracked door, hesitating. Did I really want to go in there? Whatever he had to tell me would likely drag me into Malcolm's mess, and I wasn't sure I wanted to be in the muck with him. Still, this wasn't a new revelation. I'd known the dangers of showing up from the moment I'd seen Carter Hale's text, yet I'd still come.

I was curious, that was all.

So why was I hesitating?

"I can see you lurking outside the door, Ms. Adams," Carter called from inside his office. "Either come in or leave. It's up to you."

We both knew I wasn't going anywhere.

Pushing the door open, I entered, then shut it behind me before I walked over to his dry bar. I'd already broken my vow not to drink. No sense wasting the opportunity to drink such fine whiskey. "Mr. Hale," I said without looking at him.

He remained silent as I poured whiskey into one of his fancy crystal glasses, then took a sip. I finally turned to face him, not surprised by the amusement dancing in his eyes.

"Please, help yourself to a drink, Ms. Adams."

"Thank you. I think I will." I poured more into my glass, then set down the bottle back down and moved over to a chair in front of his desk. I sat down and stared into his face. "Why is James Malcolm interested in Hugo Burton?"

He laughed. "I see you don't waste any time on idle chitchat."

"Do I strike you as an idle chitchatter?" I asked dryly, then took another sip, savoring the flavor as well as the burn as it began to hit my bloodstream. This whiskey was reason enough to drop by his office.

"No, Ms. Adams, you definitely do not," he said without malice, but some of his humor was gone.

"So?" I prompted. "What's his interest?"

He sat back in his chair and studied me for a few seconds before he said, "Mr. Malcolm likes to know the history of the places he lives, and that includes the people who live there. When he was in the federal prison in Forrest City several years ago, he had me research the current inmates in the facility as well as the previous ones."

I leaned my forearm on the padded leather arm of the chair. "You don't say." Despite the tone I'd affected, it was an interesting piece of information. Had he been looking for an inmate who he could use or was he more interested in any potential threats? Knowing what I knew about the man, I suspected it was both and a half dozen more reasons. "Okay, so let's say I go along with your *he's a history buff and is a secret member of the Jackson Creek Historical Society* explanation, why did you call me?"

"So impatient," he chided with a grin.

I took another sip of the drink. If he hadn't gotten to the point before I finished, I'd leave. Or maybe I'd have another drink.

"As I said, Mr. Malcolm likes to know the history of the place he resides, and given the accusations made against him in the past, he tends to know who is currently or previously dealing with situations that might fall into his lap."

"You mean crimes other people committed that he might be accused of committing."

Smirking, he nodded slightly.

"I take it you're in charge of research?"

"Very astute, *Detective*."

I supposed I'd deserved that one. "You've researched Hugo Burton and the Sunny Point situation." Statement, not a question.

"I have, and I have some information you might not get by interviewing men like Brett Colter and Skip Martin."

My blood turned icy, and I lowered the half-raised glass to rest on the arm of the chair. "How did you know I'd talked to them?"

His forehead wrinkled as he gave me a look of partial disgust. "Because I was told you were a decent investigator, and any decent investigator would talk to the investors."

Shit. He was right, and while I used to be a great investigator, I wasn't so sure I could make that claim anymore. I'd lost my instincts and instincts were everything. Sure, I was doing well so far in this investigation, but so far it had been an easy path to follow. The real skill would come when the leads began to dry up and deduction took over. "Yeah, right," I grumbled. "But you could still have someone following me."

"Why would we do that, Harper?" he asked with a hint of

condescension. "What makes you think we're interested in what you're doing?"

That one stung a bit, but I saw it for what it was. A way to make me think I wasn't interesting enough to deserve their attention, yet the fact he'd invited me here negated his assertion. "Then why is Malcolm so interested in what I find?"

"I already told you, he likes to know what's going on in—"

"The place he lives. Got it. Maybe it's more like he doesn't like people shitting where he eats, but sure, whatever. I still don't see why he cares about a man who disappeared five years ago. He claimed the man did something truly heinous, but he never said what the heinous act was. Do *you* know?"

"I only know what Skeeter tells me and what I find."

Which in theory meant he knew. He just refused to tell me. Still, this might not be a wasted effort. Malcolm likely didn't have just one excuse for solving this mystery. Then a new thought hit me. "Unless…"

Carter looked amused again. "Unless what?"

Unless Malcolm was one of the two original investors. Did I want to play this hand? Why not? "Did James Malcolm invest money in Sunny Point?"

What appeared to be genuine shock widened his eyes. "You think Malcolm invested in a piece of shit property here in Lone County when he was *very* occupied with the state of things in Fenton County?"

He had a point. As far as I could tell, Malcolm had been tied to Fenton County until he'd been linked to the international crime organization that had been based in Dallas, Texas. If he'd been aspiring for greater things, why move backward to a county that was worse than his own?

Still…

"You didn't answer the question, Carter," I said, taking another sip of my drink. "You evaded it with a question of your own."

His smirk was back, and he nodded slightly. "Touché. And

the answer is no, he was not an investor in the Sunny Point property."

"Was he an investor in the Martindale property?"

Confusion filled his eyes this time, and I realized he probably didn't know it by that name. "Was he an investor in *any* property that Hugo Burton had an interest in?" That question also covered the Colter Group project.

A sly grin spread across his face. "While I don't have knowledge of Hugo Burton and Skeeter Malcolm having shared investments, I do happen to know that Skeeter never backed any project in Lone County before he moved here three years ago."

"Why do you call him Skeeter?" I asked.

He shook his head slightly. "I thought you were here to find out information about Hugo Burton."

"And I want to know why you don't call him James."

Releasing a sigh, he sat back into his chair again. "It's what everyone called him back home. He decided to drop it when he came here, but old habits die hard, and I think he likes that I still call him Skeeter. It reminds him of his roots."

Had he really started using his given name to turn over a new leaf, or were there other reasons? Did it really matter?

"Okay, Carter, I'll bite. What do you know about Hugo Burton?"

He proceeded to tell me about Hugo buying the Sunny Point property, then getting the two original investors. Nothing I didn't already know.

"Do you know who the original two investors are?" I asked. "I know one was Brett Colter, but I still haven't discovered the identity of the other."

"Who do you know about?"

I spouted off the short list, watching him for a reaction to any of the names. I thought I saw a slight flare of his nostrils at the mention of Pete Mooney, but my senses were slightly dulled by the alcohol chugging through my blood. I decided to pursue it because even if I'd imagined the reaction, he might know something I didn't.

"What do you know about Pete Mooney?" I asked. "Because neither Brett Colter nor Skip Martin could tell me anything."

"He was from Pine Bluff and he died in an unfortunate robbery attempt while he was in Little Rock."

"But how did Hugo meet someone who lived about an hour northeast of us? He's the only investor who wasn't from the area."

"Who knows?" Carter said. "Word of mouth?"

Maybe, but I couldn't help thinking there might be more to it. "What else do you know about him?"

"Only that he was a later investor. He joined about a year before Hugo disappeared. The others were either in at the beginning or a couple of years later."

"Hugo was meeting a potential new investor at the Sunny Point property the afternoon he disappeared. Do you know who?"

"That would be valuable information if I had it."

"Are you suggesting that I'd have to pay for it if you did?"

"I'm not saying any such thing," he said amicably. "I'm merely stating that whoever he met that afternoon is likely key to the investigation, and from what I heard, not even the sheriff's investigators know."

"Do you have any guesses?"

He laughed. "I have a ton of guesses, from Hugo Burton's imaginary friend to the president of the bank who held the bank note." He held up a hand. "And no, he did not meet the bank president or anyone else at the bank. I checked."

Damn. Carter Hale was a good resource. If I could trust him.

"There were two original investors. One was Brett Colter, but no one seems to know the identity of the other," I said. "Do you?"

"No," he said, looking pained. "Are you sure there were six?"

"Detective Jones with the Lone County Sheriff's Department confirmed it with me yesterday afternoon."

He lifted a hand to his chin, his gaze becoming unfocused. After a couple of seconds, he turned back to me.

"Interesting."

"Have you got anything else that can help me?" I asked.

"Only an offer to help you when and if I can, not only with this case but with any future cases that come your way."

"*Why?*"

His amusement was back. "Why what?"

"Why help me? What do you get out of it?"

"I already told you. Skeeter likes to know what goes on in the area. In return, I might have some P.I. work for you in the future." He held up his hand again. "All perfectly legitimate stuff." A grin lit up his eyes. "Didn't Skeeter and I both tell you that he's turned legit?"

"Killing two men in cold blood doesn't sound very legit to me," I said without inflection.

His gaze turned cold. "And it seems to me that your silence has made you an accessory to any crime that might have been committed."

Hadn't the same thought occurred to me?

"No need for concern," Carter said sympathetically. "Skeeter has no intention of bringing you down. He's hoping you won't do the same to him."

"I've kept quiet, haven't I?"

"Skeeter's not interested in self-annihilation, and we presume you're not a fan of it either."

"You're both correct," I said, feeling unsettled. Because, hearing him say it, I knew that wasn't the reason I'd held back. No. I was glad those men were dead.

I got up again but headed for the dry bar and poured myself another drink.

What was happening to me? Sure, I'd killed before, but that had always been in self-defense or to protect someone else. I'd never killed anyone in cold blood, yet everything inside me wished I'd been able to watch the life bleed out of Dan Sylvester, just like he'd stood by and watched my sister get tortured. Except he'd gotten off on it.

"Is there anything you need to move forward with your search?" he asked as I took a gulp of the alcohol to clear my head. I needed to focus.

I started to tell Carter I didn't need anything, then decided I might as well take advantage of his offer. "Do you know anything about Larkspur Limited?" I turned to face him. "They bought the Sunny Point property from the bank, and as far as I can tell, they never did anything with it."

"Yes, from what I've gathered, it was purchased and never developed."

I nodded and took a sip, still standing next to the bar. "I was out there this afternoon, and it looks like it hasn't been touched since Hugo disappeared."

"You were out there?" he asked in surprise.

"Yeah, but I want to go back. I need to rent some kind of four-wheel-drive vehicle to go over the rough terrain."

"Why?" He seemed genuinely curious.

"To be blunt, I want to see if I can find Hugo Burton's body."

"The land is partly wooded and covered in tall grass and marsh in the low-lying ground by the river. What makes you think you'll find Burton's body when the sheriff's department couldn't pull it off five years ago?"

"Maybe because they didn't do a proper search." Not that I could do one on my own, but I still wanted to try.

He was silent for a long moment. "Okay. I'll have a four-wheel-drive vehicle delivered to the Sunny Point property by ten a.m. tomorrow morning. Anything else?"

I tried to smother my surprise. "Yeah," I said, carrying my

glass as I walked over to his desk and stared down at him. "Who is behind Larkspur Limited?"

"That, Harper Adams, is the million-dollar question." He grinned. "Something tells me you might be the one to find out."

Chapter 13

I left after that, but I knew I was in no shape to drive so I walked to the bookstore a couple of blocks away. Nate was sitting in the front window, reading a book with a fancy-looking latte on the wide window ledge next to him.

He looked up in surprise when I walked in, alarm over-taking his expression when he saw my face. He scrambled to his feet. "What happened?"

"Can I stay here for a bit?"

He stood in front of me. "Of course, Harper, but what happened?"

I shook my head, trying to pull myself together.

I was a monster. Maybe I really had killed that boy in Little Rock in cold blood and had deluded myself into believing otherwise.

Nate was good and pure and everything I wanted to be. Everything I'd thought I was before the shooting last October, but maybe I'd never been as pure as I'd believed. Maybe the monster had always been lurking underneath, waiting to be let out.

I took a step backward, bumping into the door. "This was a mistake."

"Harper? What's wrong? What happened?" he repeated.

"Just…everything," I said, surprised to discover tears were tracking down my cheeks. "Sorry. I shouldn't have involved you in my existential crisis."

"Why are you having an existential crisis?"

"My life has turned to shit, Nate," I snapped. "Wouldn't be weird if I wasn't?"

Hurt and shock covered his face and guilt flooded me. At least I could feel guilt. That meant I wasn't a true psychopath, right? I took comfort in that.

"I'm sorry," I said. "I'm having a shit day." But I wasn't. Not really. I'd reveled in the investigation. Right up until I'd dropped by Carter Hale's office.

Why hadn't I turned down his offer of help?

"I'm going home to do some meditation and self-reflection."

"I don't think you should be alone," he said.

I'd lashed out and hurt him, yet he still wanted to help me. If anything told me he was too good for me, this was the proof. "I won't be alone. I'm having dinner with my mother. I'm sorry I bothered you." I reached for the doorknob, but it took three tries to grab hold of it.

"Harper, have you been drinking?"

Instead of answering, I opened the door and headed in the direction of my mother's house. She lived about three quarters of a mile from downtown, and I needed the brisk air to clear my head. Only my head still wasn't clear by the time I got home. It was only more muddled with guilt, rage, and the need for vengeance.

I expected my mother to greet me when I walked onto the property, but she left me alone as I climbed the staircase to my apartment and shut the door. I immediately pulled out my Jack Daniel's and drank a couple of shots straight from the bottle.

So much for staying sober today.

I spent the night drinking and watching old episodes of *Schitt's Creek* on my laptop to help drag me out of this rut of self-hatred, but before long I was too drunk to follow the story-line, and I was nodding off and then startling myself awake. I told myself I had to go to the house for dinner at seven, but I drank even more at the thought of spending the evening with my mother.

I woke with a massive pounding headache that made me consider going to the ER to see if I had an aneurysm. I blinked my eyes open, surprised to see daylight streaming through the window over the sink.

How could it be morning when I hadn't gone over to have dinner with my mother yet?

I clenched my eyes shut.

Oh shit. I'd slept through dinner with my mother. She was going to kill me.

You didn't sleep through dinner. You were blackout drunk.

My inner voice had a point, and I couldn't ignore that I had a problem with alcohol, but I didn't get blackout drunk very often. At least not lately.

I forced myself to sit up and look for my phone, which I found between the sofa cushions. I looked at the screen. It was 8:42 a.m. I had five missed calls from Nate and five from Louise, along with multiple texts from both of them. They were worried about my state of mind.

I ran a hand over my head. I didn't have time to deal with them, not when I had to get ready and head over to the Sunny Point property. I sent them individual texts, saying the same thing.

Sorry I ignored your calls and texts. I'm fine. Really. I just had a moment. I spent the evening with my mother and left my phone at my apartment. I'll catch up with you both later.

I made a cup of coffee and drank it black as I started the shower. I spent a long time under the water, trying to clear my head. I couldn't remember much of last night, but when I got out, I saw that the whiskey bottle was nearly empty.

I was lucky I hadn't died from alcohol poisoning.

It hit me that I hadn't seen any missed calls or texts from my mother. She must be really pissed.

I made another cup of black coffee and added a bit of whiskey—hair of the dog—to help with my hangover. I still had some time before whatever vehicle Carter was sending to Sunny Point would be available, so I checked my email and saw that Detective Jones had followed through with the report on Hugo's car.

I took a long sip of my coffee, then tried to focus on the report. The car had been clean, no trash inside, and the seat was pushed far back.

I grabbed my phone and called Clarice.

"Sorry to bother you so early," I said when she answered, "but I have a couple of questions."

"Questions but no answers," she said in an irritated tone.

"That's the way investigations work," I said, not letting her sniping get to me. "How tall was Hugo?"

"What kind of question is that?"

"It's a straightforward one. How tall was he?"

"About five-ten, although I'm pretty sure he shrank, so probably closer to five-nine."

"Did he have long legs?"

"What does that have to do with anything?"

"Clarice..."

"Fine. They weren't exceptionally long."

"Do you know how far back he kept the driver's seat in his car?"

She paused. "You found something."

"Maybe, but don't get your hopes up. How far back did he keep his seat? All the way back? In the middle?"

"I guess in the middle."

"Great. Now one more thing. How clean did he keep his car?"

I expected her to fight me on that too, but she said, "It was always full of papers and stuff."

"So messy?"

"Yeah. It would only be clean if Anton cleaned it out."

"Did you see his car after they found it?"

"No, they impounded it and I never got it back."

"The report and the photos show that it's perfectly clean. No trash whatsoever."

"Someone cleaned it out," she said breathlessly.

"Do you think it could have been Anton?"

"I don't know. You should ask him. But text him. He can't always talk on the phone, but he can answer a text."

Yesterday she'd been reluctant to let me talk to Anton, but now she was eager for me to get confirmation from him. Maybe that meant she trusted me now. "Thanks. I plan to do that as soon as we end this call."

"Harper," she called out as I was about to hang up.

"Yes?"

"Sorry I've been such a bitch. I just…"

"It's okay, Clarice. I understand."

I hung up and sent Anton several texts.

Anton, this is Harper Adams.

I'm looking at the police report on your father's car, and I have a couple of questions for you.

Call me when you get a chance.

I wasn't surprised when my phone rang less than a minute later.

"What do you need?" he said after I answered.

"Do you know if your father's car was clean the day he disappeared?"

"It was messy," he said. "He dropped me off at school,

and I offered to clean it over the weekend if he paid me twenty bucks."

"Could he have had it cleaned by someone else?"

"Why are you asking?"

"The report and the photos show the car completely cleaned out."

"He didn't do that," Anton said in a tight voice.

"And the position of the driver's seat?" I asked.

"Not too close to the steering wheel, but not all the way back either. Somewhere in the middle."

"That's very helpful. Thank you."

"You found something," he said, sounding excited.

"I think there's evidence to support the idea that your father didn't leave his car at the airport. Someone else did."

"So he's dead," he said in a flat tone.

"I'm not sure what this means. It's only one piece of the puzzle. There's a lot more to discover. I'll let you and your mother know as soon as I know something."

Someone had cleaned Hugo's car. Why?

I scoured the report and looked for any mention of taking samples for evidence and didn't find anything, so I called Detective Jones.

"I take it you got the report," he said.

"I did, and a couple of things stuck out to me."

"Okay…"

"His car was clean."

"So?"

"His wife and his son say his car was typically messy, and they confirmed it was dirty the morning he disappeared."

"So? He got it cleaned?"

"But his son was usually the one to clean it."

"It was clean, Adams," he said, sounding irritated. "So what?"

"What about his seat position?"

"What about it?"

"It was pushed all the way back. Hugo wasn't a tall man. He usually kept it somewhere in in the middle."

He was silent for a moment. "You think someone moved the seat and cleaned the car."

"From the report, it doesn't look like anyone tested it for any kind of evidence."

"I think they took some prints, but I never heard the results for that."

"Could you check?" I asked.

"Yeah. I'll call up to Little Rock and see what they've got."

"Maybe don't mention my name."

He laughed. "Don't worry. No offense, but I'm not exactly shouting it from the rooftops that I'm working with you."

"No offense taken. I think."

"I'll let you know when I hear about those results."

"Thanks, Detective Jones."

I hung up and looked at the time on my laptop. It was 9:15, and it was going to take me about twenty minutes to get there, not to mention I needed to walk to my car, which was still parked across the street from Carter Hale's office.

I dressed in jeans and a long-sleeve T-shirt, a sweater, and a thick raincoat since the forecast called for rain possibly mixed with snow.

Had the killer struggled with Hugo in the car? Perhaps it had gotten messy, from the mud and possibly blood, and they'd had to clean it up? I had lots of questions, but I felt we were moving in the right direction.

I put on a pair of athletic shoes and carried a pair of rain boots in a bag, taking a latte to keep me warm on the walk. My mother didn't appear at the back door when I left, so I knew I must really be in trouble. I had to find somewhere else to live.

Chapter 14

When I pulled up to the Sunny Point property, the first thing I noticed was that the gate to the property was open. It looked like Carter had already come through. Funny how I'd never doubted he would.

After I turned onto the road into the property, I stopped and shut the gate behind me. While I doubted anyone would notice the gate was open and call the sheriff, I didn't want to press my luck.

I drove up the hill, noticing dark clouds in the distance. I needed to get this done before it started to rain.

A Jeep Cherokee with an open top was parked by the shed. I parked next to it and got out, bracing myself against a gust of wind that blew strands of hair into my face. I'd dressed warmly, but cold still seeped through the open spots, chilling me to the bone.

I swept the hair out of my eye and noticed the man with his back leaning against the front of the Jeep, holding a travel mug in his hand. He turned to face me with a grin. "Hello, Detective."

James Malcolm.

"Why am I not surprised to see you here?"

"Now, now," he chided. "Be careful or I might think you're ungrateful."

"*Carter* offered a vehicle."

"And you think he's paying for it?" he asked as he pushed away from the Jeep and walked toward me.

"Fine, I'll reimburse you."

He laughed, but it was short-lived. "I don't want your money. Maybe I'm here because I feel like I owe you for getting me out of Peterman's clutches."

"And what about your interest in the man who has done heinous things?"

"The two aren't mutually exclusive."

I shook my head. This was a bad idea.

"You have two choices," he said an even tone as he stopped in front of me. "You either accept my help, no questions asked, or I get in the Jeep and leave."

I was tempted to tell him to leave. I understood his involvement in my search for Ava Peterman, but this...while I believed the man he was after had done bad things, the question was what he was going to do if he got the information he needed. What if he resorted to murder again? I wasn't sure I could condone that again.

Still, he *had* provided a Jeep that looked built for the task.

I propped my hands on my hips. "Do you expect me to share what I find with you?"

"You tell me whatever the fuck you want," he said, lifting his brow in a silent challenge. "And I'll do the same."

I wasn't comfortable with this. At. All. I was considering renting my own all-terrain vehicle when he said, "A storm's due in early tonight. A mixture of snow, rain, and ice. If it rains an inch or more, this land will be untraversable for several days, perhaps a week or more if the forecast is right about the heavy rain mixed with snow. So it's either ride with me, or wait a week or more."

"Fine." I knew a storm was coming, so he hadn't lied. I

just hadn't paid attention to the expected amount, which had been incredibly stupid.

"You got a warmer coat than that?" he asked, flinging a hand in my direction.

"Since when do you care about my comfort?"

"I'm driving an open Jeep out on land for possibly hours. A cold front is moving in and it's only going to get colder."

I wanted to tell him to fuck off, but that would feel like giving him a win. "This coat is warmer than it looks, and I have a hat." I pulled a knit cap out of my pocket and tugged it over my head to prove my point. I didn't bother to tell him my coat was down lined, and I'd worn it in colder temperatures than this.

"Got any more arguments?" he asked.

"You're the one questioning my judgment in outerwear. I've resigned myself to having you as my tour guide. Do you know why I'm out here?"

"You're looking for the proverbial golden needle in the haystack. You're looking for Hugo Burton's body."

"I probably won't find it. As you alluded, it's a nearly impossible task."

"And yet here we are, standing next to a four-wheel-drive Jeep. Get in."

I grabbed my cell phone out of my car, along with my thermal mug and the map Anton had helped me create, then locked the door and popped the trunk to grab my boots. Malcolm was already sitting in the driver's seat when I tossed my boots onto the floor behind the passenger seat, then climbed in beside him.

"Do I want to know where this came from?"

"It's Misti's brother's." He shot me another look as he started the engine. "There's a blanket in the back. I don't want you whining that you're cold, forcing us to turn back."

I lifted my chin. "I don't whine."

"No, you drink." His gaze dropped to my side. "I'm guessing you have a flask in that coat pocket."

I hated that he was right. "Fuck you," I snapped.

His mouth lifted into a one-sided grin. "We've discussed my lack of interest before. Now you're just embarrassing yourself."

I bit my tongue to keep from telling him to fuck off. He didn't waste any time backing out of the space, so I grabbed a support bar to keep myself seated. "I take it you have a plan?"

"Always." He shot me a glance. "Do you?"

"I *did* have one."

"I don't intend to interfere with that, but it makes sense to start at the beginning of the property and work our way back."

He had a point, but with our limited time and the size of the property, this wasn't how I would have done it. Not without a large group of canvassers. But I held my tongue as he barreled toward the gate, then did a U-turn at the entrance and came to a stop.

He shot me a glance. "You closed the gate."

"The longer we can go unnoticed here, the better."

Malcolm kept the Jeep in place, the engine idling as we sat in silence for several uncomfortable seconds.

"Waiting for something?" I asked.

"Yeah, for you to give me directions on where to go."

I nearly argued with him over that. He'd never had a plan. He'd always intended to use mine, yet that's what I'd wanted, wasn't it? So why did I want to blow up at him?

What was wrong with me? Sure, it went against my grain to work with a criminal, but I'd done it before. It wasn't like this was the first time. A little irritation at the unwanted situation was acceptable, but this white hot anger was unwarranted. It made me question my sanity and morality even more than I had the night before.

Which made me crave a drink from the flask I most assuredly had in my pocket.

Malcolm kept his hard gaze on me, and I realized this was the face of the boss of a crime ring, not to mention a member of an international drug cartel. Sure, he'd brought that group down, but nothing could convince me he'd done it out of moral concerns. He could easily kill me and hide my body in the woods on over five hundred acres, and it would be years before anyone found me. *If* anyone found me. Especially since the only person who knew for certain I was out here was Carter Hale, and I knew his loyalty didn't belong to me.

Malcolm was still waiting for me to give him directions.

The problem was that I hadn't come up with a search plan. I'd been too busy entertaining myself in my pity party the night before.

"Or," he said, his voice a tight rumble, "we could work this out together."

A slow smile spread across my face as I turned to face him. "How hard was it to make those words come out of your mouth?"

His eyes narrowed to slits, and I suspected his red cheeks hadn't been caused by the wind.

"Look," I said. "I'm not stupid. We both know you have a special interest in this case. You have your reasons and I have mine. Maybe they're mutually beneficial."

He didn't respond.

"But if you think I'm going to hand over everything I find on a silver platter just because you showed up with a Jeep, you're sorely mistaken. This case is five years old, so waiting a week for the land to dry so I can come back out with my own four-wheel-drive vehicle is acceptable."

"I'm simply your chauffer," he said.

"Doubtful."

When he started to protest, I held up a hand. "Still," I added slowly. What I was about to say was reckless and foolish, but it felt right. "I was used to working with a partner in Little Rock. Having someone to work things through with." I lifted my gaze to his. "I suggest we work together while searching this land, then reevaluate when we finish and see if we can continue working together."

"You do realize that *I* was the one who proposed we work together?"

I simply held his gaze.

"I suspect you know a hell of a lot more about this case than I do," he admitted, looking beleaguered by his own admission, "which puts me at a disadvantage. Which also means I will let you take lead on a lot of it." I started to ask him a question, but he grunted, "And no. I will not tell you anything else about why I'm interested in your case, but I suspect you're right about the results being mutually beneficial."

It was stupid working with him on this, but working with him had helped me return Ava Peterman to her mother. As much as it pained me to admit, without him, I suspected she would currently be dead.

"I will accept your request for privacy for now," I said. "But if it becomes an issue, I'll demand more answers." I pinned him with my gaze. "And just because I don't know all the details about *why* you're interested doesn't mean you get out of telling me anything at all."

"I gave you information on Monday night," he growled. "Of my own volition, without expecting anything from it."

"Right." While what he said was true, I couldn't help thinking he'd only done it to open the door to this kind of arrangement. I couldn't say I blamed him. He knew how to play the long game, and as long as it worked to my advantage, I could live with it.

"Okay," I said grudgingly, because while I still didn't fully trust him not to withhold information, the piece of information

I was about to share was vital to figuring out where we needed to search. "Burton was meeting an investor the afternoon of his disappearance, before his son's basketball game, which started at five. His son told me the meeting was here at the Sunny Point property. He called his wife at four and told her he'd be late to the game. When his father didn't come to the game, Anton came to the property to search for him. It was dark, so he couldn't look far, but he said the utility vehicle they used to take people on tours had muddy wheels. And it was fresh, not dried, so it had likely gone out that day. Not only that," I added, "but Hugo's car was found at the Little Rock airport parking lot, and it was clean inside. He always kept it messy."

"You think someone else took his car?"

"Or at least parked it in the Little Rock airport parking lot."

He gave a sharp nod. "So you're thinking the investor killed Burton somewhere on this piece of land."

"It's a theory. And it makes sense. Why remove him from here and kill him somewhere else? Why not hide his body on this vast piece of land?"

"And the car at the airport?"

"A decoy. A sleight of hand to make the authorities think he ran off. I mean, with his financial history, I could understand the supposition that he was a flight risk, but I'm struggling to believe he'd leave without his kids. Sure, the state was opening an investigation on him, but I doubt he knew that. They usually keep those things under wraps, not to mention, from what I can tell, he didn't do anything illegal until he moved the money in his account to an offshore bank account. So it seems more likely he'd cut his losses, sell everything, and move on."

"And his wife would have agreed to moving?"

"That would have been the sticky part of the plan," I conceded. "But his kids meant *everything* to him. I think he'd divorce his wife and split custody before he'd completely abandon them."

He didn't respond.

"You don't agree."

"Seems to me you're jumping to conclusions a little too early in your investigation."

I turned to look at him. "You think he ran off."

"I don't know one way or the other," he said with a shrug. "I'm waiting to see what we find."

"I'm searching this land on the theory he was murdered. Which is probably one reason why the sheriff's department didn't search it thoroughly enough. They didn't want to waste resources because they were convinced he ran." I lifted my brow with a smug smirk. "If the killer is the one who created the decoy with his car, that's why he or she did it. And looky there. It worked. They got away with murder."

"So based on your theory that he was murdered here, where do you want to search? There's no way we can cover five hundred acres in a day, not that all five hundred acres are even accessible."

"Good point," I said. "I'm guessing this was premeditated, or at least the possibility was on the investor's mind. If you killed someone on a vast property like this, you'd have plenty of places to hide the body. Good places." My mind raced over what Anton had told me about that day. "I keep thinking about the muddy tires on that vehicle. There had been rain the day before. The main road is on higher ground as well as this higher plateau. The water would run off, making the land dry out faster."

"You think they disposed of the body on low land?"

"Maybe someplace that held water."

"The marsh?" He shook his head. "It would be stupid to bury a body there. They would run the risk of the body resurfacing."

"But it would be easy to dig down there."

"I'm not so sure. It could have been a sloppy mess, but let's go check it out." He shifted the Jeep into first gear and started driving, picking up speed until he approached the dirt road that split off to the right.

"I take it this is the road to the marsh?" he shouted over the roar of the wind.

I frowned. "How did you know——"

"I'm perfectly capable of reading maps and news reports," he said in disgust. "And I'm pretty damn sure there would have been a road leading to it given all the studies and interest." He turned onto the path.

I couldn't really argue with that, but while I knew he was intuitive, I also wondered if he'd known about the road beforehand.

"Anton said there was a shed that they housed the utility vehicle in," I said as we bounced over the uneven road. "It's at the end of the road, but it stands to reason he'd start his tours off at the top of the hill. The view probably would have helped sell lots."

The land in this area was covered in scrub brush with few trees on either side of the dirt road that I could now see had been covered in gravel. Closer to the bottom, a small grove of trees had grown to the right of the road. The road curved to the left and ended at a large flat area overlooking the river. The land didn't look like a swamp with stagnant water, but I could see a few marsh plants growing to one side.

Malcolm came to a stop and then stood in the Jeep, overlooking the land.

I pulled out my map and studied it, trying to get my bearings. The dirt road wasn't on the map, but from what I could tell, this section was pretty close to the location Anton had marked off for the clubhouse.

Malcolm glanced down. "That's your working map?" Shaking his head, he reached inside his leather coat and pulled out a folded paper. "This will prove more useful." He hopped out of the Jeep and headed to the hood. I followed.

He was already spreading out his map, and I had to admit I was impressed. This must have been the map Hugo had used to lure his investors. It showed the land with home lots and roads laid out, along with the clubhouse, pool, tennis courts, and walking trails. It not only showed the first proposed executive neighborhood, but also Phase Two with the lower-priced homes toward the south, with the entrance from the county road that Anton had told me about.

How had Malcolm gotten his hands on this?

He pointed to the clubhouse on the map. "This is where they expected to build the clubhouse. I've heard that Burton also planned to put in a golf course to the north of the river." He tapped on the area on the map. "He just hadn't bought the land yet. He figured that would bring in additional income." He snorted. "Only he forgot to take into account the fact that golf is a dying sport."

"You're right. It sounds like he had grandiose plans and an inflated sense of ego." I shot him a dry look. "Kind of like someone else I know."

He grinned. "It's not all that grandiose or inflated if you can back it up."

He had a point.

"Some water bird lives out here that was holding up his plans, but he'd supposedly come up with a work-around." He snorted. "Rumor had it he was hoping to build a dam and call it a water feature for the clubhouse patrons, adding concrete walls on the banks to keep the river contained."

"And dry up the marsh," I said. "That wouldn't be legal. Surely the river is a public waterway."

"It was fully contained on his land, and it's considered a creek. He could do what he wanted with it as long as he didn't interfere with the bird's habitat. He'd just had that pointed out to him by Colter the day he disappeared."

Scowling, I glanced up at him. "How exactly do you know that?"

"I can't divulge my source, but I assure you, it's been confirmed to be true." When I gave him a dubious look, he said, "Trust me or don't. Makes no difference to me."

Though I didn't doubt his information, I suspected I wouldn't like the way he'd gotten it. There wasn't a chance in hell he'd tell me if I pressed more, though, so I moved on.

"Seems like any potential investor would want to look at the marsh and see what was holding up the project." I turned to check out the view of the creek. While it was pretty, I couldn't imagine why it had been allowed to cause so many problems. "Why didn't Hugo just move the clubhouse, pool and tennis courts somewhere else in the very beginning? Why wait so long to change his plans?"

"That is a very good question, one I can't answer."

"What?" I said, placing my hand on my chest in mock surprise. "You seem to have the answer to everything else."

His eyes narrowed, but he didn't respond.

I headed to the side of the Jeep and reached in for my rain boots.

"You planning on walking around out there?" he asked in surprise.

I rested my butt against the foot kickboard. "That's why I brought the boots." I slipped off one shoe and tossed it onto the passenger floorboard.

"You think you're going to stumble upon a dead body?"

"God, I hope not, but who knows what I'll find." I took off my other shoe and jammed my foot into the other boot, then stood.

Malcolm watched as I stepped onto the soggy ground. There wasn't any standing water next to the clearing, but it only took walking about ten feet toward the river for water to start sloshing around my boots.

"This seems like it would be a nightmare to develop," I

commented as I continued walking around while Malcolm leaned an arm along the hood of the Jeep. "I take it you don't know what his plan was for draining it, other than the dam? I have to assume that would have been shot down, even if he owned both sides of the creek."

"Maybe he was building the clubhouse on stilts," Malcolm volunteered.

I glanced over at him and grinned. "Was that your attempt to make a joke?"

"More like an impractical suggestion. Then again, I'm not convinced Hugo Burton was a practical man."

He had a point.

I spent the next ten minutes walking around the land, not wading too far into the swampy area. "Seems to me that maybe Hugo actually planned to build the clubhouse on the ground where you parked and leave the marsh as the view."

He glanced at the map, then back at me. "Only the map shows that's where the outdoor seating for the clubhouse was supposed to be."

"It's not that pretty. And it likely smells in the summer."

If Hugo Burton had been buried out here, I suspected his body would have been washed down the creek with any of the heavy rains we'd had from his disappearance up until now. Because I had no doubt the creek flooded several feet of the banks when the water level rose.

"So where to now?" he asked as I approached him.

"West, following the hint of the road that extends from the main road."

We both climbed in, and he took off up the hill, then turned right onto the paved road and headed west. He slowed down as he approached my car, then turned down the cul-de-sac, driving slowly as we both surveyed the area.

"Looks like Hugo was ready to start selling his lots so the contractors could start building," Malcolm said.

"Only as far as I know, he never sold any of them or even

tried to. I can't help wondering why not. He would have made money on the deal."

"Which he would have had to pay out to his investors. As long as the investors were giving him money, he didn't have to pay."

He had a point. Had Hugo ever planned on selling lots? Maybe he really had decided his best bet was to hoodwink his clients and run off with the money. The more I saw, the less I thought of his business acumen.

Malcolm turned around at the base of the cul-de-sac and headed for the main entrance. I didn't ask where he was going. If he'd wanted to see the cul-de-sac, it stood to reason he'd also want to go down the longer road. I didn't tell him that I'd already seen it. Maybe something would jump out at me that I hadn't noticed the day before.

"These lots aren't developed," Malcolm said.

"It looks like he focused on the cul-de-sac first. I suspect those were the uber premium lots, and he'd planned to use them to drive interest in the neighborhood."

He shrugged. "Could be. I never saw the appeal of living someplace like this. The need to show off your wealth implies a weak character."

"Are you wealthy, James Malcolm?" I asked before I thought better of it.

He turned to look at me with an inquisitive stare. "You interested in my money, Detective Adams?"

"Just curious. You made that statement as though you were a man of means."

"I'm comfortable."

I hadn't found any financials on him when I'd originally researched him, but I knew he had money. The tavern was well built, well furnished, and well maintained. Then there was Carter Hale's setup. That all took money. He just didn't flaunt it.

Just like he didn't flaunt anything else, including his emotions. It was like talking to a brick wall.

"I bet your girlfriends have hated living with you."

He released a short laugh, then gave me a sexy leer. "I haven't heard any complaints."

"Not in bed." I rolled my eyes. "I'm sure a guy like you is good in bed. I mean, you have a reputation to maintain, it wouldn't serve it very well if you sucked in the sheets. I was talking about your poker face. Like, how does anyone ever really know what you're thinking?"

His expression went from amused to dark in lightning speed. "My personal relationships are none of your concern."

Then a realization hit me. "You don't usually have personal relationships."

"I told you my—"

"Are none of my concern. Yeah. Got that." I tilted my head, really starting to consider what kind of life he'd led before he'd moved to Lone County. As the head of a criminal organization, he would have seen a relationship as a liability. I suspected he hadn't been in any real relationships here either. According to Louise, he wasn't known to have a girlfriend, but then again, he seemed pretty private. I could see him keeping one secret.

"What's going through that infuriating head of yours?" he demanded, shooting me a dark look.

"Do you have a girlfriend?"

"Why? Are you wanting to test out your I'm-good-in-bed theory, and you're afraid you'll need to watch your back if you follow through?"

"No, I just figure if we're going to work together, I should know more about you."

"The only thing you need to worry about is what resources I have to help investigate Hugo Burton's murder. Nothing else matters."

"Murder?" I asked.

"We both know the man was murdered. We just need to find the smoking gun."

"AKA his body."

"Or some other proof, but sure, the body would be good."

I propped a hand on my hip. "I get that you're trying to take down a bad man, but somehow I don't think you're after Hugo's killer because you want justice for him. So why are you so interested helping me find him?"

"Maybe I'm a vigilante crime fighter."

"And maybe I should start calling you Batman."

"No way I'd ever be stupid enough to wear a cape," he said with a smirk.

"So you *do* joke, Malcolm."

"I never joke, Harper."

It wasn't lost on me that he called me by my first name, so I considered that exchange as a win.

Chapter 15

He headed back toward my car and the utility shed, then came to a stop at the edge as we looked over the undeveloped land to the west.

"It looks like there was a bare-bones road here once," I said, pointing to the ruts in the ground. "Do you see any roads on the map?"

He pulled it out and opened it between us. "A road was supposed to go all the way to the county road, but it obviously never got paved."

I studied it longer than I had the first time he'd pulled it out. Hugo had hired a graphic artist to come up with the layout of both neighborhoods, titled Phase One and Phase Two. The lower-priced homes were Phase Two, which helped explain the complete lack of paved roads over here. On the map, a main road tying into this one meandered through the acreage until it hit the county road. Multiple side streets broke off from it. Then something caught my eye.

"Phase Two was supposed to have a pool?"

"You can't be having the poor people swimming with the rich at the clubhouse," Malcolm said sarcastically.

"Seems like the rich would have had their own personal pools."

"Maybe so, but I bet the clubhouse and the tennis courts weren't going to be accessible to the poor people either."

"You realize the demographic for Phase Two wasn't poor people. From what I've seen, they expected homes to start at three hundred thousand."

"Still poor compared to the rich people."

Maybe.

He drew in a breath and looked out over the acreage in front of us.

He studied the land through the windshield. "The land in the lower section of Phase Two would have been soggy from the rain and is lower than where we are now. Seems like the killer only needed a shovel and the soft land would have made the job easier."

"Agreed, but there's one problem with the whole burying Hugo's body theory. If the killer was an investor, he likely wasn't used to physical labor. At least not grave digging. It's hard work."

"You dug many graves, Detective?"

"I'm a woman of mystery," I said in a playful tone. "You'll just have to wonder."

Mild surprise filled Malcolm's eyes as a tempered horror washed through me. I was letting my guard down with him, and I couldn't afford to do that, not to mention that part of me had been buried since last fall. Malcolm was not the person to let my guard down with. I could barely trust him with my life. There was no way I could trust him with my heart.

I cleared my throat and spoke in a more businesslike tone. "I say we drive across what was supposed to be the main road to the proposed entrance for Phase Two and stop if we see something. On the way back, we can check out the low-lying land and see if anything sticks out."

"Works for me."

He drove onto the unpaved road and started forward at a slow pace, not that I blamed him. Sure, he was driving a Jeep, but the tall weeds could be hiding a giant rut. I pulled my phone out of my pocket and checked the upper corner of the screen.

"Making a call?" Malcolm asked.

"Checking my service. Anton said it was a problem out there, and it still is. Nothing."

"No one was going to buy a home somewhere that lacked cell service."

"Tell me about it." I stuffed my phone back in my pocket. "One of Hugo Burton's many issues."

He continued down the hill as I scanned the land for any hints of where to look. "Let's presume they performed a decent search," I posited, "not extensive, but decent. Surely they would have seen a dead body lying out in the open."

"You're presuming the land would have been cleared. If there were a fresh body lying out there now, would you be able to see it?" he asked, nodding toward the side.

"No, *but* Hugo was still showing the land to potential investors. There was a gravel road here. Stands to reason it would have been partially cleared," I countered.

"I disagree, but I suppose that would be easy to clear up."

"I'll ask his son." Then I added, "When I get service."

I held the map open as we continued across the acreage. Most of the land was clear here, with the exception of the weeds, but there were pockets of trees scattered on either side. I'd want to look around all of those. Malcolm continued on, periodically stopping to check his map. He curved to the left as we followed the road, which veered around a large grove of trees. After we cleared the trees, a piece of construction equipment sat to the right.

"That's where the pool was supposed to be," I said, glancing down at the map to confirm it.

Malcolm slowed a little as we passed. "It's a concrete mixer. Those require electricity. I thought he didn't have utilities down here."

"Don't most pool companies bring in cement trucks?" I asked. "Pools take a ton of concrete."

"He would have needed electricity, and he definitely wouldn't have used a small mixer like that to install a pool."

"Agreed. He would have hired a pool company to put it in. *They'd* be in charge."

"Check your service," he said as he picked up speed, heading toward the road ahead.

I pulled out my phone and saw one bar in the upper corner. I opened my text app and sent some rapid-fire messages to Anton.

A few questions. 1. Was there a gravel road connecting Phase Two of Sunny Point to Phase One and the county road?

2. If so, was the land on either side cleared?

And 3, Was your father in the process of building a pool in Phase Two when he disappeared?

After I sent the last text, I realized that the Jeep was coming to a halt. We'd reached the county road entrance. There was a barbed wire fence along the road a good fifty feet before it ended, trees on either side.

"Someone put up a fence," I said, stating the obvious.

"The question is who," Malcolm said, leaning his forearm over the steering wheel.

"Could have been a number of people. Could have been Hugo's family or associates. If there was a gravel road here, nosy people could have come in and driven all over the land."

"True," he said absently, as though lost in thought.

"Or it could have been the bank or the new owners."

He sat up. "Larkspur Limited," he said in a lilting voice.

I studied him closely. "You *are* interested in Larkspur."

He snorted and turned to me. "They are an unknown, and I don't like unknowns."

"Then you must be really disappointed," I said, "because life is full of unknowns."

Rather than answer, he turned the Jeep around in a big U-turn and faced the pool, which was a couple hundred feet away. "You get an answer yet?"

I glanced down at the phone in my hand. I started to tell him no, but then a text flashed on my screen.

Yes, there was a packed gravel road, and the land was cleared. My dad said the weeds made land looked too undeveloped and trashy. He hired a guy to mow it every few weeks.

I read the text to Malcolm, and as soon as I finished, another text popped up. I read that one too.

Dad wasn't putting in a pool in Phase Two. He was focused on Phase One. Why do you ask?

"If I tell him, then I'll be admitting to trespassing," I said. "I doubt he'd tell anyone, but if someone finds out, they might have the property more closely watched."

"Tell him you drove by the fence and saw the equipment," Malcolm said.

The mixer wouldn't be visible from the road, but I doubted Anton would fact check me, so I sent him a text with Malcolm's suggestion. Seconds later, my phone buzzed with a call.

"Hey, Anton," I said as I answered.

"Are you out there?" he asked.

"I'm at the county road," I said, only slightly exaggerating. "I can see the hint of what looks like a concrete mixer about a few hundred feet from the road. It looks like it might be in the location where the pool was supposed to go."

"That wasn't there before," he said.

"You mean before your father disappeared?"

"Yeah."

"So maybe the new owners brought it in," I suggested.

"Must be," he said. "Because I was out there after he died, and it wasn't there then either."

"How long after he disappeared were you out here?"

He was silent for a moment. "The day he disappeared, of course, then every day for a few days after."

"Only a few days after?"

"Yeah, I couldn't bring myself to keep going out there."

"What do you know about the fence that goes across where Phase Two opened to the county road?"

"The bank put that up," he said. "The local teens were using it as a party spot."

"Do you know when they put the fence in?"

"The summer after he disappeared. Toward the end. We had a lot of rain that year, and their cars kept getting stuck."

"Thanks, Anton."

"Anything I can do to help."

I hung up and relayed the information to Malcolm.

"So, what's the deal with that concrete mixer?" he asked.

"Let's go find out."

Chapter 16

Malcolm pulled up about twenty feet away from the mixer and turned off the engine. He hopped out, and I did the same after folding the map in half so I could bring it with me.

The first thing I did was check out the mixer. It was gray with plenty of rust spots, about four feet tall and three feet wide. Remnants of concrete stuck to the outer walls. A squarish-shaped box sat on one side, and an industrial-looking electric cord hung out of the box.

"As you suggested, it needed electricity, but I don't see anything around here that could power it," I said.

"They probably used a generator," Malcolm said. Walking past it and stopping a few feet away, he surveyed the ground.

I stood next to him. "No hole for a pool."

"There's a whole lot of nothing here."

He was right. There were weeds, but they weren't as tall as the ones in the other parts of the property. They were also sparser. The land was flat and had plenty of space for a pool, but the wall of trees to the west would have made the pool shaded in the afternoon. We both walked around the area for several minutes.

"I haven't found anything," I said. "You?"

"No, although if kids were partying out here, they surely would have found a body," he called out from the other side of the clearing.

"I want to check the trees." I held up a hand. "Yeah, I know they would have found him in there too, but maybe he was buried, and the grave became unsettled."

Malcolm started walking back to the Jeep and I watched as he headed to the back, then emerged a few seconds later with two long metal poles. He handed one to me. "If a body is buried out there, then it's decomposed, and the ground is liable to have sunk or sink if you stand on it. If you find a suspicious area, prod it with this."

I took it and gave him a hard look. "Spoken like a man who has experience."

"Everyone's into true crime these days," he said, then turned and headed to the trees along the western edge of the property.

I made my way to the northern side. A quick glance at the map told me I should find a small creek that fed into Meadow Creek.

Young saplings were mixed in with more mature oak trees. The ground was covered in a thick layer of fallen and decaying leaves, making the ground slippery. I plunged the metal pole into the ground in front of me with every step, but all I felt was uneven ground. After about fifteen minutes of poking and prodding, I headed back to the clearing. I could still see Malcolm in the western woods, so I went over to find him.

"I've found nothing," I said as I started prodding the ground a few feet away from him.

"Same."

"The concrete mixer doesn't make sense," I said.

"It does if you want to really hide a body."

"But Anton says it wasn't here after his father disappeared,

175

and why would they leave it? Those things have serial numbers. It could be tracked down."

"Ten-to-one it was stolen," he said, his gaze on the ground as he continued to move forward, poking the dirt. "They brought it in to encase the body in concrete."

"Is that why you're really poking the ground? Looking for concrete?"

"Maybe a bit of both."

We searched a few more minutes before I noticed an object on the ground. It was brown and blended in with the leaves. I could have easily missed it. Stopping, I leaned over and picked it up.

"What'd you find?" Malcolm asked, turning to face me.

"It looks like a leather business card case."

The bifold felt wet and slimy, and I wished I had a pair of gloves. I opened it up and found a slit to insert business cards, but it was empty.

"No cards," I said, holding it up. "No name." I was about to toss it back onto the ground when my thumb ran along an indent in the bottom right corner. I rubbed at it with the pad of my thumb and could barely make out an H. If there had been any other letters, they had worn off.

"There's an H on the outside," I said. "It looks like it was personalized but there aren't any other letters."

"H for Hugo."

"Possibly." Then I acknowledged, "Okay, *probably*, but it's not proof."

We centered our search around that area for the next ten minutes. There wasn't a body, but we did find a piece of a necktie, a black dress shoe and a men's black sock. All were soaked with mud and in varying states of decay.

"People don't just leave a shoe and sock lying around," I said. "Let's presume they belong to Hugo. How did they get here? If they buried him, why is this stuff just lying around? Did an animal dig him up?"

"Anton said the concrete mixer wasn't here after his father died, but we both know he was likely dead. What if the killer left his body here and then came back later to dispose of it?"

"And I bet it made him nervous to have all those teenagers hanging out so close to a murder victim." I took a breath. "Even if they buried him in the woods. The root system of the trees would have kept them from burying him very deep."

"They might have been concerned that kids might be hanging out in the woods," he said. "What if they came back and moved it later? That would explain the mixer showing up later."

He started backing up and pointing to the items we'd found and left on the ground. His eyes widened. "They dug him up and dragged him."

"What?"

"They dug him up and dragged his body, leaving the things behind. Look, they're all in a jagged line."

I moved over to where he stood, at the edge of the clearing, and I could see it now. They had dragged him across the clearing and lost items of clothing along the way.

"That had to be disgusting," I said. "Depending on how long they waited, he was likely decomposing."

"We had weather below freezing for multiple days around the time of his disappearance. It would have preserved the body."

"Not if they waited until summer."

"True."

"You said Anton didn't see the mixer here, but the last time he was here was a few days after Burton went missing. If I were the killer, I wouldn't move the body right away either. I'd be worried about getting caught. I'd wait until things died down. And the frozen snap lasted off and on for two weeks. The killer could have moved him them."

We both stared at the path through the woods. Now that I saw it I couldn't unsee it.

"But why wouldn't they pick up his personal items and bury them with him?" I asked. "They're just a giant sign that Hugo was dead in those woods."

"They were sloppy for one," he grunted. "They left a damn cement mixer. And if they really didn't want to get caught, they probably moved him at night. Maybe under a full moon so they wouldn't have to use lights. It would have made it hard to find the shoe, let alone the other stuff that was smaller and more easily camouflaged."

"What we really need," I said, "is to talk to someone who was a teenager that summer to see if they were not only out here but saw a concrete mixer."

"I can take care of that one," he said. "Misti has a million nieces and nephews who love to party. Some of them were bound to be teenagers four years ago. I'll have her ask them."

"Okay. That's good. But we're still stuck looking for a body."

Malcolm turned his back to the trees and scanned the land. "The clearing."

"Where the pool was supposed to go?" I asked in disbelief.

"It stands to reason the person behind Larkspur Limited was the one who killed him. They made damn sure no one ever found him. They had absolutely no intention of putting in a pool."

I stared at the clearing. "So they dug him up from in the trees and moved him out into the open? That seems incredibly stupid."

"Apparently this county is full of stupid men," Malcolm said.

I shot him a look and he shrugged. I started to tell him that he lived in the county too then stopped. No one could ever accuse James Malcolm of being stupid.

"They probably dug down a bit," he said, "covered him with concrete, then covered the concrete with dirt."

It wasn't how I would have disposed of a body, but given everything we'd found, I suspected he was right.

"I heard a potential buyer for the property was considering putting an apartment complex in here," he said absently.

I whipped around to face him. "Larkspur Limited?"

"No. Brett Colter."

I narrowed my eyes. "Who told you that?"

"A friend of a friend told me that Colter was waiting for Burton to default so he could snatch up the land and build apartments. He was already preparing a proposal to put before the county planning commission before Hugo disappeared. The same commission he was a member of."

"Isn't that a conflict of interest?" I asked.

He shrugged. "It's Lone County. Who the fuck around here cares about conflict of interest. There are worse things that have been pushed through county governments."

"You sound like you speak from personal experience."

His eyes turned cold. "Let's just say the hands of justice aren't always actually seeking it. Some people use that power to fulfill their own personal vendettas."

"Someone have it out for you in Fenton County?"

"Just about everyone in the damn county had it out for me," he grumbled. "But it doesn't have a godforsaken thing to do with Hugo Burton, now does it?"

He was right, but I was still curious about his past. Honestly, I was impressed he'd shared that much.

"Okay, back to Hugo. If Colter wanted the land, then I think that rules him out as the murderer. He only had to wait for Hugo to go belly up."

"Which leaves the potential investor," Malcolm said.

"The mysterious investor..." I mused. "Okay, what about this? What if the investor was going to give Hugo money and Colter found out, so he killed Hugo because he was pissed?" I shook my head, already dismissing it. "Only he didn't get the land after all. Larkspur did."

"Maybe he thought it would be too messy to own land where the man he'd killed was buried."

"I would think it would be smart to control the area where you buried someone. Which is likely why Larkspur bought it and did nothing with it," I said. "But who owns Larkspur?" I put a hand on my hip. "You really don't know?"

An amused grin lifted his lips. "Try as he might, Carter's never been able to find out. It's a thorn in his side. He hates when he's thwarted."

From what little I knew of Carter Hale, that didn't surprise me. "Let's keep searching," I said. "We can cover this field in less than thirty minutes."

Turned out it only took us fifteen.

My metal pole hit something solid that sounded like rock or concrete, and Malcolm came over and tapped it a few feet away from my location, confirming it wasn't an errant rock. He went back to the Jeep and came back with two shovels and a crowbar.

"Wait," I said, my heart racing. "What are you doing?"

He gave me an impatient look. "You came out here looking for Burton's body, and we're looking for Burton's body."

"We can't just dig up his body, Malcolm! We should call this in to Detective Jones."

He set the tip of one of shovels on the ground and leaned his weight on the pole. "Are you serious? You want to call up the detective who blew off this case five years ago with the suspicion that he *might* be buried here?"

He had a point. "He's going to take it seriously. We found several items that could have belonged to him."

"*Could* have belonged to him. We don't know that they actually did," he said. "There were countless kids out here who could have left those items. Sure, one of them has an H on it, but that doesn't prove it was Burton's."

"If he's even a halfway decent detective he'll take it seriously," I countered, my heart racing.

Why was I so anxious? Finding Hugo's body would be a good thing. So why wasn't I hiking over to the county road and calling Detective Jones already?

"This case is five years old," Malcolm said, "and their preferred version of this story is that he ran away. Do you really think they're going to waste the money or manpower to dig up this clearing looking for him?"

I presumed they would, but then again, Jones had skimped out of several things that would have cost too much money during the original investigation, including a forensic accountant and a proper manhunt of this property. If I alerted them to the possibility of Hugo being buried here and they *didn't* dig, I'd be hamstrung.

"Besides," Malcolm drawled, as though he realized I was turning to his side but needed one last push. "You have no idea if we actually found a body. For all we know, we found a giant rock. What's Jones gonna think of you then? He'll think you're a joke."

My chest squeezed. He had a point.

"And," he continued, "he's gonna take over the case and leave you out. The credit will be all his, too."

My stomach twisted. I'd seen this case as my chance to set up my P.I. career. If Jones took over, it would still be a win for me, but it wouldn't be the big win I'd hoped for. "My job is to find out if Hugo's dead," I said, realizing as I said it that the only person I was trying to convince was myself.

"Are you really going to be satisfied with that? If you want to be a P.I. then you need to build your cred, and handing it off Jones will destroy that. You need the W in your own name so you can use it as a successful case reference."

I hated that I saw the logic in everything he said. "Okay," I finally said, reaching for a shovel. "We'll confirm whether there's a body and then go from there."

He didn't respond. Instead, he tossed the crowbar on the ground and started tapping on the ground with the shovel.

"We should find the edge," I said. "Then go all the way around to see how big this concrete pad is...presuming it's concrete."

Malcolm found the first edge and scooped out a shovel full of dirt, revealing a bumpy concrete surface underneath.

"Obviously, they weren't going for a neat job," he said. "Dump the body, cover it with concrete and dirt, then get the hell out of here. The clothing in the woods is further proof."

"Then why leave the concrete mixer behind?" I questioned. "I mean, you and I wouldn't be digging up this field if the mixer hadn't been here."

"Because no one was looking for Burton. And maybe someone was supposed to pick up the mixer later and fell down on the job. It's idiotic, sure, but they must have thought they were okay. And maybe it wasn't someone affiliated with Larkspur at all. Maybe they bought it after all of this was done."

"Maybe."

"Let's keep going," he said even as he scooped another shovel full of dirt. I knew it was wrong. We were disturbing a crime scene, possibly destroying evidence, but I couldn't bring myself to stop him.

What the hell was wrong with me?

I nearly laughed out loud at that question. I didn't have enough time to make an inventory. Instead, I pulled the flask out of my pocket and took a long swig.

Malcolm glanced up at me even as he kept digging, but he didn't comment.

I took another deep swig for good measure, then tucked it back in my coat pocket and resumed searching for an edge on the opposite side.

Malcolm started to shovel another load of dirt, but I said, "Wait."

He turned to me, irritation in his eyes.

"I'm not going to call it in. Yet," I said to appease him. "But let me at least take photos. If nothing else, we can use it as evidence for ourselves." I pulled out my phone and started taking photos of the ground and the trees around us. Then nodded for him to continue.

He was about to dig the shovel into the ground, but he dropped it and then stripped his coat off, throwing it several feet behind him. As he picked his shovel back up, he said, "I say we clear the dirt off the entire surface, then try to pry the concrete up."

"Okay." I couldn't help noticing his thick arms through his black thermal shirt. While I acknowledged they would be useful for digging, I appreciated them for other reasons I quickly stuffed down.

I was not attracted to James Malcolm. That would be a nightmare. But that didn't mean I couldn't notice that his arms were just one of many attractive features he possessed.

We got to work and managed to scrape the dirt off the concrete within ten minutes or so. While the concrete had been buried about a foot below the surface on one side, it had only been covered by a few inches of dirt on the other. There were still clumps of mud on the surface. Even without going any further, I could tell Malcolm was right—they hadn't tried to make the concrete smooth for a road or a patio. It had been a dump job to keep the body buried. The dirt still clung to the deep pockets in the uneven concrete, but we didn't bother brushing it away.

"I bet they did a piss-poor job of burying him after they murdered him," I said. "So maybe it wasn't premeditated. Surely, they would have come up with a plan to dispose of his body if their intention for meeting him out here was to kill him."

"Maybe. Based on what I'm seeing here, I'm not convinced they would have gotten it right with plenty of planning."

"They've gotten away with it so far," I said. "So don't discredit them too much."

He turned to me and held my gaze. "You ready to find out if he's in there?"

I could see he was testing me, seeing if I was about to back out, but I was just as curious as he was. And just because we found a pad of concrete under a shallow bed of dirt didn't mean there was a body underneath.

But I'd bet my mother's Blue Willow china Hugo Burton was there.

My stomach twisted. "Ready as I'll ever be."

"Use the metal pole and I'll use the crowbar. We'll see if we can lift it up on the higher side."

Thankfully for us, the perpetrators who had poured the concrete hadn't made it very thick. We put all our weight onto our respective tools, and a large chunk broke off.

"We should stop," I said as Malcolm dropped the prybar and lifted the chunk. There was a sound of tearing fabric, then he tossed it to the side as though it weighed nothing. A thick stench blew back at us, filling my nose with the odor of rotting flesh.

"I think we found Hugo Burton," Malcolm said.

"We don't know that for sure," I said, burying my nose into the crook of my arm.

"There's one way to find out."

"We proved there's a body under there. No matter whose body it is, they were likely put there for nefarious reasons. Which means we're interfering with a crime scene."

He turned back to me, picking his crowbar back up. "Is it a crime to pour concrete in a field?"

"It depends on why they poured it."

"Come on, Harper," he groaned. "If we had no knowl-

edge of a possible crime, would you still think we were interfering with an investigation?'"

"We wouldn't be here if we didn't suspect a crime. And in
fact, *we're* committing a crime by being here. When we turn
this in—because we *will* have to turn this in," I waved a hand
at him, "*you'll* be suspect number one."

He shook his head. "You do what you want. I didn't get
this close just to give up." Shoving the crowbar under the
concrete, he started to pry up another piece.

I knew I should stop him, this was *insanity*, yet I couldn't
bring myself to do it. Part of me argued that there was no way
I could stop him, he was a hell of a lot bigger than me, but
that wouldn't have stopped me from trying. I wasn't sure what
to make of the part of me that wanted to see this through.

"What's that tearing sound?" I asked, fighting the urge to
gag from the stench.

"Looks like they covered the body with a thin cloth.
Maybe a sheet. They might have used it to drag him over. It's
stuck to the concrete." He pried up a piece that let out a
cracking and ripping sound that wasn't helping my gag reflex.
"All I know is that there's a body under there that's covered in
fabric." He picked up another piece and tossed it with the
other. This time he revealed a piece of fabric that was pinned
on either side of the concrete.

"I think this is his back," Malcolm said, already starting in
on another piece. "It stands to reason. They would have
dumped him in a two- to two-and-a-half-foot grave, and if
he's on his side, like it appears, his limbs would be lower in the
ground. They take up less space. What I've exposed wasn't
covered in dirt. Just a piece of cloth, which means they didn't
toss in any dirt with him, just whatever they covered him
with."

He'd fully exposed the body's side and upper thigh before
moving around to the other side. It only took a few more
pieces to reveal what looked like bones.

My stomach roiled.

I wasn't a forensic anthropologist, and I didn't have any experience with buried bodies, but there was no doubt in my mind those were human phalanges. Especially when I spotted the gold band around one.

"It's him," Malcolm said matter-of-factly, pulling an ink pen from his pocket and poking it next to the finger bones. He pulled up the ring, then held it up, leaning in close to examine it. "There's an inscription: To my forever love, Hugo." His gaze lifted and he gave me a dry look.

"You can't touch that!" I protested. "It's evidence."

He dropped it back with the bones. "There it is, back where it belongs."

"They'll know it was moved."

He shrugged like he didn't give a shit. "I'm not stopping," he said, his jaw set and determination filling his eyes. "We came here for answers, and we're not leaving without them."

Then he pried up another piece, this time revealing another piece of cloth.

"His arm," Malcolm said, turning back to me. "You gonna help or just watch?"

He was already doing this and I was merely looking on in horror. But I was part of this, whether I fully approved of it or not, so I might as well help. More than that, I felt driven to. I'd been determined to find Hugo's body, but now that I found him, it wasn't enough. I needed to find out who killed him.

I should have been more disgusted with myself, but my morals had already sunk to low heights. What was one more rung descending into hell?

I didn't answer, just silently picked up the shovel and moved to the other end where the head should have been and put my foot on the shaft. A piece of concrete broke off, and a fresh wave of decay hit me full in the face. Gagging, I pulled a pair of gloves out of my pocket, tugged them on, then bent to pick up the piece. Malcolm had made his look ridiculously light, but I nearly put out my back trying to lift it.

He walked over to me and picked it up, tossing it behind us.

"Good job," he said. "You just found his head."

Sure enough, we'd revealed a skull, complete with short blond hair. The skull was mostly decomposed with a few pieces of flesh still attached. The stench of decay was overwhelming.

I took several steps back and vomited about ten feet from the reeking hole.

"What the hell are we doing?" I asked when I stood upright.

"Giving Hugo Burton's family closure."

I wanted to repeat the argument that we should call Detective Jones, but we both knew we were past the point of no return. But we could still walk away, and they couldn't prove we'd been the ones to dig him up. We were both wearing gloves so we weren't leaving fingerprints behind.

I squinted up at him. "Why are you doing this? And don't give me that bullshit excuse that you're after someone who did something bad."

He held his hands out at his sides. "Just trying to help you out."

"Don't insult me with such a blatant lie."

His face reddened. "What the fuck do you think I'm doing out here then?"

"Helping *yourself*," I countered. "It's pretty fucking obvious you're after something of your own, and it hurts *your* investigation if the sheriff takes over."

"I never denied I had an interest. You have to admit that you *need* this case too."

"I was hired to find him." I flung a hand toward the grave. "And I did. That's the end of my job."

His cheeks flushed with anger. "You're thinking too small.

If you want to kick off your P.I. career, you have to find out who murdered him. And you can't do that if you involve the sheriff's department." He pointed to the grave. "This is a huge step into solving it. Do you really want to give up?"

"Withholding information about a crime from law enforcement isn't exactly going to endear me to them, and it might get me arrested."

"You're going to tell them. Just not yet."

"Right…" I said sarcastically, but I couldn't ignore the part of me screaming that he was right. I wanted to wait too. Even though I knew it was wrong.

I needed to continue with this case, and not just to pad my résumé or bolster my self-confidence. I felt alive when I was investigating. It gave me purpose. My personal life might be shit, but when I was investigating, I was helping someone. I was a worthwhile member of society. I had a reason for still existing while my sister was buried in the Jackson Creek cemetery.

"Give it a week," he said. "Then you can call the sheriff's department and claim you found it like this. What's the difference?"

"You know damn good and well there's a difference," I countered without any heat in the words.

"I also know you hate your fucking job and you'd much rather be investigating than killing your soul working in your daddy's law firm." He moved another foot closer. "This benefits us both."

God, I hated that part of me agreed with everything he was saying. And I couldn't dismiss that while Detective Matthew Jones had been friendlier than expected, I didn't trust him to have my best interests in mind. Maybe it was paranoia after what had happened to me in Little Rock, but I couldn't help wondering if he was giving me just enough rope to hang myself.

"I can't hold onto this for a week," I finally said.

"Then how about this? You take it day by day," he said. "And if you feel like the time has come to turn this in, then you let me know first."

"So you can talk me out of it?"

"So I'll have plenty of notice."

I wanted to ask him why he needed notice, but I knew I wouldn't get a straight answer. I was going to have to trust him, and I hated it.

We settled into a rhythm, digging up the rest of the concrete. I pried up a piece and he hauled away the chunk until we had the body completely exposed. I started to feel wet drops on my face. It had begun to drizzle. Great.

This was about to get a whole lot messier.

Chapter 17

"Okay," I said with a deep sigh. "We need to establish cause of death without disturbing his body."

The light rain continued to fall as he moved over to the body and squatted next to the head. After a couple of seconds, he said, "That part's easy. Bullet to the back of the head."

Burying my nose into my arm, I joined him, squatting to see the round hole that was partially obscured by hair.

"No crime of passion here," I said. "Execution style."

"Punishment. Or revenge."

"So it was an investor."

"That would be my guess." He moved to the side of the body and grabbed a pair of leather gloves from his coat pocket. After putting them on, he squatted and leaned over, reaching into the pocket of the dead man's dress pants and removing a wallet.

I had to bite my tongue to keep from telling him he was disturbing evidence. That was the purpose of this endeavor, not that it made accepting it any easier.

He flipped the bifold wallet open and wiped off a film on the plastic covering the license. "The ID says Hugo Burton." He opened the side to reveal several bills. "There has to be close to two hundred dollars here, so robbery wasn't a motive." He dropped the wallet onto the ground next to the grave and reached into the pocket again.

"You can't just drop that there!" I protested. "I realize we've agreed to do this, but we have to pretend to care about the evidence at least a little bit."

He looked up at me, his hand in the dead man's pocket. "The sheriff won't need evidence if you solve the murder."

I noticed he didn't say we. *I* would solve the murder. Was that because he didn't plan on helping me or was he hoping to puff up my ego? Whichever the reason, he was challenging me. *When* I solved the murder. Not if.

"Just try to be careful," I said, wiping the drizzle from my face into my shoulder. There was no way I was wiping my face with my hands. "I don't want it looking like I pilfered his body before I report it."

He grinned up at me, water droplets beaded in his hair. "You didn't pilfer his body. You'll be able to swear to it."

I rolled my eyes. "Semantics."

"They matter," he said, returning his attention to his search.

I supposed they did to a guy like him. As long as he chose his words carefully, he could lie to the police without actually lying. It made me wonder for the umpteenth time why I was working with this man. He had an agenda, and he was using me to fulfill it. My gaze shifted to the Jeep. Then again, I was using him too, so as long as I acknowledged the fucked-up nature of the situation, I was less likely to become collateral damage.

"Found his keys." He held up a ring with several keys hanging from it, then made a production of setting them carefully on the ground.

"Asshole," I grumbled.

He grinned and continued searching.

The keys might be useless, but I was reserving judgment,

then a new thought hit me. "They drove his car to the airport."

"Yep." He shifted his search to underneath the body.

"But they left his other keys behind."

"They might not have been attached to his car fob," Malcolm said, lifting the fabric of the pants.

"How can you do that so nonchalantly?" I asked as a new wave of stench rose from the pit.

He released a short laugh. "I suspect you don't want to know."

"Experience with other decaying bodies?" I asked against my better judgment.

He looked up and winked. "I plead the fifth."

Once again, I questioned the wisdom of being out here alone with him. I knew he was a cold-blooded murderer, so why was I cooperating with him? Was it because I thought Daniel Sylvester had gotten off easy after watching my sister's torture and not alerting anyone to save her? Had the anger festering inside of me made me more like James Malcolm than the detective I used to be?

God, I needed another drink but my hands were covered in dirt and God knew what else and I wasn't desperate enough to stick one into my coat pocket. Yet.

"You haven't found a cell phone," I commented, my voice flat.

"And I doubt I will," he said as he shifted to the upper part of the body and started rummaging around in the clothing. When he didn't find anything, he rolled the body onto its back and froze.

"What?" I asked, my voice tight. It had to be something bad if Malcolm was affected.

"Nothing." He reached under the body and snatched something out before lowering the body in its original place. Then he got to his feet.

"Bullshit," I said, moving to the other side of the grave and standing next to him. "Show me what you found."

"There are perks to being the person with the gloves." Then he reached for his jeans pocket, and two things struck me. One, that there was no way he was going to get the stench of decaying flesh out his clothes and two, he'd dropped in something that looked like a coin.

"You don't trust me?" he asked with a hint of amusement. "Why don't you look under the body yourself?"

"I'm not stupid or blind, Malcolm. I know you grabbed something. Now show me what it was."

Ignoring me, he squatted and picked up the keys. "I'm done looking him over. You want a stab at him?"

Fuming, I struggled with how to handle the situation. I couldn't physically overcome him to get whatever he'd dropped into his pocket, and I couldn't make him tell me what he'd found.

Without a word, he slipped off his gloves, picked up his jacket, and started strutting back toward the Jeep.

I stomped after him. "Why did you freeze when you saw what was under Hugo's body?"

He got inside and turned to where I was standing outside the passenger side. "Are you getting in?"

"Are you denying that you knew what it was?"

His face hardened. "No."

"Then it's something important to you. Is what you found why you're interested in this case?"

"You're presuming," he said, his face devoid of expression, "and if you're going to presume, then why bother asking?"

"Do you ever give a straight answer?"

"Do you always ask questions you know you're not going to get an answer to?"

I wanted to kick him, but he was already inside the Jeep and out of reach. Instead, I turned back to face the open grave. The drizzle had turned to a light sprinkle, and we were leaving Hugo Burton's body exposed to the elements.

What the hell was I doing?

"We need to figure out our next move," Malcolm said.

"We?" I countered, spinning around to face him. "Suddenly there's a *we*?"

He spun his hand round in a circle over his head. "This whole excursion has been a *we*."

"Until it wasn't."

Resting his right forearm on the steering wheel, he twisted his body at the waist to face me. "You keep things from me, Detective. I keep things from you. We're not true partners. We each have our reasons for looking into this. Accept it or don't, but decide now, or I'll work on this on my own."

He had a point. I had a lot of information I hadn't shared with him, but somehow I knew it paled compared to what he'd found. Sure, I could search for answers on my own, but there was no denying he had more resources at his disposal, and if I worked with him, there was a chance I'd find out what he'd discovered. If I dumped him now, I'd *never* find out. But I was still pissed, and I'd have to swallow my anger if I was going to get back in that Jeep with him. Accepting that I'd lost this round was a bitter pill to swallow.

"Why stop the fun now?" I shot back sarcastically.

"That's the spirit," he said, sitting back in the seat. "Now, what do we do next?"

I wanted to be as cagey with him as he was being with me, but Malcolm was used to playing games and my brain wasn't working at 100%.

I wasn't used to holding back during an investigation. My old partner might have turned out to be an asshole, but at least he'd been a partner. Malcolm only fit the asshole qualification. He obviously had the advantage in this situation, and I wasn't sure how much I wanted to tell him.

"We need a full list of Burton's investors," I said, figuring that was a safe topic since we'd already discussed it. "These people put in a lot of money. Three of them are dead. I've already talked to Brett Colter and Skip Martin. I know Colter was one of the original investors, but I still haven't identified the other. For all we know, they're behind Larkspur Limited. Hugo's records are missing, along with his phone and laptop. Detective Jones said the desktop computer from his office didn't have any records about the property on it."

"And you believe that?" he asked wryly.

"He could have lied, but he had no reason to."

"Why would Burton not have records on his desktop computer?" Malcolm asked.

"Good question. It seems unlikely, and given the fact that nothing was found in his office, I'm guessing his computer tower was replaced."

"A decoy?" he asked. "Why? They took the laptop, why not just take the desktop too?"

"I don't know. But someone definitely cleaned out his office. His wife went to clear it out and the office manager said Hugo was behind on the rent and he'd packed up Hugo's belongings. But the only thing in the boxes were personal items. No contracts or business-related items."

His eyes narrowed. "Did the sheriff's department take them?"

"Detective Jones says he didn't find any either when he finally got around to getting a search warrant to check it out," I said. "He didn't find his checkbook either. But he *did* confiscate the computer. Sounds like that was all that was left."

He made a face, staring at the grave.

"But at some point," I continued, "I'd planned to stop by the office and see if the office manager is still there. If not, we can try to get a name so we can talk to them."

He was silent for a moment, then nodded. "Good idea."

"But I need to get cleaned up first," I said, glancing down at my jeans, which were flecked with mud and God knew what else. My hair was getting plastered to my head as the rain picked up, and even though I tried to keep my hood up, the wind kept blowing it back.

"Where was his office located?"

"Jackson Creek."

He started to say something, but I interrupted. "If you're about to suggest we split up, forget it." He'd already pocketed something, so I was sticking to him like white on rice. "We do everything together now. You're coming with me."

"To your apartment?" he asked, his lips curling into a smile.

"Don't read anything gross into it. My apartment is in Jackson Creek. It'll be a pit stop."

"Fine by me."

His quick agreement made me nervous. I'd expected more resistance.

"We need to take one vehicle," he said. "How about we drop this Jeep off, and I'll ride with you."

I liked that idea for multiple reasons, including that I wouldn't have to dodge my mother's questions about why a muddy Jeep was parked in front of her house. It was going to be hard enough dealing with her potentially seeing him walking up my stairs. But I'd worry about that later.

That seemed to be my new motto.

Chapter 18

Instead of dropping the Jeep off at the tavern like I'd expected, he parked it behind a half-deserted strip mall in Wolford. He got out and climbed into the passenger seat of my car, pushing the seat back to accommodate his long legs.

"You stink," I said, trying not gag from the stench of rotten flesh wafting off him.

"You don't smell much better."

"Actually," I said, pulling out of the parking lot, "I *do* smell better than you. I'm not carrying around something rotten in my pocket."

He lifted his brow, looking amused.

"Which means you're going to need a shower and clean clothes too."

He made a face. "Then we need to stop by the tavern before we head to your place."

"Done."

I took the back roads to the tavern and parked behind the building. When he reached for the door handle, I started to get out with him, but he shot me a look. "No need to come in. I'm just grabbing a change of clothes."

"I thought you were showering."

"Not here," he scoffed. Then he got out and shut the door. Which meant he planned on showering at my place.

Great.

I wasn't sure why that bothered me so much. Perhaps because my apartment was barely bigger than a shoebox, and his large body and ego were going to take up all the space. *My* space. And, fine, there was no denying that the idea of James Malcolm naked in my shower did funny things to my insides.

I didn't like where my thoughts were going with that image, so I shut it down quickly. We were both adults, not giggling teenagers. I could deal with it, and he'd made it clear on multiple occasions that he wasn't interested in what was underneath *my* clothes.

He was back outside within a few minutes, minus the jacket he'd been wearing and only in his thermal shirt and jeans. He was carrying a small duffel bag, which I presumed held his new clothes. It stood to reason he kept clothes at the tavern. He'd admitted he practically lived there.

After he got back, I pulled out of the parking lot, both of us silent. I had no idea what he was thinking, but I realized that I'd likely lost my opportunity to see whatever he'd pulled out of Hugo Burton's grave. For all I knew, he'd left it at his office.

Great.

When I pulled into my mother's driveway, I turned to Malcolm and said, "There's a chance my mother will come out when she sees you. Whatever you do, do *not* engage."

He grinned. "That's right, you still live with your mommy."

"Not for much longer," I said. "I'm about to start looking for my own place." I opened my door and got out.

Malcolm followed suit, casting a glance at my mother's back door, probably eager to jump into conversation with her, but the door remained closed. I was slightly worried—I hadn't seen her for days, which wasn't like her at all. But I wasn't worried enough to actually knock on the back door to check on her. She was probably peering through the blinds, pissed that I'd had the audacity to bring a man to my apartment, which had been expressly forbidden.

I led the way up the wooden stairs to my front door, opened it with the key, and walked inside, letting Malcolm follow me in.

The place instantly reeked of rotten flesh, making me gag. "How about you shower in here, and I'll take a bullet and shower in my mother's house?" I suggested, but in truth, it had been much worse in the car. It was the thought of a naked Malcolm less than twenty feet from me that had me running.

"Is she really that bad?" he asked with a smirk.

"Worse. And if she somehow missed you walking up the stairs—which is hard to believe—she's going to have lots of questions about why I'm showering in her house and not my own, an answer I still haven't worked out."

"Works for me."

"There's shower gel and shampoo and conditioner in the shower."

"Am I going to come out smelling like a flower?"

"If you're worried about it, you should have brought your own toiletries. But you won't smell like a flower. There might be a slight scent, but I try to stay away from anything strong. I liked to be scent neutral on crime scenes."

I walked out, shutting the door behind me, categorizing what I might have left lying around that he could snoop through. My laptop was in there, but it was password protected, and I didn't have anything else that would interest him. Well, other than the booze under my sink. But there was currently one bottle of Tito's vodka and my liquor of choice, Jack Daniel's.

Oh wait. That was probably gone.

Great, he'd find the empty bottle wherever I'd left it this morning.

I couldn't help wondering if I would have made these questionable decisions if my blood didn't constantly sport some level of alcohol content.

I knocked on my mother's back door, but when she didn't answer, I turned the knob to go inside, surprised it was locked. Maybe she'd locked it when she saw Malcolm getting out of my car. I hadn't brought my keys with me, and I considered going back up to get them, but I was half-worried Malcolm would already be naked, so instead, I found the fake rock my mother kept behind an azalea bush and dug out the spare key. The rock was an obvious fake, but the bush was dense enough to hide it.

"Mom?" I called out as I let myself in the back door. The house was quiet except for the tick-tock of her grandfather clock in the entryway. Where was she? Other than her occasional meetings, she was a homebody. Her car wasn't parked in the driveway, but she always parked in the garage under my apartment.

I headed to the guest bath and took a quick shower, washing my hair with the shampoo my mother kept for guests. I smelled a lot more feminine than usual, but that wasn't necessarily a bad thing. Especially if I stumbled across another dead body.

God forbid.

After I'd dried off, I realized my fatal mistake—I hadn't brought a change of clothes. There was no way I was streaking across the backyard in a bath towel, even if it hadn't been in the upper thirties and rainy. I wasn't about to let Malcolm think I was trying to seduce him. Which left me with no choice but to search my mother's closet for something to throw on.

I dug through my mother's dresser drawers, looking for the joggers and top I'd seen her in weeks ago when she'd told me that Ava Peterman was missing. (I hadn't seen her in them since.) They were in the third drawer I checked. As I started to put it on, minus underwear and a bra, I noticed that my mother's closet door was open, and her suitcase was missing.

I wasn't prone to snooping in my mother's closet, but I'd had to get something for her a few weeks ago, and the suitcase had been in the bottom left corner. Now it was gone. So was she, it would seem.

After I snatched up my clothes from the bathroom floor, I dumped them in the washing machine and started a sanitize cycle, then headed out to the garage. My father had installed a keypad, so I entered the code—my mother's birth month and date—and squatted to peek inside the garage as the door opened.

Her car was missing.

Where had she gone? Her parents were dead. She didn't speak to her sister, and all of her friends—if you could call them that—were here in Jackson Creek.

I pulled out my phone and called my father.

"Hey, pipsqueak," he said, trying out a new nickname for me. As part of his attempt to make things right between us, he'd been trying out different terms of endearment. It was a sweet gesture and not totally unappreciated, but he had yet to settle on a nickname either of us really liked. "Ehh..." he said. "I don't think that's it."

"There's nothing wrong with Harper," I said. "You've called me that for thirty-six years, but that's not why I'm calling."

"I heard you're working a P.I. case for Mitch," he said. "I didn't know you got your license. We should have celebrated."

Celebrating something that felt like it was ten steps below my previous job felt pathetic, but I kept that thought to myself. "No big deal, but back to why I'm calling—"

"No big deal?" he protested. "Of course it's a big deal."

"You know what *was* a big deal, Dad?" I said, sounding snottier than I'd intended. "When I graduated from college.

And the police academy, and then when I passed the detective test. *Those* were really big deals."

He was silent for a long second and I felt like an ass. He'd already admitted that he'd fucked up—he'd admitted it multiple times—so why did I feel the need to keep bringing it up? "Dad, I'm sorry." I rubbed my hand over my eyes to alleviate the burning. "That was uncalled for."

"I disagree," he said quietly. "I wasn't around for any of that, and I know I screwed up. But you're right. We should have celebrated *all* of those things. I've let you down in countless ways, Harper, and all I can say is I'm sorry, and I'm trying to do better."

"I know you are," I said, sagging against the door frame. "But again, there's a reason I'm calling you in the middle of the day, and it's not about the case I'm investigating." I took a breath. "Do you know if Mom was planning on taking a trip?"

"A trip?" he laughed. "Your mother doesn't travel. I used to practically have to force her."

"Well, her suitcase and her car are gone."

"What?"

"Yeah. I hadn't seen her for a few days. I hadn't noticed the lights on in the house, but I'd been coming home after she usually goes to bed, so I didn't think anything of it."

"Have you tried calling her?"

"No. I thought you should."

"Harper…"

"If I call her, she'll be less likely to answer, and if I ask one of her friends, she'll be pissed that I stirred up trouble."

"Agreed." He was silent for a moment. "Have you two been arguing?"

I snorted. "When *aren't* we arguing? But I have to admit we've been getting along better than we usually do. She asked me to go to a historical society meeting during my lunch break a couple of days ago, but I had to cancel because Mitch gave me this case. I haven't talked to her since."

"She's probably off pouting somewhere. She's not getting her way with either of us, and she doesn't know how to handle it."

"Pouting enough to pack a suitcase and run away?"

"That's her game. To make you worry and fret and then instead of apologizing for worrying you, she'll make sure you're the one groveling." He let out a tired sigh. "Don't let her win. Don't play."

"So do nothing?"

"She's a grown woman perfectly capable of taking care of herself. She's just fooled everyone into believing she's not. The biggest gift we can give her is to stop engaging. It's a fool's errand and you'll only be unhappy in the end."

Like he'd been. He didn't need to say it, because it would have been like telling me the earth rotates around the sun. It was a fact that didn't need stating.

"Okay, I'll do nothing. Thanks, Dad."

"I love you, honey. I'm sorry you're having to deal with this."

I was sorry too but saying so wouldn't help anything. I was about to hang up, but then I realized my father might be able to help me with something else. "Say, Dad, before you go—did Mitch tell you what case I'm working on?"

"No, he didn't go into particulars. He just told me you're looking for a missing person so the man's wife can declare him dead."

"So he didn't tell you it was Hugo Burton?"

He was quiet for several seconds, then finally he said, "Hugo."

"You knew him?"

"I did." But there was hesitation in his voice.

"Would you be open to having dinner tonight so I can pick your brain about the case?"

He hesitated again. "Sure." His tone was cheerful but forced. "Do you want to go to Roots?"

"Actually, I was thinking somewhere else that's more casual."

When I suggested Scooter's, he laughed. "You're kidding."

"You want to loosen up after living under Mom's thumb for so long? Trust me, this is a good place to start."

He laughed again. "Okay, kiddo. How about we meet at seven?"

"See you then, Dad."

"Love you, Harper," he said, his voice breaking on my name.

"I love you too, Dad." It was true, but I still mourned the father I hadn't had for the past twenty years. I wasn't sure I'd ever get over it.

Chapter 19

I closed the garage door and headed upstairs, forgetting that I'd left James Malcolm in my apartment until I opened the front door and saw him standing in my living room, stark naked except for the towel wrapped around his waist.

He gave me a sardonic look. "Ever think of knocking?"

It took me a second to look away from the hard muscles of his body and the tattoo of a large tree on his left pec that reached up to his shoulder. A small flower wove around the base of the tree. It obviously had meaning, but what? Not my business, but I still could appreciate that a man in his forties was in such great shape.

"Why would I knock on the door to my own apartment?" I demanded a little too forcefully as I shut the door.

His gaze drifted up and down my body and he made a face. "What are you wearing?"

"A track suit."

"Obviously, but that looks like something your mother would wear."

My brow shot up. "*You* know my mother?"

He snorted. "Figure of speech."

"Why aren't you dressed? What were you doing? I showered, washed my hair twice to make sure I got the dead smell out of it, found clothes in my mother's room, and had a phone conversation with my father. You're still…" I waved a hand toward him, then dropped it. "Were you too busy snooping through my things to get changed?"

"Please," he said, the word drenched in disgust. "You've got nothing worth snooping through unless I was looking for booze. If I was, I would have been out of luck with that big empty bottle of Jack in your bed."

My face burned, mostly because it was true, but he was also the only person who could make me feel *truly* like shit, while I clearly didn't affect him in the least.

"If my home is so far beneath you, then why were you using my shower?" I countered.

"I never said it was beneath me, just that you didn't have anything worth snooping through." He turned and snatched a pair of jeans and a shirt that were lying on the arm of the chair, then walked into my bathroom and shut the door, leaving it open a tiny crack. "What was your call with your father about?"

"Do you not believe in personal boundaries?" I asked, walking over to the sink and squatting in front of it as I opened the cabinet door. My bottle of Tito's was right where I'd left it.

"You don't seem all that close with your parents, so a friendly mid-day chat seems unlikely."

"You don't know shit about me, Malcolm, so don't go assuming anything about my relationship with my parents." I shot a glance at the door to make sure it was closed, but I caught a glimpse of him through the crack, a sliver-sized view of his naked body from behind, and parts of me that had been slumbering started to heat up.

Had he left it open so he could carry on a conversation through the door, or was he tempting me to look? Knowing him, both.

I jerked my gaze away and grabbed the vodka bottle, unscrewing the cap and downing a good-sized gulp. I was not attracted to James Malcolm. He was a criminal and looked out only for himself. He was using me, just like I was using him, and when this case was over, we'd go back to our separate lives.

I took another swig, choking when I thought of what my mother would say if she knew I was even thinking about sleeping with a known criminal. She'd be absolutely scandalized.

I should be scandalized.

"You okay out there?" he called out, and I glanced over in time to see him in a side profile. This time he was wearing skintight, black boxer briefs.

"I'm fine," I snapped, took another drink for good measure, then screwed the cap back on.

The alcohol was already warming my chest, and a familiar looseness rushed through my limbs. I closed my eyes and savored the feeling, when my world tipped from wrong to not right, but...comforting. The constant tension eased and the noise in my head dampened, giving way to peace, even if it was fleeting.

Two months ago, one gulp of vodka would have given me that rush of comfort. Now it took three. Even I, in my deep state of denial, knew this wasn't sustainable.

Taking a deep breath, I closed the cabinet as I stood, then realized Malcolm would be able smell the vodka on my breath. My go-to to take it away was gum or a mint, but he'd see right through that. Instead, I started grinding beans in my espresso machine and grabbed a muffin stuffed with blueberries out of the fridge. The muffin had appeared on my kitchen counter a few days ago. Some kind of peace offering from my mother, but I hadn't acknowledged it, not out of spite but forgetfulness.

I was forgetting a lot of things lately.

I'd already made the espresso and was foaming the milk when Malcolm walked out of the bathroom.

"Would you like a latte?" I asked, my back still to him. "Or maybe a cappuccino? I'm pretty good with this thing, good enough that I considered opening a coffee shop so this town had decent coffee."

"I thought your boyfriend made coffee at his bookstore," he said in a lazy tone as he took a seat on the sofa, stretching his arm out on the handrest.

"Nate? He's not my boyfriend," I said with a snort.

"He'd like to be."

I slowly spun around to face him, realizing that James Malcolm had ascended to a position of power because he noticed small details and used them to his advantage. One more piece of evidence that he was building a case on me, preparing to pull out the parts he needed to make me do what he wanted.

And I knew jack-shit about him.

"Nate's feelings don't concern you." I propped a hand on my hip. "Do you want coffee or not?"

He tilted his head slightly. "Can you make a macchiato?"

He couldn't have surprised me more than if he'd told me he was part elf. "Um…yeah, actually. My old roommate Kara liked them. She liked caramel on hers, but I don't have any here. But I can sweeten the milk with vanilla if you like."

Jesus, I was babbling. What the hell was wrong with me?

"Sure," he said with a hint of a smile. "Wow me."

I poured the frothed milk into my cup, then took a sip before setting it down with a sigh and grabbing a bottle of vanilla and a jar of sugar from the cabinet. I'd used vanilla syrup in Little Rock, but I didn't have any here.

I dumped the coffee puck from the machine, then started to grind more beans. When it finished, I set the machine up to make a double espresso, then turned to face him. "You seem to know a lot about my life, while you're this enigma." I waved my hand in the air.

"I suspect you know more than you're letting on."

"I know you own a tavern."

He looked amused. "Rather obvious. I thought you were a detective."

He had a point. "The stuff I do know *is* obvious. I could tell you more about what I don't know, or more accurately, what doesn't add up."

The expression on his face became more guarded, but he didn't tell me to stop playing this game, so I pressed on.

"I don't understand why you'd come to Lone County, of all places, after you got out of prison. You obviously had money if you could not only build the tavern but finish it off so nicely. You could have literally gone anywhere in the world, yet you stayed here, about a hundred miles from where you were the head of a crime organization."

He lifted a finger from the chair arm. "I was an *alleged* head of a crime organization."

I rolled my eyes. "Please. That fact is a given."

"Alleged."

"Okay," I conceded. "Alleged. So why come here?"

He shrugged his shoulders. "It seemed like a great business opportunity."

I suspected there was some truth to that. He didn't seem like the kind of man who would make a stupid business decision, but I was sure it wasn't the only reason. "Fair," I said. "Why did you name it Scooter's?"

He lifted his finger again. "Seems like the expresso is done."

Frowning, I carefully poured the coffee into a cappuccino mug, then poured the milk into the stainless steel container, doctored it with a sprinkle of sugar and a generous amount of vanilla. When it was heated, I frothed it, then carefully poured it into the mug, creating a leaf with the foam at the end.

I carried it over to him and he looked down at the foam and pursed his lips in surprise. He claimed the cup and took a sip.

My body tensed as I waited for his reaction, which pissed me off. Why the fuck did I want to impress this man?

When he lowered the cup, he looked up at me with appreciation in his eyes. "Your talent is wasted here in Jackson Creek. You should have opened that coffee shop."

"And not become a P.I.?"

He shook his head, releasing a derisive laugh. "I never said that."

"No, the key with you is what you don't say."

His eyes widened, and he lifted his mug toward me in a salute.

"Why did you name your tavern Scooter's?"

He stared down at his mug, and I didn't think he was going to answer. I was so sure, in fact, that I grabbed my own mug and the muffin and sat at the small barely two-person table.

"After my brother," he said softly.

"Is he still alive?"

"He is."

"Do you see him very often?"

"No." The word was short and deep. His gaze darkened, cluing me in that I'd breached territory he wasn't willing to delve into.

"Is he older or younger?" I asked, trying a different angle.

"Younger."

"You must really care about him if you named your bar after him."

He took a sip of his coffee, then lowered the mug, surprising me when he said, "I've tried my best to protect him his entire life. Sometimes I was successful, other times I caused him great pain." A shadow crossed over his face as he stared down at the coffee in his mug. "It seemed fitting somehow."

I wasn't sure how naming the tavern after his brother whom he'd protected and hurt made sense, but I knew better than to ask.

"Is he your only brother?"

He swallowed, his grip tightening on the mug. "Not all brothers are blood-related."

So there was at least one other person, not blood-related, who was like a brother to him. I considered pressing him on that too, but decided it was probably a landmine—one wrong step and the whole conversation would be blown to bits.

"I only had one sister," I said, then took a sip. "But then you knew that. And after Andi... well, it messed me up pretty good. I never let anyone get close to me after that."

"Not even a boyfriend?"

I thought about the string of relationships I'd had since college—all superficial. Some men hadn't cared, their own emotional maturity too shallow for them to want much themselves. Others had broken up with me because they'd claimed I was too married to my job, which was funny since I'd eventually settled into a relationship with Keith. But that had been superficial too, a convenient release for my sexual needs. We'd discussed cases, not feelings. I'd never loved him, never loved anyone actually. I was pretty sure I was incapable of it. Self-loathing followed that thought, reminding me it didn't really matter since I wasn't worthy of love. Not when Andi would never have any.

The hunger for a drink wasn't a surprise, but the strength of the need stole my breath for a moment. Pain and humiliation crashed through my head and unshed tears burned my eyes.

Why had I lived and not her? That was the question that had dogged me ever since the day that man had taken her. It would always dog me. I'd comforted myself with the knowledge that my career made a difference. I'd helped people. I'd found justice for the wronged.

Now I was pretending I hadn't found a dead man, preventing his not-so-truthful wife from collecting his life insurance.

No, I was keeping it a secret so I had more time to find justice for Anton and his sister. Hugo Burton may have been a deceitful businessman, but he'd been an amazing father. His kids deserved to know that he was not only dead, but who had taken him from them. Sure, I was hired to prove him dead, but Malcolm was right. That wasn't enough for me.

Malcolm was still watching me, and I realized I hadn't answered his question. "I mean," he said. "You asked if I have a girlfriend. It seems only fair."

"No one," I said, "and you didn't exactly answer that question."

When he didn't offer up more information, I added, "I think you and I are a lot alike. Neither of us let people get close."

He pursed his lips and surprised the hell out of me. "I have in the past, but it's always ended badly, so I've found it's better to keep people at arm's length."

The man who had been like a brother had clearly been one of those people, but I knew better than to ask if I was right. Had one of the others been a woman? Surely he'd had at least one meaningful relationship in his life. Probably when he was younger and less jaded.

"You gonna date Nate the bookseller?" Malcolm asked.

I laughed. "Why do you care?"

He shrugged, keeping his gaze on me. "I don't, but he seems like a waste of time. He's not enough for you."

He was right. I couldn't live with a normal man and have a normal life. I had too many demons to live that life authentically, and pretending would kill me.

I lifted my own mug. "I already came to that conclusion on my own, thank you very much. I've seen too much, and he's…"

"An innocent."

I shrugged. "Not the word I would have chosen. I would have likely gone with naïve, but same difference." I took a bite of my muffin. "So no girlfriends?"

"Why are you so fixated on my love life?" he asked, and I couldn't tell if he was irritated or amused. "I don't do girl-friends. Too messy."

"But a man like you has needs." As soon as I said it, I wished I could rewind time about two seconds and take it back, but now that the statement was out there, I was going to own it. I lifted my chin in challenge.

He laughed. "I do, but I don't believe in shitting in my own front yard. I take care of those needs outside of Lone County."

That was interesting. It seemed like he was always at the tavern, but then he hadn't been there all afternoon. He'd been with me.

"Tinder?"

He laughed again. "Harper, I don't need Tinder."

"That ego make it hard to fit through the door at times?"

"I seem to do just fine." He pierced me with his own gaze. "What about you?"

"You mean for sex?" I asked with a grin. "I don't need a man. I have a box full of toys that work just fine and don't insist I talk about my feelings."

"You screw a lot of men who like to talk about their feelings?"

"No, I've learned the type and steer clear." I took a drink of my coffee, wishing it was laced with whiskey.

"Thus the decision to steer clear of the bookseller," he said. "Ten to one he's a feelings guy."

I took another sip, then set the mug on the table, still clinging to it. "Nate is a great guy. He'll make some woman really happy." I lifted my gaze with a mischievous smile. "I hear lots of women are all about the feelings."

He grinned back. "So I've heard."

We sat in silence for a moment, and I knew I had to tell him about my dinner with my father, but it felt like one thing I had over him: something I knew, and he didn't. Still, I knew he was probably sticking to me just like I was sticking to him. That had to be one of several reasons I'd chosen to meet my father at the tavern instead of Roots. He probably would have found a way to sit two tables away so he could eavesdrop on our conversation.

I glanced up at him. "I'm having dinner with my father tonight."

"Okay…" He sounded bored, like I was spouting the fifty states in alphabetical order.

"He knows something about Hugo Burton."

He brow lifted. "What does he know?"

"That's what I plan to find out. When I asked what he knew about him, Dad got weird. So I suggested we meet for dinner and discuss it."

"I'll be coming to that dinner."

"You don't trust me to tell you what I find out?"

"I don't trust you to tell me *everything* you find out. You'll be selective."

"No, Malcolm, that's you," I said, my irritation rising.

"We're both parceling out information, and you damn well know it."

"Maybe that's because I don't trust you," I countered, my voice rising. "And the reason you're hiding things from me—like what you found under the body—is because you have some nefarious reason for looking into this."

"You don't trust me?" he asked, his voice cold. "I definitely don't trust you with my secrets. You're too damn on the straight and narrow, but what good has that gotten you, Detective? The Little Rock police force set you up and kicked you out on your ass."

"I quit."

"Not because you wanted to," he shot back.

"I'm on the straight and narrow?" I shouted, leaning forward. "If I was on the straight and narrow, I would have turned you in for murdering the Sylvester brothers."

"Murdering?" he asked. "It's all semantics. They're dead, and they're dead because they both did some very bad things. The world is better off without them."

"That's called vigilante justice, Malcolm."

"It's called flat-out justice, Harper. And the reason you didn't turn me in is because you agree with me."

I opened my mouth to protest, then stopped.

"Daniel Sylvester could have saved your sister from being murdered, but he took photos of her instead. His father covered it up. Then his punk ass brother kidnapped an innocent kid to set up his brother? What kind of sick ass mentality is that?" A hard look filled his eyes. "If you expect me to feel remorse for killing them, you'll be very disappointed."

I wanted to tell him he was wrong, that he should have let the justice system deal with them, but I couldn't bring myself to do it.

"You know what I think?" he asked in his now-familiar smug tone.

"Do you really expect me to answer that question? It doesn't matter what I say, you're gonna tell me anyway."

"You're right, because I think half your problem is you can't accept who you really are."

"What the fuck does that mean?" I demanded, my temper rising. "That I should suck it up and just deal with my survivor's guilt and losing the career I loved? Don't you think I'm *trying*?"

"Not that," he said, his voice gruff. "But losing your career has re-opened a chasm you can't ignore."

"For a guy who claims to hate talking about feelings, it feels an awful fucking lot like we're doing that."

"I was wrong when I said you're too straight and narrow."

I covered my chest with my hand in mock surprise. "Oh my God. Did you just admit to being *wrong* about something?"

"It happens occasionally," he said good-naturedly. "But I was only partially wrong."

"Of course," I said sarcastically.

He ignored me and continued on. "You're only *trying* to stay on the straight and narrow path. It worked while it worked, but what you're really seeking is justice. That's why you didn't turn me in for killing the Sylvester brothers. If anything, you're pissed that you couldn't mete out the punishment with me."

"That's not true," I said, even as the truth rose up inside me. *yes. yes. yes.*

"You're upset that I did it without you."

I shook my head, even as the voice inside me grew louder. *YES. YES. YES.* "I'm not a monster!"

But I was, wasn't I? I wished I had been the one to pull the trigger and kill those men, especially the one who'd watched my sister suffer. Wasn't that the definition of a monster?

"Like me?" he challenged, his voice a neutral tone.

"I never said you were a monster." But *was* he a monster? I was sure he'd done things that would make him considered one, yet I couldn't give him the label.

He slowly stood, then moved in front of me. I automatically rose, leaving my cup on the table. He set his next to mine and towered over me, his size making it clear that he'd win any physical altercation, yet I wasn't afraid of him.

"Maybe you'd think I was a monster if you knew about all the things I've done."

"You already admitted that you've killed men," I said.

"I've done more than that."

"I could tell my sister's killer disgusted you when we saw him in prison," I said. "You beat the shit out of him for gloating about what he did to her. I never once deluded myself into believing you did that for me. You did it for yourself."

"Exactly. I did it for myself."

"I know how you treat your staff at the tavern. They know you have their backs, and you care about their well-being."

"More self-interest. A happy employee is a productive employee."

"What bullshit," I said with a short laugh. "Why can't you admit that you actually have a moral code and child molesters disgust you? That you feel a responsibility toward the people who work for you and genuinely care about them?"

His eyes frosted over, and I knew I'd gone too far. "This is your attempt to make me fit the sanitized image you need so you can accept working with me. But let me be clear—I felt absolutely no remorse for killing either of those men. And I've killed plenty of others without feeling anything either." His mouth twisted, and a self-deprecating look covered his face. "Allegedly."

"Of course," I shot back sarcastically.

"Don't tuck away that monster label just yet, Detective, because I think you know it's true. What really worries you is that maybe, *just maybe*, you're a monster too."

Then he stomped out without another word, leaving me with both mugs of coffee, a slight buzz, and the fear that he was absolutely right.

Chapter 20

I thought Malcolm had left and called someone to pick him up, but when I looked out the window a few minutes later, I saw him leaning his jeans-clad ass against the hood of my car while he talked on the phone.

My mother was going to be pissed whenever she came back, because there was no way the busybody neighbor next door was missing the show playing out in the driveway.

I grabbed the vodka bottle, took two shots straight from it, and then put it back. That done, I swished my mouth out with water, then gulped the rest of my latte.

My stomach was churning with the mixture of alcohol, coffee, and self-loathing, so I threw what was left of my muffin in the trash. After I rinsed the mugs and put them and the plate in the dishwasher—fully knowing I was stalling—I changed into a pair of jeans and a light blue button-down shirt, then grabbed my coat and purse and headed out the door.

After I locked up, I headed down the steps, steeling my back for what I was about to possibly face.

"I got an address for Hugo Burton's old office," Malcolm said as I reached the bottom step.

"How'd you get that?" I shot back. "I was going to look it up."

His expression made it clear he wasn't impressed. "Did you?"

"No." I'd been too busy trying to prove my morality and failing miserably.

"Hale found it." He held out his hands. "Keys."

"What the fuck?"

"You're well on your way to being drunk."

"Fuck off, Malcolm."

"Please," he drawled, his hand still outstretched. "You can barely make it through the day without being buzzed through half of it. There's no way you didn't finish that conversation with a whiskey chaser or two."

Shame washed through me. Of course he would know that.

"Give me the keys. I suspect no one else knows," he said, his voice softening some. "I lived with a drunk for sixteen years. I know all the signs. At least you don't beat the shit out of me when you're sauced. Now hand them over."

That statement told me more intimate personal information about himself than he'd shared the entire time I'd known him. Who was the drunk? Probably his father. Or maybe an uncle? It could have been his mother, but that was doubtful. He hadn't needed to tell me that, yet he had, and that, along with his gentle tone, was what made me dig my keys out of my purse. But the vodka was catching up to me so it took a couple of attempts—further confirmation he was right to take them.

But why had he shared something so personal? To soften me up? To make me more willing to work with him after all the hard things he'd just said?

"Why are you working with me?" I asked, my hand still clutched around the keys.

"Because even if your brain's muddled from time to time, there's a good detective in there." He tapped his finger into the center of my forehead, but I batted it away. "Plus, you have access to things I don't. Now hand me the keys or I'll wrestle them from you, call Hale to send me a car, and do this on my own."

He would too, so I swallowed my shame and dumped them into his hand, then moved to the passenger door.

The car had a lingering odor of decay, but rolling down the windows had undoubtedly helped. It was faint enough that I doubted anyone would accuse of us of rolling in dog shit or playing with dead meat.

Malcolm got in, then started the car, leaving the windows down as he backed out of the driveway.

We rode to downtown Jackson Creek in silence, and it hit me that people would see James Malcolm driving my car and me in the passenger seat. Of course, the first thing they'd assume was that I was screwing him. My mother would be horrified. I wasn't sure I wanted to tie myself to him publicly, but there was no way around it. Especially since I suspected he was sticking to me like I planned to stick to him.

He pulled into a parking lot behind a three-story brick building that had a stationery store on the first floor. We got out, and he led the way into the back door of the store, sauntering up to the counter, and ignoring the open-mouthed stares of two women huddled over a candle display in front of the large windows overlooking Main Street.

I had two choices—either own the fact I was with him or stay in the background and eavesdrop. I suspected no one had seen us walk in, which meant I still had a chance to avoid being linked to him. But what I was saving myself from? My reputation was already in tatters. Would this really knock me down any farther?

I walked up to the counter and stood next to him.

The clerk was a perky woman wearing a dress that looked like it was straight out of the 1950s, minus the crinoline underskirt. Her makeup was minimal, but it made her look pretty, and her hair hung down her back in thick, dark waves. She turned her gaze up to Malcolm and a soft smile curved her lips. "I have to say you look out of place in here. Is there anything I can help you with?"

Malcolm rested the palm of his hand on the wooden counter. "Actually, there is. I'd like to speak to the manager of the office spaces upstairs."

"You thinkin' about rentin' one?" she asked, her lashes fluttering rapidly.

"Something like that," Malcolm replied, his voice full of honey. I'd never once heard that tone when he was speaking to me, and for some stupid reason it pissed me off.

"Floyd's not usually here, but he happens to be in the back workin' on the books. Give me a second and I'll get him."

"I'd appreciate that," Malcolm said, his voice still full of syrup.

The clerk smiled at the women in the front. "I'll be right back."

They didn't say anything, instead shifting their gazes to Malcolm, ignoring me as though I was invisible. That should have pissed me off more than his tone, but I had to admit I was relieved. Maybe Malcolm's presence was so much larger than life that I was invisible in his shadow. All the better.

The clerk headed down a hall and walked into a room, leaving us alone with the two women who were now openly gawking at Malcolm. Only they weren't ogling him in the same way the clerk had. Their expressions were full of disgust.

"Fans of yours?" I asked under my breath.

"They were part of the group who wanted to shut my tavern down."

"You know who wanted to shut you down?" I asked in surprise. I knew Ava's father, Todd Peterman, had set the wheels in motion, hoping to fuel his campaign for state senate with the platform of shutting down crime, but it stood to reason he had supporters.

"Of course I know who wanted to shut me down," he sneered. "Always know your enemies."

I turned to face him, the hair on the back of my neck standing on end. "You consider those two middle-aged women your enemies?"

"Anyone who's against me is my enemy."

I supposed when you lived your life in the organized crime world and ran your own empire, it made you paranoid. That must be how he'd survived in his position. But it still made me uneasy that he knew they'd supported Peterman. It felt petty. Or maybe it just made him aware.

I didn't have the mental capacity to figure it out. The vodka had kicked in full force, and I was in that nirvana of being in control of myself while my senses were dulled enough to drown out the unrelenting pain.

The clerk walked back into the hallway, followed by an older man who was adjusting the wire-framed glasses perched on his nose.

She stood to the side as Floyd stopped a few feet away, looking intimidated as he took Malcolm in.

"I hear you're here about renting an upstairs office," the older man said, rubbing his left hand on his pants leg.

"That's right," Malcolm said. "Do you have anything available?"

"What kind of business would you be operating there?" the older man asked, his voice slightly shaky.

"Shipping," Malcolm said. "International. I just need an office for my phone and an address."

Floyd swallowed hard. "And would this be…" His gaze bobbed to me. "Legal?"

Dammit. Did Floyd know who he was or was Malcolm just making him nervous? "Of course," I said, trying to make myself sound sweet and innocent, but I'd never been an actress so I wasn't sure it landed.

He glanced at Malcolm then back to me.

"We're still considering our options," I said. "We hear your office space is prime. But," I glanced up at Malcolm, "I suppose we could jump on that office space in Colter's building outside of Wolford. It is a lot more modern and up to date."

"Now hold up there," Floyd said, lifting a hand. "I have two spaces available, both on the second floor. I was just trying to figure out which would work best for you."

I didn't believe that for a minute, but I was relieved my plan had worked. "Why don't you show us both?"

"Yeah," he said, his head bobbing. "Let me get the keys."

"How about we wait upstairs?" I suggested. "Check out the general layout."

Disappointment covered the clerk's face, but she pointed to a door close to the entrance. "The staircase is over there."

"Thank you," I said as I headed to the door, leaving Malcolm to follow. I opened the door, and a quick glance back told me the women in the front were still openly gawking.

The staircase was dark and narrow, the bulb overhead barely giving the space enough light to illuminate the stairs.

"This seems like some kind of violation," I muttered as I reached the second floor and opened the door.

"This whole place is a violation."

I walked into a short, windowless hall. There were four white paneled doors with black numbers nailed to the wood. One had a wreath hanging on the door with a fake plant next to it, and a sign on the door read, "All Stars Realty." A door across the hall had a plaque that said, "Jim Palmer, Financial Planner."

Malcolm grunted. "Can't be much of a financial planner if he's stuffed into a tiny office."

"Maybe he's frugal," I said, starting to feel claustrophobic in the tight space.

"How'd you know the Colter building comment would work?" Malcolm asked, sounding genuinely curious.

"Because men like him hate progress. The thought of us preferring Colter's shiny glass building was stronger than his fear that you might open an illegal enterprise in his precious building."

He made a face. "Good call."

"Why'd you make our reason for being here sound suspicious? We almost didn't get up here."

"Because I want him to know I'm a potential threat."

"You're not going to threaten that old man," I whisper-hissed as I heard clumsy footsteps on the stairs.

He gave me a smirk and stepped to the side, making way for Floyd.

"That light bulb in that staircase is a hazard," Malcolm said when the older man emerged on the landing.

"The light bulb's fine," Floyd grumped as he shook a ring full of multiple keys. "It ain't gonna start a fire."

"Maybe not, but the dim light makes it difficult for people to see." He lifted a shoulder in a lazy shrug. "Unless you don't mind getting sued when someone falls down the stairs."

Floyd shot him a sneer, and I elbowed Malcolm in the side as the older man tried to insert a key into the door on the right. It took him three attempts with his shaky fingers before he finally got it unlocked, then pushed the door open with a flourish. "This is the larger of the two offices."

Malcolm walked in first, leaving me to follow—asshole—and I had to admit, if I'd been looking for an office, I would have loved this space. The floor was original wood with a few stains to prove its authenticity. Although the space had likely been divided into evenly sized rooms years after the building was constructed, the baseboards and crown molding looked original or near enough. Large, nearly floor-to-ceiling windows overlooked the street, light streaming in. The white walls appeared to be freshly painted.

My heart skipped a beat as I let myself consider renting

this space. My P.I. firm would need an office. Why couldn't it be this one?

"This office is five hundred square feet," Floyd said from the doorway. "Including the large closet and bathroom. The other office is four hundred square feet and doesn't have a bathroom."

"Where do the tenants go to the bathroom?" I asked as I wandered to the windows and stared down at the street. Nate's bookstore was across the street and to the left.

"Downstairs, but the rent is significantly cheaper."

"How much for this one?" Malcolm asked.

"Two thousand a month," Floyd said.

"Two thousand?" Malcolm asked with a dark laugh. "No wonder you have empty offices."

Floyd gave him a haughty look. "Quality costs, not to mention the prestige our tenants get from having their offices here."

Malcolm opened his mouth, and considering the look in his eyes, he presumably intended to argue with the man. An argument would do nothing for us, so I quickly asked, "How long has this building rented out office spaces?"

"Oh, well," Floyd stammered as his shoulder sagged into the doorframe. He stroked his chin with a faraway look. "I came on about fifteen years ago, but these offices have been leased for longer than that. I'd say about thirty years." He dropped his hand to his side and gave me a small smile.

"I'll bet you've seen some interesting tenants," I said. "You seemed worried about us having a criminal enterprise. Has that been an issue before?"

He lifted his chin. "There was someone, several years back. He ran off with a bunch of people's money."

I gasped. "You mean Hugo Burton had an office here?"

"He sure did," he said, his expression going from surprise to pride. "I guess everyone around these parts has heard of him."

"I heard he was getting investors for a land project," I said. "But that was up in Wolford so I'm surprised he had an office here."

"Like I said earlier," he said, his haughty tone returning, "there's a certain prestige that comes with having an office here."

"So you don't mind illegal businesses setting up shop here," Malcolm said with a hint of a smile.

Floyd's eyes widened. "That's not what I meant. I had no idea he was doing anything illegal. He was a good tenant. He was quiet, and when he had customers stop by, they never caused trouble."

"Because none of them fell down that deathtrap of a staircase," Malcolm said.

"We haven't had a fall in nearly two months."

Malcolm shot me an amused look, then turned back to Floyd. "What's your rent payment policy?"

"Rent is due on the first of the month. We use to take checks but now we prefer to set up an automatic withdrawal."

"How'd you handle it before?" Malcolm asked. "Say five or six years ago."

If Floyd was starting to figure out we'd come here to ask him about Hugo, he didn't let on. "We hadn't gone to automatic withdrawal then. We only started that about three years ago."

"So they paid with a check?" I asked.

"Yep."

"What's the policy if someone doesn't pay their rent?"

"Well, the law says we have to give them thirty days, and if they haven't paid we have to give them thirty more days before we serve an eviction notice."

"That sounds disruptive," I said. "Does it happen often?" I glanced at Malcolm, hoping I was coming off as worried and not constipated.

"There's no need to be concerned," he said. "We've only

had to evict one tenant in the entire fifteen years I've been here."

"Was it Hugo Burton?" I asked. "I heard he had all kinds of money trouble."

"Oh, no. Hugo always paid his rent on time."

I didn't hide my surprise. "So he was still renting his office when he ran off?"

"Yep."

"What happened to his things?"

Floyd's face darkened. "I'll go open the other office so you can take a look at it before you make a decision." He disappeared from the doorway and Malcolm gave me a warning look before he started to follow him.

I grabbed his arm and tugged him to a halt. His gaze darkened, but he didn't jerk free.

"Give him a second"—I made a face—"or twenty to get the door open first."

He grunted but stayed put, so I dropped my hold and walked over to one of two doors and opened it, revealing a bathroom with a pedestal sink and a toilet. The floor was covered in tiny white octagonal tiles with black grout. The other door opened to a narrow walk-in closet.

"You seem interested in this place," Malcolm said.

I shrugged. "I need an office for my P.I. firm, but two thousand a month is too much for me now. Nate has an apartment over his bookstore that's about to become available. I was considering it."

Malcolm crossed his arms over his chest. "You want to live with the bookseller?"

"Not *with* him. He has his own house."

He turned his gaze out the window. "Hmm."

"What's *that* mean?"

Lifting his brow, he turned back to face me. "You really think it's a good idea when the guy so desperately wants to sleep with you? What happens when he's tired of you turning him down?"

"Why the fuck do you care whether or not I sleep with Nate?" I demanded, my blood turning hot.

"I don't, but you have to admit you're not always in the right mental space to make decisions like that."

I gasped, but he chose that moment to walk out of the room and into the hallway, leaving me to follow again, as I tried to deal with his statement.

Fuck him. I was always in control unless I was in my own apartment. Alcohol consumption was legal in Lone County. I wasn't doing anything wrong.

I stomped after him, fuming at his accusation, but stopped short in the doorway when I saw Malcolm standing directly in front of the older man in an intimidating pose.

"Did Burton have many visitors?"

"His wife and kids came by a lot," Floyd said, shooting me a nervous glance.

"What about clients?" Malcolm asked.

"Yeah, but not many."

"Do you know who any of them were?"

Floyd's face paled. "We value our tenants' privacy."

"Burton ran off," Malcolm said dryly. "Do you think he gives a shit about his privacy? He lost every shred of it and put his life on full public display. He had to know that when he ran off."

Only he hadn't run off, and Malcolm knew it. Which begged the question of how much privacy he was owed considering he'd been murdered. Should Floyd really be telling Hugo's secrets to someone other than family and law enforcement personnel?

Floyd swallowed, his Adam's apple bobbing in his scrawny neck. "I didn't know most of his clients, and I'm not here all the time."

"But you're the kind of guy who doesn't like funny business going on in his building either, right?" Malcolm asked.

"I try to keep things on the straight and narrow."

"Of course, but you *must* have recognized some of them."

His gaze darted to the door then back to Malcolm. "A few."

"Who were they?"

"Bill O'Murphy," he said. "He died a good four or five years ago. He was retired."

"Okay, who else?"

"Skip Martin. He owns the Ford dealership."

"Anyone else?"

"Paul Adams," Floyd said, licking his bottom lip. "He owns the building, but he was here enough times to make me wonder what he was up to."

My heart skipped a beat, and I was sure I'd heard him wrong, but there was no denying he'd said my father's name.

My father owned the building?

He hadn't denied knowing Hugo. In fact, we were meeting tonight to talk about him. But I hadn't thought he was this deeply connected with the case. I shot a glance to Malcolm. He had to know Paul Adams was my father, but he didn't let on. I was thankful he was asking the questions now because I was reeling.

"So what happened to the shit in Burton's office when he took off?" Malcolm asked.

"Paul cleaned it out himself. I told him I'd call the family to do it, but he said he didn't want to burden them. That's why I was surprised when the family showed up to get his things, because Paul had said he was giving everything to them. But I didn't want to get him into trouble, so I just told them someone had done it, but I didn't know who."

My father cleaned out the office? Panic filled my head, but I stuffed it down. I had to keep it together and finish this interview.

"Did you confront Adams?" Malcolm asked.

"I mentioned that the family had come by, and they'd been surprised the stuff wasn't here, but he said he'd forgotten and would take care of it. We never talked about it again."

Malcolm shot me a look, probably to see if I had any other questions, but my head was still stuck on the fact my father had been part of this.

I had a whole new line of questioning to address when I saw him tonight.

Chapter 21

Floyd's forehead was dotted with droplets of sweat, so when Malcolm didn't ask anything else, the older man started for the door.

"One more thing," I asked as Floyd started to pass me. He came to a full stop, his hands shaking with anxiety.

Why was this making him so nervous? Did he suspect Hugo had been murdered? Was he worried the murderer would come after him if he gave too much away? Or, more likely, was he scared of Malcolm?

Floyd's rheumy eyes met mine, and a wave of guilt washed through me. What if we *had* put him in danger? But I'd started down this path. I might as well finish it.

"What was your impression of Hugo?"

A blank look filled his eyes. "My impression?"

"Was he a nice guy? A sleaze ball? Did he come across as a smarmy salesperson?"

"Oh no," he said, some of the tension easing from his body. "He was a super nice guy. No one was more surprised than I was to learn he'd stolen all that money. I know the news said he'd been having money trouble, but like I said, he *always* paid his rent on time."

That wasn't what Clarice had said. She'd told me the office manager had cleaned out the office because Hugo was behind on the rent.

Had my father told Clarice the rent was past due, or had she made that part up?

I gave Floyd a half smile, trying to make this feel less like an interrogation. "So Hugo didn't give you the impression that he was tricking people into investing in his properties?"

He shook his head. "No. Not at all. Honestly, for the longest time I didn't believe he'd swindled all those people. I figured there had to be a good explanation, but after a few years, it seemed pretty obvious he wasn't coming back."

No, Hugo Burton definitely wasn't coming back.

"Thank you for your time, Floyd," I said, taking a step deeper into the room. "We'll let you know if we're interested in the office."

"Stay as long as you want," Floyd said from the doorway. "I'll lock up later." Then he shuffled out of the room and we heard his heavy footfalls in the hall, leading away from us.

Malcolm turned to me, his face void of expression. "Sooo…" he finally said. "Your father."

My heart sunk. I'd held it together while we were talking to Floyd, but the heaviness of this situation was covering me like a wet blanket. "My father."

"Is he capable of murder?"

My back went rigid. "What kind of question is that?" I demanded angrily.

"A legitimate one. Someone killed Hugo Burton and your father had access to his office."

"My father didn't murder Hugo Burton."

"Does he own a gun?"

I glared at him. How dare he insinuate my father had anything to do with this. "No, of course not."

"You were estranged from your parents for years. Maybe he acquired one without your knowledge."

"My father is incapable of murdering someone the way Hugo Burton was murdered, let alone burying his body like that."

"I agree that the body disposal was sloppy, but moving his car was brilliant."

I supposed that was his roundabout way of calling my father smart, but I was stuck on the fact he was accusing my father of cold-blooded murder.

"Does your father own any corporations?"

"What?" I asked, shaking my head to clear the confusion befuddling my brain.

"Does he own any corporations?" he asked, his tone harsher.

"I don't know."

"I know he's an attorney. What's his specialty?"

The blood leached from my head, pooling at my feet and leaving me light-headed.

"What kind of law does your father practice?" he demanded, his voice hard.

Somehow I knew the question was for show, all for my benefit. He knew. There was no way he didn't, and then it struck me that when he asked questions, especially of me, in almost every instance, he already knew the answer.

Was this some kind of sick game? Did he like toying with me?

"What kind of law, Harper?" he asked again.

Bile rose in my throat, but I swallowed it down. "Property."

"Property." He said it with conviction, as if he'd just proven something.

"You're making a huge leap," I said, my anger blazing to life.

"Maybe so, but it's important to look at all the possibilities, don't you think, *Detective*?"

Detective. His mocking tone made it an insult.

I clenched my fists at my sides. "Did you already know my father owned the building?"

He remained silent.

"Of course you did, because Carter Hale looked it up. Hell, you probably have copies of the leases of all the tenants over the course of my father's ownership."

His arms hung at his side as he continued to stare me down.

"You fucking asshole," I ground out, but he still didn't respond.

"You knew, and this entire production was for my benefit. For what purpose? To hurt me?"

He finally shifted his weight. "I didn't know everything. But I knew he owned the building. I also knew that would fuck with your head, so I kept it to myself."

"Because I'm so fucking fragile?" I asked, my voice betraying me by breaking.

He didn't answer, but he didn't need to. I turned around and fled down the stairs, nearly falling on my ass twice. I told myself it was because the staircase was poorly lit and anger had made me clumsy, but deep down I knew the truth. So when I realized Malcolm still had the keys to my car, I didn't wait for him and demand the keys back. I had no business driving. Instead, I hurried across the street and down the block until I stood in front of Nate's bookstore.

Something deep inside me told me not to go in, but my instincts hadn't been on my side for the past few months, so I let my need for a friendly face, and possibly a shoulder to cry on, override what I knew was ultimately a bad idea.

Nate was behind the counter when I walked in. He beamed with happiness when he saw me, but his smile fell as soon as he got a look at my face.

"What's going on?" he asked as he hurried around the counter.

I shook my head. If I spoke, I'd break, and I was barely

holding it together as it was. I needed to take a moment to stuff everything back in and superglue it shut. The thought of doing that alone left me feeling raw and scared.

"I just need a moment and a friend."

Nate gathered me into his arms and pulled me to his chest. He smelled so good, like coffee and leather. It was comforting, and for a moment, I let myself pretend I was someone who could marry Nate or someone like him, and maybe pop out a couple of kids and live in his house that had a literal picket fence. That I could be a PTA mom who made cookies and went to Bunco nights.

That I could be happy.

But one thing I'd come to realize over the last few months of self-reflection was that I'd never actually *been* happy. Not really. Not since Andi. I'd settled for content, and I'd been the most content when I was deep in my work, seeking justice for people who'd been wronged. But other than my work, I was a shell of a woman. And while part of me desperately wanted to be the kind of woman who could marry a man like Nate and lead a small, quiet life, I knew that I would not only feel trapped, but I'd eventually gnaw off my leg to escape and bring down the man I'd tricked and any children we'd had.

I took a step back, surprised at the wet splotches on his shirt. When had I started crying?

"This was a mistake," I said, my voice breaking. "I shouldn't have come here. I shouldn't have bothered you."

His forehead wrinkled. "What are you talking about? I'm your friend and I'm worried about you. What happened?"

I shook my head, but even in my state of emotional distress, I knew he'd pursue this until I told him something, so I went with the excuse millions of children—both juveniles and adults—had used, as lame as it felt. "My parents."

Understanding filled his eyes. "I know you've said their breakup doesn't matter since you've hardly spent time with them since you left for college, but it's still hard, Harper. You need to let yourself grieve."

Grieve.

What did that mean? I felt like I'd spent my entire life in perpetual grief over my sister, and then Dylan Carpenter, the teenager I'd killed, and my career, but I'd never once felt grief over my parents' dissolved marriage. If anything, I was pissed that my father hadn't left sooner and taken me with him.

Despite the fact that we lived in the same house for four more years after my sister's murder, he'd abandoned me. My mother had abandoned me years before, but my father…

A gut-wrenching sob burst through my throat, and I dropped to my knees.

"Harper," Nate said in an anguished tone as he tried to catch me. He let me go and hurried to the door and flipped the sign to closed. Then he was at my side again, wrapping an arm around my back and hauling me up. "Let's go to the back."

I let him lead me to the back of store and guide me to the leather sofa customers sat on to read while drinking their coffees and perusing books.

Sobs poured out of me, and Nate sat beside me, his leg touching mine, my shoulder hitting his upper arm. I laid my head on his shoulder and cried and cried, but he kept his hands to himself as my heart ruptured and my emotions bled out.

Grief.

I knew I'd stuffed everything in for too long, planning to deal with it later, but later had never come and the knowledge that Malcolm was not just using me but manipulating me, piled on top of my father's involvement with Hugo Burton, was too much. Just too much weight to bear.

I cried and cried, deep ugly, gut-wrenching sobs that left me hyperventilating, and when I finally stopped, I felt empty.

Not only had I sobbed out my emotions, but I felt like I'd purged myself, leaving me behind an empty shell.

"I'm going to get you a glass of water," Nate said, patting my leg. "Cover your face with your hands. That'll help with the hyperventilation."

I did as he said, feeling like an idiot, because how many people had I instructed in the very same thing? Apparently, I'd cry-vomited all the reason out of my head too.

He returned a half minute later with a glass half-filled with water. "I don't have any ice, but it's cold."

My breathing had returned to somewhat normal, even if my face still felt numb. I reached for the glass with shaky hands, then took deep gulps of the water. It soothed the raw ache in my throat. But what I really needed was a *drink*. Alcohol was the only thing that would fill the emptiness inside me, and now that emptiness wasn't just a crack, it was a mile-wide canyon.

"When was the last time you cried like that?" he asked, squatting in front of me and placing a hand over mine, which was resting on my thigh.

I looked at him like he'd spoken a language I didn't understand. It took a second for me to comprehend the question. "Never."

"Okay," he conceded. "That was an epic cry, so how about this—when was the last time you had a good cry?"

I shook my head.

"You don't cry?"

"No."

"What about after your sister…" A sheepish look covered his face.

"No."

"No tears at all?" he asked in shock.

"Sure, there were tears, but not many. Mom took me to the doctor, and he said I was in shock. My mother was relieved to find out I wasn't a psychopath, and we never discussed it again."

"Oh, Harper."

I jerked my hand from his, and water from the cup sloshed on my jeans. "I don't want your pity."

"It's not pity."

"The fuck it's not," I shot back, getting to my feet. Maybe I'd sobbed out my grief, but the anger was still there, a smoldering furnace that only needed a short prod to fire into life.

"What happened?" he demanded, some of his softness bleeding out of him. "And don't try to tell me this is about your parents, because I'm finding it hard to believe they were the ones who finally broke you. Not unless one of them actually *did* something."

The walls around my exposed heart started climbing back into place. "It's nothing. Just everything all together. I think it finally caught up with me."

"Nothing?" His tone made it clear that he didn't believe it for a minute. Then again, I would never accuse Nate of being stupid.

I wrapped my arms around my front, hooking my fingers on my upper arms. I suddenly felt impossibly cold, my hairs standing on end. The craving for a drink was so strong, I almost ran for the nearest restaurant that served alcohol.

He released a long sigh. "Harper, I say this as your friend, but have you ever considered talking to someone?"

"A therapist? I've talked to several."

"Finding a good therapist can be hard," he said. "Sometimes you have to go through a few before you find the right fit."

"I don't need a therapist. There's *nothing* to talk about."

He lifted a brow of admonition.

"I don't want to talk about this," I snapped.

"You can't show up sobbing your heart out, then tell me it's nothing and expect me to forget about it."

"This really was a mistake." I rushed past him, toward the front door.

"You're just going to leave?"

"I told you it was a mistake," I said as I snatched my purse off the floor and reached for the lock on the door.

"I can smell the alcohol on your breath," he said so quietly I almost missed it.

I kept my back to him, momentarily frozen. "I had a drink at lunch. So what?" So my lunch had been a latte, part of a muffin, and a lot of vodka. I dared to glance back at him to find him staring at me with disappointment.

I couldn't handle his disappointment on top of everything else, so I opened the door and headed outside, wondering what the hell I should do or where I should go. I didn't trust myself to drive, and I couldn't go back into Nate's store. So I walked down to a café and slipped inside, plopping into a booth.

A waitress who looked old enough to be my mother walked over with a menu. "You doin' okay, honey?"

Oh crap. I probably had puffy eyes and a red nose. "I've had better days," I admitted, giving her a weak smile.

"You know what I find helps with the not-so-good days?" She smiled. "A piece of pie. Ernie's got someone who bakes 'em fresh every morning. We're out of most kinds, but I have some apple left. I can serve it to you with a scoop of ice cream and a fresh cup of coffee."

I almost told her no, but I needed to order something and, now that she'd mentioned it, pie sounded delicious. "Yeah, that sounds good."

"Doctor Betty, at your service," she said, saluting me, and I grinned at her attempt to cheer me up.

While I was ashamed of how I'd fallen apart in front of Nate, I was mostly horrified. How had I let that happen? I wanted to blame it on Malcolm, but my mind kept returning to my father's involvement in this mess. Would my dad tell me why he'd cleaned Hugo's things out of his office?

Could I believe him if he did?

Betty returned holding a plate with a generous piece of pie and a scoop of ice cream in one hand and a pot of coffee in the other. I turned over the coffee mug in front of me and grabbed a packet of sugar.

She set the pie plate in front of me. "Here you go, honey. This might not fix whatever's wrong, but at least you'll get a belly full of goodness."

I couldn't help laughing. Usually I hated dealing with cheesy service workers, but Betty had a genuineness to her I had to appreciate. As she filled my cup, I asked, "Could you bring me some milk for my coffee?"

"Sure will." After she filled my cup, she spun on her heels and headed behind the counter.

I picked up a fork and sliced into the pie, scooping up a small portion of ice cream with it. I nearly moaned when I took a bite. She'd warmed the pie, and the crust was perfectly flaky, just like my old roommate Kara had made it.

I hadn't spoken to Kara in weeks, and I considered texting her, then decided she was part of the life I'd left behind. Maybe it was better to make a clean break. I was never going back to my life in Little Rock. It was dead and buried.

The thought should have made me more depressed, but I'd already come to terms with it. The question was whether I should stay in Jackson Creek. I'd come to town broke, but I could have taken the five thousand Vanessa Peterman had given me and moved somewhere else. My father's change of heart had been a big reason for me staying. What would I do if he admitted to doing something illegal? To possibly murdering someone?

But that was a big leap. Just because he'd cleaned out Hugo's office didn't mean he'd done anything unsavory. But if he'd been on the up and up, why hadn't he given Hugo's stuff to his wife?

Betty returned with the milk and set it in front of me. "You let me know if you need anything else."

"Thanks." She started to turn away and then a new thought hit me. "Hey, Betty, have you worked here for a long time?"

"Boy, have I," she said with a laugh. "Goin' on twenty years." She pointed to the back. "Me and my husband Arthur own the place."

"You do?" I asked in surprise. She was wearing a blue waitress-style dress and a white apron along with white orthopedic shoes. I pointed to my half-eaten pie with my fork. "Do you bake the pies? Because this is amazing."

"No need to butter me up," she said with a grin, "especially since I didn't make it. Arthur has a woman who bakes them at home and delivers them every morning. We can authentically say they're homemade."

"Don't ever lose her," I said, moving the small cup of milk closer. "I bet a lot of people who work downtown eat here."

"A good lot of 'em do," she said. "I know 'em by name too."

I leaned closer and lowered my voice. "Did Hugo Burton ever eat here?"

Her eyes widened. "Hugo Burton? I haven't heard that name in ages."

"Was he a customer?"

She nodded. "He was a regular. Ate here at least three times a week."

"What did you think of him?"

Her eyes narrowed. "Why are you interested?"

I considered being vague, but I suspected Betty appreciated directness. "I'm trying to find out what happened to him."

She looked surprised. "Are you working for the police, Harper Adams?"

The blood drained from my face. She knew who I was, which meant there was a good chance she wouldn't tell me anything.

"No," I said solemnly. "His wife asked me to look into it."

She glanced over her shoulder at the lone customer in the diner, an elderly man who was reading the paper while he nursed a cup of coffee at the counter. Betty slid into the seat in front of me. "What do you want to know?"

I pushed my pie plate to the side. "So you remember him?"

"Like I said, I get to know the names of my customers. We get a lot of regulars, and I have a memory like a steel trap. I remember their favorite orders, how they take their coffee, the names of their kids and their ages."

"What was your impression of him?" I asked, resting my hand on the table.

"He was such a nice man. Very polite."

"Did you know what he did for a living?"

"Something about owning land and building a neighborhood. He was so excited about it when he first started on it, but right before he left, he looked tired. He was fightin' hard to keep it all rollin', but I think he knew he wouldn't last much longer."

"So you think he ran off?"

"That's what the sheriff said, but…"

"You don't believe it?"

"Honestly, I don't know what to believe. I know he loved his kids dearly. And he wasn't just talk. I saw those two pretty regular like and he doted on 'em. They loved him too, especially his son." She shook her head. "They were good kids. I always wondered how they turned out."

I didn't usually share information about the people I spoke to, but in this case I figured I could be vague and it wouldn't hurt anything. "I spoke to Anton at lunch yesterday," I said. "He's a nurse up in Wolford and seems to be doing pretty well, and his sister is in college."

She placed her hand on her chest. "Oh, that warms my heart. Thank you for that."

"Of course." I poured some of the milk in my coffee and stirred. "Did Hugo ever bring clients here?"

"Clients? I'm not sure about that, but he definitely ate here with people other than his kids." She bobbed her head toward me. "He had plenty of lunches with your father."

"My dad?" I repeated. It felt redundant to do so, but I needed to be certain.

"They seemed more like friends than business associates, but that was back when Hugo had first rented the office space down the street. Toward the end, I didn't see them together."

Had my father stopped eating lunch with him because he knew of Hugo's business troubles and was too embarrassed to be seen with him? That seemed more like something my mother would do. Then again, I wasn't sure I knew my father at all.

"Did Hugo seem depressed?"

She pursed her lips as she considered it. "Yeah, in hindsight, I suppose so. He wasn't as quick to smile as he used to be."

Which fit with everything I'd already heard. "I know that Hugo had a business lunch the day he disappeared. Do you happen to know if he had lunch here?"

"I sure do, although neither one of 'em ate. It was later in the day," she said, irritation tingeing her words. "I told that damn sheriff's department, but they didn't seem all that interested."

"Do you happen to know who he met?"

"No one I'd ever seen before."

I grabbed my phone and pulled up a photo of Brett Colter. "Was this him?"

She studied my phone and shook her head. "Nope. That's Brett Colter. He didn't eat here all that frequently, but I'd seen him enough to know it wasn't him."

"Do you remember what the man Hugo met with looked like?"

She tapped her temple. "All stored right in here. He was an older man. Distinguished lookin'. Pretty damn snooty though. He didn't seem pleased to be here."

"Do you happen to know what they were discussing?"

"They stopped talking whenever I got close, which was totally unlike Hugo. He seemed intimidated by the man. The guy just had this presence about him." She made a face.

I looked up James Malcolm from a newspaper article from three years ago and turned my phone to show her. I wouldn't call Malcolm an older, distinguished man, but we all had different perceptions of the world, and it would have been foolish not to ask. "Could it have been him?"

She burst out laughing. "Oh, my no. That's James Malcolm. He's never stepped foot in the place, not to mention he doesn't fit the description at all." She looked down her nose at me with an amused smile. "I thought you were good at that detectiving stuff."

"That's fair," I said, picking up my cup and taking a sip. "I'm surprised you know who James Malcolm is."

"I make it my business to know the business of this town. Especially with Todd Peterman struttin' around like he owns the whole damn place. I know he tried to put Malcolm's tavern out of business for no good reason. I wouldn't be surprised if he wanted to institute some kind of tax on the downtown businesses and call it a beautification tax or some such nonsense. He already tried to tell the businesses down-town that we need to have the same fabric on our awnings."

"So I heard."

"That man is trouble, mark my words."

A couple with a family walked in and Betty flashed them a

smile before turning back to me. "Now that you've been in and know I won't tar and feather you like half the town wants to, be sure to come back and have some lunch or dinner."

I pulled out my wallet and grabbed a twenty-dollar bill.

She waved a hand toward me. "Put that away. This is on the house. Can't stand to see someone look so upset." She grinned. "What I'd tell you about the pie? You look a whole lot better."

I could have taken that as an insult, but she genuinely seemed to care, although for the life of me, I couldn't figure out why.

"Now, don't be a stranger," she said as she slid out of the booth and headed to the table with the family.

I finished my pie and coffee, racking my brain as I tried to figure out who the older, distinguished gentleman could have been. One of the people behind Larkspur Limited? Had he met Hugo for pie and then murdered him?

Chapter 22

I'd sobered up enough to drive by the time I left the café but I made sure to cross the street so I didn't have to pass the windows of Nate's bookstore. My car was still parked behind the office building, and when I opened the door, I found the keys tucked under the mat.

I had to meet my father in a little over an hour, which didn't give me time to do much of anything, so I drove up to Wolford to buy more whiskey. I drove past Sunny Point on the way to Scooter's Tavern. It was dark, wet, and drizzly, but I didn't see anything out of the ordinary.

My father's car was in the parking lot when I pulled up a few minutes before seven. The last thing I wanted to do was see James Malcolm right now, but now that I knew my father had more involvement with Hugo than I'd suspected, having our conversation in a bustling restaurant seemed like a better idea than having it in the quiet, dignified Roots.

While Malcolm wasn't at the bar when I walked in, I knew better than to be relieved. For all I knew, he was in the back, waiting to crash my private family dinner.

Dad was sitting in the booth I usually occupied with Louise and Nate. He stood and gave me an apprehensive smile as I approached. He wrapped his arms around me, and I hugged him back. I was wary of what he might have done, but the lonely, desperate-for-love little girl in me relaxed into him.

My eyes burned as we broke apart, and worry filled his gaze as he cupped my cheek and studied my face.

"Is everything all right, Harper?"

A lump filled my throat and I struggled with what to tell him. That I was so needy for his love that I would lap it up like a dog at a water fountain? Or that I knew he'd kept secrets and I was worried he was guilty of things I probably couldn't forgive?

Instead, I gave him a weak smile and said, "It's just been a long day."

His worry deepened. "We could have postponed dinner."

"No," I said, then drew in a deep breath to steady my nerves. "I wanted to see you."

He studied me a moment longer, I suppose reassuring himself that I really wanted to be here, before sitting back down.

Sitting opposite him, I reached for the water glass that had already been placed there and took several long gulps.

"Have you heard anything from Mom?" I asked when I set down the glass.

"No. I tried calling her again, but she didn't answer." He grimaced. "But to be honest, she's mad enough at me that she might not have answered anyway."

"Are you sure we shouldn't be worried?" I asked. "This is so unlike her...I think."

"The leaving part, sure," my dad said, "but the manipulative, dramatic behavior? Not so much."

Kylie, who usually worked the day shift, came over with her notepad and I realized Dad already had a menu sitting to the side. "Y'all ready to order?"

I gave Dad a questioning look and he nodded. "I got here

early and looked at the menu. But you can take more time if you need it."

He ordered a hamburger and an iced tea, and I ordered a chicken sandwich and a beer. As Kylie headed to the back, I snuck a glance at the bar and saw that Malcolm still wasn't there. While I hadn't wanted to see him, now I was worried about what he might be up to.

I had planned to wait until our food arrived to ask my questions, but I was concerned that Malcolm was planning a sneak attack. I wanted to get my answers before he could pounce.

"When I mentioned Hugo Burton," I said carefully, "you said we'd talk about it at dinner."

He drew in a breath, then nodded. "That's right." But he hushed up because Kylie was headed back to the table with my beer and my father's iced tea. After she set them down, he watched her leave, and when she was almost to the bar, he leaned in closer and said, "I helped Hugo set up his corporation and the contracts for his investors."

I wasn't sure why that surprised me. He was a property attorney, so it made complete sense.

"The sheriff's department says they never found contracts."

He didn't react.

"Why didn't you tell them you created them?"

"I didn't know they didn't have them," he said weakly.

"Then why don't you seem surprised?"

"I heard they didn't have lots of things in that case. They said Hugo ran off with it all."

I held his gaze. "Do *you* know where the contracts went?"

"I already told you that—"

"That everyone thinks he ran off, but that's not the same as telling me what *you* think."

A sheepish look filled his eyes, and he dropped his gaze to the table.

"What happened to the contracts, Dad?"

He kept his gaze down for several seconds before he said, "Did you ask the sheriff's department what they think?"

Disappointment sank into my bones. He wasn't really lying, but he *was* evading the truth. "They also think he took them."

I picked up my beer and took a long pull. My father gave me a questioning look but didn't say anything.

I set the bottle on the table and held his gaze. "The law firm has copies of every contract generated in the office. I bet I could go into the file room tomorrow morning and pull them."

"They're not there," he said, his cheeks turning pink.

My heart skipped a beat. "Where did they go?"

He kept silent.

Dread settled in my belly. "What are you covering up, Dad?" I wanted to ask him about owning the building that had housed Hugo's office and cleaning it out, but I was hoping he'd admit to it instead of me confronting him with what I knew.

His gaze held mine, his face pleading for understanding. "The past is always better left in the past, Harper."

"Are we talking about Hugo Burton's contracts or Andi's murder?"

His face paled. "Of course we're talking about Hugo."

I wasn't so sure. I had questions about the aftermath of her murder, about how much he knew about the Sylvester brothers' father calling Andi's kidnapper to warn him the police were about to show up with a search warrant. The police chief had reprimanded Sylvester but hadn't pressed charges. My father had been mayor at the time, so he'd likely known something. If so, why hadn't he objected to Barry Sylvester's slap on the wrist? But I realized I wasn't ready for those answers. Not yet.

"Mitch hired me to find out what happened to Hugo. Does he know you worked with Hugo?"

He swallowed. "No, and I'd appreciate it if you didn't tell him."

"He's paying me to find information, Dad. You want me to purposely withhold it?"

"You're not bound by the law," he insisted. "You can decide what to share and what not."

"Why wouldn't you want me to tell Mitch? Why hide it?"

He took a drink, an obvious stalling tactic, and then set down the glass. "I didn't create the contracts through the firm. I worked on them at home."

"And it was wrong to create contracts outside the firm?" I asked in confusion, then it hit me. "Oh. They didn't get their cut."

He nodded. "The other two did it too from time to time." He looked down at his half-empty glass of iced tea and ran his finger on the side, swiping at the condensation. "Hugo was on a shoestring budget. I wanted to help him out."

"But why? How did you know him?"

He drew another breath, obviously not wanting to tell me, but I wasn't letting him off the hook.

"How did you know him, Dad?" I had a good idea at this point, but I was going to make him say the words.

He sat up and ran a hand over his eyes. "I invested money into his Sunny Point project. I was one of the two original investors."

And there it was. My father was the very man I'd been looking for. Had Malcolm known?

"Part of my investment was drawing up the LLC paper-work for him and the contracts for the investors."

"So why doesn't anyone know that? You had to know the sheriff's detectives were looking for them."

"I couldn't let my partners know."

"Are you serious? Surely creating contracts outside of the

firm couldn't get you into *that* much trouble. You just said the others had done it too."

Kylie appeared next to the table with our plates and my father looked all too happy to have an excuse not to answer me. In fact, he kept Kylie at our table for over five minutes, talking about the weather, the new gas station going in outside of Jackson Creek, and the current real estate market.

By the time she was called to take another table's order, I was nearly done with my sandwich and fries. I wiped my hands off on my napkin and set it on the table.

"You need to tell me everything, Dad. Start from the beginning."

He placed his hands on the table, on either side of his plate, and leaned closer, his eyes full of panic. "It's all in the past, Harper."

"Someone killed Hugo Burton, Dad, and what you know might help me find out who did it."

His face lost color again. "Hugo ran off. Everyone knows that. Why would you say he was murdered?"

Crap. What the hell was wrong with me? "I don't believe he ran off. I think something happened to him, and I plan to prove it."

He slowly shook his head. "Nooo. I saw that look in your eyes when you were a kid. When you *knew* something to be true. You got that look when your mother insisted you ate a piece of Andi's birthday cake before her party, and you swore you didn't. Turned out it was that neighbor kid..." His voice trailed off and the panic turned to terror. "You know he was murdered. You have proof."

Well, fuck. "I *never* said that."

"You didn't have to. I know you better than you think."

I held up my hands in front of my chest and waved them. "Just forget I said anything, and leave the investigation to me. But anything you can tell me—even the most insignificant thing—could make all the difference in helping me figure out who killed Hugo Burton."

"So you think Hugo Burton is dead," Malcolm said, sidling up to our table from the shadows. "Fascinating."

Great. The asshole was back.

My father stared up at Malcolm with a wary look. I could see why. Malcolm looked even more imposing than usual. His arms were crossed over his chest, and he was giving me his full, undiluted attention.

I gave him a scathing look. "If you're here to see if we need another refill on our drinks, we're good."

"You sure?" he asked. "You look like you need another beer."

"Go ahead and get another one, Harper," my dad said. "My treat."

I ignored the fact that my father was offering to buy me beer like I was a six-year-old asking for an ice cream cone and continued to hold Malcolm's gaze. "No. I'm good."

"You sure?" Malcom asked his brow shooting up the slightest bit. "Maybe you want something stronger."

"I'm pretty sure I said I'm good," I shot back. "Maybe you should get your hearing checked, Malcolm."

"Malcolm?" my father said, sounding wary.

Shit. Surely my father knew who owned this place, but he probably hadn't expected to run into him, let alone have a chat with him about Hugo Burton.

"Dad, this is James Malcolm, the owner of Scooter's Tavern. Malcolm," I said reluctantly as I gestured to my father. "This is my father, Paul Adams."

"Real estate lawyer extraordinaire," Malcolm said, extending a hand to him. "So nice to meet you."

My father stared at his hand, his eyes wide. "You've heard of me."

Malcolm shrugged. "The county's not that big. I like to stay in the know about who's who."

My father took his still-offered hand, awkwardly shook it, then snatched it back.

Fuck. Malcolm was ruining any chance I'd had of getting my father to talk.

"We're good, Malcolm," I said again with more bite. "We'll be sure to let Kylie know if we need anything else."

He smiled, but it didn't reach his eyes, then turned and headed for the bar.

"You *know* him?" Dad asked with a shaky breath.

"Yeah," I said. "I come here a lot with my friends Louise and Nate. And Malcolm's always here. So…" I let my voice trail off and insinuate that was the extent of our interaction.

"He knew who I was."

"Like he said, he pays attention to what's going on in the county. You know Todd Peterman tried to shut him down. I guess he's a little paranoid."

"Of me?"

"No, of course not," I assured him, lying through my teeth. "We just have a bit of a rivalry going on. He knows my history and I know his. It's kind of a check and counter check kind of situation."

His gaze turned to the bar where Malcolm was pulling a beer. "He seems dangerous, Harper, and he seems to be holding a grudge against you."

"I *assure* you, Dad, I'm not in any danger. That's just Malcolm. All bark and very little bite."

"He has a dangerous history."

"And he's reformed now," I said with a bright smile that I hoped didn't look as fake as it felt. "I'm fine. It's just something we do. No big deal."

Dad set his napkin on the table. "I think I'll call it a night. Maybe you should head home too."

Fucking Malcolm. What the hell did he think he was doing by walking over? Sure, I'd expected him to be here, but it had seemed safer to come here than risk him showing up if we went somewhere else. Obviously that had been a mistake.

"We can stay a little longer." I shot Malcolm a glare.

But my father noticed Malcolm watching us and pulled out his wallet, tossing some money on the table. "I need to go. I'll call you later."

"Dad—"

But he was already out of the booth and darting across the room to the door.

I was so furious, I could hardly contain my rage. I got up and strode to the bar, my fists clutched at my sides. "What the hell was that?" I demanded when I reached Malcolm, not bothering to keep my voice down.

I felt a moment of satisfaction because he seemed genuinely caught off guard by my response. But anger flashed in his eyes.

"Time and place, Detective," he grunted out through gritted teeth.

"Yes, Malcolm," I shot back. "Time and place."

He darted a glance at Misti, who was staring at us with an open mouth. Several people at the bar were staring too.

"Meet me at the back door," he said under his breath, looking like he wanted to reach across the bar and strangle me. "*Now.*"

I nearly told him that I didn't take orders from him, but I wasn't done reaming him, and he wasn't entirely wrong. This really *wasn't* the time and place.

Spinning on my heels, I marched over to the table and grabbed my purse and coat and headed outside. In case anyone was watching, I got in my car and drove to the back and parked. When I got out, Malcolm pushed the back door open and gave me an impatient look.

I marched past him into his office, and he shut the door behind us.

"What the hell were you thinking?" I demanded; my

hands fisted at my sides again. "He was telling me about Hugo, and you blew that to kingdom come. He's terrified that you know what he did."

"I *do* know what he did."

"Do you now?" I shot back, heavy with sarcasm. "Then please enlighten me."

"Just because he's your father doesn't mean he's pure as the driven snow."

"I know that, you fucking idiot," I shouted, not caring who heard me. "He was talking, and then you showed up and spooked him."

He started to say something and then stopped.

I began pacing, pressing the heel of my hand against my forehead.

Malcolm pushed out a breath. "Once he settles down, he'll talk to you."

I stopped pacing. "No, he *won't*. He's freaked out by you, and he thinks you have it out for *me*. If anything, he'll keep quiet to protect me." My anger rose along with my voice. "So thank you very fucking much!"

Malcolm cursed under his breath and walked over to his whiskey decanter. He poured himself a generous drink then downed it in two gulps.

"What did he tell you?"

"Sucks not to know everything, doesn't it?" I asked in a snide tone. "To know you've been played by someone who's supposed to be your partner."

He turned to face me, his dark eyes glittering. "I never said we were partners."

"Yeah, my mistake," I said. "Call me naïve. I knew you had your own agenda, but I never thought you'd…" I shook my head. I couldn't do this. Sure, I didn't trust him, but I never thought he'd play me like he had. But that made *me* a fool. He'd never promised to be on the up and up, and I'd gone into this knowing exactly who I was dealing with.

I headed for the door.

"Where do you think you're going?" he demanded.

I paused with my hand on the doorknob. I was burning a bridge here. Malcolm had resources and information I didn't. Did I really want to end this almost-partnership? Maybe, maybe not, but I wasn't in any frame of mind to make that decision right now.

"Home." I opened the door and stalked out of the office and through the back door, not stopping until I was in my car.

I half-expected Malcolm to come after me, but then again, he didn't seem the type to chase someone.

That was fine. I didn't need him. I should have never asked Carter Hale for help. I didn't need either one of them. I could finish this on my own.

Chapter 23

I'd intended to go home, but I still had questions for my father. I drove to his house, hoping he'd talk to me after Malcolm's interruption, but his driveway was empty. Although the front porch light was on, the interior was dark. Still, I walked up to the front door and rang the doorbell multiple times, not surprised when he didn't answer.

Where had he gone?

I pulled out my phone and called him, but it went straight to voicemail.

Had my father gone to meet someone after our dinner? If so, whom?

I went back to my car and turned it on to warm the interior while I figured out what to do next. I went over everything he'd said before the interruption. Dad had admitted to being one of the original investors and to creating the contracts for the LLC in his home office.

Were they still stored there?

Was Dad heading over to the house now to get them? Dammit. He had a good ten- to fifteen-minute head start.

I headed home, but my father's car wasn't out front. The

lights were all off, too, confirming my mother really wasn't here.

Where was she? She wasn't the kind of woman to take a vacation on a whim, and she had no family and only superficial friends. I pulled out my phone and reluctantly called her, expecting her to either screen my call or give me a tongue lashing, but the call went straight to voicemail.

That was weird.

Then again, if she was being manipulative like my father suggested, it stood to reason she'd turn off her phone. Still, I was starting to worry about her. After I looked for the contracts, I planned to go through her address book and start calling people. Sure, my father thought she was doing this for attention, but the seasoned detective in me needed to know she was safe.

I walked through the still-unlocked back door and flipped on the overhead light. The room was just as I'd seen it last. Impeccably clean. Nothing out of place. It almost felt wrong to set my purse on the kitchen table, but no one stepped out to yell at me. Trying to ignore the cold shiver that coursed through me, I headed straight to my father's home office.

I flipped on the overhead light, and surveyed the space, looking for any signs that my father might have beaten me here. A partially open drawer. A paperclip on the floor. Instead, I saw a whole lot of nothing. The desktop was clear except for a lamp and a leather-edged desk blotter. The books on the shelves were all perfectly aligned, the work of my mother. But if Dad had hidden something on the shelves and removed it before I'd arrived, he'd been careful to hide his tracks.

I searched the desk drawers, but he must have cleaned them out when he moved. All I found was a few pens, some bent paperclips, and scotch tape. If he'd kept the documents here at home, he must have taken them when he'd moved out.

Or maybe not.

My parents' house didn't have a basement, but there *was* an attic. The documents were probably ten years old, and after Hugo disappeared, Dad probably hadn't wanted to leave them lying around. The attic, accessed by a fold-down staircase in the closet of my old bedroom, would have been the perfect place to store them. If he'd stored them there, they were in all likelihood still there. I doubted he would have seen any reason to take them. The case was dead. He had nothing to worry about.

Until I started asking questions.

I turned off the light in the office and walked into my room. I flipped on the wall switch, but the overhead light didn't turn on. After I flicked it a couple more times for good measure, I pushed out a breath.

Great.

I was already creeped out by the thought of going up into the attic, and now I had to figure out how to do it in the dark. As a little girl, I'd hated that my closet had an opening to the attic. I'd had more than a kid's fair share of insomnia, especially after my sister had suggested that an army of bugs was going to descend from the staircase in the middle of the night and eat me alive in my bed.

I was too freaking old to be scared of the attic. I needed to get ahold of myself.

First, I needed to deal with the lighting situation. I didn't really need the overhead light. I knew where to access the stairs. All I needed was the flashlight on my phone so I could see the pulldown cord. It took me less than three seconds to find the cord and give it a good tug. It budged a little, but the metal hinges felt stiff. I suspected it hadn't been used in years. I gave another hard tug, and the stairs barely missed my head as they fell to the floor.

I put a foot on the first step, testing it to make sure it would hold. My father outweighed me by a good fifty pounds, and he used to climb up and down every year to get my mother's Christmas decorations, but he'd moved them to a storage unit several years ago. I made it up the stairs without more than a few groans from the stairs and then reached for the light switch in the beam of wood at the top. I flipped it on, and two bare lightbulbs in the ceiling lit up, revealing stacks of boxes sitting on pieces of plywood spread over the attic beams. About a third of the attic had plywood flooring. The rest was uncovered insulation.

I stood upright and scanned boxes, trying to figure out where to start.

The space seemed smaller than I remembered, but I hadn't been up here since before Andi's murder. Some of the boxes had been here so long they'd sunk in on themselves.

I went to the end of the plywood floor on the side closest to the stairs. Some boxes had labels written in black marker with my mother's neat handwriting, but some were bare. The top box on the end stack was unlabeled, so I was unprepared for what was inside when I opened it and started riffling through the contents.

It was full of photos and newspaper clippings. I took me a few seconds to realize it was all from my sister's kidnapping. Some of the papers were the local Jackson Creek paper, but quite a few were copies of the *Little Rock Gazette*. It was my first time seeing the articles featuring headlines calling the Jackson Creek Police Chief incompetent.

Even though every part of me wanted to go through this box, it wasn't the reason I was here, so I set it aside and opened the next box, this time finding neatly folded girls' clothing. I knew they weren't mine, because at least half of them were dresses.

These were Andi's clothes.

Tears stung my eyes, and I sank to the floor, bringing the box with me. Why hadn't I considered the possibility that my mother would have kept all of Andi's things? She'd finally turned Andi's old room into a guest room about ten years ago, so putting her things in the attic was the logical next step.

After Malcolm had killed the Sylvester brothers, I'd done a fairly decent job of not thinking about my sister, but with the clippings and photos, and now her clothes...there was no escaping it.

I pulled out a sweater and pressed my nose into the fabric, hoping to catch a whiff of her, but it only smelled musty.

Andi was dead. I wasn't going to find her in a box.

Leaning my head against a support beam, I closed my eyes and clutched the sweater. I was tired, so utterly exhausted. I felt like I'd spent the past five months fighting someone or something, and I was tired to my core.

The doorbell rang and my eyes popped open. Who would be ringing the doorbell at eight at night at my mother's house? Definitely not one of her friends.

Then a terrifying thought hit me. What if the police were at her doorstep to deliver bad news to her next of kin? I went light-headed. Could that actually be happening? I didn't think I could deal with one more horrible thing.

But it might not have anything to do with her at all. It might be James Malcolm tracking me down. I didn't want to answer the door for either possibility, but I was curious none-theless.

There was a small octagonal window in the attic facing the front side of the street, so I got to my feet and walked on the exposed studs, grabbing the rafters to keep my balance as I made my way to it. I didn't see a police car parked at the curb, thank God. In fact, there weren't any cars parked on the street.

Maybe they'd left.

The doorbell rang again. Was a neighbor at the door? Or maybe it was my father, and he'd parked in the driveway. I pulled out my phone, but there were no missed calls or texts from him. If it was him, was he here to check on me or get the contracts?

The doorbell rang a third time, and my theory that it might be my father dissolved away. He had a key, and he knew my mother wasn't home. He would have let himself in.

I walked back over to the ladder, deciding to tell whoever was at the door that my mother wasn't here, but then I heard a man say from inside the house, "Let's make this quick."

My heart skipped a beat. Someone had broken into my parents' house. I hadn't locked the back door, but they were at the front, which was surely locked.

But my mother kept a spare key out there too.

If I'd had my gun, I would have confronted them, but I was weaponless.

What were they after? It seemed too big of a coincidence for it to be a random crime. This was connected to my investigation into Hugo Burton, and possibly my father's ties to him.

The stairs were still down, so I leaned over and grabbed a step and slowly pulled it up. The bottom half started to fold in. My biggest concern was that the stairs had tight springs that sometimes twanged, so I made a silent prayer to any deity listening that I could close them without alerting the home invaders that I was here.

I got it closed without making much sound, but I couldn't hear what they were saying anymore. Their voices had been reduced to a rumble through the ceiling and insulation. The sounds seemed to be coming from Dad's office, so I scooted on the rafters over to that area and squatted, leaning my head down in the hope that I could make out some of their conversation. I heard a few words like *drawer* and *bastard* and some slamming of cabinets and doors. The sounds headed down the hall, toward my parents' room, and there was some door slamming and plenty of cursing.

The noises stopped and then they were in my old bedroom.

Shit.

What if they decided to come up to the attic? But even though the noises were louder—two men from what I could make out—no one tried to tug down the stairs.

The voices moved away, down toward the kitchen, and I sagged against a beam. They obviously hadn't found what they wanted, but the fact that they'd headed straight for my father's office seemed to confirm they'd come here for something Hugo Burton-related. Were they trying to get their hands on the contracts too? How would they even know about them? I'd just learned about them less than an hour ago.

The timing was too close to be coincidental. But how had they found out?

My breath whooshed out.

James Malcolm.

He'd already known my father owned the office building where Hugo had kept his office. He also knew my father had cleaned it out. But did he know my father had been a partner? And that he'd put together those contracts?

Rage rose up inside me. I'd let that man use me, but I wasn't going to let him get away with this.

The back door banged, and I heard voices in the backyard.

The attic didn't have a window overlooking the back, but I wasn't sure I should risk going back downstairs in case they returned to the house.

Fuck this. I needed to see what they were doing, and then I was confronting Malcolm.

I pushed the ladder down and scrambled down the steps. I quickly closed them in case they came back, not wanting to alert them that there was another place to search. Then, staying low, I made my way through the dark house into the kitchen. They must not have turned the lights on during their search, or maybe they'd turned them off afterward so they didn't draw attention from the neighbors.

Once I was in the kitchen, I squatted by the window next to the kitchen table and peered through the slats of the plantation shutters.

The garage door was open. They must have moved their search there.

Goddamn that James Malcolm.

I pulled out my phone and placed a call to his number.

"You call to apologize?" he snapped when he answered.

"Apologize?" I whisper-shouted. "After you sent your goons to break into my parents' house?"

His tone shifted. "What are you talking about?"

"The two men who just went through my father's home office and are now searching the garage."

"I didn't send anyone to search your parents' house."

"Nice try," I said in disgust.

"I'm serious, Harper." He sounded alarmed. "Where are you?"

"In my mother's kitchen watching." I sucked in a breath. "Jesus Christ, now they're headed up to my apartment."

"Stay put. I'm coming."

"You're coming to confront your own men?"

"How many times do I have to tell you it wasn't me?" he grunted. "I didn't send them, but I plan on finding out who did."

"Unless I talk to them first."

"Don't do anything stupid," he snapped.

"You're just worried I'll figure this out before you do." I hung up and watched them go inside my apartment, my anger rising. How fucking dare they violate my private space?

I wanted to confront them, but I suspected they were likely armed, and I wasn't. I glanced at the knife block on the counter. Sure, I could use a knife to threaten them, but anyone with any sense knew you didn't take a knife to a gun fight.

I grabbed the largest one and moved to the back door.

There wasn't much cover in the back. When Andi and I

had been little, we'd had a swing set with a clubhouse at the top, but my mother had gotten it removed shortly after Andi's murder. I sprinted to the open garage door and hid in the shadows to the side of the opening, straining my ears for any sound from above. The floor creaked as they walked around.

I knew I should just let them do their thing and go, but I needed to know who they were working for. Still, my gun was locked up under my bed. I hated to admit it, but finding a way to detain them until Malcolm arrived seemed like my best option.

It didn't mean I was happy about it.

I was still holding my phone, so I turned on the flashlight and started looking for anything I could use to immobilize the door to my apartment. It swung in, not out, so I couldn't just barricade it.

Maybe I could tie the doorknob to the porch railing.

My apartment was small and there wasn't a lot to search, so I didn't have much time. In fact, I was surprised they were still inside. They weren't moving around, which meant they'd either found something that had caught their interest or were coming up with a plan of action. My father didn't have anything stored there, but my laptop was out on the table. It was password protected, and I doubted they could come up with the password. Maybe they were trying anyway.

I found a bundle of nylon rope that looked to be about ten feet long and climbed up the steps as quickly as possible. Setting my phone and the knife on the porch railing, I wrapped one end of the rope around the doorknob multiple times, tied it with multiple knots, and then wrapped the other end around the wooden porch railing multiple times and tied that off too. Just as I finished, the rope grew taut and I heard a male voice on the other side of the door say, "What's wrong?"

"The damn door won't open," another man said.

I grabbed my phone and the knife and backed down a couple of stairs.

There was another hard tug. For a second, I thought the rope on the doorknob was going to slip, but it held firm.

"Why won't it open?" the first guy asked, sounding pissed.

"Dunno, but it ain't gonna stop me from getting out." Several gunshots sounded, and the door seemed to explode, metal pieces flying everywhere.

I scrambled down the stairs toward the garage and hid in the shadows. If the bastards got out, I wanted to see where they went. I shoved my cell phone in my pocket but held the knife, point down, in front of me, ready to defend myself. My heart was racing, and I struggled to breathe evenly.

More gunshots rang out, then there were footfalls on the porch.

"Where the fuck are you?" the second man shouted, and I knew he wasn't talking to his friend.

Shit. Now that detaining them wasn't an option, I'd hoped they would run. But they obviously intended to find me and teach me a lesson.

Footsteps pounded on the steps, and two men came to a stop in the driveway, both holding handguns.

I pressed myself into the darkness as much as I could, praying they didn't see me.

"Come on, Pinky. We need to go before the cops show up."

"Someone locked us in there, Mike," the other man growled. "I'm gonna make them pay."

Pinky grabbed Mike's coat sleeve and tugged. "The neighbors have probably called the police. We need to get out of here."

Mike gave him some resistance, then must have realized the wisdom of his friend's plan, because he let Pinky lead him around the side of the garage to the neighbor's backyard.

I briefly considered going after them, but Malcolm appeared as he rounded my car in the driveway, carrying a shotgun.

"Harper?" he called out.

"In the garage," I said, staying in the shadows. "Don't shoot me."

He lifted his weapon, pointing it toward the ground, and I came out.

"They ran behind the garage," I said. "We have to catch up to them."

"They have guns and you want to give chase with a butcher knife?" he asked in disbelief.

"*You* have a gun."

"And if I shoot them on the street, I'll be charged with murder. No thanks."

"Then I'll go after them." I made a move to the staircase, then wobbled, suddenly feeling light-headed.

"You're not going anywhere," he said, his voice hard. "You're bleeding."

Chapter 24

"What? Where?" He pushed me against the wall and pulled a flashlight out of his pocket, shining it on the front of my shirt. I glanced down and saw the front of my shirt was soaked with blood.

"Were you shot?" he asked, his voice tight.

"I don't think so."

"Can you walk?"

"Don't be ridiculous." But he was already dragging me across the backyard through my mother's back door. He flicked on the switch, flooding the kitchen with light.

He pushed me down on a chair and turned toward the cabinets. "Where are the towels?"

"Use a paper towel. My mother will have a cow if you use one of her dishtowels."

He was opening and closing drawers, and when he found the dishtowel drawer, he surprised me by grabbing a handful of towels and dishrags.

"That seems like overkill." I glanced down at my shirt, slightly alarmed by the amount of blood. The fabric was plastered to my chest and abdomen. But how had I gotten hurt, and why couldn't I feel it?

But I already knew the answer. Adrenaline.

He dumped the towels on the table and found a bowl on the counter. Setting it in the sink, he turned on the faucet. "Are you sure you weren't shot?"

"I already told you. I don't think so."

He knelt in front of me, and before I could process what he was doing, he grabbed both sides of my shirt and ripped it down the front. Some of the buttons popped off and bounced on the ceramic tiles.

I nearly protested, but I understood why he was doing it. Besides, I was wearing a bra, so it wasn't like he was getting a peep show.

"A two-inch-wide piece of metal is sticking out of your chest," he said in confusion. "How did that happen?"

"It must have come from my front door," I said, realization dawning.

"How the fuck did you get hurt by your front door?" he asked, shaking his head.

"I tried to contain them by tying the doorknob to the porch railing. It did the job, because they couldn't get it open, so they shot at the door. I was still on the porch when that happened."

His eyes went wide with concern. "Fuck, Harper. They could have killed you."

"I needed to know who they work for. I had to do *something*."

He rocked back on his heels, staring at my chest, but I knew it wasn't out of lust.

"How bad is it?"

"I don't think it's deep enough to puncture a lung, but it's deep. You'll need stitches. And antibiotics."

I shook my head. "No. I'm not going to the hospital. I'll have to explain what happened, and I don't want to alert the police or the sheriff that I'm on to something."

"And you don't think the police are going to show up after the gunshots?"

"Maybe the neighbors didn't hear them. I'm sure not reporting it."

"You say they searched the house?"

"My father's office and my parents' bedroom, but there's no point in looking. They didn't find anything. I already looked." Not in my parents' room, but my father never would have stored contracts in there. I glanced down, taking note of the metal embedded in my skin. A dull pain was beginning to appear, but I knew it was a precursor of what was about to set in. "Maybe we should just take it out. I told you I'm not going to the hospital, and it has to come out at some point."

"Leave it. I have someone who can take care of it."

I narrowed my eyes. "Who?"

"You'll just have to trust me."

"Trust you?" I asked with a laugh that bordered on hysterical. "I'm still not convinced you didn't send those guys to find my father's paperwork."

His body stilled. "What paperwork?"

"Great way to play dumb."

He looked like he was about to argue with me, but instead he said, "We need to go. You're as white as a sheet and about to pass out."

"I'm not sure I want to go to some dirty backroom somewhere. I'll take care of it myself." I got to my feet and swayed, reaching out for the table with my left hand for balance.

"Jesus Christ," he spat out in disgust. "It's not a dirty backroom. I'm fucking offended." Then, before I could react, he scooped me up in his arms and headed for the back door.

"What are you doing?" I asked, trying to push him away, but my left arm was pinned, and when I raised my right one, sharp pain shot through my upper chest. There it was.

"Don't squirm," he said. "You're making it worse." He

headed out the back door, leaving it open as he made his way to the passenger side of my car.

"The keys are in my purse on the kitchen table."

He went through the back door and came out with my purse, climbing into the driver's seat, then pulling out of the driveway.

"You must really like driving my car," I said, sleepiness overtaking me. "You drive it a lot."

"Maybe you shouldn't put yourself in situations where you can't drive."

"Next time I'll try to stay away from exploding doors."

The hint of smile lifted his lips.

"Where are you taking me?"

He darted a glance to me, then back to the road. "Trust me."

"Trust *you?*" I retorted indignantly. "You keep things from me. You knew my father owned Hugo's office building and didn't tell me."

"I didn't tell you because I knew you might not believe it if it came from me. Better for you to hear it from someone else."

He said it with conviction, and it made sense. I wanted to believe him, which also made me doubt myself.

"Did you know he cleaned out the office before Floyd told us?" I asked.

"No."

"Did you know he drew up the contracts for Hugo? Or that he was an investor?"

He swore under his breath. "*No.*"

"Something has him scared. He didn't want me asking questions." I released a bitter laugh. "I guess we know why." But if they came here and didn't find what they were looking for, they might go to his new house next. Or the law office. "We have to go to my dad's house."

"The fuck we do," he snapped.

"I have to warn him."

"Then send him a text or give him a call, because the only place you're going is to get medical attention."

I leaned my head back in the seat. "I've been calling him since he left. His calls are going straight to voicemail." Anger bubbled up, but I was so tired it didn't have its usual heat. "Why'd you have to come over to the table at the tavern?" I asked, trying to put some force behind the words, but I felt too damn tired. "He was about to tell me things before you scared him."

He didn't respond.

We rode in silence for several seconds as I wondered if I should call my father again and try to warn him, but I couldn't seem to find the energy to reach for my phone... wherever it was in the car.

I was surprised when Malcolm finally spoke. "I'm sure he's okay."

"He's not like you."

"No one's like me," he said, but it didn't have his usual sarcasm.

"He's never been one to get his hands dirty." I swallowed, my mouth feeling dry. "When Andi was kidnapped, he let Mom take charge. He was the mayor. He was used to leading, but when it was really important, he just collapsed."

"People handle different things differently. Sounds like your dad had lived a pretty cushy life until then, so he didn't know how to handle it when the shit hit the fan."

I closed my eyes. "He still doesn't."

"Then he'll learn pretty damn fast or..."

"He'll face the consequences," I finished.

I wasn't sure how I'd handle it if my father was murdered. For all my mother's other flaws, she was a survivor. She'd proven that with Andi. My father and I were the weak ones.

The next thing I knew, the car had stopped, and Malcolm was next to my open car door.

Had I passed out?

I looked out the windshield and saw a small house tucked into trees. "Where are we?"

"Somewhere safe. We'll get you fixed up and then figure out what to do next."

"But my dad…"

"Hale has someone looking for him."

I tried to make sense of that, but it took too much effort.

He started to scoop me out of the car, but I pushed his arm away. "Let me walk."

"The faster we get you medical attention, the better."

Ignoring him, I moved my legs out of the car but when I couldn't pull myself out of the car, his arm slipped around me and hauled me out.

His arm stayed around me as I shuffled my way across the yard to the front door. "Whose house is this?"

"Someone who will help."

The door opened and a woman stood in the opening, silhouetted by the light from inside. "Oh God. Was she shot?" She didn't seem to mind that I was shirtless.

"I think it looks worse than it is," Malcolm said. "She was hit by shrapnel."

"Shrapnel?" She shook her head and took a step back. "Bring her into the kitchen. I'll get some supplies together."

"Who's that?" I asked.

"A friend who will keep this to herself," he said in a tone that made it clear he wouldn't be telling me much else.

I let it drop because putting one step in front of the other required all of my focus.

We walked through the front door and into the warm house. I barely paid attention to the cozy furnishings as Malcolm hauled me through a living room and into a kitchen.

The woman had her back turned to us, washing her hands at the kitchen sink, but she said, "The table's cleaned off. Help her lie down."

Sure enough, a long wooden table was situated at the end

of the kitchen, chairs pulled away and scattered to the side. Nothing was on the table save for a stack of towels. The overhead lights were on, flooding the room with light, but there was also a desk lamp on the end.

The thought of lying down sent a wave of panic through me. "No," I said. "I want to sit up."

The woman whirled around to face us. She was younger than I'd expected. Probably mid to late twenties. Her mouth puckered as she took in the metal sticking out below my collar bone. "Fine, we'll try it your way. For now."

Malcolm led me to a chair closer to the table and helped me ease onto it. When my butt connected with the wooden seat, a fresh wave of pain swept through my body.

The woman walked over with a tray of medical equipment. She set it on the table next to my chair and stared into my face. Surprise filled her eyes.

"What's Harper Adams doing in my kitchen, Skeeter?" she asked in a harsh tone.

Skeeter. Carter had told me that's what people called him back in Fenton County. Was this woman from Fenton County too?

"She's here to get fixed up, Delaney."

Delaney didn't look happy, but she turned her attention to the metal sticking out of my chest. "How'd this happen?"

"Gunshots through a metal door," I said. "I was standing too close."

She lifted her gaze to Malcolm. When he didn't counter my claim, she slowly lifted a hand to my chest. "This might hurt." Her fingers began to prod the area around the shard, and I cried out.

"It's deep," she said, still prodding, "but I don't think it's hit anything critical."

"Why'd it bleed so much?" Malcolm asked.

"Might've nicked a small artery or vein," she said. "But it looks like it's slowed down. Probably gonna start back up when I pull it out." She looked up at him, her face tight. "There's a small chance we'll need to cauterize it."

"How do you plan to do *that*?" I asked, my heart rate spiking.

"Not how I'd prefer," she said, then picked up a handful of gauze. "Skeeter, hold her back in the chair so she doesn't move."

Before I could protest, he was behind my chair, gripping my upper arms and pinning me as Delaney grabbed the shard and yanked it out.

Fire radiated from my collar bone and spread out, making me see dots. I released a long string of curses under my breath.

Delaney quickly placed the gauze on my wound and pressed hard to stop the bleeding. The pain stole my breath, and my instinct was to shove her away. But Malcolm held me firmly, even as black dots in my vision seemed to grow larger and my peripheral vision faded. I was on the verge of passing out, but I couldn't let that happen. I needed to know everything that happened in this room.

"You're still conscious," Delaney said with a smirk. "That's a good sign."

I wanted to tell her to get the hell away from me, but I also wanted her to fix this. Still, I had to wonder if it was a good idea letting someone who obviously didn't want me here have my life in her hands.

After she'd applied pressure for nearly a minute, she removed the gauze and examined the wound. "It's pretty damn deep, but I think she'll be okay." She grabbed some fresh gauze and pressed it to my chest. "Obviously, she's gonna need stitches." She looked over my head at Malcolm. "Put on some gloves and keep pressure on her wound while I get the lidocaine."

He let go of my arms and took the gloves she held out with her free hand. He quickly slipped them on, then took over pressing as she reached for a needle attached to a syringe and a small bottle.

Malcolm squatted in front of me, giving me a blank look. "Did you see the guys who broke in?"

"Not that closely."

"Define not that closely."

"I saw figures and shapes. They were wearing dark clothes. I didn't see faces."

His eyebrow cocked, and it was apparent he didn't believe me. That was fair since I'd heard names and had chosen not to share the information. He may have shown up to help me, but I didn't trust him. Not after he'd withheld his knowledge that my father owned Hugo's office building.

Even though a small part of me whispered that he'd been right to let me find out on my own. I never would have believed him without proof.

Delaney turned toward me and made a face. "She's lookin' a little pale from the blood loss," she said as she pushed Malcolm to the side and took the gauze, starting to swipe the skin around the cut with a soaked betadine swab. "Skeeter, get her a bottle of water out of the fridge in the garage."

He shot her a look that suggested he didn't appreciate her request, but he strode to a door on the other side of the room. She finished swabbing and waved her hand over my chest to help it dry.

As soon as the door closed, she didn't waste time. "What are you doin' hanging out with Skeeter Malcolm?"

"Why is it that James Malcolm has someone who does emergency medical procedures on the sly?" I shot back. "I thought he was supposed to be clean?"

She grabbed the syringe and jammed the needle into the skin next to the jagged cut.

I jumped with pain from the stabbing and the burning sensation. I was starting to rethink having her stitch me up.

"Maybe you should let me ask the questions," Delaney

snapped, moving the needle to a new location and injecting more medication. "So how do you know him?"

I nearly jumped out of my seat. If she was a doctor, she'd either missed taking the Hippocratic Oath or chosen to flat out ignore it.

"Maybe you should ask *him* instead of me," I said through gritted teeth.

"Oh, I plan to. Don't you worry."

The door opened and Malcolm came back with a few bottles, unscrewing one as he walked over to us. He handed it to me, and I grabbed it with my good hand and took a long, greedy gulp, not realizing how thirsty I'd been until the cold water hit my lips.

"You're movin' around too much," the woman grunted in disgust before jabbing me again.

"You need to be so rough, Laney?" he asked after she gave me yet another jab.

"Just trying to numb her so I can stitch her up," she said in a snide tone.

"The way you're stabbing her, you might as well stitch her without lidocaine."

"Trust me, I considered it."

"Delaney, *a word*," he said, making it clear it was an order and not a request.

She tossed the needle onto the tray with enough force that it was clear she was pissed. But she followed him into the garage, holding her gloved hands upright so they didn't touch anything.

I still didn't trust her, which meant I'd need to get my hands on my own antibiotics tomorrow.

I could hear them arguing in the garage, and I was tempted to walk out the front door and leave Malcolm with her. He'd taken my car, so I wouldn't be stealing his. But a glance down at my wound made it clear I couldn't go home and fix this with steri strips. If I left, I'd have to go to the

ER, and I didn't want to be asked questions I couldn't answer.

So I stayed, my ears straining to make out what they were arguing about, but failing.

A few seconds later, they walked back in. Delaney's face was red with anger, and it was obvious she hadn't been appeased by their discussion. But when she opened a package with the sutures, she seemed to do it with more care.

She prodded the skin around the cut. "Do you feel this?"

"Just pressure," I said. "No pain."

She nodded and picked up the needle and thread and a pair of forceps. "You're gonna have a scar," she said as she inserted the needle into my skin. "I know how to suture, but I'm not a plastic surgeon."

Did that mean she didn't usually suture people? But who had suture kits lying around their house?

None of us talked while she worked on my chest, then covered it with a bandage.

When she finished, she ripped off her gloves and tossed them into the plastic suture tray. "My debt is paid, Malcolm. Don't come to me again."

He didn't agree or disagree.

I took a swig from my water, finishing it off. I wanted to get out of here.

"Keep your sutures clean and dry. They'll be ready to come out in a week." She shot Malcolm a dark look. "I won't be the one removing them."

"Thank you," I said, getting up, but a wave of dizziness nearly made me fall over. I grabbed the back of the chair.

She picked up the tray and carried it to her trash can. "You lost a lot of blood," she said, keeping her back to me. "Be sure to keep drinking water."

I'd already thanked her, so I limped to the front door, gasping when the cold night air hit my bare stomach and chest. Malcolm didn't follow me out, so I walked around the back of the car, headed toward the driver's door. I only hoped he'd left the keys in the car.

I reached for the car door as Malcolm called out, "You gonna drive in nothing but your bra?"

"I'm also wearing jeans. And besides, I rode here this way. I can ride home this way." I pulled on the door handle, and it wouldn't open. Dammit. Once again, I hadn't thought something through. He had the keys, and the door was locked.

He descended the steps toward the car. "You really think going home is a good idea? You want to stay in the place you just got shot at?"

"They shot at the door, not me, and I sincerely doubt they'll come back."

He walked up next to me. "The door to your apartment is ruined."

"Then I'll stay in my mom's house. She's not there, so she won't know."

Malcolm pulled my keys out of his pocket. "I'm driving. You lost a lot of blood, and I don't want you passing out and killing us both after I went to all that trouble to get you stitched up."

I wanted to argue with him, but I had to admit passing out was a possibility. I walked around the front of the car to the passenger door. The car beeped as Malcolm unlocked it. I grabbed the handle and pulled the door open, feeling a tug and a sharp pain. I stopped and let the pain pass before I got into the car.

We were silent for the first few minutes of the drive. The numbing medication was still working, but there was a deeper ache in my chest. I again wondered why Malcolm had Delaney in his back pocket. People involved in organized crime often had their own doctors to patch up injuries that would draw too many questions in an ER.

Was this proof he was up to no good here? Maybe he hadn't left his life of crime behind after all. Then again, I supposed I already had plenty of evidence of that. Murdering two men in cold blood was about as criminal as you could get.

"So do you have Delaney on speed dial or did you have to search up her contact info?" I asked sarcastically.

He was slow to answer, but then he glanced at me with a grin. "Jealous?"

"Jealous?" I asked with a laugh. "Hardly. I'm trying to find out how deep you are in criminal activity and if it's too late to cut ties with you."

He laughed. "Sorry to disappoint. Delaney's a customer at the tavern, and she owed me a favor. That's all."

Maybe that was true, but I suspected it wasn't a legal favor.

He pulled into the driveway of my parents' home. The door to my apartment was gaping open.

"I need to get the doorway to my apartment boarded up until I can get the door replaced," I said as Malcolm turned off the engine.

"Deal with it tomorrow." He opened his door and got out.

I opened my car door, and to my surprise, Malcolm appeared at the opening and offered a hand to help me out. I almost refused, but I was exhausted and sore, and I decided it wouldn't be the worst thing to accept his help.

I took his hand with my left hand, feeling the rough calluses on his palm. He easily pulled me up, then released my hand. After he shut the door, he stayed by my side as we walked to the back door.

After he opened the door, I was greeted with the bloody mess we'd left on the kitchen table. My stomach sank at the sight.

"Clean it tomorrow," Malcolm said gruffly. "You need to go to bed."

"Good idea," I said. "We'll talk about what to do next in the morning."

He nodded but didn't make any move to leave.

I nodded toward the back door. "This is your cue to go."

He chuckled. "I'm not going anywhere. While it's doubtful those men will return, I plan to be here if they do."

"Why?" I asked skeptically. "I don't mean shit to you."

"Because we haven't found out who murdered Hugo Burton, and I can't let you get murdered until after I have the answers I need."

"For the questions you refuse to share with me," I said bluntly.

"You have your agenda, I have mine. Neither one of us has ever made a secret of that."

"Just like last time," I said. "Tell me, will anyone end up dead this time?" As soon as the words left my mouth, I regretted them. With Ava Peterman's kidnapping, his agenda hadn't been to kill anyone. He'd wanted to stop Todd Peterman from blackmailing him.

Beating up John Michael Stevens had been a bonus. Killing the Sylvester brothers had been part vengeance, part cleanup.

"Go to bed, Detective," he said, exhaustion creeping into his voice. "I'll sleep on the sofa."

I opened my mouth to protest, but something in his voice stopped me. It made me see him not as the hardened crime boss he'd been purported to be, nor the no-nonsense bar owner I'd gotten to know. No, the exhaustion in his voice and the flat light in his eyes was something I saw every day in myself, defeated by life and plodding through.

Funny, how I'd never given a single thought to the fact this man had given up his entire life to come here. As far as I knew, the only person he brought with him was his attorney. Not friends or family. He'd named the tavern after his brother but left him behind in Fenton County. Was he lonely too?

Maybe the blood loss had gone to my head, making me soft. "Do whatever you want," I said, turning my back to him and shuffling out of the kitchen. "You seem to do it anyway."

As I walked into the dining room, my mother's sideboard caught my eye. I saw a couple of wine bottles she must have bought for some upcoming dinner she hadn't told me about but would probably require me to attend. My mouth watered and my fingers itched to grab one. The need for a drink hit me full force, and I didn't have the will power to deny it. Why would I? I'd had a hell of a day, and I was on edge. A drink would help me settle down and go to sleep.

I grabbed one of the bottles, relieved to see it was a screw top, then saw Malcolm standing in the doorway, watching.

"I really don't need a lecture right now," I snapped.

He lifted his hands in surrender. "No lecture. Now doesn't seem like the best time to give up alcohol."

"I'm not an alcoholic," I said, turning my back to him and heading to my room.

"Just don't get so shitfaced you can't work tomorrow. And take some water with you. You're already dehydrated. The alcohol's only gonna make it worse." He disappeared into the kitchen, and I continued on to my room.

I turned on the lamp on the bedside table and sat on the bed. Opening the bottle, I took a long pull. The liquid slipped down my throat, appeasing my thirst, but I knew Malcolm was right. I needed water too.

I kicked off my shoes, nearly collapsing right then and there. But I knew I'd be uncomfortable sleeping in my jeans, so I took off my pants and started to crawl into bed in my bra and panties. I caught glimpses of the blood on my chest and stomach, but didn't care, I'd clean myself up tomorrow.

I was just starting to pull up the covers when Malcolm pushed open the door and walked into the room, holding a tall glass of water and a shorter glass.

"Ever hear of knocking?" I asked, but I couldn't muster up the heat I'd meant to put behind it.

"I knew you'd tell me to go fuck myself, and I'm too tired for that game. We'll save it for tomorrow." He handed me the water and I took it. Even though part of me wanted to throw it in his face, I knew my anger was irrational. I needed the water, so I drank it. He picked up the wine bottle, not looking surprised that it was already open, and began to pour it into the juice glass.

I nearly called him on it, but part of me was grateful. If I didn't fall asleep within a few minutes of getting into bed, there was a risk of me drinking the whole thing. I hated that I'd admitted my drinking needed to be policed, but in this instance, I decided it was okay. I needed to be as alert as possible in the morning.

After I drank half the glass of water, I set it on the night-stand, and to my surprise, Malcolm held out the half-full juice glass to me.

I took it, looking up at him. "Do you ever get tired of it all?"

Surprise flickered in his eyes, and he cleared his throat. "You've been through a lot today. You need to go to sleep."

I took a long sip. "I'm slipping," I said, then to my frustration, my eyes began to sting. "Investigating. I used to be good."

He took the juice glass from my hands, then said more softly than I'd expected, "You found Hugo Burton's body when no one else has in five years. That doesn't sound like slipping to me."

"But—"

"Stop," he grunted. "You need sleep. We'll start fresh tomorrow."

He walked out, shutting the door but leaving it cracked. I closed my eyes, feeling the tears well behind my eyelids but refusing to shed them.

I was a mess. Did I have any business letting people trust my investigative skills? But Malcolm was right. I'd found Hugo's body. That had to count for something.

I finished off the wine in three gulps, then followed it with a long drink of water before I turned off the lamp. As I lay in the dark, I realized he'd never answered my question—did he ever get tired of it all. But I could still see the pain in his eyes, the way the muscles of his face had sagged just a little.

And I knew we were more alike than either of us would ever admit. He was tired of it too.

Chapter 25

My head was pounding when I woke up, but for once it wasn't because of a hangover. As I roused, the smell of coffee filled my nose, making a promise I planned to accept.

The area over my collar bone throbbed, but I didn't feel any sharp pain. I sat up and let my head adjust to the wave of dizziness that washed through me. Once it settled, I reached for what was left of my water. I'd drank nearly the entire glass, plus the water bottle at Delaney's, and I didn't feel an overwhelming urge to pee. I'd obviously been dehydrated.

It felt like every muscle in my body ached, proving I was out of shape. Then again, how did one train to dig graves?

I didn't have any clothes in my old closet, so I left my room and walked over to my parents' room, deciding it didn't matter if Malcolm saw me. I was wearing more than some women wore to public swimming pools.

I found another track suit of my mother's—deep purple velour. I tugged on the pants as best I could with one hand after realizing the hard way that I shouldn't be making any abrupt movements with my right hand. Then I slid on the jacket and zipped it shut, the movement tugging at my stitches. I was sure I looked like shit, but I headed toward the kitchen to face Malcolm and the bloody aftermath of last night.

Except it didn't look like I'd imagined at all. When I walked in, it was clean and Malcolm was sitting at the kitchen table in front of an open laptop and a coffee cup, the picture of domestication. His legs were extended under the table, his ankles crossed, and his hair was slightly rumpled like he hadn't bothered to straighten it after he woke up. It looked a hell of a lot sexier than my bedhead probably did.

No. James Malcolm is not sexy.

But I'd have to be an idiot not to recognize that a lot of women probably *did* find him sexy. I just wasn't one of them.

He looked up when I walked and gave me his trademark assessment, only it didn't seem as harsh as usual. "You'll live."

"If you call hurting over every square inch of my body living," I muttered. "But I guess it's what I should expect after getting stabbed by part of my front door and digging up a body. Full day, yesterday." I shuffled to the coffee maker, then reached for the cabinet above it with my left arm to grab a mug. "I see you found my mother's coffee maker."

"It's hard to miss on top of the kitchen counter."

"What happened to the mess?"

"I cleaned it up."

I turned to glance at him, lifting my brow. "You? You don't seem like the kind of guy who'd clean up messes that aren't your own. And I suspect you have people to clean up your messes for you."

He crossed his arms over his chest. "Do you want me to send you a bill or is there a point to this?"

I poured my coffee into the mug and then set the pot back on the heating element. "Sorry. Just making an observation. What are you doing?"

"Nothing to do with this case," he said, turning back to his laptop and tapping some keys. "Tavern-related bookkeeping."

I wasn't sure I believed him, but I wasn't going to call him on it. I was still thrown that he'd cleaned up my blood. Why had he done it?

"I've been thinking about the men who broke in last night," he asked as he picked up the coffee cup next to him. "We're presuming they were after your father's contracts, but could they have been after something else? This seems like a lot of trouble just for contracts."

"I've seen people do worse things for a lot less than a stack of contracts," I said as I grabbed creamer from the fridge and poured it into my mug. I was really missing my espresso machine right about now and considered wading through the debris of my apartment door to use it. "Besides, what else could it be? I keep case notes on my laptop and it's password protected. But it was on the kitchen table in my apartment."

"Your purse was still on the kitchen table, and I checked your wallet after you went to bed. There's cash in it, so simple robbery wasn't the motivation. I take it you haven't gotten in contact with your father?"

I felt guilty that I hadn't even tried again since my attempt the previous night. It made sense that they would have targeted his new place next. "No. I should check my phone to see if he texted or called back." But the phone was in my jeans pocket, and I really didn't feel like walking back to my old bedroom yet. At least not until I drank the rest of this coffee.

"We need to plan our next steps," Malcolm said.

"I have to find out what my father cleared out of Hugo's office. I was checking the attic to see if he'd stored Hugo's things up there when those men broke in last night."

"Find anything?"

"No," I said carefully. "But I'd barely gotten started before I was interrupted."

"I'll head up and look after I finish my coffee."

"*We'll* head up after we both finish our coffee," I corrected.

He shot me a look of disapproval. "You have no business climbing up into the attic."

"If you think I'm going to let you go up there and search my family's things without me, you obviously don't know me very well."

"Fine," he grunted. "But no lifting anything, or you'll bust your stitches."

"Careful, Malcolm, or I'll start to think you care about my well-being," I half-teased.

He snorted. "I already told you. We need each other to work this case."

"Seems to me that I might not need you as much as you need me. Sure, you provided the Jeep to tour Hugo's land, but I've supplied all the other information."

His face screwed up. "What the hell are you talking about? I got Burton's office address. I knew your father owned the building."

"I could have gotten that on my own," I countered. "Hale just beat me to it."

He gave me a deadpan look. "Are you saying you want to do this on your own?"

Was I saying that?

Something had changed the night before. I hadn't expected him to care so much about my well-being, and while we could play this game that we needed each other for our resources, I knew it had been more than that. I was used to taking care of myself, but I'd *needed* him, and it made me feel vulnerable. But I also saw concern in his eyes and the way he'd taken care of me. I was used to being on my own, and I was already starting to rely on him. That was a dangerous game.

Especially when I couldn't trust him.

Sure, I was grateful he'd taken me to see Delaney, but I still didn't trust him. I'd bet good money he didn't trust me either. Still…

"No. We should continue to pool our resources."

He held my gaze for a moment, and I was pretty sure he was adding the same silent caveat that was running through my head.

For now.

I leaned my backside against the counter. "Before we go up in the attic, I need to see what kind of damage is inside my apartment and see if my laptop's still there. I also have to find a handyman to replace my door."

"I've already got someone coming to fix it," he said, turning back to his computer and picking up his coffee mug.

I stared at him, my mouth dropping open, but I quickly closed it. "While that's super convenient, I'm afraid I need to turn down your offer of help."

"It's not an offer of help," he said, his gaze still on his screen. He started to tap on his keyboard again. "If we can find Hugo Burton's murderer, call it payment."

"Why are you so interested in Hugo Burton that you're willing to pay me for it? What did this person you're after actually do?"

He set down his mug and turned to face me again. "We've both admitted multiple times that we have our own reasons for wanting to find out the truth about Hugo Burton. Your goal is to find his murderer and bring them to justice. I have my own motivations. We both bring our own resources into this endeavor, and I plan to reward you for your help." He tilted his head to the window. "Like fixing your door."

"So you mean you've hired me."

Aggravation covered his face. "That's not what I said. That's what you're choosing to believe."

He was right, and while I knew I should kick him out, I needed him more than I'd like to acknowledge. Especially since I was hurt.

Instead of answering, I downed a couple of ibuprofen

tablets with my coffee, then walked out the back door to check out my apartment and change.

In the light of day, it was obvious my door wasn't the only thing that needed to be replaced. The railing around the porch was splintered. The intruders had been using a high-powered handgun with ammunition that wasn't meant to just wound. For a moment, I let myself consider what would have happened if they'd found me in my parents' house or had managed to shoot me on their way out of my apartment.

I could be dead right now, and it would have been because of my own sloppiness.

After I climbed the stairs, I got a good look at the damage. The door was shut, but there were multiple large holes close to the doorknob.

Stepping around debris on the porch, I pushed the door in and surveyed the room. I expected it to be trashed, but everything looked in place except for a few pieces of the door on the floor inside. My laptop was missing. I wasn't surprised, but it seemed to confirm they were looking for something related to Hugo's death. They were going to be sorely disappointed, because there was no way in hell they'd ever crack my password. But now I'd need a new laptop. Great. There went a portion of the five thousand dollars I'd been saving for my practice.

The first thing I did was brush my teeth while I started my espresso machine and made a latte. I rinsed my mouth out multiple times before I took a sip, sighing with satisfaction. Taking my cup with me, I went into the bathroom and stripped, staring at my bloodstained, bandaged body in the mirror. I was lucky. I could be dead right now.

Days ago, I would have been okay with that, but today...

Today, I was grateful to be alive. Something had changed. Maybe finding myself at death's door and surviving had given me this newfound desire to stay alive.

But I'd also be lying if I refused to believe it had something to with James Malcolm. If he considered me worth saving, maybe I was.

After washing off the blood with soap and water using a washrag, I patted my skin dry and then wrapped a towel around my body so I could grab some of my own clothes to wear. I half expected Malcolm to be in my apartment, waiting for me to come out, but the room was empty.

After grabbing clean undergarments, a pair of slacks, and a button-up shirt, I changed in the bathroom and brushed my hair with my good arm. I planned to pull it back into a low ponytail, but the stitches in my chest strained when I lifted my arm, sending a fresh round of throbbing through my upper body. I'd have to leave it down, because I sure wasn't asking Malcolm to pull it back for me.

After putting on a pair of flats, I made a fresh latte for myself and a macchiato for Malcolm, then headed back to the main house.

I half expected him to be in the attic searching without me, but he was still at the table in front of his laptop, an open spreadsheet in front of him.

I set the macchiato down next to him.

He glanced down at the cup, then back up at me. "Is it poisoned?"

I released a genuine laugh. "So suspicious." I set my cup down and took a sip from his drink, watching him over the rim, before lowering it and grabbing my own again. "We need a plan for the day. We started discussing it before we got side-tracked."

He picked up his mug, lifted it under his nose, and then drank. "Obviously, checking the attic is priority."

"I've been thinking about that." I sat in the chair next to him. "As paranoid as my father acted last night, if he had anything up there, I feel like he would have come home to make sure it was still there."

"You don't think he did?"

"No, because I left soon after he did. I went to his house, but he wasn't there, so I came straight back here. I suppose he would have had enough time to check, but I don't think he did. The attic staircase was sticky, like it hadn't been opened in a while."

"So you don't want to go up to the attic?"

"I still do, but I guess I'm saying we should temper our expectations."

He took another sip of his drink. "I take it you have a plan for afterward?"

"I need to talk to my father. He should be at work. He won't be able to run from me at the office. At least, not without drawing suspicion, and my father has always preferred to fly under the radar."

"Even when he was mayor?" Malcolm asked in surprise.

I leaned back in my chair as I considered his question. I hadn't really given much thought to my father's job back then. He'd been the mayor for twelve years at the time of Andi's kidnapping—almost my entire life back then, so I hadn't known him any other way. He was mayor for a couple of years after her death, but his heart hadn't been in it. "My father is an affable man. People like him. He's not full of swagger and arrogance. He has a quiet authority...or at least that's how I remembered him as mayor. But I was a kid." I shrugged. "So my recollection is probably skewed."

He sat in silence for a moment. "Okay. That works."

"But you can't come with me." I felt like I was stating the obvious, especially given the way my father had run scared from Malcolm last night, but it had to be done. "I know part of the reason you're sticking with me is to make sure I don't keep anything from you, so you're going to have to trust me on this."

He gave me a smirk. "Trust that you'll tell me sensitive information regarding your father that could get him in trouble?"

"I get your point, but you can't come in and I'm not wearing a wire or carrying my phone in on mute. You'll just have to trust that I'll tell you anything I think you need to know."

His jaw clenched.

"Look," I said, holding out the cup in my hand in a beseeching manner. "You're holding shit back from me, supposedly telling me what I need to know. This is no different."

He took another sip of his macchiato, then set the mug on the table as he got to his feet. "I guess we'd better get started on the attic."

Chapter 26

The attic quickly proved to be a bust. I supposed that I should have been more embarrassed that Malcolm was riffling through forty-plus years of junk my parents had accumulated, but I didn't have the energy. When he made a move toward the stack of Andi's things, I told him I'd already gone through them the night before. I was fairly certain he saw Andi's name written in black marker on the side, because he let it go without a fuss.

Going down the ladder was harder than going up, but Malcolm stood at the bottom, patiently waiting, as though ready to catch me if I fell. Once we were both down, he folded the stairs back up and then we grabbed our things and headed out the back door.

"Where's your car?" I asked as he headed for the driver's side of my car.

"Hale had someone pick it up," he said as we both got in.

"How'd you get here so quickly last night?"

"I was already in town."

"Doing what?" I asked skeptically.

"Nothing that interests you," he said as he started the car, but it didn't have his usual edge.

We were silent as he drove toward my father's law office. Funny, I technically worked there too, but I didn't consider it mine. I couldn't wait to tender my resignation. I'd do it as soon as I closed this case. I'd only taken the job because I was desperate for money, and while I had no guarantee I would make enough money to keep myself afloat, if I worked one more hour in that file room, I was going to drink myself into oblivion. I'd figure out a way to make it work, and if things got dire, I'd take Carter Hale up on his offer to toss me some work.

As though realizing the optics of him pulling into the parking lot and dropping me off, Malcolm stopped at the curb half a block away. "Text me when you're done."

I gave him a questioning look. "No coaching on what to ask?"

His grin was more of a smirk. "If you need me to coach you on this, then you're not as good as I thought you were."

I got out, letting his compliment hang in the air. While he'd said he needed me, he'd never told me that he considered me to be a good investigator. Was it a ruse to get me to play nicely, or had he meant it? With Malcolm, there was no way of knowing for sure. Any niceties should be taken with a healthy measure of distrust.

When I walked into the office and headed to the back, Becky was one of the first people who noticed me. She shot me a glare so dark I almost needed a flashlight but remained silent as I made my way toward the hall leading to the partners' offices.

I passed Mitch's open door, and he caught a glimpse of me as I walked by

"Harper!" he called out, and since I was still in front of the doorway, I stopped. "How's the investigation going?"

"It's going well," I said, refusing to elaborate.

"Anything to report yet?" he asked, anticipation on his face.

"Nope. But I'm making progress and I'm hoping to have something soon."

His eyes lit up. "You found his secret bank accounts." His enthusiasm was greater than I would have expected, but then it occurred to me that while I was playing P.I. for him at my filing clerk salary, he probably took Clarice as a client so he could get a percentage of any money I found, including the life insurance policy if I proved Hugo was dead. It wasn't surprising, yet I was still disgusted by the possibility. I told myself that maybe he'd planned on giving me a bonus, but I knew better.

Mitch Morgan had always been a greedy man. Whether it was money, women, or attention.

I left his office and headed down the hall to my father's. The door was only open a crack. I studied his name on the plaque attached to the heavy wood.

Paul Adams

Attorney at Law

I'd visited his office more times than I could remember when I was a kid, and I'd always viewed his name plate with a certain awe and respect, but now I felt like my father wasn't the man I'd thought him to be. To be fair, he didn't know me all that well either.

I knocked on the door with my left hand but didn't wait for him to answer. I pushed it open and found him sitting behind his desk. His white dress shirt and blue tie were neat and pressed, but dark circles underscored his eyes. He looked older than he had the night before, when I'd meet him at the tavern.

I couldn't help the twinge of guilt that crept in. I'd done this. I'd given him a sleepless night and filled him with anxiety by dredging up the past again.

Maybe he regretted persuading me to come back to town. I'd done nothing but bring up memories he'd rather forget.

"Harper," he half-whispered when he saw me. "I owe you an apology."

I walked in and shut the door, the soft click filling the room. I used to love hearing that sound when I was a kid, because it had felt like a privilege to come here with Andi— for us to take part in our father's separate world that excluded our mother. But now it sounded ominous.

I didn't say a word as I lowered into one of the chairs in front of his desk, trying to hide a grimace from the pain that shot through my collarbone. Once I was seated, I studied him, not as my father but as someone who knew more than he should about a missing man who'd been murdered and then hidden in a shallow grave.

"I suppose you're here to finish asking your questions," he said softly. He placed his hands on his desk and then flinched, as though realizing the pose looked too formal, and put them back in his lap. A slight sheen from the sweat on his palms remained on the wood.

Still, I didn't say anything.

He drew a deep breath and closed his eyes, his chin quavering.

My father was about to cry.

The last time I'd seen him cry was when Chief Larson had shown up at our front door to tell us they'd found Andi's broken body. Dad had sobbed and sobbed and sobbed until there was nothing left. He hadn't cried at the funeral or any time after that I'd seen. It was like he'd climbed into his well of emotions and bled it dry, and when he'd emerged, he'd left part of his soul behind with his dead daughter, and what was left was too miniscule to be shared. I wasn't the only one he'd abandoned. He'd abandoned the fun-loving father I'd known, leaving behind a shell that had continued plodding through life.

And now, that same man looked like he was about to break down in tears.

My heart froze. Oh. God.

"What did you do?" I asked quietly, my mind racing with what I was going to do if he confessed to murder.

"I got involved with some not-so-great people, Harper," he said, his eyes shiny.

I took a moment to wrap my head around that. "Okay," I finally said. "Are you still involved with them?"

He shook his head. "No, and what I did…"

"What did you do, Dad?"

He swallowed, looking terrified, and then said, "I worked on some projects for a man who turned out to be a criminal, but I didn't know it at the time. He held it over my head."

Criminal? Was he talking about James Malcolm?

Oh. God.

Was that why Malcolm was so interested in this case?

Had he been using me to get evidence on my father?

"It started after you left for college," he continued, looking ten years older. "Some simple sales and lease contracts, and honestly, I was flattered."

If he was talking about Malcolm, I was having trouble making the pieces fit. Why would Malcolm have hired my father over a decade ago, when he was embroiled in his own messes in Fenton County?

My father took a breath, then made an apologetic face. "He was a well-respected businessman, by everyone in the state. His father had been a senator, for God's sake. I had no reason to guess what he was doing was illegal."

"Who are you talking about, Dad?"

"J.R. Simmons."

My brow shot up. I remembered news coming to light that one of the most influential men in the state had been arrested for multiple crimes, including murder, but then the headlines had petered out because he'd escaped police custody and then died in an explosion in Fenton County.

Fenton County.

My blood ran cold.

When I'd researched Malcolm weeks ago, I'd concentrated my search on his ties to the international crime syndicate. But I'd seen articles tying him to Simmons the year before.

Was this why Malcolm was interested in Hugo Burton's murder?

"What did you do for Simmons?"

"I told you. Contracts and such."

"Supposedly J.R. Simmons had his hands in things all over the state. Did you do business for him in Lone County or all over?"

He looked down at his desk, the sweat marks now appearing as greasy spots. "Southeast Arkansas."

I shook my head. "The man lived in El Dorado. Why would he hire an attorney sixty miles away in a podunk town?" I asked in disbelief, then added, "No disrespect to your skills or reputation."

A sheepish look filled his eyes. "I wondered that too, but he charmed me, and I fell for it hook, line, and sinker." He shook his head. "I'm a fool, Harper." His gaze lifted to mine. "I should have known not to move forward when he told me our work together had to happen outside of my law office. That it was between us."

"*Oh, Dad.*"

"Nothing I did was illegal. At least not in the beginning. Simple contracts. I rarely even saw the man. We talked on the phone and used email."

"When did it change?" I asked, terrified to hear his answer.

"With Hugo Burton."

My stomach churned and I swallowed the bile rising in my throat. "Tell me everything."

His chin quivered again. "J.R. was paying me good money to draw up his property contracts, so I had money to invest. I knew Hugo through mutual friends, and he told a small group of people at a party about Sunny Point. He hadn't done anything with it yet. He'd just bought the land. It was still in the first phase, with the executive lots. The second phase wasn't announced until a few years later." He drew a breath. "Anyway, he said he was looking for investors, and I was flush with money, so the next day we went out to lunch, and he showed me his business plan and his forecasts for net worth." He put his hands on the desk again, his thumb absently picking at the skin of his finger. "I'm not a stupid man, Harper. It all looked legit."

"No, Dad, you're not a stupid man." Maybe that was why I was so upset he'd gotten involved in this. He should have been smarter.

He nodded, looking grateful for my acknowledgment, then swallowed hard. "My mistake was in telling J.R. I'd drawn up the contracts for the investors. I knew Hugo needed more capital, so I mentioned it to J.R., who asked me to set up a meeting."

"Did Simmons invest?"

He shook his head. "I have no idea. If he did, I didn't see the contract. And I didn't ask questions. J.R. and I didn't have that kind of relationship. But I brought it up with Hugo later. While he acknowledged JR had contacted him, he seemed reluctant to tell me more so I let it drop."

"Did you make a boilerplate contract for Hugo to use? Or did people have different terms?"

"He used the same contract for almost everyone. I gave him the template with spaces to fill in with names and addresses and the amount invested. He changed the terms for a couple of people and had me look over the alterations. Otherwise, he handled the contracts himself."

"That's unusual, isn't it?" I asked.

"It depends." He made a face. "Smaller operations will use a boilerplate template for the first phase. But he kept hitting setbacks and then he purchased the second property, which made him cash-poor and land-rich. While it would have been in everyone's best interest for him to have an attorney look over every contract, he simply couldn't afford it. He asked me, of course, but I told him it would be imprudent for me to help him with the other contracts since I was an investor." Guilt filled his eyes.

"But you did it anyway."

He paled. "I did, because I'd invested money, and I needed it to all come through. But I was beginning to have doubts. He started suggesting I look at contracts pro bono, so I told him to find someone else." His mouth twisted to one side. "I've always wondered if that was a mistake."

"Did he provide you with a yearly update? Anything official?"

He hesitated. "At first, yes. It was all on the up and up, but he took hit after hit, and the reports weren't good..." He paused. "He stopped sending them, and I stopped asking. He always looked so defeated."

"Did you know who the other investors were?"

"I knew of some, but there might have been others."

"Who do you remember?"

"Brett Colter. Skip Martin. Billy O'Murphy. Tim Heaton. And some guy I didn't know much about. Pete something."

"Pete Mooney."

He made a face. "Yeah. That could be him."

"Did the others know about you?"

He shook his head. "My one request was that I have anonymity. It would be unseemly if it got out that his own attorney had invested in his projects."

"Not to mention you were keeping the contract work from your partners."

He made a face. "Yeah."

"Do you know if the other investors were unhappy?"

"I didn't talk to them outright, but rumors got around."

"Were any of them upset enough to kill Hugo?"

His eyes widened. "I don't know," he said in a whisper.

"And J.R. Simmons, you're not sure if he invested?"

"If he did, I never saw his contract, and neither he nor Hugo mentioned it."

"How soon into the project did you mention it to Simmons?"

Dad shifted in his chair. "I'm not sure. I'm guessing a year into the project."

"And who'd invested at that point?"

"Just me and Brett. And Bill O'Murphy."

"Did Hugo seem concerned about getting more investors at that point?"

"No, but Tim and Skip joined shortly after that. Oh, and that Pete guy. He got special terms."

That caught my attention, especially since Mooney had been murdered. "What kind of special terms?"

Dad shifted in his seat again. "I'm not sure exactly. I never saw Mooney's contract, but Hugo told me Brett was pissed Hugo had brought in an outsider and given him a better deal." He shrugged. "Maybe he was just pissed there was another person to get a split of the profits."

"So you told Simmons about the investment, but you're not sure whether he invested," I said. "Do you know if Simmons was behind an LLC called Larkspur Limited?"

He gave me a stunned look. "What?"

"After Hugo disappeared and the land foreclosed, it was purchased by a company called Larkspur Limited, but I don't know who's behind it."

He shook his head, confusion in his eyes. "I don't know anything about Larkspur Limited."

"Are you sure?"

Irritation replaced his previous stoicism. "Yes, Harper. I'm positive."

"I had to ask, Dad."

Defeat quickly melted his steely posture. "I know."

"You said you regretted introducing Hugo to J.R. Simmons. Why?"

"When news broke that Hugo went missing, J.R. called me. He knew Hugo had been renting an office from me, and he wanted access to it."

"When news broke?" I asked. "When was that?"

"The day after he went missing. J.R. asked if the police had supplied a search warrant to search Hugo's office. When I said no, he told me he was sending someone to Jackson Creek within the hour and I was to meet them there."

"And you did?" I asked in disbelief.

So my father hadn't cleaned out Hugo Burton's office personally. He'd just let the big bad wolf in.

"I'd learned that J.R. Simmons was a scary man, and he seemed even scarier toward the end. I was afraid to piss him off, so I agreed."

"You helped him interfere with a police investigation, Dad," I said in disgust.

"I know, but…" He drew a shaky breath. "I was afraid."

I was in shock that my father had gotten involved with the notorious J.R. Simmons, but then again, a decade ago, J.R. Simmons had simply been known as a savvy businessman. I could understand why the attention and opportunity would have flattered him.

"So what happened when you met J.R. Simmons's man?"

He looked down, his cheeks turning pink. "When I pulled up, he was already in the parking lot. He got out and took multiple boxes out of the car. I asked him what he planned to do with them, but he just gave me a dark look. I didn't ask any more questions. I took him inside and let him into Hugo's office."

"That was wrong on so many levels, Dad."

"I know," he moaned, placing his face in his hands. "I know," he repeated more quietly. "It still haunts me. Taking everything from Hugo's wife and kids."

My brows pinched together. "Wait. What does *that* mean?"

"He cleaned out everything except the family photos…but everything else. The only thing left was a desktop computer."

"Why would he leave a computer?"

He looked sheepish. "I think he switched it out."

"You didn't watch what he took?"

"No, he told me to go, and he was the sort of guy you'd do better not to mess with. So I left for a while, and when I came back, I noticed the keyboard on the computer looked different. When I mentioned it to J.R.'s guy, he told me to stop asking questions. I thought about it for a long time afterward, and that's when I realized he must've switched out the computer."

"What happened after that?"

"After they found Hugo's car, the police arrived with a search warrant. They questioned where the files had gone, and of course, I couldn't say that J.R.'s guy had taken them. I told them I didn't know."

"You lied to the sheriff detective, Dad. That's bad."

He looked like he was going to be sick. "I know."

"And Floyd, the office manager, thinks *you* took the stuff from Hugo's office."

His eyes widened. "You talked to him?"

"Yeah. I'm guessing he didn't tell the police it was you?"

"No, but Floyd has always been pretty loyal."

We were silent for a moment before I asked, "Why did J.R. Simmons want Hugo's files?"

"I don't know," he said quietly.

"Did you ask Simmons about it?"

"No," he said in a rush. "I only spoke to him once after that. I'd emailed to inform him that I could no longer act as his attorney. He called to tell me that I was a disappointment, not that he was surprised, but insisted he'd send me a check for twenty dollars every month to keep me on retainer."

"To ensure his client privilege," I said.

He nodded. "I didn't cash them, but I saved them." He opened his desk drawer and pulled out a long envelope, opening it to show me a thin stack of checks. "But not long after that, he got into his own mess of trouble, and after he died, the checks stopped coming."

"And you didn't go to the police then?" I asked.

"No. Hugo was gone. J.R. was dead. What good could have come from it?"

"Maybe finding Hugo Burton?" I prodded.

He shook his head, his jaw tight as his eyes glittered with defiance. "Hugo's long gone. He took the money and ran."

"You don't believe that," I said, dread building in my chest. "You freaked out last night when you thought I had proof that Hugo was murdered. That's part of why you ran." I held his gaze. "You think he's dead, and you believe J.R. Simmons was responsible."

His face lost more color. "I never said that. I never even *implied* that."

"Still, you don't believe he ran off. Did J.R. admit to killing him?"

He shook his head, his eyes glassy again. "No. I never asked, and he never admitted to anything."

"But he was there within a day, cleaning out Hugo's paperwork and switching out his computer. Sounds pretty damaging to me."

"J.R. Simmons is dead. There's no point in rehashing it."

I'd never been more disappointed in him, but at least he wasn't a murderer. "What about Hugo's wife and kids? I had lunch with Anton two days ago. He hasn't gotten over his father's disappearance. Finding out what happened to Hugo won't bring him back, but at least his family will get closure."

He stared at me in silence.

"That's it? You're not going to tell me anything else?"

"There are dangerous people out there, Harper. You need to stay away from this."

"Why?"

"Because me, Brett, and Skip Martin are the only ones who've survived this mess!" he half-shouted. "Bill, Tim, and Pete Mooney all died after Hugo left."

Then a new thought hit me. If the men searching the house and apartment weren't sent by Malcolm, then... "Who did you talk to last night after you left the tavern?"

He looked stricken. "What?"

"Someone broke into the house and then my apartment last night. They were looking for something, Dad. It happened right after we had dinner. I checked out Hugo's old office before we met up. I think the person who was behind it knows what I'm doing and thought I found something."

"That's impossible, J.R. Simmons is dead," my father said, his face pale.

"Well, someone is interested in this case, so if not him, then who?"

He pinched his lips together, remaining silent.

"Dad," I said, leaning forward. "If you know more, like who might have broken into your house and my apartment last night, then you need to tell me."

Fear filled his eyes. "Let this case go, Harper." He swallowed. "But I see that filing isn't enough for you, and you really like investigating, so how about I help you set up your P.I. practice?"

My heart leapt at the suggestion of him helping me, but I knew it wasn't genuine. It was merely an attempt to get me to leave this alone.

He wasn't going to tell me anything else, so I got up and started toward the door.

"Have you heard from your mother?" he called out behind me.

I stopped and turned to face him. "No."

"What if she'd been home when those men broke in,

Harper?" he pleaded. "Something could have happened to either one of you."

Was he trying to protect my mother, me, or himself? I was going with the latter, and it hurt more than I'd thought it could. He'd disappointed me again, worse this time. "I don't give up that easily, Dad. But then you wouldn't know that since you really don't know me at all."

"Harper…"

Ignoring him, I walked out, trying to decide what to tell Malcolm. Did I want to admit to everything and make my father look as complicit as he'd probably been, or should I protect him? My instinct was to protect him, but did he deserve it?

Chapter 27

I needed a drink in the worst way, so I ducked into the bathroom and hid in a stall while I pulled out my water bottle. It was only a quarter full, but I took a couple of sips, chasing the heat of it, then closed my eyes as I leaned my back against the metal wall.

Had my father been more involved in Hugo's murder than he was letting on?

And, if so, what the hell was I going to do about it?

If I'd still been a Little Rock detective, I would have gone straight to Detective Jones to report that my father had suppressed potential evidence and information. But I wasn't Detective Harper Adams of the LRPD. I was no longer someone I recognized. Going to Detective Jones wasn't even on my long list, and I wasn't sure what to do with that acknowledgment either.

I needed time to sort this out without Malcolm watching my every move, but he wasn't about to let me dodge him. And if I went to him in my current state, he'd know something had shaken me.

Basically, I was screwed.

I took another swig from my water bottle, then tucked it

back in my purse while grabbing my phone. After a couple of swipes, I typed *J.R. Simmons James Malcolm* into the search engine.

Multiple results popped up.

Alleged Crime Boss Brings Down Successful Arkansas Businessman

J.R. Simmons Faces Murder Charges in Fenton County Dust-Up

I scanned the articles, and sure enough, Malcolm had set up a sting to bring down Simmons. It had involved a Fenton County woman and the Fenton County Sheriff's Department.

Why would Malcolm put himself on the line by setting up a sting like that? That wasn't the action of an organized crime boss. It sounded like a great way to paint a target on his back. It made absolutely no sense.

Another article said Simmons had escaped custody when he was being transferred from the hospital to the county jail. It hadn't done him any good, because a few days later he'd been found dead with multiple gunshot wounds in a burned-down warehouse, along with a few other bodies. I couldn't ignore that the situation had been pretty convenient for Malcolm, since he hadn't needed to testify against Simmons in court after all.

It couldn't be a coincidence that Malcolm was interested in a case that had ties to J.R. Simmons. So what was he after?

I closed out the search app and took another long swig from my water bottle. The tightly wound ball of anxiety in my gut was already beginning to unravel. After I closed the cap, I popped a breath mint in my mouth and left the bathroom, strutting past Becky and somehow finding the willpower to resist flipping her off on the way out.

Malcolm was parked on the street, but he started inching my car forward as soon as he saw me walk out the front door. When I got inside, he turned to me with a grim look. "Well?"

"Impatient much?" I snapped as I struggled to get the seat belt secured without irritating my injury.

After several fumbled attempts, he leaned over me,

grabbed the seat belt, and pulled it across my body, clicking it into place. "What did he say?"

"My father created Hugo Burton's contracts, but he did it under the table. So there's no record of Hugo being a client of the firm."

He pulled away from the curb. "We knew that already."

I ignored him. "My father said it was because he wanted to invest in the property too. He created a boilerplate contract as part of their arrangement, but he didn't see any contracts after that."

"What else?" he asked, his voice low and dangerous.

"What else what?"

I still hadn't decided whether to tell him about my father's connection to J.R. Simmons, and I sure wasn't about to admit I knew Malcolm had played a role in that man's downfall. I wanted to see how long it would take for him to admit to that piece of information.

"It didn't take you that long to learn only that. What else?"

I turned to face him, my back stiff. "He's my father, and my mother took off out of town without telling us where she went. We had things to discuss that have nothing to do with you."

"Do you expect me to actually believe that bullshit?" he ground out through gritted teeth.

"Why would I lie to you, James Malcolm?"

"To keep the upper hand."

"If you think I'm hiding something, then why don't you tell me something you've been keeping from *me*. Maybe it will jog something loose in my own memory."

"Don't play games, Detective," he snapped.

"You're the one playing games," I shot back. "Why did Delaney call you Skeeter? Why does Carter?"

He flinched and hesitated for a fraction of a second before he said, "It's a nickname."

"Why doesn't anyone at the tavern call you Skeeter?"

I didn't think he was going to answer, but after a few seconds of silence, he said, "Because that nickname belonged in Fenton County."

"Then why did Delaney use it?"

"Because she has a cousin in Fenton County. That's how Hale found her."

"Because you needed access to medical attention on the down low here in Lone County?" I asked smugly. "*Why?*"

"Because sometimes fights break out in the tavern, and I need some help patching people up."

"Why don't they just go to the ER like most normal people? Why didn't *you?*"

He gave me a wry smile. "What can I say? I provide a full-service experience."

I didn't believe him. Not for a minute. "Why did you move to Lone County? And don't give me a bullshit reason like you saw an opportunity for the tavern."

"I needed a change of scenery, and I didn't want to leave Arkansas."

"Why?"

"Why didn't *you* leave Arkansas?" he shot back.

"You know why," I said, getting pissed. "I was flat broke after everything that went down in Little Rock. My father brought me back home."

"You hate this town. You'd rather be pretty much anywhere else. Why have you *stayed?*"

"Because my sister's here," I spat at him, then instantly wished I could reel the words back in.

"She's dead, Harper," he said, quieter this time.

"You didn't leave for the same reason," I said, certainty setting in with the words. "There's someone you care about in Fenton County. Maybe someone other than your brother. You feel a tie to the place."

He released a bitter laugh. "I burned every fucking bridge

I had to that shit heap. The only person who would talk to me was Hale."

"So why stick around Arkansas?"

He pulled up to a stop sign then turned to face me with a slow, predatory smile. "I know how things work here."

"No," I said, studying his face. "I think you have unfinished business."

His eyes turned cold. "Everyone has unfinished business. *You* have unfinished business. You've never forgiven yourself for what you see as failing your sister. Then there's the mess you left behind in Little Rock. Do you expect me to believe you plan on letting them get away with the way they treated you? After they took everything from you?"

His questions surprised me. I *had* planned to let it go, because the people who'd mistreated me were the law, and there was no way to find out what happened within the system from outside of it.

But what if I used other methods that wouldn't be condoned for someone wearing a badge?

What if I could get retribution after all?

"There it is," he said with a dark smile as he drove through the intersection.

His comment made me feel dirty...but also empowered. I wasn't used to playing the victim, and I relished the thought of shedding that skin. Nevertheless, I knew he was trying to distract me. "What unfinished business are *you* working on? Does it have something to do with the people you left behind in Fenton County?"

His body tensed with a raw, angry edge that filled the car. If I didn't know he wanted to work with me, I might have jumped out of the car and run.

"I left those people behind, and I've never looked back," he said. "What I'm looking into is something else entirely."

He could have been saying that just to protect them, but the conviction in his eye convinced me. "Okay."

"Okay?"

"I believe that you're not doing this for anyone in Fenton County." But I still believed it had some connection to that place. Especially since he'd expressed multiple times that semantics mattered.

His shoulders seemed to relax.

"You told me a while back that your brother Scooter's in Fenton County," I said. "Did he turn his back on you too?"

"I got his girlfriend killed."

"*You killed her?*" I asked in shock.

"No," he spat out in disgust. "She was murdered by my rivals. To hurt *me*."

"And he didn't forgive you?"

"I didn't forgive myself." He shuddered slightly as though realizing he'd shared things he hadn't meant to share. "We're not talking about me. We're talking about the parts of your conversation with your father that you haven't shared with me yet."

"What are you talking about?"

"Don't play dumb," he growled.

I turned in my seat to face him, trying not to flinch at the pain from my chest wound. "How about you quit pretending that I'm dumb? You have a specific question to ask, Malcolm? Ask it. If I know, I'll tell you. God's honest truth."

"You're expecting me to ask specific questions about the conversation you had with your father when I have no idea what you discussed?" he demanded.

"I suspect there's something specific you want to know, and no, I'm not going to just give it to you. You've been keeping this piece of information from me, and I suspect it *does* have something to do with Hugo's murder. So pull on your big boy pants, Malcolm, and *ask*."

His teeth were clenched so tightly, I was sure he'd ground his molars down a few millimeters. "Fuck you, Adams."

I gave him a saccharine smile. "No thanks. Not interested."

His face turned bright red and a vein in his forehead throbbed, and for a brief moment, I wondered if I'd gone too far.

He took several deep breaths. "Not now."

I suspected he was buying time so he could figure out a way to get me to confess without giving me anything of his own. I'd let him have it for now.

"Okay."

"You gave in too damn easy."

I just shrugged. "So where are we going?"

"To the tavern."

That surprised me, but then it made sense. He probably had to work the lunch shift. He'd missed a good portion of the day yesterday.

After he'd driven about five minutes in silence, he said, "Does your father know who broke into your house? Did they break into his?"

I'd told him to ask the questions he wanted answers to. I'd just hoped it would be a different question. "He seemed surprised and claimed he didn't know who'd broken in. I forgot to ask him about his house." But I'd bet money his place had remained unscathed, which made me even more certain he'd called someone. Could I get my hands on his cell phone?

Malcolm was silent for a moment. "He was scared last night when you were asking him questions about the case. Was he scared today?"

"He said I'd caught him off guard last night. He seemed prepared to see me today."

"Do you believe that?"

It didn't feel like a betrayal to answer truthfully. "Yes, but I think he was still scared."

"Did you ask him what he did with Burton's things from

his office?"

"He says he didn't take them. Someone else did."

"And you believe him?"

"Yes."

He was silent for a long moment. I could tell he was dying for me to verify that I knew about J.R. Simmons, but he couldn't bring himself to ask.

"Feel free to ask a very specific question, Malcolm. Once I know we're on the same page, I'll be happy to fill you in."

He remained silent for several more seconds, his jaw locked, before he said, "Was J.R. Simmons an investor?"

There it was, sort of. Maybe he simply suspected Simmons had ties to the case but didn't know the details. "My father admitted that he'd introduced Hugo to Simmons, but he had no idea whether Simmons had invested."

He remained silent.

Now that he'd mentioned Simmons's name, I had a few questions of my own. "What do *you* know about J.R. Simmons being connected to Hugo Burton?"

"Who said I knew anything?"

"Give me a fucking break, Malcolm," I said in disgust. "I can read between the lines. You're interested in this case because J.R. Simmons was involved."

He remained silent.

"The question is why *you're* interested."

More silence.

"Even if he killed Hugo Burton, then there's no possibility for vengeance or revenge, if that's what you're after. Simmons is dead."

"I'm very well aware of that," he spat out.

"So why do you care about this case?"

The tavern appeared ahead, and Malcom pulled into the parking lot, heading behind the building. He turned off the car, grabbed his laptop from the backseat, and got out, leaving me to follow him in through the back door and then into his office.

"I need to work the lunch shift," he said once we were inside. He walked around his desk and set my car keys and his computer down before he started to write something on a sticky note. "*You* need to rest and drink more water. You lost a lot of blood last night. So hang out in my office and take a nap on the sofa. Or use my laptop if you want to work. Here's the password." He stuck the sticky note on the laptop. "You need food too, so feel free to come up front and order at the bar. I'll get someone to cover for me after the shift ends, and we'll figure out where to go from there."

"You trust me alone in your office?" I asked in disbelief. "And access to your *laptop*?"

He released a short laugh. "You think I have something incriminating for you to snoop through? Go ahead and snoop. You'll be bored with what you find." Then he turned around and headed to the door.

I stared at his back as he walked away. He was so full of contradictions I got whiplash trying to keep up.

While I could have used a nap, I got to work instead.

I sat at his desk and opened his laptop and entered his password. I couldn't believe he had just given it to me. It was tempting to snoop through his files, but even though he'd given me permission, I couldn't bring myself to do it. I doubted he'd have anything helpful to the case on here. He definitely wouldn't have anything to do with J.R. Simmons. So instead, I started researching J.R. Simmons.

When he'd been arrested and then murdered four years ago, the entire state had been in shock—but I hadn't paid much attention. I'd been firmly invested in my own cases. So I gave myself a crash course on what had been posted about him in the press.

It appeared he hadn't been on the state police's radar for long. Not much was known about his fall from grace, but it had all come to a head in Fenton County when Simmons had allegedly kidnapped a Fenton County woman, Rose Gardner. The details were pretty nonexistent about why he'd done such a thing. The rest of the story was even stranger. He'd murdered a man—Mick Gentry, a Fenton County large animal vet—in front of multiple eye-witnesses, including law enforcement, which had led to a charge of second-degree murder. No kidnapping charges had been filed, but I knew it wasn't uncommon to arrest someone on a single charge and then add others later. With murder charges, Simmons would have faced a hefty bail, or if the judge had deemed him dangerous to society or a flight risk, he could have been held without bail.

One article mentioned that the woman Simmons had kidnapped, Rose Gardener, was the girlfriend of the Fenton County Assistant District Attorney, Mason Deveraux.

Had Simmons kidnapped Deveraux's girlfriend because the Assistant DA was building a case against him?

Did Malcolm's interest in Hugo Burton's case have some-thing to do with what happened in Fenton County? J.R. Simmons had been part of both. I needed to know more about what happened there and how it might tie into this case.

I needed to talk to Mason Deveraux. But would he talk to me?

There was only one way to find out.

I looked up the Fenton County Courthouse, but Deveraux wasn't listed as the DA. It appeared he'd been replaced by a woman named Marsha Poindexter nearly four years ago. A further search revealed he'd moved to the Arkansas Attorney General's office. He was now lead attorney in the criminal department. There was a phone number for the general line listed on the website, so I decided to see if I could talk to him.

After some runaround, I finally got a gatekeeper at the criminal department and asked to speak to Mr. Deveraux about a case he'd handled in Fenton County.

"And who may I ask is calling?" the woman asked in a bored tone.

"My name is Harper Adams. I'm a licensed private investigator, and I'm looking into a case that involves a man named J.R. Simmons. Mr. Deveraux filed murder charges against him in Fenton County."

"I'm sure the Fenton County DA's office can help you with anything you need to know," she said, making it clear she was the end of the line.

"*Actually*, I think Mr. Deveraux will have more information given Simmons kidnapped his girlfriend at the time, Rose Gardner."

The woman paused. "And what exactly is it that you want to know?"

Interesting. Had there been other calls about this case?

Guilt stabbed me in the gut as I cast a glance at the closed office door and lowered my voice. "I need to know what involvement James Malcolm had in the case. I'm currently investigating a case with ties to J.R. Simmons, and I think Malcolm might be involved."

She hesitated. "I can pass along your request to Mr. Deveraux, but he's preparing for a trial and might not even see the message until next week."

"That's fine." While I felt a sense of urgency, Hugo Burton had been dead for over five years. A week wasn't going to make any difference. I shifted in the desk chair and pain radiated outward from my stitches. Then again, my life might be on the line. "Maybe add that I'm investigating a missing man named Hugo Burton in Lone County, and I think J.R. Simmons had some involvement in his disappearance and murder."

"I'll be sure to add it to the message. Now if I could get your contact information…?"

I gave her my name, phone number, email address, and my license number to prove I was legit.

When I hung up, a sense of dread hung over my head, and I felt surprisingly slimy. Had I just thrown Malcolm in front of a moving bus?

Six months ago, I wouldn't have had any qualms with reaching out to the former ADA and requesting information about people related to a case. I wouldn't feel like I'd betrayed someone who didn't want to be labeled as a friend, but in many ways had acted like one. But then again, I'd already firmly acknowledged I was no longer that woman.

I'd just made a huge mistake.

Chapter 28

As I began to freak out, I reasoned that Mason Deveraux had moved on with his life. If Rose Gardner had been his girlfriend, and it hadn't worked out, there might be hurt feelings in the mix. And the chances of him discussing a case of a personal nature with someone who wasn't in law enforcement were slim to none.

He probably won't call me back.

I took several deep breaths and the panic faded. Even if he called back, I'd find out more about Simmons and downplay anything to do with Malcolm.

My stomach growled, and I realized it was past noon. Bringing the laptop with me, I headed down the hall to the dining area, bypassing the doorway leading behind the bar, and took a seat at the counter in front of Misti.

She gave me a huge smile. "I heard you might come up front."

I set the laptop down. "What are you doin' here? You usually work nights."

"I'm pullin' a double." She gestured to Malcolm, who was working at the opposite end of the bar. "He wasn't sure he'd be in for the lunch shift." She leaned in closer. "What are you two workin' on anyway?"

"What did Malcolm tell you?" I asked cautiously.

"Not much. Just that you're a P.I. now and he's helpin' with a case."

All true, but I still wasn't sure I was comfortable with the world associating us as a package deal. I almost gave her some vague blow-off answer, but Misti seemed to know a lot about a lot of people. Maybe she could help. "We're looking into a missing man. Hugo Burton. He disappeared about five years go. Ever heard of him?"

She laughed. "Everyone who's lived here longer than a decade knows about Hugo Burton disappearing." Her nose wrinkled. "When was it? About three years ago?"

"Five."

She shook her head. "Time sure flies."

"Do you know anything about him?"

"I know people are torn about whether he ran off or was murdered."

"What are your thoughts on it?"

"I didn't know him very well."

"You actually knew him?" I asked in surprise.

"Sure. Before James opened the tavern, I used to waitress at a diner out on the highway, about halfway between Jackson Creek and Wolford. Hugo used to have business lunches there sometimes."

My eyes widened. "Really? Do you happen to know who he met there?"

"Some of 'em, sure, but others." She shook her head. "I have no idea."

"Do you remember what they talked about?"

She released a short laugh. "That's easy. It's all Hugo ever talked about—his property. Sunnyside or something or other."

"Sunny Point."

"Yeah," she said, her face brightening. "That's it."

"Do you remember what they were saying?"

"Not really. That was ages ago."

I pulled out my phone and Googled Brett Colter and held up the photo. "Could this man have been one of them?"

She took my phone and studied the image. "Maybe," she said as she handed it back to me.

It didn't matter. I already knew Brett Colter had been an investor. On a whim, I looked up J.R. Simmons and showed her a photo. "What about him?"

She looked at the photo and shook her head. "I don't recognize him."

I wasn't surprised. J.R. Simmons didn't seem like the kind of guy who would conduct business in a diner…

Except maybe he was.

"You gonna order something?" she asked.

"No," I said, sliding off the stool. "I need to be somewhere else."

"James said you were sticking around here all day," she said, her forehead crinkling with confusion.

"If he asks, tell him I'll be back." I headed back to the office. Setting down the laptop, I grabbed my keys and then headed out the back door before Misti could snitch on me. Because I knew Malcolm would chase after me. I had no delusions that he was trying to keep me safe, or whatever excuse he'd pull out to make me think he cared. The cold, hard truth was he didn't want me to find out anything else without him.

He called my cell as I pulled out of the parking lot, but I ignored the call and drove to Jackson Creek. Twenty minutes later, I was sliding into the last open booth at the café on Main Street. Betty saw me and smiled as she walked by, carrying a couple of plates with burgers and fries. "You're back! I'll be right with you in a moment," she called out as she walked by.

"No problem."

I grabbed one of the menus at the end of the table and scanned the lunch specials. While I waited, I pulled up the search page on my phone.

By the time Betty returned, I had pulled up multiple images on my phone.

"You know what you want?" she asked with a warm smile.

"I'm trying to decide between the chicken club and the hamburger. Can you point me in the right direction?"

She laughed. "Obviously, you can't go wrong with either. Everything we serve is good."

I grinned. "Well in that case, I'll take the chicken sandwich, sweet potato fries, and an unsweet tea to drink."

"Good choice," she said with a wink, then wrote down my order.

"I know you're busy, Betty, but could you look a couple of photos for me?"

"Sure, I guess," she said, moving closer to me.

"You said you never forget a face. Is that true, or was that just a figure of speech?"

She preened. "It's true. Orders too. My memory's like a steel trap. It comes in handy with the customers, because everyone likes to feel remembered."

She had a point. I felt good when she'd recognized me.

"You said the day Hugo Burton disappeared that he met with an older man here. Could this be the guy?" I turned my phone so she could see the screen, then swiped through several images of J.R. Simmons, mostly of him in suits, his hair impeccably styled.

She squinted for a moment, then nodded. "Yep. That's him."

My heart skipped a beat. "You're sure?"

"Sure as rainstorm in October. That's him."

Excitement bubbled in my stomach. I'd just tied Simmons to Hugo Burton possibly hours before he was murdered. "I know you told me what little you knew about their conversation, but can you remember if it was heated? Did they argue?"

"They weren't yellin' or nothing like that, but it seemed tense."

"Did you hear the older guy threatening Hugo?"

"No, but like I said yesterday, I didn't really hear their conversation. I could read their body language, though, and neither one of them was happy. Of course, I probably remember it so well because he disappeared that night."

"That's really helpful. Thank you."

She thumbed toward the back. "I've gotta get your order in and check on the other customers."

"Of course," I said apologetically. "I'm sorry to have kept you."

As I tried to figure out what to do next, I thought about Hugo's body, lying out in the open. I should have never agreed to dig up that grave, yet I was finding it hard to feel guilty about it. I *did* feel guilty that Anton, Mary Ann, and Clarice Burton were still living in the agony of not knowing what happened to their father and husband, but not enough to tell them yet. I hadn't figured out how to explain how the grave had got dug up, but maybe I could claim I found it that way. I'd work it out later.

Betty brought out my sandwich and I ate, turning my attention to searching more about James Malcolm. I knew I should let it go and focus on J.R. Simmons and his involvement in Lone County, but my curiosity was gnawing at me. I tried to reason that the more I knew about Malcolm the better equipped I'd be to find Hugo's murderer, but some small part of me acknowledged that I was doing this for myself. Then again, I was committing crimes with this man. It would be prudent to know more about him.

I'd done a similar search weeks ago, but now that I'd worked with him, I felt like I had a better understanding of the man and things might hit me differently. The top results were about his connection to a crime organization called Hardshaw Group. There was little information on it other than it had collapsed nearly four years ago. Malcolm had cooperated with the FBI to bring them down, but he hadn't fulfilled some part of his bargain, so he'd gotten thrown into federal prison.

Why had he set up the Hardshaw Group? And what had he done to piss off the FBI?

I doubted searching on the internet was going to answer that question. If I wanted it, I was going to have to get it out of him, and hell would freeze over before he ever told me anything more than what he wanted me to know. Had there been personal reasons?

I looked up the articles about the sting with J.R. Simmons again, this time taking more time to read every word. Most articles were vague about the sting, but it had involved the kidnapping of Rose Gardner. Had Malcolm worked with the ADA to help save Deveraux's girlfriend? Or had he known her personally? That part seemed preposterous, but then, most people would never suspect me of working with Malcolm either, so maybe not as preposterous as one would think.

How had Malcolm known Rose Gardner?

Maybe *she* was the key.

I searched Rose Gardner next, surprised at the multiple hits. She owned a landscaping business called RBW Landscaping as well as Gardner Sisters Nursery, which specialized in plants and landscaping. I found a business spotlight piece about her in the *Henryetta Gazette* from about a year ago. Though the focus was on her businesses, it dipped into her personal life. She lived in a nearly hundred-year-old farmhouse with her husband and four kids, two of whom were the children of her deceased sister. The article also mentioned her dog Muffy, who seemed to be well known by her clients. But it was her husband's name that caught me by surprise. Rose was married to Joe Simmons, the recently elected sheriff of Fenton County.

Simmons.

Could he be any relation to *J.R.* Simmons?

It only took me about twenty seconds to discover that Joe

was J.R.'s only son. Was it a coincidence that Rose Gardner had been the ADA's girlfriend during the Simmons sting, and then married Simmons's son? And that Malcolm had been involved in the sting when she'd been kidnapped?

Why had James Malcolm, a crime boss, saved the now-wife of the chief deputy sheriff? Who *was* James Malcolm and what was he doing now?

The only thing I could surmise was that his organized crime past was perhaps a front to help law enforcement bring down other organizations. He'd vanquished the elder Simmons, and then Hardshaw Group.

Shit. Was he undercover *now*? Was I helping him work his own cases?

The idea filled me with equal parts relief and rage. But at the same time, I *knew* he'd killed the Sylvester brothers. There was no way he would have done that if he was law enforcement. So what was he up to?

My phone buzzed and I saw Malcolm's name on the screen. I almost let it go to voicemail, but then changed my mind.

"Where the hell are you?" he demanded as soon as I answered.

"I'm getting lunch in Jackson Creek."

"Why?"

"Because I was hungry," I said flippantly. "Guess who Betty remembers seeing here in her café?" I asked good-naturedly.

"I'm not playing guessing games," he grunted.

"J.R. Simmons. Having pie with Hugo Burton the day he disappeared."

"We knew Simmons was involved," he said without hesitation. No hint of surprise. Had he known?

"Yeah," I said, letting the word drag out. "I suppose we did. But what *I* didn't know was that *you* were involved in Simmons's arrest in Fenton County shortly after Hugo's disappearance." Not technically true, but I hadn't known until a few hours ago. I just hadn't mentioned it.

There was a long pause before he said, "We need to have this conversation in person."

"Who is Rose Gardner to you?"

The phone felt electric from the silent tension coming from the other side.

"Who is she, Malcolm?"

"You diggin' into my past? Have you found my speeding ticket from the Lone County Sheriff's Department three years ago? And the ticket I got for the bullshit charge of not wearing a seat belt a week after that? But I guess there's no record of the dozen or more times they pulled me over for bogus reasons, only to harass me and let me go. All because they were trying to make it clear they didn't want me here. But guess *what*? I'm still here."

"Does any of this have a point?" I spat out.

"You can dig into my past all you want, but if you're looking at the official record, you'll only find half-truths and a metric ton of bullshit."

"So you're saying Rose Gardner means nothing to you?"

"It means you have no idea what you're talking about."

"Then tell me."

"I'm not having this conversation over the phone."

"You mean you're *actually* going to tell me in person?" I asked. "How can I believe you when you never once told me you knew J.R. Simmons?"

"Why would I? Up until this morning, I had no reason to." He paused. "Come back and we'll talk." Then he hung up.

Damn him.

I flagged down Betty and paid my bill, leaving her a generous tip, but just as I started to walk out, I remembered I hadn't shown her the other set of photos on my phone.

"Say Betty, do you happen to remember seeing this man

when Hugo Burton was alive?" I held out my phone to her
and she took it, shuffling through the photos before handing it
back to me.

Her mouth twisted to the side, as she considered it then
said, "Yep. A couple of times."

"You're certain? This probably would have been five years
ago."

"Yep. I know him. He had this habit of biting his thumb-
nails, sometimes down the quick. Plus, he wasn't a very nice
man. Very abrupt and rude. I never liked seeing him walk
through the door."

"Was he ever with Hugo Burton?"

"Usually alone, but once with him." She glanced over her
shoulder, then turned back to me, lowering her voice. "The
day after Hugo disappeared, I saw him across the street, going
into the office building. When he came out, he had a couple
of boxes."

The only office building across the street was Hugo's.

"The day after?" I asked, trying to contain my excitement.
"You're sure?"

"Positive. He came in for a piece of pie once he finished
his job."

"Thank you. This is *very* helpful."

I'd just tied Pete Mooney to J.R. Simmons and possibly
Hugo Burton's murder.

Chapter 29

My first instinct was to head back to the tavern and confront Malcolm, but I sat in my car for a few minutes and thought this through. Even if Pete Mooney had killed Hugo, someone else was involved. Otherwise, why would someone have broken into my parents' property? There were two investors still here—Brett Colter and Skip Martin. If they were involved and thought I was digging up information to implicate them, they could send someone to look for it. The thought made me feel better about my father's recent involvement with all of this. Colter and Martin both knew I was searching for Hugo, so they wouldn't need someone to alert them that I was looking. Maybe they were hoping to find proof of what I'd found.

But how was I going to prove it was either one of them? I had the names of the guys who'd broken into my place. I could possibly use that to my advantage. Skip had a car lot and likely had a lot of employees. Maybe they were two of his men.

I decided to pay a visit to Skip's car lot and ask around for Pinky. It was an unusual enough name that if he worked there, someone would know.

I headed to Wolford and parked in the dealership parking

lot, trying to decide where to start. The service department seemed like a great place to look. The two men definitely had blue collar vibes. It seemed to make more sense that a mechanic would be one of his henchmen rather than a salesman or finance guy.

So I walked through the service doors right up to the counter and gave the twenty-something guy behind the counter a big smile. "Hi. Could you do me a favor and tell Pinky that I'm here with a check?"

His nose scrunched up. "Who?"

"Pinky. I was told he worked here."

"Don't know a Pinky," he said. "What's his last name?"

"I don't know."

He gave me a skeptical look. "I thought you had a check for him. Wouldn't you have to put his last name on it?"

"I didn't write it," I said. "My boss gave it to me in a sealed envelope, and told me to bring it to him." I shrugged. "I'm just doin' what I was told."

"Sorry," he said, relaxing after my answer. "Like I said, no Pinky here."

"What about Mike?" I said. "My boss said his real name might be Mike."

He shook his head. "Nope. No Mikes either. You sure you're at the right place?"

"My boss must have gotten it wrong. Sorry for taking your time."

"No problem," he said. "Good luck with your search."

I turned around to leave, and ran right into a man. I took a step back and tried to keep from crying out as pain shot through my shoulder.

"Harper Adams?" the man said in surprise, and I realized I'd bumped into Skip Martin.

"I'm sorry," I said. "I should have looked where I was going."

"I shouldn't have snuck up on you like that," he said with

a laugh. He stepped around me to hand a folder to the guy behind the counter. "Here's that report for you to look at."

"Thanks, Skip," the guy said as he took it.

Skip turned back to me. "You havin' car trouble?"

"No, nothing like that," I said, not wanting to reveal the real reason I was here.

But the guy behind the counter said, "She was looking for someone named Pinky or Mike."

Skip's brow shot up. "Is that part of your case?"

"She said she had a check for him. From her boss."

Skip narrowed his eyes. "I thought *you* were your boss."

Shit. But then I remembered my real boss. "I may have forgotten to mention I work for the Morgan, Hightower, and Adams law firm."

"You were delivering a subpoena?" the guy behind the counter asked in alarm.

"No. I really *was* delivering a check," I said, trying to look beleaguered and not concerned I was about to get caught in a lie. "He won a minor settlement. Mr. Hightower sent me to hand deliver it to him, but obviously they gave me the wrong place of employment." I made a face. "Again, sorry to have taken up your time." I considered asking Skip if he knew about J.R. Simmons, but there was still a chance he was involved, and I didn't want to tip my hand. Also, if I confronted him, I wanted backup, as hard as that was to admit to myself.

I headed out the door, and to my surprise, Skip followed me.

"Have you gotten any closer to finding Hugo?" he asked.

I stopped on the sidewalk in front of my car and turned to face him. "No, I'm sorry, but it's bound to take longer than a few days."

"I thought of something else after you left," he said. "I'm not sure how important it was, so I didn't call you."

"Oh?"

He leaned in, close enough I could smell a hint of garlic on his breath. "When Hugo was asking for more money, Brett Colter called me. He was pissed that Hugo had fucked away the money he had." He cringed. "Sorry for the cursing. No offense."

"None taken."

"Anyway, he made an offhanded comment that something had to be done with him or we were gonna lose everything we'd put into the property. I thought he meant going to the Secretary of State. But now I wonder…" He frowned.

"Wonder what?"

"Well, what if that's not what he meant? He was really pissed at Hugo and thought he'd mismanaged the whole project. He said he'd sunk a hundred grand into it, and he was worried Hugo was going to get off scot-free."

I chose my next words carefully. "You think Brett Colter may have harmed Hugo Burton?"

He held up his hands in front of him. "I didn't say that. Brett's a stand-up guy. He's done a lot for the community."

"But…" I prompted.

"I keep thinking, what if he confronted Hugo and demanded his money back? Hugo probably got an additional hundred grand from the investors before his disappearance, so it would have been enough to cover Brett's investment. What if Brett forced him to return the money and then something happened to Hugo?"

If Brett Colter had confronted and killed Hugo, then he might have gotten Hugo's password first and made the wire transfer. It stood to reason a guy like Colter would have a foreign bank account.

"Plus," he continued. "Brett has a temper, but he's never caused anyone physical harm that I know about. Just thrown things and screamed at employees."

"His realtors?"

"He owns more than just a realty," he said. "He has a

construction business too. He's notorious for throwing fits at job sites."

So he had a business with blue-collar workers he might recruit to be his henchmen from time to time.

"Thank you, Skip," I said. "That's very helpful information."

A guilty look filled his eyes. "Then why do I feel like I've done something wrong? Brett and I have known each other for over twenty years, and I feel like I just implicated him in something really bad."

"Don't worry," I said, patting his arm. "What you told me doesn't mean he's guilty. Just that he needs more looking into." I lowered my hand and said, "Did you happen to mention any of this to the sheriff's department back when they were investigating?"

"I did, but not as much as I told you. Just that Brett was pissed about possibly losing his money. Not that I was worried he'd do something to Hugo." He cringed. "Should I tell them now? Will I be in trouble for not telling them sooner?"

"I doubt you'd be in trouble. You didn't have facts, just a feeling. Still, let's not tell them yet," I said. "I'll do my own investigating first, and *then* we'll inform the sheriff's department."

"I just want to do the right thing," Skip said, looking like he was about to be sick. "And I'm sure Brett wouldn't really have hurt Hugo."

"You're probably right," I said, taking a step back. "Thank you for being so forthright."

"Anything I can do to help."

I got in my car and headed toward the tavern. I was dying to meet with Brett Colter, but if Skip's concerns were legit, I needed Malcolm for backup. Still, I could set up the appointment. I pulled over in a strip mall parking lot and called Brett Colter's office, asking to set up a meeting with him.

"May I ask who's calling?" the receptionist asked.

"Harper Adams."

She put me on hold, then returned about ten seconds later. "I'm sorry, Ms. Adams, but Mr. Colter says he has nothing further to tell you."

"So he won't meet with me?"

"I'm sorry," she said, sounding like she genuinely meant it.

"That's okay," I said. "Thank you for your time."

I hung up, my mind whirling. It was suspicious behavior, and it seemed totally possible the men who'd broken into my house were members of his construction crew. What if I dropped by a job site and started asking a few questions? But one problem with that plan was that construction crews often subcontracted labor. Even if I dropped by a job site like I was tempted to do, the people I talked to might not know either Pinky or Mike. That was even if I could find a job site to investigate.

Instead, I called Detective Jones. I figured I could ask him if he knew of a criminal named Pinky.

"Detective Adams," he said congenially when he answered. "Making progress?"

"Oh, you know these things take time," I hedged. "Do you happen to know anything about a criminal in the area named Pinky?"

"Pinky?" he asked incredulously. "Any last name?"

"For all I know that is his last name," I said.

"Can I ask what prompted this inquiry?"

"I'd rather not say at the moment."

He was quiet for a couple of seconds. "I don't know anything about a Pinky, but I can ask around and see if anyone else has heard of him."

"Thanks. I'd really appreciate it."

"So how's the case going?" he said.

"I already told you it takes time," I said good-naturedly, but the way he was pushing me felt off. Like he was too interested. Then again, maybe he was worried I'd find the ways he'd screwed up during his investigation. I decided to push back to see what he gave me. "I may have stumbled across something that more definitively suggests Hugo Burton was murdered."

"And this has something to do with the mysterious Pinky?"

"I think it's all related."

"And you're not going to tell me what you stumbled across?"

This was tricky. Technically, it was still an active investigation, so he was within his rights to haul me to the station and try to force me to answer, then charge me with impeding an investigation if I didn't. But I suspected Detective Jones had a full plate and didn't want to shove his cases to the side to work a five-year-old crime. Even if it was a murder. "Not yet. But I promise I'll tell you what I've found when I have more concrete information."

He was quiet again, then said, "Well, I guess that's all I can ask."

"Thanks for trusting me, Detective," I said. "That means a lot."

"Call me Matt, and we both want the same thing, right? Hopefully, you'll be able to break this case."

"Thanks."

"And I'll let you know what I find out about Pinky."

"Thanks for that too."

When we hung up, it struck me that he wasn't the only source I had for nefarious people in this town. Malcolm might have information, but there was someone else who could dig even deeper.

"Harper Adams," Carter said when he answered. "I hear you had a minor mishap last night."

"I suppose you heard it from Malcolm."

"Who do you think he called to fix your door?"

"He called his attorney for that?"

"I'm an all-around fix-it guy. Now, to what do I owe the pleasure of this call?"

"If you have time," I prefaced, realizing I didn't have the right to order him to do anything, "could you look into a couple of thing for me?"

"I can certainly try."

"First, can you see what you can find out about a guy named Pinky? He was one of thugs who broke into my house. The other guy's name was Mike, so that's less helpful. Pinky's definitely more unusual."

"Agreed. I'll see what I can find."

"Also, I just heard that Brett Colter has a temper and was pissed at Hugo Burton. Skip Martin was worried Colter might have done something to him."

"You want me to check his criminal history?"

"Yeah." I could have asked Detective Jones, but I hadn't wanted to tip my hand. "Thank you."

"No problem. Shouldn't take long. Where will you be?"

"You can call me on my cell, but I'll probably be at Scooter's Tavern."

Malcolm had a lot of explaining to do.

Chapter 30

When I arrived at the tavern, I walked straight up to the bar in front of Malcolm and said, "We need to talk. Now."

He was wiping out a glass with a towel and stopped to level me with a glare so menacing a customer on a stool a few feet away shrank to the side. "I'm busy."

"You won't be too busy for the information I've just discovered."

"About my past, you mean?" he grunted, resuming his wiping job.

"I found several things, and one of them pertains to the mysterious Pete Mooney."

He stopped wiping and leveled his gaze on me.

I took a step back from the bar. "I'm not having this conversation out in the open. Not after what happened at my house last night. Besides, you're the one who demanded I come over to chat." I suspected he was being obstinate because I hadn't come directly to heel, and I was the one doing the demanding now. James Malcolm was a man who didn't take commands.

His forehead creased with a scowl, but he set the glass

down and turned to Misti, telling her he was taking a break. Then he motioned me toward the door leading to the back.

He was already in the hall that led to his office by the time I'd gone through the door. We were both silent until he'd shut us into the office.

"What do you supposedly know about Pete Mooney?" he asked, his voice tight.

"I had lunch at the café, and Betty, who's both an owner and a waitress, remembers him."

Some of his anger faded. "Remembers him how?"

"She says he was in the café around the time Hugo was alive, and she saw them eat together once."

He moved to his desk and leaned his butt against the edge. "So? We already knew he was an investor. It stands to reason he'd meet with Burton to discuss the project."

"True, but that doesn't explain why Betty saw him carrying boxes out of Hugo's office building the day after Hugo disappeared."

Malcolm's eyes widened slightly, but he remained silent.

"This ties Pete Mooney to J.R. Simmons," I said emphatically. "Who ordered my father to let someone into Hugo's office the day after his disappearance."

He pushed away from the desk, his agitation back. "Hold up. You told me your father didn't remember what he did with Burton's office shit. Now you're telling me Simmons ordered him to let someone in there?"

Oh. Shit. He was right. I'd withheld that piece of information.

His body went rigid. "I think you need to level with me. Now."

"That's a two-way street, Malcolm. You need to level with me about what happened with J.R. Simmons in Fenton County."

His expression was deadly before he walked over to his dry bar and poured two glasses of whiskey, handing one to me.

"Sit." It was an order. I was tempted to tell him to fuck off, but something about the way he handed me the drink suggested he was going to share some of his secrets, so I sat on the sofa as he lowered his large frame into the armchair across from me.

He took a sip of his drink, then lowered the glass to the arm of his chair, holding it with his fingertips around the top. His bluster faded as he said, "Some of my past is a secret for a reason."

When he remained quiet, I changed tactics. "Why were you working with the girlfriend of the assistant district attorney? How did that come about?"

"Just because we're working this case together doesn't give you the right to know about all of my past. Let's just say she and I had goals that intersected. She was trying to protect her then-boyfriend, Mason Deveraux, the assistant DA in Fenton County, and I was trying to bring down J.R. Simmons. We decided to pool our resources and deal with him together."

I shook my head. "How did that arrangement even come about? You both must have run in very different circles, and why would bringing down Simmons protect Deveraux?"

He drew in a breath and slowly released it. "Simmons owned one of the judges in the county as well as the DA. Deveraux was new to the county and was a by-the-books kind of guy. It didn't take him long to realize something was fishy in the county courthouse. Simmons wasn't pleased and decided Deveraux needed to be eliminated." He lifted his glass. "It's more complicated than that, but it's enough of an overview to tell you what you need to know."

"So Deveraux used his girlfriend to get to Simmons?" I asked in disbelief.

He shook his head. "Deveraux had no idea what she was up to until the end. In fact, her participation in the takedown cost Rose her relationship with him."

Dammit. Now I really regretted making that call to Mason

Deveraux. "And you're not going to tell me how you became allies in this endeavor?"

"It's not important." He took a sip of his whiskey. "But that answers your question of how I came to work with Rose Gardner. She was a tool to help bring down my enemy."

Something about the way he said her name suggested she had meant more than that, but I let it go. There was a bigger question to ask. "Why were you so dead set on bringing down J.R. Simmons?"

"Because he was a cancer that had infiltrated most of the state and I wanted him out of my county. Unfortunately for him, that meant he had to be eliminated."

"Was he trying to encroach on your criminal activities?"

"My *alleged* criminal activities," he said before he took another sip.

"Alleged," I amended absentmindedly. "Was he really all that bad?"

He lowered his glass. "He was a nightmare. You'll likely never meet a more vindictive, petty, sorry excuse of a man who took great pleasure in inflicting pain on others." He paused. "Even his own kids."

"Joe Simmons? The sheriff of Fenton County?"

"Someone's been doing her homework," he muttered as he took another drink. Then he lowered the glass and held my gaze. "J.R. Simmons took great joy in raping and killing and flat out torturing anyone who stood in his way. Including children."

I'd seen how disgusted he was by my sister's rapist and murderer. He looked just as pissed now.

"Simmons wanted me gone just as much as I wanted him gone. It was a death match."

"Why would he want you gone?" I asked. Then it hit me. "Oh. You stood in his way."

He gave me a smirk. "I didn't approve of his methods. He

wanted in my county, and I wanted him out. So yes, I stood in his way."

"You had it out for J.R. Simmons," I said, trying to work this through. "Simmons is dead, so why are you so interested in Hugo Burton's murder? Do you plan to enact some type of revenge against the man's children?"

Oh. God. What if he was? I wouldn't condone that at all.

He released a bitter laugh. "As you already stated, his son is the sheriff of Fenton County, and although not as straight and narrow as you used to be, he has a strong sense of right and wrong. Unjustified murder and harming others for the joy of it isn't his thing." He took another sip, finishing off his glass. "Simmons's daughter is dead, but she was a piece of work when she was alive. Her father made her the psychopath that she was." He got up and walked to the dry bar. "I have no quarrel with Joe Simmons."

"So why are you interested in this case?" I asked again.

He poured whiskey into his glass. "Simmons Sr, might be dead, but his dynasty didn't get stamped out with him."

"So you're after whoever took over?"

He set down the decanter and looked at me. "Yes."

"Why?"

"Because I suspect they're just as evil as Simmons."

Why did he suspect the person who'd taken over was evil? I made a note to myself to look up murders and missing people over the past five years.

He walked back over with both the glass and the decanter and set the decanter on the side table next to him. "Now tell me how else your father was involved with J.R. Simmons."

I took a sip of my drink, barely restraining myself from closing my eyes to savor the rich warmth as it passed my lips.

"My father did some legal work for J.R. Simmons," I said. "Simmons asked him to work on some contracts for him. My father also told Simmons about Hugo's investment property. Dad had no idea if Simmons invested, but the day after

Hugo's disappearance, Simmons called and said someone was coming to clean out Hugo's office and Dad was to let them in."

"Which is why the office manager thought your father had cleaned it out."

"Yes." I took another sip of my drink. "My father showed up to let him in but claims he didn't stick around to see what the guy took. But he did confirm Mooney switched out the desktop computer."

"That had to be Mooney's idea," Malcolm said in disgust. "That man was an idiot. It never would have fooled the police and only made it look more suspicious. Not that it did a hell of a lot of good." He tilted his head. "Did the investigators accuse your father of taking the original?"

"If they did, he didn't admit to it." I studied him. He'd let slip that he knew Pete Mooney, but then again, I was pretty sure Malcolm didn't let anything slip. "How did you know Mooney?" I asked casually.

The corners of his mouth ticked up, but the smile didn't meet his eyes. "He was one of J.R. Simmons's lackeys."

"He was murdered in Little Rock less than a year after Hugo disappeared. Do you know anything about that?"

"Not for certain, but I suspect Simmons had him murdered. Mooney was getting sloppy—especially if the waitress saw him at the office building. Simmons was probably cleaning up."

"So you think Simmons killed him himself?"

"No," he said with a snort. "Simmons rarely did the dirty work himself. He paid others to do it for him. And he had a lot of people on his payroll."

I studied him through narrowed eyes. "You're going after the people on his payroll."

His smile spread, but it looked deadly. "I never said that."

"You said you were after Simmons's replacement." I paused. "You're after him or her."

"Him," he clarified. "Simmons was a chauvinist through and through and never worked with women." Something flickered in his eyes, and he took another sip. "And yes, someone's still around, otherwise you wouldn't have had your apartment and your parents' house broken into. They know you're looking for Hugo and they're terrified you'll discover the truth."

"So why break in?"

"Your car was in the driveway," he said, holding my gaze. "Did it ever occur to you that they weren't looking for information? They were looking for *you*."

My mouth dropped open because it *hadn't* occurred to me. "They were searching for something. I heard them."

"They might have gone in there and shoved something in frustration."

Was I in real danger?

"The real question is the timing," Malcolm continued. "It happened right after you spoke to your father, but was that coincidental?" he mused, glancing at the wall. "I've been going over that in my head, and as much as I hate coincidences, there's a chance it could be one."

"So my father didn't alert anyone that I might have proof Hugo Burton is dead?"

"Did you tell your father that?"

"No, but I was sloppy and said Hugo had been murdered. I think my father took it as proof."

"Then I rescind my coincidence statement. Your father left the tavern in a state of panic and called the person who killed Burton."

"You don't think Mooney killed him?"

"No," he said, then took another sip of his whiskey. "Mooney was in Pine Bluff that day. I've verified it."

I narrowed my eyes. "Care to tell me how you verified it?"

He met my gaze. "You'll just have to take my word for it."

"The two guys broke into my house," I said. "Their names

were Pinky and Mike. I'm trying to figure out who they work for."

His eyes bulged. "You didn't think their names were pertinent information last night?"

"I was a little distracted by the metal sticking out of my body and all the blood," I snapped, but he was right. I should have told him last night. I'd kept the information like currency.

Shaking his head, he took another drink and finished off the glass, then set it on the table next to the decanter. "I've never heard of a Pinky, which is a memorable name, and Mike…" He shook his head. "Don't know."

"I've already done a little sleuthing." I told him about going to the dealership and the service guy saying there was no one there by either name.

"That was foolish," he grunted. "If it's Martin, you tipped your hand."

"Maybe," I admitted, "but Skip Martin gave me some valuable information." I told him about his concerns about Brett Colter having something to do with Hugo's disappearance and the revelation that Colter had a construction crew that could have provided his muscle.

"Also," I said, prepared for him to be pissed. "I asked Detective Jones and Carter to look into who Pinky might be."

"You involved Jones?" he asked with a foreboding look. "Did you tell him everything else too? Like where to find Burton's body?"

"Don't be an idiot," I said, overcome with exhaustion. "I only asked about Pinky and didn't tell him why." Then, to help make amends, I added, "There was a money transfer after Hugo's disappearance. Around nine p.m. that night to an unmarked account, probably offshore."

If he was upset I'd withheld that from him, he didn't let on. "You think Colter forced Burton to transfer the money, then killed him?"

"And had some help to do it," I said. "I tried to make another appointment to talk to Colter, but his receptionist said he had nothing else to tell me."

"So maybe he's running scared."

"Could be. Also, we already suspected Colter was after Hugo's land," I said.

His frown deepened. "But it was bought by the corporation."

"What if Colter is behind the corporation? We both admitted it would be smart to own the land where you bury a body. Only he didn't want to make it so obvious. He's probably planning to wait a few years, then 'buy' the land for whatever he originally intended it."

He rested both hands on the arm of his chair. "Brett Colter?" The way he said his name suggested he'd never considered him to be Simmons's replacement.

"I didn't say he did it himself. If he's behind it, then he likely used his goons. Think about the sloppy way Hugo was buried. Colter would have been more careful." I made a face. "Not that I see him getting dirt under his manicured fingernails."

He was silent for a long moment. "He does seem ambitious."

"So the person who took over the area would be ambitious?"

He lifted a shoulder in a lazy shrug. "Simmons liked his underlings to be ambitious, but not *too* ambitious."

"He didn't want them taking over," I suggested.

"Exactly." He drummed his fingers on the chair. "We need to have a chat with Colter." His eyes darkened. "We'll do it tonight. I'll see if he has any events on his schedule. We can ambush him when he gets home before he goes into his house."

"He might call the police when we arrive or after we leave," I said.

He smiled but it didn't reach his eyes. "Then we'll be polite. They can't arrest us for asking questions."

It wasn't how I would have handled it as a detective on the LRPD, but I wasn't opposed to the idea. "How will you get his schedule?"

His grin looked foreboding. "Leave that up to me."

My reaction was disquieting. A month ago, I would have been horrified, and now…I was willing to do what was needed to find the truth.

Chapter 31

I spent the rest of the afternoon in Malcolm's office, mostly because I didn't want to go back to my apartment or my mother's house. I was beginning to suspect he was right, and those men had been after me. Besides, the intruders had taken my laptop, so I couldn't do any research there.

My injury must have sapped more energy out of me than I'd realized, because I was soon overcome with exhaustion and ended up taking a three-hour nap.

When I woke up, I was still alone in the office, but I had a blanket spread over me. Although my wound throbbed, the pain and discomfort were bearable. I grabbed my purse and dry swallowed some ibuprofen before taking out my phone. I was surprised to see it was not only 6:10, but I'd missed a slew of calls. Five were from my father, one from Clarice, and one from a number I didn't recognize. My father had left messages; the first four were him begging me to call him so he could explain, pleading with me to keep his involvement with J.R. Simmons to myself. His last message simply said to call him, that it was important. Clarice called asking if I had an update, and the unknown number turned out to be Mason Deveraux.

This is Mason Deveraux returning Harper Adams's call. Feel free to call me on my personal cell phone.

Then he rattled off the number.

First, I was surprised he'd gotten back to me so quickly. His assistant had said he was busy with a court case. Second, his request to call him on his personal cell was unusual. Law enforcement officers had a separate phone for work. We took photos of crime scenes with our phones, and there was a chance they could be taken as evidence. No one wanted their personal phone—including texts, photos, and who knew what else—submitted to the court as evidence. That could only mean what he had to tell me was of a more personal matter. That didn't surprise me given Rose Gardner had been his girl-friend at the time of Simmons's arrest. What did surprise me was that he was so open to talking to me about it.

I stared at the number on my screen. Did I want to call him back? Calling him now felt even more like a betrayal. I decided to put off making the decision until tomorrow. Hope-fully, I'd be in a better headspace to figure it out.

Plenty of customers were spread out across the dining space. Misti was still behind the bar, and Malcolm was mixing drinks down at the other end. I started to walk toward him, then changed my mind and sat on a stool in front of Misti.

"Hey, Sleeping Beauty," she said with a wide smile. "Or are you Goldilocks and about to run off before I can give you your bowl of porridge?"

I laughed at her mixed metaphor. "I'm not running off. Not without your boss anyway." Then I added, "Hey, thanks for putting that blanket over me while I was sleeping. I was *out*."

Confusion crossed her face, then a sly grin lit up her eyes. "I didn't cover you with a blanket."

I narrowed my eyes. "So who did?"

"James," she said, shooting him an appraising look before she turned back to me.

"Are you sure?" I asked. It definitely didn't sound like something he'd do.

"He wouldn't let anyone else back there. Said you needed your sleep. He even made sure the back door was deadbolted. He said he didn't want some random supplier walking in and waking you up." Her eyebrows waggled. "So what exactly is going on with you two?"

"It's strictly work related."

"Are you sure?"

I laughed. "Positive."

"Well, too bad, because he's been different over the past few days."

"Maybe he's just getting off on helping me investigate this missing person case."

Misti made a face. "Maybe…"

He walked over and set a glass of ice water in front of me. "You hungry?"

"Sure."

"Good, because I put in an order for you. Now drink that water."

He started to walk away, but I called after him, "Do we have plans tonight?"

Misti waggled her eyebrows again.

I rolled my eyes at her as he turned back.

"We'll hang around here for another couple of hours and then head up to Wolford."

Which mean he'd gotten Brett Colter's schedule. I was sure Carter Hale had something to do with that.

I picked up my water glass and took a long drink as he walked to the other end of the bar. Less than five minutes later, Malcolm hand-delivered a plate with fried chicken, mashed potatoes and gravy, and green beans, then walked off before I could thank him.

"I don't remember ever seeing fried chicken and mashed

potatoes on the menu," I said as I stared at the plate, my mouth watering.

"Petey cooks something for the staff every night," Misti said, giving me a pointed look.

"What?"

"He's never given the staff's dinner to anyone but us." She shrugged. "Well, other than Carter, but he's still staff."

I knew I should give more thought to what that might imply, but my mouth was watering. I couldn't remember the last time I'd had fried chicken. I savored every bite, surprised when I ate everything on the plate.

"I'm gonna need another nap after that," I said as I put my napkin on the plate and pushed it away. "And I'm gonna need to find a way to get on Malcolm's payroll."

Misti laughed. "I thought you were working for your daddy's law firm."

The thought of my father sobered me. "Maybe not for long."

"You plannin' to do P.I. work full time?"

"I'm considering it."

My phone vibrated in my pocket. I pulled it out and cringed when I saw it was my father again. I ended the call and set my phone on the counter, then read his voicemail once it posted.

Harper, I really need to talk to you. It's important. Call me back.

While I agreed it was important that he'd lied to the sheriff's department, I didn't agree it was urgent for us to talk about it before I was ready. Maybe tomorrow. Tonight, I wanted to focus on how to bust Brett Colter. We needed to come up with a plan, but first I needed to know where Malcolm planned to meet him.

Malcolm was busy at the opposite end of the bar, and I couldn't seem to get his attention. I considered going down to his end to ask him but discussing it in the open seemed like a bad idea.

My phone buzzed again, this time with a message from Detective Jones.

I have something important to discuss with you. Can you meet me somewhere as soon as you're available?

Several things in the text caught my attention. One, that he didn't want to meet in the station. Two, that he wouldn't discuss it over the phone. And three, that he seemed to think it was urgent.

Sure. Where?

Malcolm would likely disapprove of this, but I couldn't imagine the detective would talk if Malcolm was there. And Jones had said it was important.

I'm in Jackson Creek so I can come to you. Where are you?

There was no way I was having him come here, and I wasn't sure my door had been fixed yet. And after the strange vibe I'd gotten from him after our last phone call, meeting in a public place seemed like a good idea.

I'm headed to Jackson Creek. How about Betty's Café downtown? I can be there in about twenty minutes.

That was sure to make him suspicious, but at least he already knew I was working a case.

Good. See you then.

The whole thing felt off, but if he knew something, I wasn't *not* going to find out what it was. But how would I explain leaving?

I wouldn't.

"I'm going to head to the back," I said to Misti. "Tell Malcolm I'll wait for him there."

A frown creased her forehead. "Okay. Are you feeling okay?"

"Just a slight headache," I said. "No big deal, but it's quieter in the office."

"Okay."

I went to his office and found a piece of paper and wrote him a quick note.

Detective Jones has some important information that he wants to tell me about right away. I'm meeting him at Betty's Café. I'll let you know what I find.

Not bothering to sign the note, since he'd immediately know it was from me, I set it on the blanket on the sofa. Then I headed out the back door and drove out of the parking lot.

But the closer I got to Jackson Creek, the more concerned I became about the whole setup. Why hadn't Detective Jones *called* me to set up the meeting? What if he was tied up in this mess somehow? I knew I was being paranoid, but being framed by some faction in the Little Rock Police Department had made me suspicious of everything.

I called Carter Hale.

"I still haven't found anything about a Pinky in Lone County. And Brett Colter's record is clean as a whistle."

"The latter's not surprising," I said. "He's a prominent businessman. He's probably found ways to avoid arrest or people were too scared to report him." I paused, then added, "Probably a lot like J.R. Simmons."

He hesitated before saying, "Aww. That's a name from the past."

"Don't play stupid. I know Malcolm's interested in this case because of Simmons's involvement. He claims he wants to bring down the person who took his place here in Lone County."

"That part's true."

"Which part's not?" I demanded.

"All of that is true," he amended.

"*Carter...* What aren't you telling me?"

"Skeeter has a very personal interest in this case."

"Because of his vendetta against J.R. Simmons."

"Yes, but there's more to it than that."

"*And...*"

"It's not my place to tell you, but be careful. I think you've gotten caught in something bigger than you realize." He paused. "I'm worried that you might become collateral damage."

"Malcolm's using me?"

"Not like that," he hedged. "But I think you could be on the other side's radar and..."

"Become collateral damage," I finished.

"Just stick with Skeeter. He genuinely cares about your safety, otherwise he wouldn't have taken you to Delaney."

"He only did that to save his own hide." I'd be a fool to think he actually cared about me, but then again, he'd covered me with a blanket and made sure no one disturbed my rest. He'd made sure I got medical care. I could try to reason those things away, but the plain truth was that those were the actions of someone who cared.

I was starting to second guess this decision to see Detective Jones on my own, but it was too late to turn back and get Malcolm now.

"Where do I fall on *your* loyalty scale, Carter?" I asked.

"Weeellll," he said, drawing out the word. "You know Skeeter's my boss, so his instructions supersede all others. But..." He paused. "I like you, Harper, and investigating these cases with you has ignited a spark in him I haven't seen in a long time. So, the answer to your question is I'm loyal to you *and* I'm loyal to him. But I think the real question you're asking is you want to know if you can trust me to keep your secrets and protect you, and the answer is yes to both."

"But you won't protect me from Malcolm."

"He won't hurt you, not how you think. Once he takes someone under his protection, he'll move heaven and earth to protect them."

"Who's to say he's taken me under his wing?"

"Trust me, Harper. He has."

This conversation was confusing, but I didn't have time to work through what he was telling me. So I got to the real reason for my call.

"I'm about to meet Detective Jones at Main Street Diner, but the whole thing feels fishy. Like it might be a setup."

"So don't go."

"I *have* to go. I need to find out what he's up to, but I left Malcolm back at the tavern and didn't tell him I was leaving." I ran a hand over my head, pulling on my stitches. I stifled a gasp, then said, "It was stupid. I was worried he'd refuse to let me take the meeting."

"There's one thing about Skeeter Malcolm you need to know right away—he's loyal and protective, and sure, he'll try to boss you around, but here's the clincher—he's a reasonable man. And if you give him good reasons for what you're doing, he'll come around."

"So you're saying if I'd told him I was meeting Detective Jones, he would have been okay with me going?"

"Hell no, not alone," he barked out with a laugh. "But he would have gone as backup. He recognizes your talent, Harper. He's not going to squelch it."

"This sounds an awful lot like we're talking about a relationship, and he and I aren't like that. At. All."

"There are many different kinds of relationships," Carter said. "But all are important. Especially to a man like Skeeter."

"I can't turn around and go back," I said. "I'm almost to Jackson Creek."

"Call him. He might have someone around to play backup."

Headlights of a fast-approaching car appeared in my rearview mirror. "Hang on, Carter. Someone's speeding up behind me."

"Like they're about to run you off the road?"

"I love how you just jump to worst-case scenario." But he was right. I hadn't hung up for that very reason.

Speed up or slow down and see if they passed? I had a bad feeling about the whole thing, so I pressed my gas pedal to the floor. Especially since Tim Heaton had been run off the road.

"How far are you away from Jackson Creek?" Carter asked.

"About five minutes," I said. "So five or six miles."

"Dammit," he said under his breath. "Try to make it into town. If you do, I can get a sheriff's car to intercept you."

I knew what he was really asking. Did I want to involve the sheriff? The car behind me was closer than before, even though I was pushing eighty. "Yeah. Do that."

"Done." I heard him making a call, probably on his land-line, telling the dispatcher that I was being pursued on the highway into Jackson Creek.

"Can you tell what they're driving?" Carter asked.

"A truck," I said, shooting a quick glance up to my rearview mirror, then back to the road as I approached the back of a car in front of me. "A pickup. But I don't know what make or model. I'm about to pass a car. I hope to God the truck doesn't hit them."

Carter passed on the information to the sheriff's department as I passed the car with the truck in hot pursuit. But I'd slowed down to switch lanes, and the truck seemed to have accelerated. The beams of its headlights filled my car and then suddenly I felt a hard jolt.

"It's ramming into my bumper," I said, jerking the car to the left lane, thankful there wasn't any oncoming traffic.

"They say help is on the way," he said, sounding distracted. "And so is Skeeter."

The news that Malcolm was on the way was more comforting than that the sheriff's department was sending someone. But I didn't have time to be too relieved, because the truck rammed me again, this time harder. My car lost control, spinning around several times before I saw trees rushing toward me. Metal crunched and the airbag exploded in front of me, and the last thing I heard before I faded into darkness was Carter calling my name.

Chapter 32

When I woke, I was in a dark room with cinderblock walls, sitting upright in a hard chair. Moonlight streamed in through a small rectangular window close to the ceiling. My head was pounding, my eyesight fuzzy, so it took me a while to piece things together: I'd been run off the road, and whoever had done it had kidnapped me and put me in what looked like an old cellar. I'd been tied to a wooden chair with spindles at the back. My arms were secured behind me, and pain radiated from my stitches. A quick glance down at my shirt revealed multiple dark spots, which were likely blood. My legs were tied snugly to the chair legs.

Whoever had taken me had done so for a reason. They could have just killed me, but instead they'd tied me up. Did they want to question me about what I'd found? Probably. But if Carter was right, they might be holding me hostage to lure Malcolm here.

Would he come for me? Before my chat with Carter, I would have been fifty/fifty. But now, I was sure he would, if for no other reason than to mete out the justice he seemed set on doling out. Perhaps saving me would be a bonus.

If it had been anyone other than Malcolm, I would have

been worried for their safety. But from what I knew about him, I figured the people who'd taken me should be worried for theirs.

I only hoped I'd have a front row seat to witness the retribution.

A few minutes later, I heard the sound of squeaky hinges and then a single lightbulb hanging from the ceiling came on, casting most of the cellar in shadow. Footsteps landed on the staircase, and soon a pair of boots and jeans appeared, followed by the rest of the man.

Skip Martin.

He gave me an apologetic look. "Sorry we're meeting under these circumstances."

"You're not the person I was expecting to see," I admitted. "Kudos for the misdirect."

"Still, you were getting too close." He dragged a wooden chair from the wall so it was a few feet in front of me and sat down. "I see you found Hugo's body. You were modest when you said you hadn't found much."

I shrugged, then regretted it, but steeled my face so he couldn't see my pain. "No one likes a braggart."

"True." He leaned forward. "Did you find the money?"

"You mean the money that was transferred to your offshore account?"

He shook his head. "No money was transferred to *my* account."

"You're trying to tell me you didn't kill Hugo for the money?" I asked in disgust. I was starting to see two of him, and I was struggling to figure out which one to focus on.

"Of course I killed him for the money," he snapped in disgust. "And also for revenge. That man was running around like he hadn't stolen my money. He had to learn you don't cross Skip Martin."

If Skip wasn't behind the transfer, who was?

"I guess he didn't learn it for very long," I said. "Maybe

not at all since he was shot in the back of the head. Did he even know it was coming?"

"Oh, he knew it was coming all right. And you're correct, he didn't live with his lesson for long, but long enough that he pissed his pants, cried like a baby, and begged for his life. I took satisfaction in that before I put the bullet in the back of his head."

"Funny," I said. "I didn't think you had it in you to kill someone. I figured you'd left that to Pete Mooney."

Surprise washed over his face, then he chuckled. "You really were modest about what you found." He leaned back in the chair and spread his legs wide, resting a handgun I hadn't noticed on his right thigh. "Mooney was an idiot who thought he was the favored one." He shrugged. "I suppose he was. Until he wasn't."

Then a new thought emerged through the sludge of thoughts in my head. "Did you kill Pete Mooney?"

He laughed. "No, but I'm sure he outlasted his usefulness."

"So you worked with J.R. Simmons?"

"Are you asking if I was one of his Twelve?" His jaw set with disgust. "No. He never found me good enough, but then I guess Simmons got what was coming to him in the end."

"One of the twelve?" I asked in confusion.

"I figured you'd know about the Twelve since you're working with Malcolm." He drew in a breath. "J.R. had twelve men spread across the state, ruling their own empires but tithing to him. He set the Twelve up in their sections and they had to do J.R.'s bidding when he asked."

I shook my head and instantly regretted it as pain shot from one temple to the other. "What does that have to do with Malcolm?"

He laughed again. "You idiot, Malcolm was one of the Twelve."

His image came back together, then split apart again. A

wave of nausea hit me, and I leaned to the side and threw up part of my dinner.

Disgust covered his face. "Gross."

"I think I have a concussion, so I'm not going to apologize," I said, wishing I could wipe my mouth with the back of my hand.

He looked like he wanted to douse me with water, not that he had any to use.

"So why am I here?" I asked. I'd gotten my confession, not that it would do me much good if he killed me before Malcolm showed up. "Why keep me alive instead of letting your assholes kill me at the scene of the accident?"

"Because," he said, "I need to know who took the money."

"I already told you I don't know. I thought it was you."

"And I told you it *wasn't* me."

"So we're clearly at a stalemate."

"You had access to his bank statements," he said insistently. "You could see where the money went."

"I already told you it went to an offshore account. I couldn't find out. I'd take you to my apartment to show you the bank statements, but I'm sure you already looked them over." I closed my eyes as another wave of nausea hit. When it subsided, I opened them again. "What time did you kill him?"

"Who?"

"How many people have you *killed?*"

"Enough to know I'd get the electric chair."

I shouldn't have been surprised given how much pleasure he'd obviously gotten from killing Hugo, but I still found him utterly revolting. "Then what time did you kill *Hugo?* The transfer took place at about nine p.m. on the night he disappeared."

He made a face. "I killed him when he was supposed to be at his son's basketball game. Kept whining about how he was letting his son down."

"You're a sick bastard, Skip Martin."

He leaned closer and an evil look filled his eyes. "You're about to find out how sick I am. I'm gonna get the name out of you one way or another."

"What happens when I never give you the name? Because I don't know where it went."

"Then I'll dump your cold, dead, mutilated body on Malcolm's doorstep and let him deal with the fallout."

Well, shit. That meant he wasn't using me to lure Malcolm here after all.

I was in deep trouble.

Skip looked a little too pleased with himself. "How do you think Malcolm will handle it? You think he'll hide your body to avoid being involved, or will he deal with being a suspect in your murder?"

"Why would he be a suspect? There are plenty of witnesses who will testify that we weren't enemies."

The hint of a shadow appeared at the base of the staircase, and I heard Malcolm say in a deadly tone, "Or maybe I'll blow your brains out, Martin, and bury you next to Hugo Burton."

Skip sat up, then grabbed my chair and dragged it across the floor to use me as cover. "How the fuck did you find us here?"

My heart nearly burst from my chest, and I struggled to keep it together. Somehow Malcolm had shown up, but I could still become collateral damage.

"Never you mind that," Malcolm growled as he stepped into view holding a handgun. "I'm more interested in the topic at hand—your attempt to frame me."

"Not that I'm about to kill your girlfriend?" Skip sneered.

"Girlfriend?" Malcolm said in disgust. "Someone's been misinformed. She's a P.I. who investigates things for me. She's my employee and people don't fuck with my employees and live to tell about it."

My heart twisted in my chest, although I wasn't sure why.

Possibly because neither thing was true: I was neither his girl-friend nor his employee, and yet he was here anyway, risking himself for me.

"This changes my plan," Skip said, pressing the muzzle of the gun into my temple. "But I've always been a go-with-the-flow kind of guy. Hell, while people were dissing electric cars, I was first in line to get the new electric trucks."

"Wow," I said sarcastically. "How green of you."

Skip snorted. "I don't give a shit about the environment. I like money."

"It's gonna be hard to spend it in hell," Malcolm said. "But before you go, I need to ask a few questions."

"I'm the one with the power here," Skip said, shoving the gun hard into my temple, sending a wave of pain through my head. "How about you answer some questions for me? Why'd you off Simmons?"

Malcolm's eyes were hard and dangerous. If I'd been Skip Martin, I would have been scared shitless, but then again, maybe Skip *was* scared. The gun pressed into my head had a slight tremor. "Simmons got what was coming to him."

"Why are you here in Lone County?" Skip asked. "If you're lookin' for the treasure, then you're on a fool's errand. It ain't here."

"As in you took it or someone else did?" Malcolm asked.

"As in it doesn't exist."

"Oh, it exists all right," Malcolm said. "I've seen it." Then, before I had time to prepare, I saw a flash of light and a loud boom and the gun to my temple was gone.

My ears rang as I turned to see Skip flopped back on his seat, the gun on the dirt floor. A bloody hole was in the center of his forehead.

I swung back to face Malcolm, but he was already untying my legs.

"You okay?" he asked, his voice gruffer than expected.

"You killed him."

"I got what I needed, and we both know he was never going to let you go alive." He started working on my other leg. "I did what I needed to do."

"They're going to tie this to you," I said, my brain working a million miles a second, scrambling for ways to hide his involvement.

"I'm one step ahead of you." He got my second leg untied, then moved my chair so he could reach my wrists. "This is Pinky's gun."

With a start, I realized he was wearing gloves. "Pinky?"

"We had a nice little chat outside when I showed up. He's a shit guard." When he finished untying my wrists, he said, "We have to get out of here. Can you walk?"

"I'll crawl if I need to."

"It won't come to that." He grabbed my elbow and helped me stand, though a wave of dizziness washed through me as soon as I was on my feet.

"I'm pretty sure I have a concussion from the accident."

"We'll deal with that once we're out of here."

I nodded and regretted it again, then took a step toward the staircase and nearly fell. Malcolm scooped me into his arms and carried me up the stairs, turning sideways so we fit through the narrow staircase.

When we reached the top, I saw two men I didn't recognize standing guard with shotguns. They cast a glance at us as Malcolm carried me to a black sedan. But as soon as we passed, they turned toward a man sitting on the ground, his legs extended.

I had a feeling I knew how this situation was going to play out, but I had to know something first.

"Wait," I said, and Malcolm came to a halt. I pushed on his chest and he got the message that I wanted down. He lowered my legs, and it took me a second to gain my balance before I took couple of steps toward the man.

"Pinky?" I asked, staring down at his defiant face.

"What's it to you, bitch?"

"Manners," Malcolm growled.

To my surprise, the guy flinched.

"Did you help Skip kill Hugo Burton?"

"Why do you care?"

"Answer her question," Malcom said menacingly.

A sneer lit up his face. "Did I pull the trigger? No. But I had plenty of fun with him first if that's what you want to know."

I turned to Malcolm, shocked at myself when I said, "Do what you want."

"What's that supposed to mean?" Pinky demanded, but I was already walking to Malcolm's car.

I didn't even flinch when the gunshot echoed behind me.

Chapter 33

The whole not sleeping with a concussion thing is an old wives' tale. But the waking the patient up every few hours to make sure they know who's the current president is not.

Malcolm took me to his office and helped me remove my clothes, leaving me in my bra and panties so he could look me over for injuries. When he deemed that I didn't need urgent medical attention, he gave me one of the T-shirts he kept there and settled me on the sofa to sleep.

Then woke me up every three hours.

When I woke up on my own, the sun was streaming through the blinds in the windows. Malcolm lay asleep in one of the armchairs, his legs extended onto the coffee table.

I studied him, grateful there weren't two of him.

He seemed to sense I was awake, because his eyes cracked open. "You need more sleep."

"I could sleep for weeks," I said, sitting up and then crying out in pain. Every muscle in my body hurt.

"Maybe you *should* sleep for weeks," he said, sitting up. "You're lucky you're still alive."

"Thank God you showed up or I wouldn't be," I said.

"I was talking about the car accident. There was no doubt you'd survive Martin."

"How'd you find me?" I asked.

He gave me a half smile. "I put a tracker in your pocket when you were napping last night."

"That's not creepy as fuck," I muttered. "Not to mention stalkerish."

"I had a feeling you'd take off again. I also had a feeling the people who'd tried to kidnap you two nights ago might try again last night. So you're welcome."

"You could have told me."

"Would you have removed it?"

That was a good question. Would I have? Probably.

"There you go," he said in satisfaction.

"I didn't even answer," I said emphatically.

"Your non-answer was answer enough."

I supposed there was no arguing with that.

"Did the sheriff show up to the crime scene?" I asked after a couple of moments of silence.

"Yep."

"Do you think they're going to buy that it was a murder-suicide?"

"Yep. Especially after Mike tells them Pinky was planning to murder their boss."

"You found Mike?"

"Yep."

"And you're letting him live?"

"Unless he fucks up and tells someone? Yeah. I do have mercy." He tilted his head. "No recrimination for killing two men last night?"

"No," I said, meaning it. "Skip would have killed me. I got all I needed from him, and if you did too, then why try the whole *you put your gun down, no you* scenario. We both know he wasn't going to let me go."

He studied me for a moment before he asked, "And Pinky?"

"Pinky tortured Hugo Burton without remorse. Skip admitted to having killed more men than Hugo, and I suspect Pinky helped him and enjoyed every moment of it." I lifted my chin in defiance. "We could have had them arrested, but that ran a risk for you and we both know someone like Skip Martin could have gotten out on bail. And even if he didn't, all he had to do was have us assassinated. No witnesses to testify—the greater chance of him going free."

"You're okay with this?" Malcolm asked in disbelief.

I considered it for a long moment, then said, "Yes. But I need a drink."

Malcolm left the room, then came back with two bottles of water. He partially unscrewed the cap of one and handed it to me.

I swung my legs over the side of the sofa so I was totally sitting up and took the bottle. "This wasn't the kind of drink I was talking about."

"It's the kind of drink you need," he grunted and took a long gulp from his own bottle. I watched the bob of his Adam's apple as he swallowed and tried to ignore the hint of longing in my chest.

I took a drink too, relishing the cool water as it eased down my throat.

"I have a few questions," I said after another drink.

"Okay…"

"Were you one of J.R. Simmons's Twelve?"

Malcolm lowered his bottle. "I guess Martin did some talking then?"

"He did. He confessed to killing Hugo and plenty of other men, but he denied killing Pete Mooney and said he wasn't one of Simmons's Twelve. But he said *you* were."

He took another drink before lowering his bottle again. "I

was. But I quit about five years before I set out to destroy the man."

"Why'd you quit?"

He stared down at his bottle, swirling the liquid. "He wanted me to kill a child. The boy was the sole witness to a hit and run, and Simmons didn't want him to testify. Refusing him wasn't allowed, so I quit, which also wasn't allowed. Simmons killed the boy himself." He worked his jaw and took another sip.

"I'm sorry."

He stared at me in surprise.

"I know what it's like wondering if you could have saved someone by doing something slightly different. In my case, it's wishing I'd convinced my sister to go straight home like our mother told us to instead of letting my sister talk me into checking out those stupid baby birds." I took another sip as he stared at his bottle again. "I bet you wished you'd killed Simmons then."

His gaze slowly lifted to mine. "I didn't have the balls to do it then."

"We all grow at our own pace," I said. "A half year ago, I didn't have the balls to condone what happened last night and look at me now." I finished off my water, relieved that the pounding in my head was beginning to subside. He was right. Water was what I needed, not that I'd ever admit it to him.

"You're turning out to be one scary woman, Harper Adams," he said with a genuine smile.

I playfully lifted an eyebrow and misquoted Taylor Swift. "I'm a daydream dressed as a nightmare."

He studied me again, then lifted his bottle. "That's what I'm afraid of."

Chapter 34

At my insistence, Malcolm took me home soon after our conversation. I wasn't sure what to tell the sheriff about my crashed car, but Malcolm told me that Carter had placated the sheriff's department. I could give my statement later. The story they'd been told was that Carter had stopped by the scene of the accident and picked me up, and I'd refused medical attention. The sheriff's department had had my car towed to a repair shop at his request. It was a miracle they took his word for it, which led me to believe Malcolm had someone in the sheriff's department on his payroll.

That should have given me more pause, but better or worse, I had decided to trust him.

After I took a shower, I covered the bruises on my face with makeup, then I rented a car and drove out to Clarice's house. Once she let me in, I had her sit down and told her I'd discovered that her husband had been murdered but couldn't give her a full report until later.

She seemed satisfied with the information and didn't ask any of the expected questions—who'd killed him, where was his body, and how had he died. If I hadn't known Skip Martin was the murderer, I would have been suspicious of her involvement, but as I pulled out of her driveway, the truth hit me.

Clarice hadn't killed her husband, but when he hadn't come home that night, she'd transferred the money herself. That was how she'd managed to stay afloat for five years. Now she was merely interested in getting the life insurance money. Once I'd assured her she would have the means to get it, everything else had become superfluous.

I called Anton next and arranged to meet him in my car outside of the clinic where he worked. He had a lot more questions—the ones I'd expected and a few I hadn't, like why I had bruises on my face. I assured him that I'd tell him what I could, when I could, but I'd wanted him to know his father hadn't abandoned him.

After I left Anton, I headed for the sheriff's office, ready to give my statement about my car accident and also tell Detective Jones I'd found Hugo's body exposed on his land.

Only when I got to the sheriff's station and Detective Jones came out from the back, he looked exasperated and concerned at the same time.

"Are you okay?"

"Yeah, I'm fine. Sorry I didn't make our meeting last night."

"Why didn't you stick around to give your report about the accident?" he demanded.

"I had a slight concussion and obviously wasn't thinking straight," I said. "I'm here to give a statement now and to tell you I think I found Hugo's grave."

His lips pressed into a tight line. "A guy named Mike Anderson came to us early this morning and told us his friend Edward 'Pinky' Farrell confessed that he'd helped Skip Martin kill Hugo Burton, and he'd dug up Hugo's grave to make sure he was there. Then he lured Martin out to an old, abandoned farmhouse and murdered his boss and then himself."

I tried to act surprised by his news, especially since he was obviously gauging my reaction. "I must have made Pinky nervous asking all those questions around town."

"You must have," he said, and I wasn't sure he entirely believed me.

"If he confessed this morning, that can't be what you wanted to talk to me about last night," I said.

He sobered at that and took my arm, leading me to the waiting room chairs. Once we were both seated, across from each other, he said, "I'm so sorry to have to tell you this, Harper, but yesterday we found your mother's car submerged in the Red River up at the county line."

A rushing sound filled my ears. "What?"

"I'm equally sorry to tell you that when we pulled her car from the river, her body was inside."

I shook my head slowly. "No."

He gave me a sympathetic look. "I'm sorry, Harper, but your mother is dead."

My world just turned upside down.

Harper Adams Mystery #3 coming in Fall 2024

About the Author

Denise Grover Swank was born in Kansas City, Missouri and lived in the area until she was nineteen. Then she became a nomad, living in five cities, four states and ten houses over the course of ten years before she moved back to her roots. She speaks English and smattering of Spanish and Chinese which she learned through an intensive Nick Jr. immersion period. Her hobbies include witty Facebook comments (in own her mind) and dancing in her kitchen with her children. (Quite badly if you believe her offspring.) Hidden talents include the gift of justification and the ability to drink massive amounts of caffeine and still fall asleep within two minutes. Her lack of the sense of smell allows her to perform many unspeakable tasks. She has six children and hasn't lost her sanity. Or so she leads you to believe.

denisegroverswank.com

Made in the USA
Las Vegas, NV
01 February 2024

85150842R00225